MW00389811

The Marsh Bird
by Anne Brooker James

© Copyright 2021 Anne Brooker James

ISBN 978-1-64663-365-4

All rights reserved. No part of this publication may be reproduced, stored in a retrieval system, or transmitted in any form or by any means—electronic, mechanical, photocopy, recording, or any other— except for brief quotations in printed reviews, without the prior written permission of the author.

This is a work of fiction. The characters are both actual and fictitious. With the exception of verified historical events and persons, all incidents, descriptions, dialogue and opinions expressed are the products of the author's imagination and are not to be construed as real.

Published by

◤ köehlerbooks™

3705 Shore Drive
Virginia Beach, VA 23455
800-435-4811
www.koehlerbooks.com

The Marsh Bird

a novel

ANNE BROOKER JAMES

VIRGINIA BEACH
CAPE CHARLES

FOR

GLADYS ROBERTS OLIVER

1904—1994

GEECHEE

AUTHOR'S NOTE

In the middle of the eighteenth century, ships with cargos of African women, men, and children arrived on the savage beauty of the lowcountry coast. These enslaved people brought the skills needed by plantation owners to cultivate rice, cotton, and indigo. The planters, fearing uprisings against them from a race they considered bestial, separated families and tribes. But the Africans developed powerful means of survival and crossed plantation boundaries to join with different ethnic groups to maintain their rich culture and spiritual tradition. Together they fostered music, herbal crafts, oral history, spiritual practices, and mystical beliefs. They developed an English- based creole language, the only distinctive African-American creole in the US today.

They named their language *Gullah* in the Carolinas and *Geechee* in Georgia and called themselves by those names. When the Union army invaded the lowcountry during the Civil War, plantation owners fled, leaving thousands of slaves to fend for themselves. Some travelled north, but those who stayed began a new life in the wild beauty surrounding them, with the lush marsh grasses abundant with sea life and crawling and winged creatures, where sunsets and sunrises swallowed the sky with outrageous color and where lagoons, streams, inlets, and rivers flow through the marsh to the sea. For many years they remained relatively safe, secluded on the multitudes of coastal low country islands. But trouble was never far away.

This story is inspired by the remarkable Gullah Geechee people who live on the coastal lands of their once-enslaved ancestors. In writing this book, I have used dialect suggested to me by Victoria Smalls, a respected Gullah native of Beaufort, SC. Victoria has written about the Gullah Geechee language in the last pages of this book. That is fitting. It is theirs. Not mine.

During the winter of 1993, I lived with my mother in her warm, sunny Florida home away from the mountain snow. I planned to begin the novel about a story I had always longed to tell. However, except for a few short stories, I had only written non-fiction for publication. The *Phantom of the Opera* was playing on the stereo, and I had recently attended the Gullah Festival on St Helena Island in South Carolina. I began a tale of unrequited love, two orphans who grow up in a Gullah community, fall in love and come to a sad ending. I named it *The Monkey Vendor*. It was for practice never intended for publication. I married soon after I began the story, and it went on and off the shelf for many years. At last, with many changes, it has come to life as *The Marsh Bird*.

I once lived on an island shaded by ancient live oaks and surrounded by a great tidal marsh. My island was one of hundreds on the South Carolina lowcountry coast. A coastal plain rich with wildlife and webbed with tributaries running into rivers that run to the sound and the sea. Where sunrises and sunsets over the golden marsh grass and blue water are unworldly with brilliant colors that engulf the sky. I called upon memories to create the settings for *The Marsh Bird.* The map below will show you the entire area I worked—from Savannah to the Beaufort complex of islands. I pulled together parts of Savannah and Beaufort for the town, Belleview.

The Gullah community and its close environs is predominantly drawn from Spring Island, a rare treasure of natural beauty that has been wisely preserved by its developers. It is here that I wrote of primordial oak forests, one so dense and old and crooked that I would not drive through it at night alone when I lived there. The tabby ruins of the antebellum plantation are on Spring Island, much as I described it. The magnificent three-hundred-year-old oaks still line the road to the ruins.

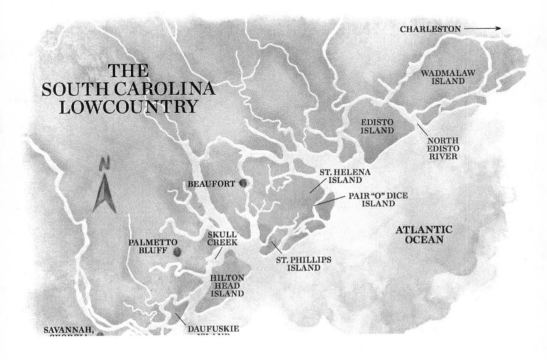

1912—1920

It was white. Everything was white. The white house, the white columns, the white men shrouded in white cloaks whirling around a white cross. And thunderous. Howls of laughter, screams, the hateful outrage, unthinkable cruelty. And then it was red. Everything was red.

CHAPTER 1

The mist hovered over the great marshland and then rose with the first pink edge of dawn. Flushing life to flight, it rolled over the mudflats and tidal pools, over the scrawny arms of creeks and estuaries that reached through the reeds and tall marsh grass, until it came to rest where the river curved against the stone-cobbled banks of the town. There it left the wild beauty behind and crept into the strange, haunting beauty beyond the shore, mingling with the heavy scented air of jasmine and magnolias, and the ancient live oak, their crooked arms draped with moss like mourning shawls. It trailed over wide green lawns and columned mansions and then settled into the mystery of the Lowcountry. Here the Gullah lived along the coastal shores where their ancestors were once enslaved.

As the early morning light moved across their treasured land the Gullah market was coming to life. Gaily dressed women in turbans and long cotton dresses and men in white shirts and black pants held up by suspenders gathered jovially, glad for a new morning, dayclean they called it. The vendors began to set up neat rows of fruit and vegetables brought from the nearby fertile fields. Tables were iced to hold the mounds of clams, crabs, shrimp, and fish so fresh their eyes were still clear with surprise.

One of the vendors, stacking second-hand clothes, called out, "It's gonna be a beautiful day, Aunt Letty. We're goin to be busy today."

"Mebbe," the woman called back. "If those uppity town cooks take a notion to shop."

The vendor laughed. "And just when ain't the town's Missus's sent for your pies and cakes?"

"Humph!" Aunt Letty said and put her attention back on wiping off the morning dew from her table.

The vendors all laughed. "You're not goin to spoil our fun today. What's got you so ornery, anyhow?"

Aunt Letty ignored them. She didn't feel ornery. But she was upset, and she didn't know what to do about it. She threw oil cloth over the long boards of her table and leaned down for a basket full of buns and biscuits still warm from her wood-burning ovens. She was still able at middle age to do that with ease. Though not tall, she could seem so when she rose to an occasion. She had a well-rounded figure and a comely face with lips as plump as a ripe peach, which she was fond of bunching up. Her large brown eyes were keen and took in all around her, and her posture was of one who had gotten her way long enough for it to show. She was aware of this and used it to her advantage as often as needed. Nevertheless, she was loved and respected, and she knew this as well.

She looked out over the sound to the river where a small bateau brushed through the lush shoots of spartina, being paddled by a boy not more than twelve. Baggy short pants, the color of his sun-bleached yellow hair, hung on the notches of his bony hips, and mud from the oyster flats clung to his legs and arms. He steered through the crooked finger of the tidal creek where it emptied into the great river, then pulled his boat onto its muddy bank.

⤳

The boy sat on the bank and watched other flat-bottomed boats return from the creeks, their nets laden with the small shrimp gathered from the spawning fields amidst the marshland islets. The catch would be sold at the daily market, or at back doors of fine houses, or hawked along the shell roads.

"*Swimps, swimps. Raw, raw swimps.*"

A small, square sail caught his eye as a boat skimmed by. He would like a sail like that and meant to have one soon. He thought of the schooners that made their way gracefully along the river, their huge white sails billowing in the warm salt air. Someday, he dreamed, he would captain such a ship and leave behind the oyster flats and small fish that brought only pennies at the market stalls, or occasionally a breakfast of hominy and fish cakes or bacon from a Gullah cook at one of the great houses on Washington Street. He would sail the tradewind islands where there was sweet fruit or to Africa where King Oosafella lived with wild animals, haunting music and magic.

The air was already thick, and he wiped away the rivulets of grime and sweat from his forehead, swiping at the mosquitoes that hummed in the marsh grass. He slid from the bank into the cool, amber water and rolled with the wake from the paddle wheelers that steamed the local ports. He watched it churn by and sighed. He loved this river and all that flowed with it. He spent his days on the river, foraging along the ebb and flow of the marshland, attuned to the rise and fall of its heavy breath. And, at night when the screaming of the gulls had quieted and the cicadas had begun their incessant chatter, he slipped into the ruins of one of the old warehouses stretched along the wharf, climbed the rickety stairs to the top floor where he had made his home, and imagined the groans and cries of slaves who once slept there.

He had no family, none that he knew of. He had been left behind, it was thought, by sharecroppers and was found in the marsh on a mud flat by Ben Clary, a white drifter, who gave him his name for want of a better one, cared for him the best he could, and taught him all he knew of the rich low country until the day he wearied of life. The boy stayed in the old slat shack until the rats and water took it over, then moved to his present home where the rats were larger but left him alone.

The boy washed the mud from his body and paddled across the murky channel. Long Robby and his men, the best fishermen anywhere around had pulled into the docks. Long Robby was the strongest man he knew. He didn't look like any of the other Gullah. Tall and dark as a moonless night he always wore a shirt, black vest, coat, and pants held up by a cord above his ankles. And he never wore shoes. Not winter nor summer.

When he cleaned up his boat after a haul, he piled the nets in a bucket and balanced it up on top of his tall black hat. Long Robby was a show all to himself. He made Ben's bateau for him a couple of years earlier and that was one of the reasons the boat was so special to him. Long Robby told Ben the enslaved people brought the knowledge of making the bateau with them from West Africa and was used to navigate these rivers and creeks at low tide. He loved Long Robby as much as anybody. Maybe more than anybody. And, even though Long Robby never talked about it, he was kin to Bones.

Ben had never seen Bones, and he was not alone there. But Bones was out there somewhere. He started to stop and see what they brought in, but hunger gripped his ribs as he smelled the scent from Aunt Letty's tables. He had a few pennies in his pocket for a hot cross bun from the baker.

As he got to Aunt Letty's booth, Ben saw something move under her white cloth-draped table and fell to his knees. Staring, unblinking with feline assessment were the largest, darkest eyes he had ever seen. At first, he thought he was looking into the sooty face of a panther cub, but as he leaned closer, he saw it was a child, a very dirty child with long black hair tangled hopelessly around its small face and crouched on bare feet like a marsh bird prepared for flight. One of her grimy hands was gripped a sugar roll from the colored woman's mound of golden-crusted breads, raisin-filled cakes, and juicy pies.

So jealously did Aunt Letty guard her wares and so keen a trader was she that Ben, who was fairly certain of her favor, had only managed after considerable cajoling and the best of his catch, to part from her a coveted bun. And even then, if the crabs were too small, there was often an extra chore that if not done to her liking brought forth her famous wrath. No one, he thought, dared steal from Aunt Letty. For despite of her round frame she could run faster than a barnyard hen about to be plucked. Once he had seen her take to flight when some of the little Gullah children had sneaked a biscuit from behind her back. He had bent double, choking with laughter at the sight of her voluptuous body, its ample parts bouncing in every direction like a vendor's balloons on a windy day.

Ben raised his eyes in wonder of Aunt Letty as she loomed above her stall. Unprepared for the threatening storm he saw about to erupt, he jumped to his feet, confused as to just where this fury was directed.

"Aunt Le . . . Letty," Ben stammered, backing away.

"Wrap up your mout, boy."

Ben quickly pointed to the obvious culprit and saw to his increasing dismay that the child was gone. "B . . . but. There." He pointed.

Aunt Letty, her kindly face once more smoothed out, beckoned to him, took his hand, and placed upon his palm a warm sugary bun. Surprised, he looked up at Aunt Letty, who pulled her generous pink lips in such a formidable bunch that he blinked.

"You ain't seen nothin. You heah me boy. Now, come sit over heah by me. I want to talk to you."

Surprised, Ben sat on the ground and leaned against the oak tree.

"You didn't fish today, did you, Ben?"

Ben stared at her. "How'd you know that, Aunt Letty?" He bristled, thinking, *What business is it of hers, anyway?*

"Just thought you didn't. Don't look so squirmy. What you do ain't up to me."

"Then why'd you ask, Aunt Letty?"

"I've been thinkin bout you, Ben. You don't have no friends. All you do is run around in your boat all day it seems like, and when you ain't out on de water you are at de docks with older men."

Ben squinted his eyes at her. "I do too have friends, Aunt Letty. Long Robby, Jimmy, and the fishermen at the wharf are my friends, even if they are older. And Ragbone, when he's around. And sometimes Rufus when he ain't with his school friends from the island. That's all the friends I need."

"You need friends your own age is what you need. You been around grown ups too long for your own good."

"Aunt Letty, what's got you onto me bout friends all of a sudden?" He frowned. "You know the boys from town don't like me. And I sure don't like them."

"They don't like you because you live near Gullah an in dat ole tumbling down warehouse. Ain't there no one else your age, Ben?"

"You know there ain't. Long Robby's kids are younger, and Rufus is older. Anyway, why do you care? I'm happy with the friends I got."

"It's too bad those boys gave you such a bad time at school. Can't say I blame you for leavin."

"Those truant people ain't never gonna find me and I sure ain't never going back to that hateful place. Anyway, Pa Clary taught me to read and write since I can't go to the island colored school."

Aunt Letty chuckled. "Well, I guess dat's de way it be. For now, anyway." She smiled to herself.

"There's somethin else," she said as he got up to leave. "Henny told me he was talkin to one of de fishermen de other day bout de yellow fever dat took so many people bout twelve years ago. De fisherman, don't know which one, said there was a whole family of Swedes livin down de way on de marsh. He didn't know de family but saw all these yellow-headed kids runnin around when he trolled down dat way. He saw de mama with a baby in her arms once. Then one day there wasn't no one there. He heard they all died. Dat got Henny to thinkin, Ben. Maybe they was your family."

Ben got up from the ground in a huff. "Aunt Letty, what's got you and Henny so interested in what I do and where I come from all of a sudden?"

"You're growin up, Ben. And don't you want to know somethin bout yourself?"

"Good golly, Aunt Letty." He rolled his eyes. "I dunno. I been getting along fine just being me. I can't think bout being someone else now."

Aunt Letty chuckled. "Well, Henny said he had a mind to go see Miss Becky's husband. Mr. Morton might know somethin bout dat family, being a lawyer."

"You got me all twisted up. Asking all these questions. All I wanted to know was who that kid was under your table."

"Dat's my first customer comin, Ben. You just skedaddle now. You don't need to know everythin. Git!"

⁓

For many mornings after that as Ben carried out his trade in the market, he casually searched the under-pinnings of the various stalls, always with Aunt Letty's words echoing in his ears like a proclamation from God. In fact, encouraged by an already vivid imagination, the apparition consumed his thoughts. As he pushed his small boat around a thicket of tall grass, Ben was sure he saw enormous black eyes watching him. And at night he gathered his arms around his thin body, wide-eyed with bone-deep certainty that through some magic of Aunt Letty's race, a secret ritual that only she and her kind understood, a beastly thing had been conjured up to do her bidding. Most likely in the dark of the night.

His heart pounded as he saw in the shadows of his room the haunting, gleaming eyes of a creature that could change with unearthly speed to a great black bird that swept down and stole the eyes of children and used them for its own. Or a giant, demon cat that could melt idle boys with its burning black eyes. *A plat-eye,* he thought, his eyes widening. There were ghosts, and then there were plat-eyes, the most fearsome of all goblins.

With those ominous thoughts in mind, he avoided Aunt Letty's stall and the sweet buns he cherished. So, it was by chance one early spring morning, when the mist was still heavy on the leaves of oaks, elms, and magnolias, that he saw the child again. Ben was standing under the leafy branches of a dogwood, letting its dewy drops cool his back, when he happened to look to the trunk of an old oak near Aunt Letty's table. Hiding behind it was a girl, younger than him, but so small in her dirty and torn gingham dress it was hard to tell. Like a rag hanging on a stick. She leaned against the tree and timidly stared at Aunt Letty's back.

Rooted to the ground, he watched as the child slowly edged her way to the soft, white apron that encircled Aunt Letty's body. With a small tug on the apron she turned large, luminous eyes up into the disturbed expression of the colored woman and held out to her a twisted piece of cloth. Aunt Letty shot a quick, nervous glance around the market where every vendor was watching and listening as they could. She drew her formidable bulk even taller, thrust her plump lower lip to full extension, swished her skirts away from the waif, and muttered, "G'on, chile. Git. G'on from heah."

Undaunted, the girl yanked on the woman's skirts, refusing to be ignored. Aunt Letty, who expended much effort to hide the loving heart that beat under her ample breast, was genuinely distressed and brushed at the small hands that gripped her white apron.

"Git, I said, chile. You ain't got no bizness heah."

As Aunt Letty's perplexed pout swelled, the girl grew more persistent, until tears struggled through the grime. That was Aunt Letty's undoing. She looked down at the child and then fixed a defiant glare upon the market. Slowly, she removed the twisted rag from the girl's fingers, long and slender for her size, she noted. She would grow like a reed in the marsh. Her face even now showed the beauty to come. Aunt Letty unwound the cloth and stared at its gleaming contents: a simple but lovely gold locket on a twisted gold chain. She looked at the child once more before she opened the smooth top. Without expression she studied the picture of the lovely woman within and saw the same dark eyes as the child's. She raised her eyes to the river, let them rest upon the reeds and grass of the marsh and beyond to the sound and on to the cerulean sky where the gulls soared over the sea. When her eyes once again met the child's, she smiled and pried open the small hand to take the locket. The child's expression crumpled, her eyes fixed on Aunt Letty's tables.

Aunt Letty, without another thought, dropped the necklace down into the vault of her bosom and began to package an assortment of her pastries, occasionally glancing over at her fellow vendors as she carefully wrapped her wares. The girl took the parcel from the weathered hands and fled away.

In lowered voices, the vendors' gossip traveled from stall to stall. The child, Ben heard, had come with a white man a while before when the early summer rains and the heat consumed the air. They had come from Louisiana, the gossipers insisted, but no one knew for sure. They drifted in one day so poor it had sucked out their spirit. The man was sick, anyone could see, whether from hunger or the inclement clime. His cough hacked through the air as if it were an omen, like the eerie feared hoot of the screech owl. And then there was the child. The vendors shook their heads and clucked. Instead of the pale hair and complexion of her companion, she was tawny, a golden-skinned urchin tanned from breeding more than sun. They had settled in an old, abandoned shack well behind the square, a squalid area on any account, neither in the colored section nor white trash but off where old rusty metal and broken wagon wheels and other junk was thrown and lived there without notice for awhile. Mr. Trainey, at the compound's store, took their pennies for food while they lasted and then he gave to them out of pity.

Nothing that Ben could think of had happened like this before. No one just came and took up with anyone here. The Gullah didn't trust other people—colored or white—just settling into their commune. Henny Findley, the only white person living near the Gullah compound beside himself, didn't have anything to say about it, which was peculiar to him. Henny almost always had something to say but he just kept his head down knitting the strings in the cast net.

A few days later, Ben was sitting with Henny in a shady area next to the market watching him make his nets. Henny said a Gullah elder taught him how to knit them when he was a kid. It was an art, he told me, brought over from West Africa, and they were proud of that. "Most Gullah fishermen used to knit their own fishing nets. They made a needle outta palmetto wood. Like this one I'm using."

"Henny, look!" Ben interrupted, pointing toward the market. "That girl. Looks like something's wrong."

The child was running to Aunt Letty's booth, her dirty face blotched red and tear streaked. Aunt Letty took one look at her and called over to Nellie whose stall was next to hers to watch over her table. She threw a linen cloth over the baked goods and walked quickly away with the child.

Miss Emmy, who was hanging clothes in her stall, shook her scarf-bound head. "This ain't comin to no good. No Lawd, this be bad news come to sit on us." Miss Emmy put her hands on her hips, watching the girl and Letty as they left the market. "For soul for soul."

"Dat ole she-she," Ben heard one of the vendors say to another and chuckled. He knew *she-she* meant talkety woman in Gullah, the language they spoke. It seemed to him they were all she-she.

Not long after they left, one of Long Robby's boys ran back with the news that the sick man the girl had come with had died. The buzz of the market stilled for only a moment then hummed on in renewed speculation.

"Well, I reckon Letty's done let herself in for it now," Henny Findley said to Ben as he set down the net he had been working on.

Ben twined his fingers through the webbing of the net and asked, "So what's Aunt Letty in it for?"

"Well, let's just say that this time she's gotten herself in deeper than a bear stuck in a log with a pole kitty at the other end," Henny answered and spat out a stream of chewing tobacco.

"Ah, Henny," Ben said and laughed, not believing for a minute Aunt Letty would let herself be in trouble about anything. "You're always talking that way." He looked out toward the river. "Ya know, Henny. I never been too far down that river and where the tributary runs off it. I think I'll go explore a little and see if there are any good creeks for shrimp or crab."

"Boy, I thought you knew every stream, creek, and waterway around these parts," Henny said.

"Mebbe not all. Not down there, anyway."

Henny chuckled good naturedly. "I reckon stories from down the river are a little scary, huh?"

Ben frowned. "I ain't scared of nothin, Henny."

"Just teasing you, boy."

⌒

Ben whistled as he paddled down the wide river toward where a large tributary angled off. Henny had struck a nerve, and Ben still felt it. He had avoided this part of the river with its heavy marshes and dead cotton and rice fields. He'd heard too many stories about the slaves who worked at the plantation farther down the river than where he intended to go. Jimmy, one of Long Robby's fishermen, said he heard moans and cries all around him every time he went by that place. He'd heard that Junie Savage, the old master, wasn't there no more, but it was still just too spooky for him.

Ben pulled into a creek that looked promising. He didn't even see any gators, which was unusual. Just shoots of grass along the banks and woods on either side of the narrow creek. It was so pleasant he lay back against the hull, his arms behind his head, and felt the spring sun warm on his eyelids as his boat gently moved along the still water.

Startled, he jumped up in the seat when he heard dogs barking. "Holy mackeral," he yelled to himself. Where in tarnation did they come from? He started backing out as fast as he could as three vicious-looking hounds got closer, ferociously barking. He had barely gotten out of the creek and turned into the river before they were at the edge of the bank, no more than two feet away, looking like all they wanted was to tear him apart.

His heart was beating so hard it shook the boat as he hightailed it back to the docks. Long Robby was sitting on the edge of the dock chatting with the fishermen when Ben pulled in so fast he almost hit Long Robby's boat.

"Whoa, Ben. What's got into you, boy? You look like you been seein some ghosts." Long Robby's big grin spread across his kindly face.

"Long Robby." Ben struggled to get his breath.

"Slow down, son." His laughter faded into concern. "What's goin on?"

"Dogs," Ben said, "the meanest dogs I ever seen came after me. They'd a had me too if I hadn't gotten outta that creek so fast."

Long Robby's face was clear of amusement now. "Just where was this, Ben?"

When Ben told him, Long Robby looked off down the river. Old dread, misery and loathing, drawn back into his senses.

"Whose dogs are they, Long Robby? I ain't never seen dogs like that."

Long Robby's attention returned to Ben. "I'm sorry dat happened to you, son. I know whose dogs they be. I'd just stay a little closer to home."

Ben let out a long sigh. "Long Robby, you sure don't have to tell me that. I ain't never going back there."

After Ben left, Long Robby turned to his fishermen, whose faces showed the fear they were feeling. "Well, looks like Satan and his dogs are back, men."

The next day Ben tied his small craft along the wharf, whistling as he thought of the bounty in his boat. He sure didn't need to go down that river again. It had been an especially productive day, and as he slung hampers of iced fish over his shoulder and grasped the heavy buckets of clams and crabs, he thought of how he would barter his choice catch. He could choose from the stacks of used clothing on Miss Emmy's tables. Or maybe Aunt Letty would part with some of her buns or biscuits. He had a fleeting thought that he hadn't seen her in a couple of days, but it left his mind as the excitement of his possibilities returned.

His step quickened as he remembered Moss Hill, sitting on the town square behind a pretty iron fence. On the square, with its tall monument of the town's founding fathers, the richest people in town lived in white columned houses surrounded by oaks and Spanish moss and hills of red azaleas and their own idea about what was rightfully theirs. Ben had shied at venturing into this privileged world, but Aunt Letty told him one day, in a rare burst of confidence, that her sister, Orie, the best cook in the Lowcountry, held forth in the kitchen at Moss Hill and was especially partial to the juicy white meat of she crabs with their pink clumps of roe from which she made scrumptious soup. Orie was the familiar, needed link to the coveted back doors of Ben's fancy.

Like her sister, Orie was tall and kindly, but here the resemblance ended. Orie was as thin as Aunt Letty was stout, and her face a wonder of light even in its darkness, the suggestion of laughter forever there under her turbaned head. With the least excuse her rich, musical voice rippled through the air like the peals of St. Michael's bells.

Ben walked across the cobblestones past the tall brick warehouses to the market, never suspecting that he walked toward an encounter that would change his life forever.

Aunt Letty was at her stall talking to her sister. His eyes lit up as he saw the mounds of pastries on her tables—hot cross buns oozing with sugar and cinnamon, sausage biscuits, breads, pies, cakes.

He saw the girl standing almost hidden behind a big oak, scrubbed from head to toe, her small amber body glistened under a freshly washed callico dress from Miss Emmy's tables. Her tangled web of hair, washed, combed and plaited into two long ropes, was held securely by blue ribbons. She was clutching something, but he couldn't see what it was. *She gives me the creeps,* he thought. *I'll come back later when Aunt Letty ain't busy.* He passed behind Aunt Letty and Orie chatting but heard enough to slow him down.

"Her name be Tilly." She shook her head. "Orie, dat chile can't say one word. She just can't talk."

"Did her daddy say why?"

Aunt Letty shook her head woefully. "It was her uncle, not her daddy, and I ain't sure how dat happened, him being white. He just said dat she ain't talked since they left home. Poor man's so sick he could hardly talk. Musta been somethin' real bad."

"Real bad?"

"Real bad. But I never did get all of it his voice be so low. He said he thought she would talk again when she remembered things. He said they come a long way. From New Orleans."

"How old is she?"

"I asked him dat an after a fit of coughin he asked what month and year this was. I figured de fever affected his memory. I told him it was September of 1912. He closed his eyes an didn't say nothin for de longest time. He never did open his eyes but said in de saddest voice, 'We left home nearly a year ago.'

"I asked him again how old she was and he said, 'She's ten. She'll be eleven in November.' Dat poor man had tears runnin down his face and he say again, 'Just a little girl.' Then he wouldn't talk no more."

She threw up her arms and closed her eyes as if beseeching an answer from above. "Just what am I goin to do with her, Orie?"

"Oh, Letty, I be so sorry."

"She got somethin in her hand and won't let go of it."

"Did you ask her uncle bout dat?"

"He just say it be all she's got left and to leave dat alone. Nothin else. Even when she puts on her clothes, she keeps it tight in her hands and watches like she thinks I might grab it from her. And she's always so hunkered over." She frowned. "Gets me down."

Orie searched her sister's face thoughtfully. "Letty, I know how hard this be for you, but it seems to me dat whatever she's clutchin onto be de only comfort dat chile got."

"Mebbe."

"I been helping Miz Becky raise all four of her children an they have one toy dat's special long after dey put all de rest aside." Her face softened and she reached for her sister's hand. "You know somethin bout that."

"Get off dat, Orie."

"Letty, I believe dat child was sent to you. It has been a long time now. You need someone to love."

"Well, we ain't gonna talk bout dat." Letty started to turn away, disturbed by the way the conversation was going and said softly but emphatically, "An it don't answer de question of what I'm goin to do with her."

Orie smiled. "I know your big heart. You will." Orie put her hand on Letty's arm as if to comfort. "Letty, there be somethin I got to tell you."

Aunt Letty furled her brows into a wary frown. "What?"

Orie put her hand to her mouth and looked down at the ground. "It be Junie, honey. Long Robby says he be back."

Aunt Letty, visibly shaken, walked over to the chair by her stall and sat down. "How does Long Robby know dat?"

"Ben ran into some dogs down dat way and then Jimmy and some other fishermen were comin down de river draggin a load of tree logs behind em. They passed Grandterre and there was Junie, plain as daylight, standin on dat big ole porch of de plantation looking out at em."

Aunt Letty closed her eyes and let out a long sigh. "Guess things was goin too good."

"Try not to worry, Letty."

"Nothin is gonna ease my mind but to see dat devil in de ground." She shook her head. "An I got this girl now." She looked up at the sky. "Lord, why are you puttin all this on me?"

"I gotta go to work but I be seein you tomorrow. The Mortons are goin out an they need me to see to de children and master Beau. Letty, if I ain't there when dat boy wants somethin he be havin a fit."

Orie kissed her on the cheek and started to walk toward town. "Beau'll be askin me why you don't come see him an bring those cinnamon buns," she said over her shoulder.

"Orie, hold on."

"I'm goin to be late, girl." Orie turned and looked at Letty's distressed face. "I know what you goin to say, Letty. You gotta stop blamin yourself. I can't say Beau's name without you grievin up."

"How can I? You know well as me I caused dat infliction to dat boy."

"Miss Becky don't think so and neither do I, Letty." She looked at her impatiently. "Why don't you believe what we say instead of carryin on with this ache you keep in your heart? Beau is thirteen years old now and you and I been going round and round about this for thirteen years."

"Orie, I ain't been bringin in babies for long back then, and I didn't know what I know now. Dat baby's feet coming out before his head. I hurt him, Orie, and dat be de second worse thing dat ever happened to me in all my forty-five years." She looked painfully at her sister. "Why won't dat boy let a doctor see his foot?"

"How do I know dat?" She softened her expression. "I gotta go. And you got enough to worry about without frettin over Beau."

CHAPTER 2

*H*oly Moses, Ben thought, picking up his stride toward town. *That girl they call Tilly can't talk. I never knowed no one that couldn't talk. Poor Aunt Letty if she is stuck with her. Guess that's what Henny meant.*

It was a beautiful day and Ben was happy. He sold all his seafood so quickly he ran and whistled all the way back to the market for . . . he couldn't make up his mind between a sweet bun or biscuit.

Aunt Letty saw Ben just ahead and smiled. "Hello, Ben." She cocked her head, coyly. "I bet you got your eye on a sweet bun?"

"Can't make up my mind, Aunt Letty," he answered, pleased with the pennies and nickels in his pockets.

"Umm mm, sounds like you did good today. Make your choice, Ben. You don't have to pay today." Smiling, she called the child to her and clasped her hand on Ben's shoulder. "Ben, this be Tilly. She goin to be with me now."

Hesitantly, Ben looked at Tilly, remembering what he'd heard, and reddened at her intense gaze. "Well, I reckon that's nice, Aunt Letty," he said, ignoring the girl. Uncomfortable, he backed away from her grasp. "I gotta go now. I sure do thank you for the biscuit."

Aunt Letty lowered her voice and said, "Tilly don't know nothin bout what's around heah. It would be nice of you to show her."

Alarmed, Ben sidled away, shaking his tousled head. "Can't, Aunt Letty. I got things to do."

She let out a long sigh and closed her eyes as he started to walk away. Shaking her head slowly, she said almost in a whisper, "Please, Ben."

He stopped and stared at the ground. He kicked the hardened dirt and slowly turned around. "Aw, Aunt Letty." He looked at Tilly, who had walked over to lean on a tree. "What would I do with some girl?" He nodded toward Tilly. "Specially one that can't talk."

A glower darker than a soot froze on Aunt Letty's face. "And just how do you know dat?"

Oh Lordy, Ben thought, blushing. "I'm sorry, Aunt Letty. I heard you tell Miss Orie when I passed by you this morning."

"What?" Her head thrust back as she pondered this. "You listened in on my talkin?" She suddenly grabbed his ear and held on like a crab.

"Ouch! Aunt Letty, that hurts." He jerked away.

"You let dat be de last time you listen in on me. You heah me?"

Ben screwed up his face in pain and rubbed the side of his head. "Jeez, Aunt Letty."

"Wal, you deserve dat." Her voice softened. "Ben, this be good for you, too. You be always alone. You need a friend almost as much as she does."

Angry, he glared at her and then over at Tilly. "You know she'd be a heap better off with some girl or . . . someone."

She put her hands on her hips and glared at him. "Mebbe so but dat ain't for you to say."

He felt his face burning and balled up his fists in frustration.

Aunt Letty smiled. "Just show her around, Ben."

She called to Tilly sitting under the tree, holding onto her legs. Tilly turned her face away.

"She don't wanna go, Aunt Letty."

"You hush up!" Aunt Letty walked over to Tilly and pulled the child up in front of her. "What's de matter, chile?"

Tilly dropped her head to her chest and covered her mouth with her small fists.

Aunt Letty walked over to the stall and slumped in her chair. "Tilly, I dunno what to do." She shook her head sadly. "I ain't figgered out how to be with you."

Tilly looked over at Aunt Letty, her eyes stinging, got up, and walked with her head down over to Ben.

"I'll be right here, Tilly," Aunt Letty said, relieved as she watched them leave.

"C'mon," he growled, thinking that he would take her far away from any chance of seeing anyone he knew. *I'll go to my boat and just sit there all afternoon tying some of the knots Henny Findley showed me.*

Tilly followed behind Ben to the little cove where his boat was pulled up on the bank. The water was stained winey by the trees that closed in on the edge of the creek. She looked up and down along the small hard mud shore, took off her shoes and socks, placed them on the bank, by the boat and started walking toward an old driftwood stump, broken and split, but large enough to hide her small body.

Ben reached in his boat and pulled out a circle of small rope. Without looking at her he said, "I don't care whatcha do, just don't cause me no trouble." When he looked up and saw her walking down the stream, he yelled, "Don't you go off nowhere."

She disappeared behind the tree stump, ignoring him. She leaned against the light dead wood of the trunk, put her face in her hands, and shook with sobs. Slowly, as the grief and drowsiness from the sun overcame her, she closed her eyes and leaned back against what was left of the tree and slept.

When Ben had enough of tying ropes, he walked over to the tree where she was sleeping. "Hey, you." He looked down at her. "Let's go."

She looked up at him with her large dark eyes as if she had not seen him before. For a moment she didn't know where she was, but she quickly picked up something from her lap, followed him back to the boat, got her shoes, and returned to Aunt Letty's stall.

That evening, Ben lay back in his boat and drifted the steamy waters of Possum Creek, watching the sun set over the day. It was quiet, except for the occasional deep croak of a bullfrog or the gentle splash of an egret diving for dinner.

Girls, he thought, *stupid girls.* At least she had left him alone. *It weren't right of Aunt Letty to make me take that girl.* He picked up an oyster shell that slid across the wooden bottom of the boat and threw it out, watching it skip across the surface of the creek. *One thing I know for sure, I ain't going near that market any time soon.* He sighed and leaned back against the back of the bateau, watching an Osprey soar above. He wrinkled his nose and rubbed his head. *Wow, Aunt Letty sure can get mad.*

Several days later Ben, tired from a long day of working the creeks and inlets, walked towards the shade of a big oak with the lemonade he had been hankering for all day. He jumped when Henny put his hand on his shoulder. "Henny, you scared the life outta me."

"What are you doing back here, anyway? Hiding?" he asked, amused.

Ben looked away, embarrassed. "Aw, I guess so."

"Wouldn't have nothing to do with Aunt Letty and that little girl, would it?" He laughed. "Well, you ain't far enough away to escape her eyes if she wants to find you, boy."

"Henny, that woman's trying to ruin my life."

Henny chuckled. "Well, I can see how you might feel that way, Ben." He squatted to look into Ben's face. "But Letty's going through a hard time right now. Most everybody here knows that."

"What kind of hard time?"

Henny looked down at the ground for a bit before saying with a sad tone, "She was hurt bad once, Ben. Ain't never got over it."

Ben frowned and looked at Henny. "How was Aunt Letty hurt?" he asked as if he couldn't imagine her being hurt by anything.

Henny stood up. "Ben, you might think about helping her out with the little girl. Now, I ain't saying to do that. I just mean you might think about it." He ran his hand over Ben's head and walked away.

Ben watched him leave, wondering what all that was about. He caught a shadow out of the corner of his eye and turned to see Aunt Letty standing there.

"Well now, if it ain't Ben," Aunt Letty's rich voice bellowed.

Ben dug his toes in the ground and rolled his eyes to the sky, wondering why there wasn't someone up there to help him. He started shaking his head and said, "I ain't gonna take that girl nowhere, Aunt Letty, not again. You gotta find somebody else."

"Ben," she said softly, "there ain't nobody else. An ain't goin to be."

"Why?"

Aunt Letty studied him for a minute or two, then closed her eyes and took in a deep breath, finally letting it out with a long sigh. "Ben, you know these people. You know how supersticious they be. They think Tilly come with some kinda spell around her." She shook her turbaned head and bunched up her face, not telling him the other reason Tilly was shunned by the locals. "She needs somebody to be with, Ben. I can't keep her with me all de time."

Ben turned that around in his mind. *Spell?* He knew a little about spells, and it took a root man like Bones to get rid of a spell. So, why didn't Aunt Letty get Bones to fix her?

"Aunt Letty, no matter what, I ain't gonna take that girl nowhere."

Suddenly, Aunt Letty seemed to rise to the heavens and stomped her foot so hard the earth shook. "Dat's it. Dat's all I'm goin to take from you. You be de most selfish boy I know without one tiny thought of anythin but yourself. Now, I ain't askin, I tellin. You take Tilly outta this market and you be nice to her."

Stunned, Ben stood mouth agape staring at her.

Ignoring him, she walked quickly back to her table as he angrily followed behind.

Ben's eyes narrowed and followed Tilly's down to where they were fixed on her new high-button shoes. He surily brushed the sand off one bare foot with the other and had a longing to see the shiny brown leather of her shoes scratched and muddy.

"C'mon," he ordered, yanking his arm around. He made a steady track away from the market, weaving through the thickets of palmettos and tall weeds. "You better keep up or a bear will get ya." Never looking back to see if she followed. *Maybe a rattler will get her*, he thought.

After walking a good distance through heavy brush and a thick growth of pines and hardwoods, he came to a trillium-banked stream flowing over moss-covered rocks and stepped over them to the other side. He looked back, the thought crossing his mind that Aunt Letty would kill him if anything happened to that girl. A chill ran down his back. *Or worse*, Bones. She was okay, walking close behind him staring at the ground. His anger began to ease as they came out on a dirt road where huge old live oaks, their massive limbs forming a long arch, lined the way down to a building facing the marsh.

When they neared the end of the road, the ruins of an exquisite tabby house that faced the marsh came clearly into view. Much of the outer structure of oyster shell, lime, sand, and water was intact, but it was just a frame for the almost bare interior. Ben always wondered who had owned it. And why they left it. As beautiful as it was, it looked so forlorn and forgotten. It wasn't like the large plantations along the river he had heard about. It was just this one house without the outbuildings. He looked at the majestic oaks with sweeping limbs gracing the lawn to the water. Off some distance to the side was a walled-in area with honeysuckle falling over the tabby, and inside the rusty iron gate were the remains of a garden and a bench overlooking a pond.

This was his favorite place in the world. It had a ghostly beauty. He had never been here with anyone before. In fact, he had never seen anyone here in all the times he had come since he found it after Pa Clary died. Often, he would lie down on the grass and let the salty breeze put him to sleep. Surprisingly, it didn't bother him that Tilly was there. As long as he didn't have to be with her.

"You can do what you want," he told her without a trace of malice. He pointed to the walled-in garden. "I'm goin over there. I'll find you when I'm ready to leave."

Tilly watched Ben until he disappeared then walked to the house. She ran her hands over the old and worn surface of the tabby shell and slowly edged her way to a large opening that must have been an elaborate entrance once. She stepped over broken-off pieces of the structure and went inside. The interior was gutted by weather and time with only the partial remains of walls leading up to where the loss of roof framed a deep blue sky, giving the illusion of a painted ceiling. Where she stood at the front door, a wide space that would have been the entrance hall passed directly to an opening where the back door had been. She walked carefully over the broken and rotted remnants of the wide plank floors, more dirt than debris, and looked out the back open space to weeds, shallow woods and off to the left the oak lined drive.

She went back outside and ran to a ground-hugging limb of an old live oak, crawled up on it, leaned against the trunk, and watched two gulls screaming and fighting in the air over one's catch, only for it to drop back into the water. She quickly turned her face away from the marsh, squeezed her eyes shut, and shuddered.

Suddenly in the stillness she heard something and quickly moved to the edge of the limb. She heard it again, an unfamiliar sound in the distance. She jumped down and ran toward Ben, looking back every other step. She saw him through the gate lying on a bench, his knees bent, his eyes closed. She watched him for some time, almost going to him, but a black cloud passed under the sun, encasing the garden in a mantle of gloom. She wrapped her arms around herself and faced the marsh. Dark patches of the dying winter grass swayed in the wind, catching beams of sunlight in the tall reeds then casting it out as the spartina rippled over the pluff mud. She sucked in her breath, feeling the marsh's sinuous fingers reaching for her.

She ran back to the house and crouched close to the wall, watching shadows under the trees forming ghostly shapes. Tears welled, and she got up to run back to Ben when she heard a cracking noise close by. Twigs were breaking by the side of the house. She squeezed her eyes shut and made a ball of herself as footsteps neared then stopped. She jumped up, ran to the front opening of the house and stepped across the entrance, careful not to make noise. When she straightened, she looked directly into the repugnant face of a man with a head of unruly graying hair, holding a half-empty bottle of whiskey. A faded black cotton shirt seemed pasted over a bulging belly. His khaki riding pants, tucked into high boots, were held up by a wide belt with a gun holster. Both shocked, they stared at one-another.

"Who the hell are you?" the man slurred.

Tilly put her hands behind her and started backing up.

His face twisted in a sneer. "Cat got your tongue? You must be one of those pickaninnies across the woods. I ain't your pappy, am I?" He laughed raucously, moving toward her. "What you got behind your back?"

Tilly turned and started to run, but he grabbed and twisted her around.

"I asked what ya got in your hands," he said, pulling out the arm holding her little toy.

"What the hell is this?" He leaned his head back and looked maliciously at the broken object she held tightly. "Now, a big girl like you don't need some broken up toy, do you?" he mocked.

She yanked her arm away as he tried to take it from her, glaring with ferocious intensity, and kicked his shin with all her might.

"Oww!" he howled. "Why you fuckin' little shit." He grabbed her dress as she turned to run and swung back the whisky bottle. "I'm gonna whop the hell outta ya." He was pulling her to him when Ben ran into the house.

"Let her go," Ben yelled and pushed the drunk backwards, catching him off balance. The man stumbled, dropping his bottle on a sharp edge of a piece of broken tabby.

"You fuckin' river rats. I'm gonna kill ya." He reached for his gun as Tilly and Ben ran for the door. Suddenly his hand froze on the pistol.

Startled, he stared at it. He tried to yank at it with the other, but that one wouldn't move either. Bewildered, he stared at his useless hands and hollered, "What the hell?" He struggled to get up but was as stiff as a stone statue. "What's happened to me?" he yelled. His face took on a mad, grotesque expression. "Why can't I move?" he wailed frantically. "Somebody help me."

Ben looked back, wondering what the drunk was screaming about, and thought he saw a flash of red moving behind the house, but he dismissed it and ran with Tilly into the woods toward home. Angry and frightened, he yelled at her, "It's all your fault, you stupid girl. We coulda got killed."

When they arrived back at the commune, Ben sat on his haunches, sweat pouring down his face, bewildered about what to do. Aware Tilly was standing beside him, he looked up at her tear-streaked face, her mouth hanging open. His chest tightened, and he hung his head down, then stood.

"I'm sorry. I didn't mean what I said. I was just scared." He looked her up and down and asked, "Did he hurt ya?"

She avoided looking at her reddened wrist and shook her head side to side.

"Where did that guy come from?" Remembering she couldn't answer, he said, "Oh lordy, you can't tell me nothing."

He wiped his face on his shirt and looked toward Aunt Letty's booth and winced. "Oh Lordy." He looked over at the docks and saw no one. He looked at Tilly standing beside him.

"Tilly, that had to be a drifter maybe looking for a place to spend the night. I guess no one needs to know. As long as you're okay."

She nodded slowly.

"I ain't gonna say nothing to Aunt Letty." He looked sideways at her. Again, she nodded.

Aunt Letty saw them coming and smiled until she saw their faces. "What in the world is wrong with you two?"

Tilly went to her and folded into Aunt Letty's arms.

"Just tired," Ben said hesitantly. "Had a long walk."

Aunt Letty pushed the little girl away to look at her face, but Tilly looked down, not letting her see her eyes. Aunt Letty shifted her gaze to Ben. "I've been pushin you too hard, Ben. I knew Tilly didn't wanna go off. I guess its been a hard day for you. I won't ask again."

⁂

As Ben walked to his bateau before dawn the next morning, he saw Long Robby with his men getting his fishing boat ready to go out, but he decided not to say anything about the night before. *Just some old drunk drifter,* he told himself. *No need to worry anyone. Probably slept it off and already down the road.*

After selling his morning catch in town, he walked down the main street to Mr. Moody's general store.

"Hi, Mr. Moody. Are your seed books in the back?"

"Yep, they sure are, Ben. You planting a garden?"

"Mebbe. Mr. Moody, do you know anything bout that tabby house on the marsh down the way?"

Mr. Moody laughed. "Ben, I don't think anyone knows about it. Why you asking?"

"Oh, just wondered," he said as he walked to the back of the store.

Two minutes later, a sour-faced man holding a rifle case walked up to the counter.

Mr. Moody looked at him, surprised. He forced a smile. "Mr. Savage. I heard you were back in town." He looked at the case, curious. "Ya going after turkey or hogs?"

"Neither," he said wearily. "Getting my rifle cleaned. Moody, do you know who that tabby house down the way belongs to?"

Mr. Moody whooped, and said, "I'll be dang. I have never been asked about that place since I been here and not five minutes ago someone else wanted to know the same thing."

"Who was that?"

Mr. Moody noticed the flicker in Savage's eyes and was already sorry he had said anything. "Oh, just some kid who comes in here. Don't know his name."

Junie Savage studied Mr. Moody's face. "He still here, Moody?"

"Well, he was in the back awhile ago."

Savage looked toward the back of the store. "Maybe he still is."

Ben had been listening, alerted to danger. The man's voice. He had no doubt that man was the drunk from last night, and he had to get out of there. He ran behind the barrels and out the back door before Savage could see him, hightailing it back to the commune.

"I don't see anyone back here, Moody," Savage said gruffly.

Mr. Moody bit his lip. "He'd been here a while. Probably left while I was busy."

Savage walked to the front and slapped his hand on the counter with a menacing glare and stormed out the door.

⌒

Ben didn't stop until he got to the docks. Long Robby was just pulling in, and he hopped on one foot and the other until he could get his attention. Long Robby waved.

"You wanna see me, Ben?"

"Yeah, I do, Long Robby," he hollered, panting.

"I'll be awhile. I'll come find you."

Ben sat on one of the benches, winded.

"Hey, young fella, what's got you lookin upset on this pretty day?" Long Robby called as he approached.

Ben jumped up from the seat. "Long Robby, I gotta tell you something that happened yesterday. I did . . . "

"Hey, slow down." Long Robby laughed as Ben's words stumbled out all at once. "Let's just sit down here and you can tell me all about it."

Ben told him of finding Tilly with a drunk, the skirmish that followed, and what just happened at the store. "I thought he was a whiskey drifter, Long Robby, but now I know for sure it was Junie Savage."

Long Robby sat looking into space. "You sure he didn't hurt Tilly?"

"I asked her. She just shook her head."

"Ben, we need to tell this to Aunt Letty."

"Ohhhh," Ben groaned. "Long Robby, I don't think I wanna do that."

Despite the seriousness of the situation, Long Robby laughed. "She can be a little hard when she dont like somethin, but you saved Tilly's life, it sounds like. She'll be grateful."

"I ain't so sure bout that, Long Robby. I didn't tell her about yesterday, and she ain't gonna like that."

Long Robby chuckled and put his arm around Ben. "Maybe not, but I'll be there with you."

Aunt Letty surprised them. After Long Robby repeated what Ben told him, she just shook her head. "I been dreadin this. And wonderin why he come home. Why now?" She frowned. "Long Robby, why do you think he was at dat house?"

"No tellin, Letty. It's always been a mystery what goes on in Junie's head."

"I think someone else was there, Aunt Letty. When I was running into the woods, I looked back and saw something red moving behind the house."

A smile began to curl at the edges of Aunt Letty's mouth. "Mebbe so, Ben. Mebbe so."

"Why did he leave here?" Ben asked.

"We think he was broke. He wasn't paying his people and there wasn't no one to work the cotton. Then came the boll weevil. No one could fight dat. He been gone bout seven years. Now dat devil is back. We have to be aware of dat now, Letty. Ben, I would be careful goin back to dat house. He may have just been nosying aroun, but hard to know with Junie. I don't think you have nothin to worry bout. Just keep your eyes open."

"I sure hope you're right, Long Robby."

The following afternoon, Ben paddled down the river to where
he had left his traps at a little dock near his favorite swimming pond.

It was so quiet he jumped when he heard what sounded like low
voices and a rustling of leaves. "What in tarnation?" he whispered to
himself. He rowed quietly to the dock and tied the traps to the back
of his boat. No one went in those woods much, except to shoot a deer.
He got shivers.

He rowed quickly back to the cove where he kept his boat just
beyond Henny's house. He pulled it under the chinquapin and checked
the tin wire traps. He had two dozen or more big blues, and at least
half of them were she-crabs full of roe. He could sell all of them to the
colored cooks up on the Square. They loved those she-crabs for soup.

After he sold all the crabs, with nothing better to do, he roamed
the woods toward the railroad tracks that divided the colored shanty
town from the shacks of the poorer whites. Drowsy from the heat, he
lay back on the ground, welcoming the shade from a large oak, and
slept until a falling acorn awakened him. Dusk was casting its gray
shadows upon the tracks. With one foot before the other, he inched
his way along the rails toward home.

As he came closer to the shacks, imagined perils stirred his
mind. On one side were white-cloaked shapes undulating like candle
flames. On the other side were the spectral shapes of black figures
circling cauldrons of mystic brew to the beat of the drums. He was so
spellbound by his fantasy that when a large dark form loomed from
the trees, he was certain he had just taken his last breath. Flattening
himself to the ground alongside the rails, he watched as the figure lit
across the tracks. "Aunt Letty," he gasped into the packed dirt, swiping
at his dusty eyes lest he lose sight of her. Before he could blink, another
movement caught his eye.

Creeping from the darkness of the shanties, a creature emerged,
the like of which he had only heard about in the muffled gossip of the
market. "Bones." Ben's hair stood on end. Like an elongated skeleton,
the blackest man Ben had ever seen hobbled across the tracks, his shiny

head thrust forward and beamed on Aunt Letty's path. His face was bony and scarred with brows of an eagle hooding his sunken eyes and he was bare, except for a faded red cloth draped about his waist. Ben's heart pounded where he lay against the crushed oyster until his body was cooled by the darkness.

Lying on his pine mat that night, his ears pricked to every creak of the wide boards or sigh of the cracked wood plank walls, he pondered what he had seen. Aunt Letty's daring was not too surprising. She had more gumption than a minnow chasing a sea bass, but surely even for Aunt Letty, venturing across what he thought was a forbidden line was odd. And Bones. Now that was something else again. *Bones*, he repeated over and over until sleep finally shut out the commotion of his mind.

CHAPTER 3

As soon as Ben had taken care of his business the next day, he ran to the market looking for Henny, but he was nowhere in sight. Dark clouds were approaching, and he guessed right that Henny would be on his porch. Sitting next to him was Tilly.

Panting, he blurted out, "What's she doing here?"

Henny lay his hook and string in his lap. As kindly as he could, he said, "Ben, Tilly is visiting. Now come on up here and sit down with us."

"I wanted to talk to you, Henny. Without no one else here." He was so upset his voice cracked. He turned to walk away.

"Ben," Henny called, "hold on." He walked out to Ben, putting his arm over his shoulder. "There's no reason to get your feelings hurt, son. Aunt Letty needs help with Tilly right now. She and I been friends about all our lives so when I can I'm gonna help her."

With his arm on Ben's shoulder, he turned to face him. "I pretty much know how ya feel bout her. Letty told me she felt bad being so hard on you."

Henny sighed and looked back at the porch where Tilly sat quietly. "Ben, she don't have a soul in the world to care about her except for Letty and us. It won't hurt you none to be nice to her."

Ben looked down at his feet, thinking that he had never felt alone.

He'd grown up with all the people here and was made to feel like family by them. He never felt different being white.

"I'm sorry, Henny. She's okay. I just didn't expect her to be here with you."

Henny smiled and hugged Ben's shoulder. "Tilly being here don't change a thing between you and me. We're still best buddies, right?"

Ben looked up, the heaviness easing out of his chest. "We sure are, Henny."

Henny ruffled Ben's mop of hair affectionately and said, "Okay."

"Henny, what's she holding onto?"

"I asked Letty that, Ben. She just don't know, an that little girl sure can't tell her. Before you came, I asked her if I could see it and she folded it in her dress, staring at me like I'd take it from her. She'll find a way to tell us when she's ready."

Henny patted Tilly's knee as he sat back in his chair, noticing the sadness that seemed to always be there in her eyes.

"Ben has somethin he wants to tell us, Tilly."

"It's about Bones and Aunt Letty. I saw them last night, Henny. They were crossing the tracks going over to the poor white shanties."

"Hmmm," Henny murmured and leaned his straight back cedar chair against the house, his scruffy old boots resting against the rail, and studied a buzzard circling in the sky.

"Isn't that kinda peculiar?"

"Ben, how old are you now anyhow?"

Ben, surprised, said, "Before Pa Clary died, he told me he'd found me about ten Christmases ago. That was 1910. I remember that because he said it would be easy to know how old I was each year. Pa died about three years ago, so I must be almost thirteen."

Henny chuckled softly. "You're growing up, boy." He winked at Tilly and settled back in his chair.

"Why you wanna know that, Henny?"

"Well, just thinking you're about the age Judson Savage was when he went after Bones."

"What d'ya mean?"

"I'm gonna tell you." He settled back in the chair, spat out another amber stream across the porch rail, and said, "But remember, sometimes you're better off the less you know.

"Bones' folks was enslaved at Granterre from the time the Africans landed here. It was the grandest plantation on the coast then. Still is. With the cruelest masters around. Bones' mama ran the house for the third generation of Savages. Bones was a queer fella, they say—sulky and quiet as a tree stump. And odd to look at, too. Black as mules' blood, legs like stilts, and his head slick as a melon. He'd thrust that head forward with his eyes staring straight before him like he was seeing into another world.

"There was talk, even then, that he had acquired the mantle, a gift of vision it's called, from King Oosafella who came over from Africa. He refused to work the fields, and he weren't fit for the house. Nobody couldn't make him do nothin, and his mama didn't try. She knew he was special and just let him be.

"Judson Savage weren't as old as Bones but decided he'd see to it Bones did his work. So he took to the whip." Henny scratched his chin. "But it didn't do no good, and Judson finally figgered he'd have to think of somethin else to save face with his daddy.

"Judson knew the Gullah was terrified of the water because of all the stories of the slaves dying in the bilge of ships bringing them over, all those dying of malaria and other sicknesses out in the rice fields. No matter what the weather or how sick they was, they died without a decent burial, lottsa times being thrown out dead in deeper water to float down stream. But it was the devilfish that Judson decided to use to get Bones. You ever hear of a devilfish?"

"Yeah!" Ben's eyes widened. "I sure have. From Pa. He used to go out at night when the tide was low and find em. He said watching them play was as much fun as he found on the water. He never did gig em."

"No, I didn't neither. Gentle souls that they are. But oh my goodness did they look menacing. They was a sight for your eyes."

"Pa said they was big as his boat."

"Ben, their wings spread twice the width of a six-foot-tall man. They would jump ten feet outta the water and do somersaults over and over under the surface of the water. It sure was a show. It was the horn-like fins next to the head that gave them their name. Made them look evil. There wasn't one Gullah anywhere along the coast that would risk being near somethin they believed was sent by the devil. An, of course, that's what the slave owners told them. Said they was there to catch any slave that thought about escaping across the water."

"So, what'd Judson do?"

"He told Bones to take him out for a boat ride an if he didn't take him, he'd do somethin bad to his ma. Bones knew he would, too. Bones didn't know nothin about boats, but Judson got a Gullah who did. Bones was shaking so hard the boat swayed and dipped, and when they found the devilfish not far from shore, he started moaning. There was a whole school of em. I can just see Bones looking down at those monsters, the way they swam with their mouths open, expecting they was just waiting for em. Judson told Bones to stand up. He knew Bones couldn't swim. He was shaking so bad he fell over before Judson could push him. Right in the middle of those mantas. Judson told the other feller to take him on back home, leaving Bones flapping around in the water moanin."

"Bones can do anything, Henny. Why was he so scared?"

"I reckon if you're so scared of somethin, you might forget that." He frowned. "Don't ask so many questions, boy. Lemme finish my story.

"Anyway, Judson went to bed smiling, but it wasn't long before he felt somethin crawling round his feet. There was enough moonlight for him to see a snake as big round as his daddy's bulging waist with mean, small beady eyes and hissing with deadly intent. Judson opened his mouth to scream, but nothing came out. He tried to move but couldn't move. He was paralyzed from fear. The room filled with nasty critters crawling in bed with him. There's no telling how scared he was. All anyone heard was his story, which no one believed. By the time the varmints had slid away, Judson's natural eliminations had let go and left a pool of foulness on the bed. His scream was heard throughout the house, and his pa, ma, and all house servants on duty rushed to see Judson crying in his mess like a baby. His father turned on him and said he didn't want to see him until he grew up. His mother was horrified but pitied him. The house servants hid their grins until they were safely out of the house. It's said he didn't go around no one for a long time, hiding out wherever he could."

Tilly had her hands clasped over her mouth, but her eyes were twinkling.

Ben was laughing so hard he wiped his eyes. "What happened to Bones?"

"Like I told you, Bones had ways. The Gullah boy who rowed em out to the devilfish went back to look for Bones. He couldn't be sure but thought he saw a body on top of one of the rays, floating down the river. No one saw Bones again for many a year." He winked at Ben. "I don't think there's much doubt about Bones seeing his chance to get away from that place without it causing trouble to his mama.

"'He'll be back someday,' his mama said, 'when he is good and ready.'"

With the end of his story, Henny pushed the white shirt sleeves up on his arms and with boots resting on the rail settled back and gazed at the grey swirls of clouds moving out to sea.

Ben looked with consternation at Henny. "Well, what was Aunt Letty doing with Bones anyhow?"

"Patience, boy, patience. Only so many hours for story telling in a good day."

"Aw, Henny." Ben grasped the arm of Henny's chair. "Dagburn it, Henny, that's what I wanted to know in the first place."

Henny, studying his bony hands, said, "I don't know about last night, Ben, but I can guess. Bones don't come around much. Letty can handle most things on her own."

"What d'ya mean?"

"Letty's the midwife. She brings all the little Gullah babies into the world an sometimes the poorer whites. On occasion she takes care of some of the problems folks get themselves into. Both Gullah and white." He got up and leaned over the porch rail and spat out a wad of tobacco. "Letty has gifts taught her by Bones."

"Gifts?" Ben looked at him, puzzled.

"Ways to take care of some evil things."

Ben's face brightened. "I know about some evil things, Henny. I know about plateyes and boodaddies. What kind of ways does Aunt Letty have?"

"Ways with spirits. To the Gullah, spirits are as alive as you are to me sitting there." He stopped to reason with this. "The Africans brought beliefs over with them, and they passed them down and not just witchcraft but knowledge of herbs and roots and other things. They live and breathe spirits."

"Do you believe in spirits, Henny?"

"Well, reckon I do." He shook his head slowly. "I've heard some stories makin it hard not to believe. I know Pop did."

"Whew," Ben muttered. "I never knew nothing like this about Aunt Letty. How did she get to be so close to Bones?"

"Well, that's another story for another time, son, and nothing you really want to know. There's just sadness in this world, and sometimes it's hellbent on finding a body no matter whatcha do. Letty was just a girl when she run off from home." He looked out toward the river, lost in his thoughts. "After some speculation, most folks thought Bones had found her. She learnt his ways an in time began caring for the sick and bringing babies into the world."

"So, Aunt Letty and Bones was helping some sick person last night? Some white sick person?"

Henny shook his head and sighed. "Not sure about that, Ben. More likely something dark musta been around. Bones is special, Ben. He's different from the rest of the Gullah. You know that. One thing I know is you're not likely to ever know what they was up to so mights well get it outta your head."

Henny stretched his arms, yawned, and looked down, surprised to see Tilly sitting at his feet. He had been so caught up in his story he had not seen her move. He started to lean down and speak to her but quickly steadied himself, shaken by her expression. She sat stiffly on her bent legs, her eyes as alert as a frightened small animal. On her lap, her long slender fingers held the object of wonder she had clung to so guardedly. A tiny white painted bird sat on top of a mast, most likely from a sailboat, where two torn cloth sails hung forlornly. It was hand carved and well done.

Ben had leaned over to look at it with Henny. An odd, somewhat sad, feeling lodged in his throat. He looked at Tilly and smiled.

She stared back and after a while smiled back and clasped the fragment of her past to her chest.

Henny wanted to pull her up in his arms and make all her heartache go away. Instead, he smiled and said, "Thank you for letting me see your treasure, Tilly.

"I'll tell you what, Tilly. That's a cute little bird on top of the mast. He's looking out like he's enjoying the ride. I bet he's a little marsh bird." He thought, *One step closer to Tilly. Certainly, her trust.*

Henny pushed himself out of the chair. "Just so happens that I have a pot of beans and rice on the stove just waitin to be heated and eaten. How bout that?"

Ben took his time walking home along the dirt river banks, skirting the shallow laps of amber wake and poking at the fiddlers with his bony toes while his mind dwelled on Henny's story. The big swamp, the scary one, was down off the river, beyond the dark blue-green expanse of the pine barren. He'd been there once chasing after a wild turkey and had gone further than he realized until there, beyond a sumpy clearing, was a swamp, as dark and ominous as the devil's mouth. Steam rose from blood black water and the ghoulish corpse of cypress were entangled in strands of moss, spun from limb to bony limb like giant spider webs awaiting prey. It was still, so still, but he knew something was there, slithering through the mist. Then the hoot of an owl jolted him back, and he bolted through the woods barely breathing until he fell, heart pounding, on the solid ground of Christ Church.

He turned toward the wharf and sat on the low stone wall, the eerie foghorn of the side-wheeler filling his ears. *Things sure is strange sometimes,* he thought. Aunt Letty and Bones. Bones did magic. Everybody knew that. He made plat-eyes and hexes and boiled black cats for their bones. *I like being with Henny,* he thought. *And Tilly's okay.* He climbed the rickety steps of the warehouse as it began to rain and lay on the remnant of an old sail, listening to the haunting whistle of the wind.

CHAPTER 4

Aunt Letty had put aside a dozen cinnamon buns, and after she cleaned up for the day, she put them in a box. Orie told her that morning that Miss Becky was going to Savannah and it would be a good time to visit Beau, who had been on her mind ever since they talked. She was not a coward, but she did have a hard time facing Miss Becky and Mr. Michael Morton. She felt their blame even if they didn't accuse her.

She knocked on the back door of the Morton house on the Square, expecting Orie, but it was Rebecca Morton who answered.

"I know you were expecting Orie, Letty, but she and Brian have run an errand for me in Savannah. She told me you were coming." She smiled sweetly. "I'm so glad to see you, Letty," she said, holding the door open. "Come in and sit in the breakfast room with me. I want to talk to you." She looked at the box in Aunt Letty's hand and smiled again. "If that is what I think, I know someone else who will be glad to see you."

"It be for all de children, Miss Becky."

"Then they all will be pleased. Beau has missed you, Letty. He cares about you. I mean that, Letty."

They sat across from one another, Rebecca Morton with her arms resting in her lap, Aunt Letty sitting up as straight as the pine chair.

"Letty, Orie told me how you worry about being responsible for Beau's deformed foot. I want to tell you something, and I want you to put your mind at rest and never think of blaming yourself again."

Letty shifted her gaze a little to the side. She had heard all that before.

"Letty, you listen to me. I see that look on your face," she said impatiently.

"Miss Becky, you can talk yourself blue in de face. I ain't never gonna believe I didn't cause dat foot to be dat way unless some doctor say I didn't."

"Look at it this way. Beau would not be alive, and very likely neither would I, if you had not been the bravest young woman alive and come to me when we couldn't find old Doc Holly. I was in so much pain I was delirious. You saved our lives, Letty. If the birth caused Beau's foot to be deformed, that is little to pay for his life."

"Mebbe so, Miss Becky."

Rebecca threw her hands up in the air. "I can't talk to you. You are impossible. Just go on believing what you will, Letty. But I cannot see the sense in anyone making themselves miserable. You know the way to Beau's room."

When Letty got up, Rebecca said, "Wait a minute, Letty. I wanted to tell you that my husband told me Mr. Savage was back in town. He is interested in that tabby house across from your community."

Aunt Letty frowned. "What he want dat place for, Miss Becky?"

She sighed. "We have no idea what he wants with it. Mr. Morton said Mr. Savage wanted to find out how he could get it without paying for it since it had been vacant for so long. By squatting or homesteading or other ways. Frankly, Letty, I think most people have forgotten it's there, but anyway, when Mr. Morton told him to stay away from that property or he would see to it he was fined for trespassing, Junie got angry and ran out of my husband's office yelling he was going to report my husband for not performing legal matters responsibly or some such nonsense. My husband said he couldn't take any action against Mr. Savage for going there, but he suspected he was up to no good and hoped what he said would stop him. My husband is the only lawyer in this small county, and that prevents Junie Savage from going any further legally with this matter. I think he did scare him away from going back to that house. I hope so." She put one hand on the table and leaned slighty forward. "I'm so sorry he came back, Letty. I know of all the wretchedness he has caused you and your people."

"Yes'm, he sure done dat."

"He is an evil man, Letty. No telling what he'll be up to now."

Aunt Letty laughed. "Dat's what everyone says." She frowned. "For de life of me. Miss Becky, I never could understand how your great aunt, Miss Jenny, the sweetest woman in de world, could be married to Junie Savage's father. He was worse than his son."

Rebecca was quiet for a moment. "She had no choice, Letty."

Aunt Letty knew Miss Becky wasn't going to say more, but she had always wondered about that. "Miss Becky, if it ain't been for Miss Jenny, I don't know what woulda happen to Orie. She was just a little girl and Miss Jenny saw to it dat your grandmother took her in. I'll never forget dat."

"I wasn't born yet, but my mother loved Orie like family."

Yeah, she be like family, but she calls you Miss Becky, follows behind you, an takes care of you. She sure don't eat with you or use your toilets and never did, I bet. She sits in the kitchen and eats out back. She only felt a little ashamed for thinking that. Orie would never say anything against the Mortons. But that was the way it was. Letty knew what she thought was true. She was just grateful that Orie had a good home.

"From what I heard, you are rignt, Letty. Judson Savage was worse than his son. If that is possible. I never knew Aunt Jenny. Letty, the story my mother told me about how the Savages hurt you breaks my heart." She looked with compassion to Letty. But when Aunt Letty looked down at the floor, Rebecca remembered she had crossed the line. No one spoke to Aunt Letty about that. She quickly changed the subject. "Beau is waiting for you, Letty. I won't keep you any longer."

CHAPTER 5

It had been a hot and humid spring, and today was the worst day of all. Clouds of mosquitoes needled after every inch of Ben's body; not even the stinky silt kept them away. He had been pining for a swim at Goose Neck pond all morning, hardly thinking about anything else but the clean, cool water of the spring. He headed his boat toward the pond when he thought of Tilly and Aunt Letty. *Tilly would like Goose Neck*, he thought. *Aunt Letty needed some help.* He felt right proud of himself as he turned his boat around.

Tilly saw him coming before Aunt Letty and moved quickly behind the woman's back to hide her smile. Aunt Letty, taken by surprise, a rare and she thought dangerous reaction on her part, gathered her composure. "Well, if it ain't Ben. Good to see you, Ben." She smiled in that inscrutable way that made Ben not sure what to do next. "Ben, have a biscuit. I know they be your favorites."

Ben was watching Tilly come out from behind Aunt Letty's skirts. He had a moment of hesitation, but the sweet smell coming from the sausage was more powerful than his doubt. "I sure thank you, Aunt Letty."

"What you up to, Ben?"

"Well," he said blushing, "I thought Tilly might want to go with me to Goose Neck for a swim."

Aunt Letty looked down at Tilly, who was now grinning so widely that the woman almost laughed. "Ben, I think she just might like dat." She looked puzzled and asked, "Tilly, can you swim?"

Tilly nodded up and down.

"But she's gotta have somethin to swim in." She looked over at Emmie and called, "You got somethin Tilly can wear to swim?"

Emmy rifled through her piles of clothing on her table and pulled out a child's flowered jumper with pantaloon legs. She held it up. "This do?" She looked it over and laughed. "She can have it if she'll wear it. I'll cut off some of the bottom."

Aunt Letty was beside herself with something between gratitude and triumph. "Why don't you take some of dese bittles just in case you get hungry?"

Ben was lightheaded with pleasure. *Bittles*. The Gullah word for food. He managed a half smile at Tilly and said, "C'mon."

They walked to the wharf where Ben had tied his boat. "You'll like where we're going, Tilly. It's my favorite swimming hole."

She smiled at him.

He pulled his boat onto a bank where the woodlands and marsh met and tied it to a myrtle limb. "This is where we get off."

He took her hand and pulled her out. "Let's go get in that water. The only way to get there is to run. As fast as you can."

She laughed and Ben did, too, until he realized she wasn't making any sound. *Holy Moses*, he thought. *That girl don't know how to laugh, either.*

He ran into the forest, Tilly behind him, and yelled, "Wahooo, Goosey Pond, here we come." They laughed as the startled wild turkeys gobbled and flew away. It was quiet but for an occasional rustle of a black-faced squirrel and Ben slowed his pace, inhaling the earthy smells of the forest dampness until he saw the pond ahead. With another shout, he looked back at Tilly. She looked happy, maybe for the first time since he saw her. She looked around the pond for a place to put her toy, then with arms flailing, jumped into the shallows of the inky-black spring-fed water, rolling, laughing, and splashing until they felt the draining heat of the day washed from their bodies.

They lay on their backs listening to the occasional trill of a songbird in the stillness. There were several spring-fed ponds nearby, but this was his favorite, secluded as it was. At dusk a white blanket of wood storks would fill the leafy space around the spring, roosting on every limb like tiny soldiers guarding the pond. Reluctantly, he said, "Guess we gotta go now."

She followed him out of the dark water colored by tannin from the hard woods and stood to let the soaked jumper drain some.

Ben smiled to himself. Whatever he did she did.

"Hey, Tilly," he teased, "I'll race you back to the boat."

They were both laughing so hard by the time they got to the boat they were oblivious to anything but themselves until a noise sounding like a gunshot followed by angry voices rebounded across the river. Startled, he glanced back at Tilly, who was looking at where the sounds had come from. "You hear that, too?" he whispered.

She nodded.

The voices had stopped, but Ben kept staring at the woods. *Just like yesterday*, he thought. His inclination was to paddle away as fast as he could, but he was curious. He looked at Tilly. "I gotta see what that is." At her fearful expression, he said, "Likely just someone hunting for something."

He rowed across the river slowly, keeping the oars from splashing. His voice barely above a whisper, he said, "Tilly, you stay put. I mean it. I promise I won't be long." He was pretty sure of that.

He stepped gingerly on the hardened surface of the leaves. He didn't see anyone, but he could hear voices. He was getting ready to move up behind a large oak when a hand clasped hard on his shoulder. He almost yelped, but a deep gravelly voice stilled any movement he might have made. "What are you doing here, boy?" A tall, thin, middle-aged man with black hair slicked to his head, black straight brows, and a long pointed nose, yanked Ben around. "Answer me," he demanded, his black eyes narrowing.

Ben's voice cracked. "I just got my traps, sir."

"I don't see no traps. What are you doing in these woods? And if you don't tell me the truth, boy, you have seen your last day."

Ben saw the butt of a gun in the man's belt and began shaking so hard he felt his pants slide on his hips. "I thought I heard noises and was just looking to see." He was thinking fast. "But I guess I was wrong."

The man chuckled sardonically. "Yeah, boy, I reckon you were. Now you listen to me. Don't you ever come near here again. And, if you do have traps, you find another place to put em. I'm letting you go now, but if I ever see your hide again, I'll slit your throat." He removed a knife from a sheath on his belt and slid the flat of the blade across Ben's neck. "Easy as that. Now GET!"

Ben started running to his boat and heard someone else running ahead of him.

"Hey, what's that? You got someone with you?"

Oh, Lordy. Tilly. "No sir, just a squirrel," Ben called back and ran faster than he ever had, leaping into the boat. Tilly's eyes were so wide open he didn't say anything. Besides all he wanted to do was get home.

When he pulled his boat into the cove, he said to Tilly, "You don't open your mouth to say nothin, Tilly," forgetting she couldn't. "Don't you dare tell Aunt Letty or I won't ever take you no place again."

⁓

When Ben finished telling Henny every detail of what happened, even to the way the man talked, he sighed and sat down on the porch floor.

Henny leaned back in his chair, frowning. "Ben, I been listening to every word you said, and for the life of me, I'm dumbfounded. I don't like what you told me, but I don't know what to do bout it."

"Could it have been thieves or somethin like that?"

"I thought of that, but what would they steal? And I thought about bootleggers, but that's not a good place for a still. I'm pretty sure it weren't the Kluxes. Never been any around here."

"Should I tell somebody else?"

"Well, that would be Long Robby." He thought a moment. "Ben, if I was you, I'd just stay away from that area. Let's just keep quiet and see what happens."

Ben's eyes got so big Henny laughed. "Going back there ain't worth getting my throat slit."

After Ben left, Henny knit his brows and leaned back in his chair, thinking about the men in the woods.

CHAPTER 6

As spring slipped into summer, Ben stopped more often at Aunt Letty's after work was done to take Tilly to swim at other ponds or just to sit by the docks and watch the boats go by. One day he noticed she no longer carried the little bird toy. He had never had a friend his age before. Rufus was nice to him, but he had his own friends from the school. Though he would have been loath to admit it, even understand it, he accepted her place beside him as if he had been waiting for her. He hadn't realized he was lonely. Except for Henny and the fishermen who had their own lives, his friends were the wild birds of the marsh and other speechless forms of life.

Early one morning, before the sun cast its first shimmer of light, the last of the summer squalls exploded onto shore without warning. Curled in a ball under a scrap of canvas from an old sail, Ben was awakened by the loud banging of the wood shutters. He ran to the window to fasten them before they broke off from the rusty hinges, already loose from years of wear.

"Holy Moses," he gasped, as he stared wide-eyed at the roiling gunmetal color of the sky. He closed the shutters, pulling the old warehouse wood slats across them, and winced as he remembered his boat. Instead of his usual mooring place, he had pulled it up on the bank of the river without tying it to anything. Usually, it was safe to do this,

but not in a strong wind. He grabbed his coat and squeezed into it, the
sleeves so long last year now halfway up his arms. Bracing against the
cold gusts of wind, he raced to the river, pushing at the brush on his way.
The little boat was where he left it but full of water.

Coulda been a lot worse, he thought, whistling a sigh of relief
between his teeth. He turned it over to drain out the water that had
poured into it, set it upright and pulled it away from the bank, pushed
it under a thick clump of brush, and wiped salt spray from his eyes. A
perch floundered on the edge of the water where it had been washed
in by the waves. He ran to it and threw it back in the river.

Wind wailed through the pines and thunder rattled the sky after
each jagged streak of lightning cover the marsh. *It's getting really bad
and I ain't going back to that cold place with misery pushing in through
every crack in the boards.* He looked toward Henny's home snuggled
against the woods. *Maybe I can get there without being blown away.*

He started to make a dash for it when a blinding stream of light
stretched across the sky, landing down the river with a crack that shook
the ground. He stopped, stunned at how close it struck.

"Oh my gosh," he yelled out loud. "That's about where Goose Neck
is, and that streak sure hit somethin." He ran to the edge of the water to
looking for any sign of fire. It was nearly impossible to see for the hard
rain and wind, but in the distance where he thought the lightning had
struck, he saw a strange glow. *That ain't no fire.* Shielding his eyes, he
stared at the light flickering in the wind and felt goosebumps all over his
body. *That's creepy. I've never seen that before, day or night. That sure ain't
no fire.* Another clap of thunder sounded nearby, and he turned and ran,
pushing against the wind and the slapping limbs and branches toward
the lights he saw in Henny's house until he jumped up on the porch and
banged on the door.

Henny reached out with one arm and yanked Ben inside. "Good
grief. You're as soaked as a drowned possum, boy. Get by the fire and
take off those rags. I'll get some towels."

He returned with towels, a flannel shirt, pants, and socks.

"Here, get them on. They're old clothes of Pop's but a sight better than what you're wearing." He studied Ben in his ragged pants. "Are those all ya got?

"Mostly."

Henny shook his head. "Well, keep what ya got on." He looked at the shivering boy and asked, frowning, "What are you doing out in this hellacious storm, anyway?"

"I had to get my boat further up on land. But, Henny, there's somethin mighty weird going on down the river."

Wide-eyed and still shaken from what he had seen, Ben told Henny about the light. "I mean it was spooky, Henny. I ain't never seen nothing like it. Henny, it wasn't no fire. It was just an eery kind of glow."

"Well, what do you think it was?"

"That's what I hoped you would know."

"Now how would I know that when I ain't seen it?" He raised an eyebrow at Ben.

"Henny, it was strange. Just about where Goose Neck is, I'm thinking. It was spooky."

"Okay, Ben, I believe you," Henny said. "But I can't give you no answers."

After a thoughtful while, Henny said, "Mighta been those ghosts that live in those woods."

Ben gave him a dirty look. "That light wasn't no ghosts."

"Aunt Letty might tell you different."

"That wasn't no ghosts, Henny," he said emphatically.

CHAPTER 7

The next morning, with the waters too swollen for Ben to think about fishing, he waited until he saw Aunt Letty and Tilly setting up the stall and ran to them so fast it startled Aunt Letty.

"What's got into you, Ben? You runnin from a ghost?"

His jaw dropped. "You been talking to Henny. It ain't funny, Aunt Letty. I been awake all night wondering bout that light."

"Am I supposed to know what you're talkin bout?"

Ben looked puzzled. "You ain't talked to Henny?"

"Not since yesterday."

Ben sighed with frustration.

"Lightning struck hard down the river last night, but when I looked, there wasn't no fire but an odd glowing light shining through the storm."

Aunt Letty's expression sent a shiver down Ben's spine.

"Where'd you see dat glow, Ben?"

"Looked to me near where Goose Neck Pond is."

"Well, you stay away from around there. Ain't safe."

"Why's ain't it safe, Aunt Letty?" Ben asked, perplexed.

She bunched up her lips and looked around at visions only she saw. "You just be smart and do as I say." She turned to Tilly. "And dat means you, too. Now ya'll git. I got work to do."

"Well, I came to tell you that Dicky gave Henny some ribs and he wants us to help him eat em tonight." As he walked away, his thoughts were not on dinner but on that light, and if the river calmed down the next day, he was going back there. No matter what Aunt Letty said.

After every succulent morsel of Dicky's barbecued ribs had been gnawed to bare bone, Aunt Letty, Henny, Ben, and Tilly settled around the warmth of the fireplace. Aunt Letty wriggled around until she was satisfied all her body parts fit then turned her gaze on Ben until he squirmed.

"Ahh, Aunt Letty. Why are you looking at me that way?"

"Cause I know what you be thinkin. You have it in your head to go down de river where you saw dat light."

Ben blushed. "Well, what's wrong with that?"

"What's wrong with dat be someone else be goin with you."

Tilly dropped her head, smiling.

Ben shook his head and said, "I'd never . . . "

"Don't you go on about what dis and what dat. I know you two," she said, her eyes gettin as big as the moon loomin over the river. "Dat's why I'm goin to tell you bout those ghosts in those woods.

"An, for your information, Long Robby went down dat river to the creek that runs off there, and there ain't nothin more than usual going on in dat swampy good-for-nothin land."

Ben, genuinely surprised, asked, "Long Robby went down there? Why'd he do that?"

"Well, maybe I'll tell you bout dat later. Maybe, but now I'm gonna tell you about those ghosts dat would eat you up if you even think bout goin in those woods."

She settled back and lay her hands in her lap.

"Long time ago, before I was born, de first master Warren ruled the plantation with a whip and an eye for pleasure." She stopped, thinking how she could delicately word what she had to say.

"Dat mean devil liked to play with de young ones. Particularly de young lil girls. There was one family with four boys and a lil girl. He come around the cabin often lookin at de boys and thinkin they would soon be strong enough to work de rice fields, but he also was watchin de pretty lil girl growin up.

"De family knew what de master had in mind and made plans to escape. They sneaked away on a dark night, not even tellin their families, fearin it would bring trouble to them if they knew. They walked close to the riverbank til it narrowed enough for them to cross over de rocks to de little island you be talkin about, Ben. It was so swampy and black it looked like de treetops be tied together, and they felt safe enough bein there while making plans to move along and get help on de underground railway like others had. But they had bad luck. One of de master's friends, maybe there for a deer, caught sight of two of de boys. The master got up a bunch of buckras and with a pack of dogs swarmed every grain of sand and mud until they found de family huddled together between a big clump of buttonbush and cypress. Those evil men shot every one of dat poor family and left them to rot and be picked over by de buzzards and critters.

"By and by most folks forgot about those folks." She shook her head sadly. "Dat sorta thing happened so much of de time. Then, not too long ago, Sherrif McTeer from de next county heard there was a good-sized still near dat swamp. So, he and some others went in one night to catch the moonshiner. They sneaked in just where those poor slaves were murdered when a strange light began to glow all around them and all of a sudden a low moanin sound started outta de swamp, so scary dat those men ran away so fast their feet didn't touch ground. To this day there be talk about dat light, bright as a full moon right where those slaves was murdered." She looked at Ben, satisfied she had gotten her point across.

CHAPTER 8

Autumn kicked out summer with the wrath of the furies, hurling torrents of rain and lashing winds. "Ain't heard of nothin like this in over a hunnerd years," could be heard throughout the market, which was no match for the gusty weather, even without the rain. Goods bellowed up from the tables where rocks had been placed on them. A pair of bloomers from Miss Emmy's pile of dainties swept up, just as a section of roof flapped back, as if they had been waiting for the chance. The vendors hung blankets and oilcloths from post to post to protect their wares, but some days it was senseless to try. Then all stayed home.

Finally, the winds stilled, and the constant patter and throb of water dwindled to a drizzle. The whoops and cries of the housebound Gullah could be heard to the marsh.

"Tilly, come on, chile," she said, as she placed a large basket on her head. "An watch your feet. This land be wet enough to drown a goat."

They joined a cheerful stream of gaily dressed women in colorful long dresses and bandanas wrapped around their hair, with baskets filled with fruit, vegetables, jars, and clothes balanced on their heads as if they grew there. They were all laughing, singing, or chatting gaily, ignoring the light fall of raindrops on their faces or sudden splashes of water as they passed sodden branches of small trees.

Nellie called over to Aunt Letty, "Ain't no day for sellin, Letty."

"It's goin to clear, Nellie."

The skies did clear and the market filled. The chatter and laughter were infectious with everyone happy to be outside again. Tilly was looking longingly toward the wharf. It had been about six months since Ben had brought Tilly back to her, barefooted and disheveled. This past week was the longest time they had been apart since that day. Tilly's large brown eyes were shining now and rarely dimmed back to the sadness that had been there when she came.

She watched Tilly carefully placing the buns on the table. Her chest suddenly ached, and all the pent-up hurt and longing burst out of her heart so quickly she steadied herself against the table. Tears sprang to her eyes, and she turned away quickly, but not before Tilly saw the crumpled expression on her face.

Tilly reached her arms around Aunt Letty as far as they would go and leaned against her soft body.

Aunt Letty looked up to the heavens and cried inwardly, "Oh Lawd, Oh Lawd, please not again," until she became aware of the little hand reaching up to touch her face. She quickly jabbed at her wet cheeks with her flour sack apron, turned and tenderly wiped away the tears spilling down Tilly's face, and smiled. "Well, look at all these people comin with their money, Tilly. We got work to do. Besides dat, look who I see comin."

Tilly ran grinning to Ben. He grabbed her arms and swung her around, laughing.

"Phewww!" Aunt Letty held her nose. "You smell like a pole kitty dragged through de swamp. Where you been, boy?"

"I tried to wash off in the river, but all that silt just stuck to me. I'm sorry, Aunt Letty."

She looked him over. "You look like you could use some bittles on those bones."

Ben grinned. "Oh, Aunt Letty, I'm so hungry my ribs are tied to my backbone. I'm just going to stand under Henny's rain barrel til I feel my skin instead of dirt."

"Go on." She waved him away. "Then come back and tell us what you been up to." She smiled to herself. One thing she knew was he hadn't been down the raging river.

⁙

Ben got back to Aunt Letty's stall just as Long Robby walked up. "Hi, Long Robby," he called.

"What brings you here?" Aunt Letty asked. "Tired of eating fish?" She laughed jovially then sobered at the look on his face.

"Letty, I wondered if you or Ben heard about anythin unusual goin on down where de creek goes in de river?"

Ben's heart thumped. He saw Tilly staring at him. They both knew she wouldn't let Tilly go anywhere with him anymore if she knew about the close call with that man on the island. Best to not mention that.

"What sorta thing you talkin about?" *Aunt Letty's mind is still on ghosts.*

"Well," Long Robby took off his hat and scratched his head, "Jimmy was comin down de river a few days ago and caught sight of some white men on a small barge in de creek. He didn't wait around to see what they were doin. Could of been just some strangers on de river explorin or lost." He looked doubtful. "Just seems a little strange to me. I was down there yesterday, but everythin looked okay to me."

"I heard bout dat," Aunt Letty said with a side glance at Ben.

Long Robby shook his head, the tall hat staying firm on his bushy head. "Still bothers me. One of de other fishermen saw a large ship out in de sound a few days ago. Said it looked like it'd come from Nassau or Jamaica."

Ben's stomach knotted, wishing that he had told Long Robby about the men he heard in the woods and the gun shot. But what Jimmy saw probably didn't have anything to do with those men or the one who threatened him.

Aunt Letty studied Long Robby for a moment or two and said, "No one with any sense goes around dat putrid island, Long Robby.

You know dat. Must be two different things. An boats come and go. You know dat. I don't think it be nothin to worry about."

"I hope you're right, Letty. I don't like what I hear from down de river these days." Long Robby looked so worried Aunt Letty held out a biscuit to him.

"Cheer up, Long Robby. The rain has stopped, and de sun is out."

"Aunt Letty, I left my boat down at the docks and Tilly and me are going to get it if that's okay?"

"Go on, get outta here."

"Bye, Long Robby," Ben called.

Aunt Letty watched the two running toward the dock and smiled.

"Seems those two are never apart, Letty. Mighty good they have each other."

"Yes, it is." She raised her arms to the heavens and said, "Ahhh Lord, life is good. Yes, it is."

Long Robby looked off and said again, somberly, "I sure hope you're right, Letty."

CHAPTER 9

"Hey, Ben," Rufus called as Ben and Tilly walked toward the wharf. He was with a few of his friends down by Long Robby's boat. Ben didn't know any of them and usually shied away when he saw Rufus with other boys, but he was waving him to join them, and it was too late to turn around. He sighed and walked their way, Tilly reluctantly behind him. They were okay.

Ben felt funny around them. He didn't think they liked him for one thing, but at least they weren't mean like the white boys that tormented him when they saw him, throwing rocks and calling him "nigger lover" and "white trash". Fortunately, that didn't happen often, unless he passed them in town.

"Hi, Tilly," Rufus said and threw his arm around Ben's shoulders. "Y'all know these guys," he said, grinning at them. They all nodded their heads without much expression. "We're talking bout what to do on Halloween. We've been thinkin bout goin to Hallellujah cemetery. What do you think bout dat?"

Ben's eyes widened and his mouth fell open before he could think about it, causing all the boys to roar with laughter.

Tilly hung her head and got behind Ben so fast they could not see her expression.

"I didn't think anyone went to the cemetery on Halloween," Ben mumbled.

Rufus laughed. "Joe Taylor saw a Jack O Lantern dancin in de woods on his way home de other night and we ain't never seen one. There's sure to be one showin off its light on Halloween."

Tilly put her head in her hands.

"Well, you know there's a BBQ at the market."

"We're not missin that, Ben." He winked and rubbed his stomach and smacked his lips. "I wouldn't miss the first BBQ of the year, roasted pig and coleslaw, pies and cakes an all de fixins. Anyway, we'll have our bellys full by the time the sun goes down." Rufus made an eerie sound and shook all over, laughing. "Come on, Ben, you and Tilly go with us."

Ben felt his stomach turn inside out, but he also felt a little proud that they seemed to want him to go with them, and before he gave his words much thought, he said, "Well, okay, for a little while, maybe."

"What are you doin back there, Tilly?" Rufus said, pulling her out of hiding.

Ben didn't have to look to know she was upset. He was, too. He had never been to Hallelujah and had no intention of ever going.

He'd heard things all his life about Hallelujah, and some of the stories would make your skin shrivel. He knew about Jack O Lanterns. He knew of people who had gotten lost in the woods following the strange light of the Jack O Lantern. He knew people who had been chased by a beast that was tall as a cow and looked like a mean dog, as black as the swamp with fierce red eyes and flashing gold teeth. Some had gone so crazy, going in circles following after that spooky light that they just babbled on with wild-eyed looks for the rest of their lives. Jack O Lanterns hung around the cemetery and not just Hallelujah, he knew that. And then, of course, there were the boodaddies and haints. And they weren't just around on Halloween.

On Halloween, as Ben approached the clearing next to the market, Tilly, who had been waiting for him, ran toward him smiling from ear to ear and grabbed his arm, pointing to the scene before them. Ben stood, wide-eyed in wonder at the miraculous transformation that had taken place. The market and all the area around it were ablaze with color. Each stall had been festooned with garlands, streamers, and ornate lanterns, which swung from the rails that held up the canvas tops. Balloons in every hue bobbed in the crisp air. Long wooden tables out in the clearing had been covered in yellow, green, and red checked oil cloth and held large platters of steamed and fried shrimp, crabs, clams, and catfish; bowls of cole slaw, red rice, corn, and peas, sweet potatoes baked in ash, biscuits, bread, corn pone, and every kind of pie and cake. Huge seasoned black iron cauldrons full of shrimp boil or Frogmore stew sat on iron hangers. More than one ladle reached for the thick stew filled with fish, potatoes, onions, sausage, and whatever else the cook had on hand. To the side, corn was roasting on a wood-fired grill.

The Gullah were everywhere, gussied up in their Sunday best, looking like bright ornaments that belong on a Christmas tree. The women were gaily dressed in long gowns of every color they could buy or dye, mixed-up colors, striped, checked, polka dotted, all covered with fancy bib aprons to the end of their skirts and turbaned in beautiful hand-dyed bandanas. Shirts from yellow to purple were colorful under vests and coats with felt hats topping their heads and little girls pretty in dresses below their knees and big taffeta bows in their plaited hair played with boys splendid in knickers and suspenders.

Tilly was grinning so widely that Ben broke out laughing. "Come on, I see what we came for."

The pulled pork, along with stacks of bread and sauce, had been brought to rest on a long table covered with red oil cloth to the ground. Miz Emmy's husband, Billy John, exclaimed with a full mouth of meat, "Just makes you slap your brains out lickin your chops." And then he doubled over laughing at himself. Ben fixed a sheet of heavy paper full of the pulled pig meat and sloshed on some sauce for him and Tilly.

They looked at each other and rolled their eyes to the heavens.

Aunt Letty was with some of the women laughing and talking, not paying any attention to Tilly or Ben. These gatherings didn't happen but about three or four times a year, with or without a pig, and they lasted way into the night while they sang spirituals, did ring dancing, or sometimes went to the prayer house for shouts.

Ben knew how important the Prayer House was to the Gullah. When the masters of the plantations didn't want the slaves attending their churches, they built small, one-room buildings where the slaves could worship. They would gather together to pray, and the praying and singing got louder and louder, shouting for joy, shouting for sorrow, shuffling and clapping hands, shaking their heads, dancing and whirling in reverence for the Almighty, some getting so loud and riled up they dropped to the floor in a trance. If there was room, but more than often the room was so packed, they just passed out standing up.

Ben wasn't worried about getting back here before the fun was over; it was getting out of here that was the problem. He hadn't seen Rufus in some time and decided he and his friends had gone ahead. Tilly had shaken her head when he asked if she had ever been to Hallelujah. When he casually asked Henny earlier how to get to the cemetery, Henny had scrunched up his eyebrows and asked, "What you want to know that for?"

"Just curious."

"I ain't too sure, Ben. I never had no reason to go there. And I don't think anyone that's not Gullah are welcomed." He scratched his head and said, "But I think the way is down that shell road back over there."

When the sun slowly dropped toward the horizon, Ben and Tilly started looking for Aunt Letty, but he didn't have to worry. She was having so much fun with all her friends she barely noticed them.

He and Tilly ran behind the market along a well-worn path. He began to feel guilty. She trusted him. He'd never done anything to betray that trust since he and Tilly had become friends. Although he'd told her over and over that she didn't have to go.

As the path divided, Ben turned toward the shell road Henny thought was the way to Hallelujah with Tilly following close by. The road narrowed to nothing but a trail of compressed leaves and shallow ruts leading into the creepy darkness of a live oak forest.

"Oh my gosh," Ben muttered.

The two stopped dead, staring at the mass of long, broken limbs of the ancient trees, their limbs bare and shrouded with moss as frizzy as a witch's hair. Grapevines as thick as a big man's arm twisted and hung like ropes on the gnarled limbs—so crooked and bent they arched eerily over the path. There was so much growth: palmettos, large ferns, and other plants in between and under the trees. Anything could have been hiding there. It was the spookiest place besides the swamp that Ben had ever been.

It was nearly dark now, and Ben said to Tilly as she moved close to him, "It's only woods, just plain old woods." But he struggled to keep his legs still.

They began to run and finally burst into a clearing, but there was no cemetery and no Rufus. The full moon was higher now, and there was nothing in sight but an old cabin and more woods. He couldn't see anything that looked like a cemetery, but he called anyway, "Hey, Rufus. We're here." He stared out at the woods all around and called again.

He looked at Tilly, who was staring at the ground and so still it made him feel awful. "I know they're here, Tilly. They told me they would be."

She looked up at him, her lips quivering.

"Tilly, don't worry, they're here somewhere."

But his insides told him they weren't, and he sure didn't see any cemetery. His knees began to wobble when suddenly Tilly, jumping up and down, pointed to a distant light moving through the woods.

"They're here, Tilly," he yelled. He was beside himself with relief, seeing the glow moving toward them. "Hey, Rufus, we're over here."

But the expected call back didn't come. It was so quiet that Ben could hear Tilly trembling when out of nowhere something whirred by close to their heads. They grabbed each other, clinging wide-eyed with terror as the eerie *hoo, hoo, hoo* of the hoot owl sounded from a nearby tree.

Ben knew that meant death to someone. He gulped for air and said, "Tilly, we gotta go."

He whirled around at the sound of galloping hooves coming in the distance from the direction of the light. "Ohhh," he groaned. He grabbed Tilly's hand and started running, the pounding hooves getting closer with every breath he took.

"It's that red-eyed beast, Tilly. That's what it is," he gasped.

They fled back onto the rutted path through the woods, their feet barely touching the ground, back on the old shell road, and at last back onto the market grounds. Surprised, they skidded to a stop and looked into the anxious faces of the Gullah. Instead of reveling or chatting and laughing as they were when he left them, they stood looking out at the woods as if they expected him and Tilly—or something. *They hear it, they hear the beast,* he thought through a veil of fear and fell panting at Aunt Letty's feet. Tilly ran to Aunt Letty and clung tightly to her.

"Tilly, you gotta get back of me," Aunt Letty said desperately. "Let go, Tilly." But Tilly grasped her dress in a wad around herself.

Ben lay on the ground, his head in his hands waiting for the vile creature to come and eat them all with its gold teeth, but the only sound he heard was the whinnying of horses. Surprised, he jumped to his knees and turned to look. "Oh no!" he gasped. He spun around and quickly crawled under the oil cloth that covered the table holding the pork.

A few feet away stood three scruffy white men on horses with a few hounds scampering around them. One heavily built man with a ruddy unpleasant face was sneering at Aunt Letty.

Her black face had lost its color and her eyes were squinted to slits. Long Robby and a few of the other large Gullah men were gathering around her, watching the men cautiously.

"Well, well," the red-faced man said, reining in close to her. "Lookie who we got heah. If it ain't Letty." He smirked maliciously as he took his whip and let it slide down her shoulder. "Remember me?"

He looked contemptuously at the Gullah, his words slurring. "I reckon y'all know who I am. I am Junie Savage. Judson Savage the Fourth, owner of that plantation down the road where most of you was likely born. And I just might be some of y'alls daddy."

He nearly fell off his horse laughing.

Letty began to tremble, and Long Robby reached around her, pinning her arms to her sides as the other Gullah men moved closer without an expression on their faces.

Junie Savage threw back his head and guffawed. "You trying to protect her from me? You think I want any part of her?" He turned to his friends. "That old fat cow wasn't much to moan over when I was just a horny kid."

Tilly, terrified, slid in back of Aunt Letty, the cloth still wrapped around her, but not before he saw her.

His face contorted into a venomous glower, his eyes cold as ice drilling into Aunt Letty's. "I shoulda known that little nigger bitch was yours. D'ya think I couldn't get to her, hiding behind your skirts, and give her what's coming to her?" He looked over at the dogs. "I think I should let her play with my dogs. What d'ya think about that?" He looked at Letty, screwing his face into a grimace until his teeth bared. "I bet she'd just love to play with these sweet dogs."

Letty lurched forward against Long Robby's arms, her face an expression of unbearable loathing. Long Robby leaned close to her ear and whispered, "Hold on, girl. Not a word. You know dat's what he wants, and you be dead fore you take a step. Nothing we could do but be dead with you." Letty, rigid as an oak, glared at the man but didn't move.

A low *hoo, hoo, hoo* moaned through the night.

Junie quivered. "I ain't gonna bother with that half and half tonight, Letty. I'm gonna wait. Just wait. Me and the dogs. An you'll never know when I got her."

He looked out at the gathering, his nostrils flaring. "You apes hide behind that half-wit freak ya call Bones, thinking he's gonna take care of ya. He ain't nothin but pluff mud. Where is he now? He ain't always around, is he?" Junie laughed, but with an edge of uncertainty. "But

I am." His face burned red in the full moonlight. "I'll get ya. All of ya." He looked threateningly over the Gullah. "Ya can count on that."

He lifted his head, sniffing the air. "I think y'all been cooking pig." He rode around the table where there was a mound of pulled pork left.

He turned toward the men standing near the table. "Why don't you boys just wrap up the rest of that pig in that oilcloth?"

"Too big to carry, Junie," one of his friends called back.

Junie poked one of the Gullah men with his crop. "Put it in that old flour sack you been sopping it up with and hand it over to my friends here."

He swung around to Letty, his face as hard as the pig bones. "You ain't nothing but a nigger, Letty. Might as well get off that high horse you perch on and accept that. You ain't nevah gonna be nothing but a nigger."

Grabbing the sack of pig meat, he yanked his horse around and cantered off with the other two men.

There was not a sound nor movement until the men were out of sight, then only hushed mumbling. Long Robby reached out one long arm, swooped up Tilly from behind Aunt Letty, and with Billy John's help, each put an arm around Letty and took the pair home, Orie right behind them.

The rest, a somber lot, stayed to clean up, all the happy excitement of the long day forgotten. Henny looked around for Ben. He saw him standing alone watching after Aunt Letty and Tilly, looking sad and bewildered. Henny walked over to him, placed a hand on his shoulder, and said gently, "Come on, son, let's go home."

CHAPTER 10

Long Robby and Billy John eased Aunt Letty down on the edge of the bed, where she slumped like a lifeless form, her red-turbaned head falling over her large bosom, and placed the terrified Tilly next to her, where she burrowed into Aunt Letty's side.

Orie dropped to her knees in front of the two, throwing her arms around Letty.

"Oh, Letty, I know what you must be feelin. I feel it, too." She whispered out the words as if they were too full of their shared anguish to be said aloud.

Orie had become so worked up with pain and grief, Long Robbie gently pulled her away. Orie looked at Long Robby, tears running down her face. "Oh, Robby, dat vicious man. Why'd he come heah now? He's never been heah on our place. Not in all these years."

"I know, Orie, I do know." The tall, muscular man looked down sadly at them. Letty's eyes were glazed over as she slumped on the edge of the bed, seeming to be in a semi-conscious state, and the little girl who counted on Letty for all that was safe grabbed onto her for dear life. Long Robby longed to say or do anything that would ease their pain, but he knew that nothing he could say or do would help.

Billy John, looking as miserable as Long Robby and Orie, said, "Wherever Bones be, he's knowin about dis, Letty."

When there was no movement from Letty, he said, "Ain't no sense in talkin now, ya'll. I don't think she knows we be here. Just too much for her after so long." Her face was drained of any emotion, and he was drawn back to that day she buried her baby girl and her mama at Hallelujah. It was in Orie's mind and heart as well, and all the sadness welled up in him again.

"I'm gonna stay with them, Robby. I can't leave my sister now."

"If dat's what you want, Orie," Long Robby said. "But she ain't goin to know you was here."

Orie looked over the room, expecting to see something. Someone. She nodded her head and followed Long Robby and Billy John out the door.

Tilly lay in a ball against Aunt Letty's side, neither of them moving, with the eerie light of the full Halloween moon shining through the branches of the trees, casting flickering shadows throughout the room.

It wasn't long before there was just the slightest sound in the room, but Tilly's keen ears heard it. She struggled frantically to hide behind Letty as a dark, bony shape came into view.

Letty, as if she had expected him, roused and sat up on the edge of the bed, reaching for the black hands held out to her.

"He be dead fore dayclean, Letty." Bones looked down at Letty, his usual stoic expression transformed into a look of overwhelming compassion. Tilly peeked out from behind Aunt Letty when she heard his soothing, deep voice, unable to stop staring at this unearthly apparition that had appeared so suddenly.

Letty pulled Tilly out onto her lap, holding her close. "Bones, this be Tilly. My little girl now."

"I know dat, Letty. I've seen Tilly," he said, smiling at Tilly, her face a picture of wonder, her fear melting at the kindness she felt in him.

"I figgered dat." Letty managed a weak smile. "Dat's why I don't worry bout her." Her expression became strained with the deep emotions she was feeling. "Bones, I don't want you to do nothin to dat monster." She gave him a resolute look. "He's mine, Bones."

CHAPTER 11

When Ben woke up the next morning, later than usual, Henny had a fire going and coffee made. He sat in the chair next to Henny and said, so seriously that Henny held back a smile, "Thank you, Henny, thank you so much for letting me stay here last night."

"You're more than welcome," Henny said and handed him a mug of coffee. "Here, warm your innards."

Ben grinned. "My innards are already warm. I don't know if I ever slept so good."

Henny chuckled. "Not surprised at that." He let his gaze rest on Ben for some time then settled back in his chair. "I think you had a pretty bad time last night."

"The worst thing I ever been through in my whole life." He raised his head to look at Henny and said soulfully, "I don't know where I was, but that shell road didn't go to any cemetery I could find. It went through the worst forest of tangled trees I've ever seen."

"Oh, Lordy, Ben. I know where you're talkin bout. If I had known you had any idea of going to Hallelejah. I thought you were just curious." He shook his head at the floor and looked back at Ben. "Ben, that's the Gullah cemetery. It's somewhere off one of those roads." His expression darkened as he stared into the fire. "I've only been there once." He looked at Ben incredulously. "What in the world gave you the notion to go there, anyway?"

"To meet Rufus."

"Well, maybe I can get the whole story sometime and how you got mixed up with Junie chasing you." He cleared his throat. "I'm sorry it turned out so bad for you. Son, the Gullah'd rather be dead than go through those woods."

"Henny, I just remembered somethin I been meaning to tell you. Bout those men with Junie Savage. At least one of them. He was the man at the river. The one that wanted to cut my throat."

Henny looked at Ben. "You sure about that?"

Ben raised his eyebrows and nodded emphatically. "I'd know him anywhere."

Henny turned that around in his mind. "Well, that puts a different light on what I been thinkin." He stared at Ben and rubbed the top of Ben's sunbleached yellow head. "We'll talk more bout that later."

Henny picked up the net he was making and let his bony hands rest on it, thinking of Ben's yellow hair. He remembered the conversation he had with Joe, the fisherman, about the Swedes who died down the coast not far from here. Ben looked like someone who could be from what he knew of that country. Tall, blond, fine features. One of these days he was going to talk to Michael Morton about that family. He had a notion Ben was that baby the fisherman saw. But he had a sad story to tell Ben now. He thought about where to start.

"This ain't the kind of story I like to tell, Ben." He hesitated and looked down at the rope thoughtfully as if he could see the past in its twists and turns. "I told you some time ago it weren't a good story."

Ben, without getting up, edged nearer to Henny.

"I'll try to make it short and fast," Henny said. "No sense in going into all the suffering that had been going on for so long at Grandterre." He slowly shook his head. "But, with all the beauty of that place, and nothing around to match it, that's where most of the suffering was and most always had been.

"Letty was born at Grandterre, like Bones, but after the war. Her mama, Aunt Sally, ran the house so her youngins had more leash than other servants. Mostly because the mistress of the house, Miss Jenny. She woulda had her say to anybody that harmed a hair on Aunt Sally or her kids' heads."

Henny cleared his throat, the sound as shrill as a crow's caw, and spat into the hissing fire. "That was about all she had any say over—what went on in her house, and sometimes not then. Judson Savage kept a mean hand on what went on around him. I reckon he was the most evil man I ever knowed and was raising his son, Junie, just like him.

"Junie was just a little kid when the slaves was freed. The only ones that stayed was old or sickly or had no place to go. Whipping was outlawed after the war, but Judson didn't pay a mind to that. Nor Junie. Aunt Sally said she could never forget Junie with his daddy's lash whipping one of the old house slaves' crippled legs, making him hop like a broken-leg turkey til he fell on the ground and the master slapping his knees and choking with laughter. That boy hated Gullah from the day he was born. He watched Letty grow up. She was a spunky kid. Skinny as a bar of soap after a hard day's wash. Didn't take nothing off nobody, including the master's son. She'd just hold that little head high and walk right past trouble.

"As the years went on, she became right shapely. Enough for Junie to notice. One day she come stumbling home bruised, her dress ragged and bloody and her mouth as clamped shut as a bear trap. Not even her ma could pry it open, but a few months later, her little belly told the tale."

Henny put his nets aside and reached for his pipe, shaking his head in wonder. "She was just old enough to get that way. About thirteen. Your age, come to think of it. Poor Aunt Sally. She knew who done it an couldn't do nothing. Pet, when she come, nearly killed her ma and fixed it so she'd be her last. But Letty took one look at that baby and knew she had a reason for living. Pretty little thing. Skin like milky chocolate and eyes big as her face and sweet as a spring day. Aunt Sally kept Pet, Orie, and Letty in the big house right beside her."

Henny leaned toward the fire, his arms resting on his knees. "Everybody loved that little child. Everybody but Judson Savage and Junie. Not that the old man didn't have plenty of his own, but he'd send em outta his sight.

"Pet loved Miss Jenny, and that lady was foolish over that baby. She fussed over her like she was her own granchile, which I guess she was. Miss Jenny stayed mostly in her room for her heart problems—an no doubt to keep away from her husband and son. Letty and Orie was there to take care of her, and Pet followed right along beside them. If it was food or a glass or tea, Pet would beg to carry it to Miss Jenny. Regardless, she was right behind her ma when she went to the mistress's room and would get up on the bed an stay there til Letty come to get her, talking to the Missus just like she was a grown up, telling her everything going on around the plantation. That really rankled Savage and Junie. That a Gullah was accepted in his house like she was family. Savage would yell and carry on to Miss Jenny, but she had a blank ear.

"Pretty soon, Aunt Sally let Pet start carrying small things upstairs when the Savages weren't around. Most of the time her ma was right there with her."

Henny stopped, lit his pipe, and watched the curls of smoke, feeling sick with remembering.

"The happier Miss Jenny was with Pet, the madder Savage and Junie got. It was eating them up they was so filled with hatred. Anybody coulda seen that." He raised his eyebrows and shook his head. "But no one did. Not Letty, not Miss Sally, not Miss Jenny. The time musta come when Savage and Junie decided to do something bout little Pet.

"Letty never let Pet alone when the Savage men were nearby, but one sunny day when Letty was helping Miss Sally with her baking, they didn't see Judson come in the house. Letty sent Pet up with a plate of cookies, the rag doll the missus had given her under her arm.

"Ole man Savage walked over to the child as nice as could be and told her the missus was waiting in the garden, sitting in the shade of the elm tree. Pet knew her mama didn't like the master, but she was just a little thing and didn't know evil, so she set out across the lawn without a thought but getting to Miss Jenny.

"When Letty saw Pet wasn't with Miss Jenny, she ran looking all over everywhere. When she got to the porch, she saw her baby girl crossing the lawn. She started screaming, calling her back.

"They heard the old man say, 'Let em loose, Junie.' A pack of the most vicious dogs on God's earth ran straight across the lawn toward Pet, their teeth bared. Letty was running and screaming so loud the field hands came up. That little baby girl turned, smiling, and raised her lil hand at her ma. She was still waving when the dogs got to her. Everybody heard the howling of the dogs and Letty's screams and came running fast as they could, yelling and crying, but it was too late. She was tore apart. That little body thrown every which way all over that grass.

"Savage and Junie beside him called off them dogs like it was some terrible mistake. Letty flung herself over Pet, sobbing like a crazy girl, trying to piece her baby together.

"It was a while before anybody noticed Aunt Sally sliding to the ground like melting wax. With help from some of the old-timer slaves and field hands, Letty and Orie carried Aunt Sally and Pet back to Hallelujah.

"The two was buried together that day after the graves were dug in Hallelujah. Letty walked off."

He paused, remembering the pain of that day. "No one knew where she went, but Bones musta found her. That's pretty certain. Considering the closeness of the two. That finished Miss Jenny, too.

"Orie was just a little girl herself, but she went back to Granterre to try to get the missus to leave, but she wouldn't and sent Orie, who didn't have no place to go, back to her sister in town that was Miss Rebecca's granma, Miss Eloise. We heard a few days later that Miss Jenny had swallowed all her heart medicine. I don't reckon the old man cared, but Junie worshiped his ma, in spite of all he did that hurt her, and blamed it on Letty."

Ben felt tears sting his eyes and looked toward the fire.

"Ben, there'd be something mighty wrong with you if you didn't feel bad about that story. There's no shame in that." He got up and put his arm around Ben's shoulder. "Come with me."

They walked to the back of the house and entered a room with a single bed with a quilt on it, a chair, and an old pine chest. It would have beeen a bright sunny room on a nice day.

"This was Pop's room."

Ben, who had already looked around earlier, said, "I bet Pop really liked this room, Henny. It sure is nice."

"I been thinking, Ben. Well, I been thinking it's time for me to have someone live here with me." He looked over at Ben and spoke softly. "An you got no business trying to make do in that crumble-down filthy old building with all those rats running around waiting to take a chunk outta ya. How would you like to live here? This'd be your room."

Ben's mouth fell open, and he stood staring at the space before him, unable to speak.

Henny laughed. "What's the matter, boy, it take you this long to make up your mind?"

"Oh, Henny." Ben's voice broke, and unable to speak, he flung his arms around Henny and buried his face in his faded denim shirt.

Henny patted Ben on the back. "Now, now, no need to make such a fuss."

But all the emotion of the past two days and all the pent-up aloneness of his young life welled to the surface. "Ah, Henny," Ben said, tears streaming down his face, "nothing in my whole life has ever happened to me so good. I'd rather live here with you than anything on this earth."

CHAPTER 12

When Aunt Letty saw Ben and Henny walking toward her stall, she smiled at Henny and said before he could say anything, "It's all right. No need to talk about it." She looked at his doubtful face. "It was just a shock."

"I'm so sorry, Letty. Junie's got to be the meanest creature alive."

"He sure is dat." She put her arms around Tilly's shoulders. "But he ain't goin near Tilly again. Bones is seein to dat."

"I have a feeling that Junie knows that," Henny said, looking up at the sky. "We might have a shower, but that won't keep us from having a party. Why don't you and Tilly come for dinner tonight? Ben an I got some news to tell you," he said with a sly smile.

Aunt Letty and Tilly both whirled around and looked at Ben and Henny.

"What kinda news you got, Henny Findley?" she asked, a grin beginning to spread across her face. "I hope it's what I think?"

"I don't know if it's what you think, Aunt Letty, but I'm gonna live with Henny." Ben was obviously so happy his words sang out.

"Thank Heaven above." Aunt Letty spread out her arms like wings and wrapped them around Ben, who was still grinning.

Tilly went to Henny and reached her arms out for him.

"Well, I reckon we do have a reason for a celebration." She winked at him. "An maybe a lil bit of libation to help de celebrating?" She laughed and hugged both of them again. "I'll bring de bittles." *An mebbe put Junie and last night outta my mind.*

~

The market day seemed to go on as usual, no one wishing to give the night before any more thought. It was best forgotten. Junie Savage had never come to the market. He had no use for them, the vendors chatted from stall to stall.

"He was just curious and followed those little kids here," Emmy said.

"Yes," they all agreed. "We seen de last of dat buckra no matter what he said."

"Dat's de trute," they all chorused, ignoring Junie's threats.

That was what they all longed for, their feelings deeper than the spring at Goose Neck Pond. Junie's appearance was just an unfortunate accident, but fear had surfaced that night, and it couldn't be forgotten. Jim Crow sat on every branch of every tree watching them and waiting for one move out of line—the white line. Knowing this was as much a part of their lives as eating, sleeping, and working. At the end of the market day, after the booths were cleaned and ready for tomorrow, the vendors would walk home with one thought: *What was Junie doing there and why had he really come home?*

~

"Would you look at that?" Henny whooped at the array of food Aunt Letty and Tilly had brought.

"Wow, look at that cake," Ben said, wide-eyed, not able to conceal the pure joy that had taken over his being.

Henny reached behind bottles and jars in a cabinet near the kitchen and brought out a mason jar of peach brandy. "Pop was a dandy at making this."

He handed a glass to Aunt Letty and a small glass to Ben and Tilly, who were eagerly standing by him. "A thimble full won't hurt ya." Pleased with himself, he smiled. "In fact, it will tickle your inards and warm your outards."

At sundown after a wonderful evening of delicious food, laughter, and enjoying being together, they walked out onto the porch, holding their arms across their chests to break the chill. The clouds had cleared after what they felt was a clean-up shower, and there was a blaze of stars against the black sky. The fresh air smelled of pine.

"It sure is nice out after a good rain." Henny took a deep breath as if inhaling all the sweet night air and hugged his body tighter as the cold made his loose-limbed body tremble and said, "I think this has been a good party."

They all agreed.

"Time for us to go home. My bed is lookin mighty good to me." Aunt Letty hugged Ben and walked down the steps with Tilly.

Ben lay in bed thinking about the day, overcome with happiness. For the first time in his life, he had a real home. He was living in a house, a nice house, with a room of his own and a chest of drawers full of Pop's clothes. He'd have real food, and best of all, he'd have a real friend to talk to. He had loved Ben Clary. He'd been the only father he'd ever known, but this was different. This was real different. He had a good friend to be with and one who treated him like a man. He felt the glow of the brandy in his body until his eyelids, too heavy to keep open, covered his eyes. His last thought was that except for the talk about Aunt Letty and Pet, this had been the best, most perfect day of his life.

The next day, Rufus found Ben after his school day and asked what happened. "We looked all over for you."

Ben told him he got lost and let it go at that, which Rufus seemed to accept.

"Well, you didn't miss a thing, Ben. There wasn't a Jack O Lantern in sight." He slapped him on the back. "I heard the good news about your livin with Henny. I'm really happy for you, Ben."

CHAPTER 13

Tilly, neatly stacking the biscuits in a box, had been watching Aunt Letty furiously packing up everything they had just finished baking.

"Tilly, I want to get to the market early." She hesitated for a moment and added, "I got somethin on my mind."

When the two arrived at the market, Aunt Letty looked around to see who was there. "I'll set up the table, Tilly. I been thinking dat it be a beautiful day for you to spend with Ben."

Tilly cocked her head as if to ask why.

Aunt Letty ignored her and looked around the market again.

Tilly tugged on her skirt.

Aunt Letty waved her hand out toward Henny's house. "Now git."

She watched, hands on her hips, as Tilly walked toward Henny's house, looking back at Aunt Letty from time to time. Tilly couldn't be here when she talked to the market vendors.

⌒

Ben was walking out of the house with a bucket in one hand and a hammer in the other when Tilly got there. He stopped, surprised. "Tilly. What are you doing here?" Tilly rolled her eyes and shrugged her shoulders, then pointed back to the market, giving Ben a look of resignation.

Ben laughed. "Well, I'm glad you're here. Wanna go on the boat with me to the salt marsh?" He looked at her shoes. "We need to get you a pair of Pop's boots. You'll ruin those in the pluff mud. Stay here." He ran back in the house and got a pair of worn-down boots that were going to be too big, but at least she would be able to get out of the boat. "Here, put these on. We're going to the oyster beds. Hard to get on the beds without good shoes. We gotta be there when the water is low, leaving the mud flats bare and piles and piles of oyster shells on the beds at the edge of the marsh grass." He got on one knee and helped her change from her shoes to Pop's old working boots.

Tilly nodded her head so many times Ben laughed again.

As Ben rowed his boat through Coosaw Creek, skimming past fragments of dead trees and brush, bands of palmettos and palms, he showed Tilly the rosy sweet grass that grew on the edge of the water that the Gullah made into beautiful baskets like the ones she had seen on their heads. He pointed to a couple of blue herons looking for small shrimp or fiddlers and toward a few gators basking on the bank after their morning swim. Ben could tell how happy she was as she noticed everything around them with such delight. He had never taken her this far. But, as they neared the open salt marsh, he noticed she was trembling.

"You okay?" he asked, concerned.

She held tightly to the rim of the boat with a troubled smile, like something was bothering her. Maybe she and Aunt Letty fussed about something. He dismissed it from his mind.

"Look, Tilly, have you ever seen anything so beautiful?" Before them, radiant in the morning sun, was the serene beauty of the vast tidal basin. Fed by freshwater rivers and salty sea, it was painted by nature with golden fields of spartina grass rippling over the blue water almost as far as their eyes could see.

"This is the prettiest place on earth, Tilly. The tide rises and falls two times a day, and you gotta know when that is. I come here sometimes

when the tide's low and just sit watching the wading birds and wild ducks
as they come in. There's all sorts of herons, terns, egrets, and the marsh
rabbits chattering away. And turtles, too. There's a tall bird that struts
around called an Oyster Catcher that's got a black head and bright red
bill he uses to open up the oysters. An clams and mussels, too. There's
lottsa fish. Croaker, drum, spot. There's flounder, but it's about to go
back to sea now that winter's almost here, and when the tide is higher
there's schools of jumping mullet. There's lottsa little animals, too, that
feel safe here and come to feed in the grass when the tide is low like it is
now." Ben pointed. "Look at that, those little periwinkles digging down
in the mud."

Tilly sat, unmoving, her eyes fixed on Ben while he was talking
to her. Ben saw her looking at him and turned away, confused at the
change in her within a few minutes.

He said, "The grass is turning from gold now to brown for the winter,
and it'll stay that way until its back green in spring and summer and then
gold again in the fall. It's always changing but not changing, too. There's
so much life here in these waters, Tilly. It's my favorite place." He pointed
to a dead limb of a cypress that had fallen in the water. "Look at those
cormorants and gulls. They don't like to ruffle their feathers so you can
always tell the way the wind is blowing 'cause they face into it. There's
always somethin to see. I've seen deer swimmin aroun looking for fresh
waters from island to island. They're amazing swimmers. Gosh, they can
swim fast." He looked out at a dolphin surfacing. "Look over there, Tilly.
Have you ever seen a dolphin?"

She shook her head solemnly.

"You can't believe the show they put on catching fish. And they
learned it, Long Robby says, and teach it to their young. And this is the
only place in the world they do this, Long Robby says. They find a school
of fish and circle them pushing the fish up on a mud bank so fast and
lie on their sides there eating the fish with all these birds waiting to get
what they don't eat. They go right up pretty high onto that mud, too,
but not so high they can't wiggle down. I'll bring you out sometime to

watch if Aunt Letty'll let me. Some nights I come out and lie back in my boat waiting for the dolphins to come swimmin around and listen to them blowing out through their blowholes. Sounds like somebody with a cold saying, 'Hi there.'" He smiled dreamily. "On a full moon, it's near perfect."

He pointed to an island in the far distance across the sound, barely noticeable. "Someday, I'm going there. Long Robby said it is the prettiest place he's seen around here. No one has ever lived there, like on most of these islands, and the fish almost come to you and say, 'Here I am.'" He gazed out over the spartina, swaying gently in the breeze and let out a long sigh. "Someday.

"You gotta muck around in the mud and get to those beds. But ya gotta be careful. As small as you are, you would sink to your neck through that pluff mud." He laughed at her making a face and holding her nose. *At least she doesn't seem so nervous.* "You don't like the way it smells, d'ya? Well, a lot of plants and animals die in the marsh, so I reckon some folks think it stinks, but to me it smells like heaven might.

"I'll show you how to break apart the clusters so you can leave the smaller oysters to grow. They can cut you real easy, so let me do the hammering on them." He plodded through the mud and leaned over the huge pile of shells. "Wow, there's a lot of really good ones here. We start harvesting in October and stop in April. We got a lotta time to eat oysters, Tilly. We gotta watch our time, though. One thing you sure don't wanna do is go against the tide with a boatload of oysters."

He started to help her out of the boat, but she hesitated just long enough for him to know something was upsetting her. *She's never been afraid of the water,* he thought.

"You don't have to get out, Tilly. You can just sit in the boat and watch."

She immediately got out of the boat without Ben's help and smiled at him, pointing to Pop's shoes surrounding her small feet and laughed.

Ben felt relieved. *Maybe she's cold.* It could get pretty chilly out in the marsh. He was mighty glad for Pop's warm jacket. He'd seen that Tilly had on a short coat. Winter had come as fast as fall had come fast after summer. He was growing, too. Henny joked that it was the clothes that just made it seem that way, but he could see his bones getting longer.

"We'll get as many as we can, Tilly, and take some home for dinner."

He watched her moving cautiously around the bed. He wished she could tell him what's bothering her, but she usually found a way around that with her hands or expression.

Aunt Letty had been waiting for the right time to set the vendors straight about Tilly and what they thought. After Tilly was out of sight, she smoothed her apron, pulled herself up tall, and strutted into the middle of the stalls, hands on her hips, and called out to the vendors, "Ya'll stop what you're doin and listen to me. I ain't goin to say this again."

Taken by surprise, the vendors looked up from their booths.

When she was certain she had their attention, she spoke in a tone they would remember. "Ever since Tilly come heah, ya'll skittered away from dat chile like she be poison ivy. I know what you think. I heah the gabble. I ain't deaf an I sho ain't dumb." She glared around at the faces, most beginning to stare at the ground.

"Not all of you mebbe, but most of you think Tilly got some kinda root put on her. Don't go lookin at me dat way. Dat's what I hear." She raised her voice to a near shout. "And dat ain't so! There's no more spell put on dat chile than on Jesus." She nodded emphatically among the gasps and stunned looks at words they considered blasphemous. "And don't get so high horsed. I know most all there is to know bout Tilly, and she can't talk cause she just can't."

She looked around the market. "And it ain't none of your bizness why." She pointed over to Freezy, who was trying to hide behind a post.

"Freezy, shame on you. I heard about all your she-she talk, and yesterday I saw you runnin away from Tilly with your gran. Tilly ain't nothin but a sweet lil girl wantin to see dat baby." She glanced around and said, "Now dat's dat.

"As for de color of Tilly's skin. Just who you think you is?" She gave them all a disgusted look. "You treat Tilly like de white man treats you. Look at your own skin. Where you think you get all these different skin colors from? Ain't nobody here have blood straight from Africa. But Bones. And most of you don't have to go far back to find when your skin got lighter. There wasn't a master of no plantation around here who didn't have a passle of slave chillun. You hate the word mullato. That's what you call Tilly. You hate light skin. And you look down on it 'cause it reminds you of de shame. There ain't no shame except on de bukra what did dat to your kin. As for Tilly, she ain't like us. She ain't lighter cause some master dirtyied her mama." She puffed out her chin. "And I ain't gonna talk bout dat. Tilly be my lil girl now, and if you don't accept her, you can just get your biscuits elsewhere."

And with a final nod, she walked back to her booth, satisfied she'd gotten all she had wanted to say for so long said. She knew there would be talk, but she also knew that they listened to her. All the fear surrounding Tilly and the man who came with her had been slowly fading away.

CHAPTER 14

Late one November morning, Aunt Letty and Tilly saw Ben running toward them, grinning from ear to ear.

"Hi," he called as he got nearer. "Tilly," he said loud enough to turn the heads of those at the market. "I just sold three boatloads of oysters." He was so excited Tilly grinned back and made a sign asking to whom? They were together so much now that certain looks and gestures were all they needed to understand each other. Not that it was the answer, not that they could share thoughts and information and feelings, but unless Tilly could speak, it was what they had.

"To the Hackneys in town. Miz Hackney's cook, Gladys, saw me come into the dock with the first load and got em on the spot. Tole me to get two more loads and she would send Plummer down to get em. They're gonna have a big oyster roast." Ben was out of breath with excitement. "That is more money than I ever made. And, not only that, but Gladys said she bet the neighbors would be wanting oysters as well for their own parties.

"Aunt Letty, can I take Tilly to town for an ice cream cone?"

"Ben, I'm really happy for you. And I know how excited you are, but I have to say no."

At their crestfallen expressions, she said, "I'm so sorry, Ben. I ain't sure dat's a good idea right now."

Tilly pulled on her arm, pleading with her eyes.

"Tilly, Mr. Trainey have ice cream and it be a lot closer."

"It's not the same, Aunt Letty, and he don't have cones."

"But he got popcicles. Ain't dat close?"

"Not quite what I had in mind, Aunt Letty, but that's all right. We'll go there."

"Ya'll run ahead, then. I'll be at Henny's."

Aunt Letty watched after them, knitting her brows.

Henny swung aside his axe where he was chopping wood and walked over to the porch steps and sat down. He drew in a deep breath of the crisp, pine-scented air as his eyes swept over the pleasant surroundings. He and Pop had settled on this little plot of land, backing up to the pines and running to the river, when Long Robby told him it wasn't a part of the Gullah commune. Asking around, it seemed no one knew anything about the property. Most of the uninhabited property was available for purchase in this county or homesteading and land grants.

There wasn't a hill or much of a rise of land anywhere around. This was the low country. And it was low.

Pop told his Gullah neighbors he was just up the hill from them. Not close enough to be a bother in their community but close enough to wave. That caught on.

He smiled as he saw Letty struggling toward his house. She was leaning forward with arms flailing for as if they could carry her along. He walked out to greet her.

"Letty, what brings you here?" He would have laughed, but she was so out of breath he was concerned and took hold of her arm for the few steps left to the porch.

"Lemme," she panted. "Lemme sit down."

"And when you've got your breath, let's go sit by the fire and sip on a little brandy." He winked.

After the cracking and popping of the fire, along with a little peach brandy, had soothed her considerably, she said, "Henny, I've been hearin news about soldiers bein seen around heah. What do you know about this?"

Henny rubbed the back of his neck then reached for his pipe. "There's that fort everyone's been talking bout starting up across the river. I'm not sure the soldiers are there yet. But I don't think these people here will hold any interest to them. I don't think so, anyway. The coloreds who're in trouble are the ones whites consider get in their way, and we don't have that around here. At least so far."

"Well, I sure hope you be right." She sat back and rocked. "I didn't let Tilly go into town with Ben just now. I feel bad about dat, Henny, but it ain't just fearing de law. Ben and Tilly ain't children. We think they are, but they ain't. Belleview people are okay. They seem to have respect for us in their way. But a white near-grown boy and a girl, small for her age, who might pass for white, worries me."

"Letty, do you know how old Tilly is?"

Letty shook her head. "I know she was almost eleven when she came here. Why you want to know that?"

"Just thinking about what you said. That was a year ago now that she came, Letty." He mused. "From what Ben told me, he must be close to fourteen. They're growing up, Letty, right before our eyes." He looked out of the window onto the grounds. "And speaking of that, there they are now, walking down to the river." He smiled at the two young people enjoying being together. "I wonder where this might go?"

"Don't think that don't keep me awake. They're friends now. I don't think they even thought of being nothin else. But another year or two and there'll be something wrong with them if the changes in their body don't put ideas in their heads." She looked over at Henny. "You know dat's de truth."

"I expect you're right, Letty." He chuckled. "Well, let's enjoy their youth while we can." He watched the two youngsters walking arm in arm down to the river. "That's a beautiful girl, Letty."

They sat staring at the fire, thinking about all that had happened since Tilly and the man everyone had assumed was her father at the time walked into their lives.

"Thanksgiving's just a few days away. You going to the market square this year?"

He turned to face her. "You know I ain't going, Letty. You know I never go to your Thanksgiving shenanigans."

She gave him a dirty look. "Don't you be disrespectful."

"I'm not disrespectful, Letty. It's just not my idea of enjoying a day. All that singing, praying, dancing." He rolled his eyes. "And listening to your Reverend Barnwell spouting more religion than one sane man can handle in a day."

Letty poked her lower lip out wide enough to sit on and started to get up. "You sure don't have to share our day with us, you old heathen."

"Sit back down. I'm sorry if I hurt your feelings. There's more I want to talk about." Henny moved around in his seat, patting the back cushion before leaning against it. He cleared his throat. "Letty, you and me have been friends for as long as I can remember. We played together when we was children."

She turned sharply to him. "What are you gettin to, Henny Findley?"

"Tilly. I wanna know about Tilly, Letty."

"Dat's what I thought." She pushed on the rocker chair arms, trying to get up.

"Sit back down or I'll push you down."

She glared at him, her black eyes flashing, but she did.

"I reckon you know everything about Tilly, Letty. Why don't you tell folks why Tilly can't talk?"

Letty folded her hands together and looked at them so long Henny was about to ask again. "I can't, Henny. Just can't." Her voice was so low he barely heard her.

"Letty, you know you can trust me. Maybe not like Bones, but you know you can. All we been through together." He let his words rest with her for a minute or two. "That child spends almost as much time here with Ben and me as she does with you. I think I got a right to know somethin bout her."

Letty raised her hands to her face, then let them fall back in her lap. "I don't know, Henny. And dat's de truth. I know she saw some terrible, terrible things no chile should ever see. I was told she just stopped talkin all of a sudden."

Henny thought about that, bewildered. "Well, will she ever talk again?"

"Only God knows dat, Henny. I guess de blessin, if there be a blessin, is she don't remember nothin. Least, dat's what de man wno brought her here say." She stared into the fire. "It was mighty hard to hear dat poor sick man, Henny. Whisperin and soundin like jibberish. I leaned as close as I could, but he was so far gone he just wasn't makin sense. Kept saying somethin about getting Tilly here. Said, 'I got her here. I got her here.' Over and over like dat was what he was here for."

"Mebbe it was, Letty."

"I drive myself crazy thinkin I missed somethin I need to know."

"That was a hard time for you, Letty. Bound to have been. Can't blame yourself for anything."

"Dunno, Henny."

"Do you know what happened?"

Letty sighed, still staring at her knotted hands. "Not much, Henny, but dat be where we stop. I done told you all I'm goin to."

"That man that brought her, Letty. Was that her father?"

"No, that man was her uncle." She turned sideways, stretching out her arm to the arm of his chair. "Henny, if you ever say anythin about this, Bones'll be looking at you before you blink."

Henny knew how serious she was and felt a chill at the thought of Bones coming after him. "Letty, rest yourself about that. I love Tilly, too."

"I think de uncle was a gentleman, Henny. You know what I mean." She furled her brow and looked at Henny. "I don't think he was poor. Least hadn't been poor. Just somethin about em. And de way he talked. Like he was a lot more than de way he looked lying there dying." She looked up, remembering something. "He gave me an envelope with some papers in it. They looked old. Which I guess they was. Said they were for Tilly." She looked down, shaking her head.

"Good Lord, woman. Didn't you read em?"

She turned a fierce look at him. "No, I didn't, you old fool." She looked away, mumbling, "You know I didn't have no chance to learn. Neither did Orie. Old Savage didn't allow any of his enslaved people to read or write and no one who worked for him, neither." She whirled around to face him. "And it ain't done me no harm."

"No, Letty, I reckon it ain't." He smiled kindly. "I can read those papers for you, Letty."

"We'll see. I don't know where they are now." She got up and started walking toward the door and stopped. "Henny, have you heard any more about what Long Robby said? About the boats and men down de river?"

"Not anything to worry bout. Just gossip. Let's hope whatever and whoever was there are long gone."

CHAPTER 15

Letty washed up the pots and pans and looked at the display of pies on the long table. She plopped down in the cedar armchair, threw the muslin towel over her shoulder, and sighed at how different this year was from the last. There was so much to be thankful for. Thanksgiving was the biggest celebration her people had. She was tired, but the excitement that flowed through her seemed to overcome that. There was something else to do, and for her it was more important than the day coming. She got up and went back to the house. She had left Tilly with Ben and Henny last night, partly because of Tilly's begging and mostly because she needed this time alone. She was not afraid of the darkness through the fields and woods. She had made this trip every year since she left the deep forest. She changed quickly into dark clothes and threw a black shawl around her shoulders. The weather was chilly, but it would be a beautiful day according to Mae Brown, a fisherman who was rarely wrong about the weather.

She walked through the woods on the back property of Grandterre. At this hour, even if she were closer to the grand house, no one would see her. There were few house hands left there, and all the workers lived in their own homes now. It was the dogs that kept her at a safe distance. These woods were sacred to the Gullah, as it was the place of worship and singing during slavery; it was where the spirituals were born. Many of the slaves were buried here, their little tombstones lying on the ground, mostly broken. She passed a tumbled-down prayer house and breathed in the past—feeling her kin, and those of her friends, singing out their hearts and long-lost dreams of going home. When she walked through these old, neglected woods, she knew she had company. She felt the spirits with each step she took. It was so quiet. Rarely a bird call or sound of a critter as if it had been consecrated into a silent sanctuary for the spirits of her people. She walked out of the woods onto a barren stretch of tangled weeds, nettles, palmettos, and dried prickly brush. She was careful to feel with her stick for any scum mold patches in this wetland. Letty was fairly certain no one ever passed through this rodent- and snake-infested back land. It didn't hold any use but for critters, along with the fact that walking through the tangled mass of growth was tricky. But she knew that if she were in trouble, Bones would be by her side. This was where he had found her all those years ago. Lying on the muddy ground covered with bites, bleeding from being scratched by thorns and half dead, a cloth doll clutched in her hand. He had picked her up and carried her to his home in the deep forest. He had treated her with herbs, plants, mojo, and tender care, often holding her in his bony arms like a loving father as she sobbed out her grief. In time, she fell into the life Bones lived, learned his art as well as she could, and healed as much as her heart would allow.

It was dark this early morning, with only the sliver of a moon for light, but she felt the way, led by years of knowing every inch of the land. She always knew when she was close to the forest. It called to her. The closer she got, the more she felt change in the space around her, a lightness, a welcoming, the air gently caressing her. Her heart beat faster now. She was so close to this special place, which was lost to the world except for Bones and her. Possibly no one had ever walked through this sylvan woodland except for the Waccamaw Indians several hundred years before. The river dwellers had moved inland when the first settlers arrived with illnesses for which they had no natural immunity. She and Bones had found sacred mounds and relics of their being there and felt good about that and often felt the Waccamaw's presence.

During the spring, summer, and early fall, the branches and leaves of the old mixed hardwoods were so dense it blocked out the sky. She would lay on the ground at night watching the fireflies against the darkness where there would have been stars. It was autumn now, and the ground would be a mass of golden, red, and yellow greenish leaves. In daylight the sun would beam its rays through the trees where they would flicker as the branches swayed. She had played games with the dazzling light as it moved, jumping from one sunlit spot to another.

The trees were old, gnarled, scabbed, and burled, the bark so thick and cracked a small critter could hide from a predator. Often, she had watched, amused, the chase of a hawk and squirrel until the bushy tail squeezed through a handy hole in the bark, then would peek out with eyes as big as acorns as if to say, "Not this time, fella." Many of the huge trunks, their roots spreading out so high and far over ground and rocks, were cavernous, the large, deep warrens forming shelter for forest animals.

When rain seeped through the heavy boughs, she would sit inside one of the hollows with small rabbits or chipmunks in her lap. Ferns, older than any other growth, were taller than her, and there were plants and wildflowers she had never seen elsewhere. Bright green ground covers joined the brown earth and stones, and every trunk or limb was covered with lichen, fungi, vines, and moss. It was a place so magical in its verdant beauty it seemed to be another world. She was fifteen when she came to this fairyland, and it had never ceased to enrapture her.

Over the years she was accepted by the natural inhabitants, the many and varied types of wildlife: chipmunks, muskrat, mink, beavers always working the banks of the streams, raccoons, bobcat, black bears, owls, hawks, eagles, deer. There were so many of God's creatures she often felt the Ark had landed there. Her friend, Nanda, the cougar, named for Bones' father, romped with her over the forest and slept by her side like a kitten.

Bones, who communed with the nature spirits, helped her see their sparkle among the lush growth. She had only known love here, and even when her grief was intolerable, she had felt peace. Unlike the silent woods she had just walked through, this eerie, beautiful jungle was bustling with life, a symphony of sounds. Whether its magic drew Bones to it or whether Bones created this unearthly haven he would never say. She suspected it was both. Bones and the forest lived as one. His own sweet, pure nature, long past the earthly realm, was at one with the divinity of the forest. Nothing unseemly could enter here. It was guarded by Angels.

She cherished her life there with Bones and never wanted to leave, but as she grew into her middle twenties, Bones persuaded her that there was another life for her. A life with family and her people. He was her people, she argued. They had become as close as skin would allow—perhaps closer. He was her brother, her father, her companion and friend. She only put her own wishes aside when she realized that Bones was spending increasingly less time with her, retreating more and more into the mists of the deep forest. As much as he loved her, he wanted to be alone now. To go where she could never go. She was aware he possessed powers that were beyond her imagination. She also knew he only used them for good, unlike other root doctors. And sometimes he didn't use them when she hoped he would. He only listened to his heart and soul and God.

So, one day she walked back into the other world she had left so many years before and made a life. It was the hardest thing she had ever done besides accepting Pet's death. She and Bones were too attuned for her to think she would lose him. He let her know over and over he was only a breath away. And that had been true.

As she walked into the forest now, she felt as she always did. At home. Her true home. She sat on a fallen log and leaned against a tree beside it, waiting.

"I been spectin you, Letty."

"I shouldn't never left heah, Bones."

He laughed, his voice deep and kind. "You say dat every year, Letty."

"Yeah, I know. And every year I feel it." She looked at his dark, chiseled face. "Bones, of all de blessings I got, I'm most thankful for you. You know dat."

Bones sat beside her on the log and took her hand. "We be a part of each other, Letty."

Letty looked up at the starlit early morning. "I love it when the leaves fall and open up to de sky. I never forget being here, Bones. I never forget what you gave me."

He picked up a golden leaf and turned it around in his hands. "Letty, I see trouble comin."

She turned sharply and stared at him. "Where's there goin to be trouble?"

"Can't say. Just know it goin to be, Letty. I can't stop this." He looked at her seriously. "Letty, this trouble comin goin to change everythin for all of us."

"What you talkin bout, Bones? Can't you stop this trouble?"

"Not this time, Letty."

Letty didn't press him. She knew Bones was always right. She pushed away her fear but shivered. "Well, I hope what you see don't happen." But she knew it would. "There's still so much evil, Bones. Will it never end?"

She leaned her head against his shoulder. "I ain't got long here, Bones. I just want to set here with you and take in all I can to last for another year."

CHAPTER 16

God bestowed a glorious day for his people on Thanksgiving. Tables were loaded with an assortment of everyone's favorite dishes from succotash and sweet potato casseroles to roasted wild turkeys and wild game to Letty's assorted pies. Bunches of golden Chrysanthemums and other late-blooming flowers, pumpkins, and gourds were woven in every empty space.

When she saw Ben and Henny coming toward her smiling, Aunt Letty turned her back so they would not see the surprise on her face. When she turned around, she said, "This goin to be a blessed day for all of us, ain't it, Henny?" She cut her eyes at him with a pleased smile.

"At the look of what's on these tables, I'd say so, Letty. Thanksgiving is all about food." He rubbed his stomach and laughed.

Letty gave him a dirty look and waved a hand at him. "You be food for de devil, Henny. Dat's what you be. I'm gonna sit down and rest a spell," Letty said. "Ben, you kids don't have to hang around here, but don't go too far off. We're goin to gather for de ring before we eat."

After Ben and Tilly left, he said, "Letty, why don't we have a little libation to celebrate the day?" He winked at her, a mischievous expression in his eyes.

She turned and gave him a disgusted look. "Humph! If you ain't somethin today, man."

Henny, not in the least phased, said, "It'll put a sparkle in your eye and a tap to your toes." He cackled and elbowed her shoulder.

She said, whispering, "Where from? Tobiah Higgins?"

He cocked his head, raised his eyebrows, and said, "Who else? Best moonshine around."

A slight smile was on Aunt Letty's lips. "Henny, we've got a lot to be thankful for today. I think a little nip is fittin."

It took three rolls of the drum to get everyone's attention. Finally, when it was quiet enough for the preacher, Mr. Jeremiah Barnwell stood up on the small, improvised platform and waved his arms. He greeted the crowd with the same enthusiasm as he did every year.

"Welcome, welcome, dear family."

"Amen, amen," came shouts from the crowd.

"This be de day we wait fo all year to gather and share our love we feel for one another and raise it up to the one power we believe in so fervently, who both give and take our lives. The God we worship with every breath who seen us through baaaddd times and with us through the good."

"Hallelujah," the crowd shouted.

"This be de day we pray for our ancestors and those not so long gone who can't be here with us today. This be de day we pray for all those who suffered under someone else's hand not by their own doin. We never forget them. We hold them in our hearts til kingdom come."

Amen, Amen!

"Now that's all I'm saying."

A chorus of *Amen, Amen* and shouts of laughter followed.

Reverend Barnwell joined in and told them, "Ragbone is goin to sing a spiritual for us fore we start the rings. Come on up here, Ragbone."

Everyone clapped and yelled a greeting to their beloved friend who was dressed in a yellow cap and yellow tie and a checkered vest under his brown coat, which had a yellow chrysanthemum in the lapel.

"Folks," Ragbone called, almost on his tiptoes because of his small frame. "Folks, later we'll be startin the fiddlin for you to shake a leg."

Everyone laughed. "Now, I got a little spiritual I'd like to open with fore all dat, if dat is fine with you. This is an old spiritual my mama taught me, passed down by her mammy and her mammy and who knows how many mammies back."

He began singing, so sweetly there was not a murmur.

> "O sweet Lawd, watchin oba me
> Somewheres my chillun is, what wus taken from me
> O sweet Lawd watch oba dem
> somewheres dey mama is, loss crossin de sea
> O sweet Lawd watchin oba me
> somewheres mi bruddah, mi sista, mi whole famlee
> when we takun fum our lan
> is wonderin where we be.
> O sweet Lawd watchin oba me
> Our souls will meet in hebben
> when de time cum to be.
> An, all de hurtin in de heart we feelin on dis lan
> I know be gon when all we be in your lubin han.
> O sweet Lawd look on we
> who long to be togeddah in de promise lan
> All de trubbles we have knowed
> Be gone when dat day come
> We all be togeddah in de promise lan."

There was silence as tears flowed. After a reasonable time, the preacher stood on the platform and said, "Ya'll start de rings now. Then we'll all eat bein as I don't believe de Holy Spirit goin to keep our gravy warm." Everyone laughed and began looking for their kin or friends to form the circles.

Letty and Tilly grabbed Ben's hands and joined a ring, but Henny walked back to a bench and dipped into his pocket for a little salvation of his own before sitting down and watching.

The rings were as much a part of the Gullah as eating was. Maybe more so. The ring shouts were as old as the first slaves. Whenever the Gullah were shuffling, clapping, and praying in a circle, singing their hearts out, they remembered all their families who had been enslaved, about them being separated from family and children losing everything familiar to them, everything they loved. But the enslaved found a way to grieve through music—songs from Africa and songs they made as they sang, expressing the emotions they couldn't and wouldn't talk about. They would often go to the woods and spend hours, walking in circles, pouring out their souls to God in music, many of them dying or half dead from malaria or yellow fever. The rings were sacred rituals. They still were. All the elements of music were present in the rings. Blues, spirituals, call and call back, cries.

The preacher sang out gratitudes for everything he could think of, and those in the ring responded until all were hoarse. "An now let us dig in before our bountiful feast is cold as a heathen's heart." And he laughed joyfully.

Ragbone came over to Aunt Letty and thanked her for the delicious pies. She got up and hugged him but felt a shiver run down her spine. *Now, why did I feel dat?* she wondered.

After all had eaten and talked to as many people as they could, Ragbone's drummer, Matt, began the roll for the final event of the day. As Ragbone had said, it was shaking a leg time.

Henny had enough of food and prayer and said his goodbyes, but Aunt Letty, Ben, and Tilly were just getting in the swing of things. There wasn't much moonlight, but the light from the kerosene lanterns lasted until Long Robby put them out and all went home.

CHAPTER 17

November weather had been delicious enough to eat, the Gullah all agreed, and the first week of December had them still smiling. Ben, who had been cleaning his boat down by the river, swung the buckets of clothes and brushes up the hill singing at the top of his lungs. Henny, watching, would have laughed but noticed everyone in the market running toward the docks.

He yelled to Ben, "Look over there. Something is going on. Drop your buckets and let's get down there."

As they came closer to the large crowd gathered on the docks, Ben said, "Oh, Henny, it must be bad. Look at em."

The Gullah already on the docks appeared to look on the ground and quickly turn away, crying, screaming, yelling, "Praise be de Lawd," and other religious chants.

"Better be prepared, Ben," Henny panted as they reached the dock, out of breath from running. He looked down on the floor of the dock and moaned, "Oh, no. No," tears springing to his eyes.

Ben just stared. Mouth open, he dropped to his knees.

Long Robby, sobbing uncontrollably, held Jimmy in his arms, tryin to make his head stay on his body. Jimmy's neck, slit to the backbone, lay open, blood pouring out like a gurgling spring. "I told him," Long Robby said between sobs. "I told him not to go back down dat river."

He rubbed his hand gently over Jimmy's head. He raised his head to the sky, his face a mask of agony. "Why, Lawd? Why you let this happen to this sweet boy?" He was sobbing so hard he lost his voice and dropped his head onto Jimmy's blood-drenched body.

Rufus put his arms around his dad's shoulders. He knew Long Robby would stay there crying his heart out until the other fishermen lifted Jimmy away, wrapped him up in clean sail cloth, and took him out to sea. This was the fishermen's oath: that each of them would be laid to rest in the water they loved.

Henny said to no one in particular, "I just made Jimmy a net to go with his new boat."

Ben stared at the ground, overwhelmed with grief, and said almost in a whisper, "I shoulda told Long Robby bout those men, Henny."

"Nothing you coulda told him woulda made a difference, Ben. Jimmy knew better."

Henny saw Aunt Letty and Tilly coming and grabbed Ben's shoulder. "Go stop them, Ben."

Ben sat like a stone as if he had not heard Henny.

"Ben!" Henny shook him and shouted, "Come on. Now." Softening his voice, he said, "I know you was close to Jimmy. So was I, and it hurts, but get a hold of yourself. Let's go."

Aunt Letty and Tilly were still far enough away not to see or hear the people on the dock. "Letty doesn't need to see that gruesome scene."

"Hey," Henny greeted them. "There's too many people down at the dock, so we was going home. Come on with us."

"Why they down there, Henny?"

"Aw, Jimmy got cut, and Long Robby's trying to stop the bleeding." He looked away from her. "Let's go have some coffee and sit on the porch for a change."

Letty stared at him. "What's going on down there, Henny, dat you don't want us to see?"

Henny looked at her, allowing his sadness to show. "Yes," he sighed. "I am, Letty. Jimmy was killed. In a bad way. It's torn everyone up."

His eyes welled, and he wiped his face with his shirt tail. "I just didn't think you and Tilly needed to see it."

Aunt Letty covered her face with her hands, took them away, and said sadly, "I got to go to Robby, Henny. He raised dat boy. Ever since his ma run off and his pa drank himself to death. I can't bear to think what he's feeling."

"Ain't no time to see him, Letty. You gotta trust me on that."

"Tell me what happen?"

"I heard Rufus say his boat come floating out of the river into the sound, Jimmy stretched across the boat seat. His neck was slit."

"Oh Lawd. Oh Lawd." She put her head in her hands again and rocked back and forth.

"Nothing we can do now, Letty. C'mon, let's go up to the house. Ben and Tilly are already there."

Tilly was sitting on the steps, looking upset.

"C'mon, honey, let's go inside. Where's Ben?" Henny asked.

She pointed toward his room.

"He's feeling pretty low, Letty. He and Jimmy were close. And I think he feels bad not telling Long Robby that day at your stall bout some men down the river he ran up against."

Aunt Letty glanced over at Tilly, who was pretending to play with the edge of her dress. "And I can bet he had company, right?"

Tilly hung her head.

"Well, now is not the time to go into dat."

"If ya'll will excuse me." Henny sighed. "I think I'll go set his mind at rest."

He knocked on Ben's door then walked in. He was sitting in a chair looking out the window.

"Ben."

"I know I ain't alone in hurting over Jimmy, Henny. I just wish I could go after those men. I never knowed hate before."

Henny laid his hand on Ben's head and stroked it like he was a small boy. "I expect you're not alone there either, boy. Now, let's go join Tilly and Aunt Letty and try to find a reason to feel better."

"You really think we can, Henny?"

Jimmy was laid to rest at his favorite fishing spot with all the fishermen and his friends in boats surrounding Long Robby's boat, which carried Jimmy, the soulful spirituals sung from their hearts sounding out to sea. They were all too grieved then to think about anything other than Jimmy, but fear was comin in like the tide.

CHAPTER 18

The next day, Jimmy's friends gathered in the prayer house to talk about him and how he was killed and who did it and why. There wasn't anyone there who didn't want to go down the river and hunt for the murderers.

"You know well as me dat we can't do nothin about this." Long Robby shook his head sadly. "I'd be de first to skin those varmints."

Rufus said, "There's a lot of talk about dat island, Dad. People from outside this county go over to the school to take supplies and sometimes food. Some of them know something about what's going on there . . . have some evidence of it."

There were "dat's de truth."

"Yeah, dat's what I heah."

"Rum runnin! Them was rum runners, dat's what I heah."

"Dat's what I heah, too," Long Robby said, sadly. "Dat been goin on for as long as I can remember. But I think we know who's runnin dat outfit. If we go after those men, we'll be dead before dayclean. Even if they didn't know it was us, they be comin after us no how. Not only us but our wives and chillun." He looked around. "If I heah of any of you goin against my word, you be facin me." He looked around to see how they felt about that. "Okay, hard as it be, we have to let this go, but not forget. The good Lord has a way of takin care of evil."

Later, after talking to Rufus, Ben told Henny, "They're all talking bout Jim Crow."

Henny's brow furrowed, and he let out a long sigh. "Yep. There sure was a lot of talk about Jim Crow today," Henny sighed.

"They say Junie's bringing Jim Crow to em."

"I know." He shook his head in pity.

"What do you think, Henny? Is Jim Crow coming here?"

"I sure hope not, Ben. These people don't deserve anymore cruelty. Slavery was a dark, dark time and left a dark place in the mind and soul of the Gullah. They hurt too much to talk about it. So far, back in these islands, it's like we ain't been seen. But looks like that's changing now."

"Because of Jim Crow?"

"Maybe. Jim Crow or the Kluxes may not have been here, but it has in just about every other place in the South. First the Ku Klux Klan came. The government finally put a stop to it, but it'll be back. Too much hate for it not to. And then Jim Crow."

"What does Jim Crow do?"

"It's a law that all but gives any white man the right to do as he pleases where colored people are concerned. They called it Jim Crow."

"Why they call it Jim Crow?"

"There was a show where the white actors painted their faces black and called it Jumpin Jim Crow an it caught on an they hatefully got to calling the colored people 'nigger.'"

"Why do they hate colored people, Henny?" Ben asked, troubled by how anyone could hate the people he knew.

Henny raised his brows and shook his head. "I reckon fear, son. Fear and ignorance."

"Why're they afraid?"

"I dunno. I think a lot of it's not knowing what to expect. The bad trouble started when they began running for office. The white man couldn't stand the thought of former slaves they considered more like

a brainless animal havin power over them. Their contempt grew to
loathing. They put it out that colored men were raping white women,
and that stirred up more of a ruckus than a rabbit in a snake den. The
mobs gathered hunting down the coloreds yelling, 'Get the nigger.'"
Henny shook his head again. "When they'd find a colored person,
whether he was old and crippled or a baby, they'd beat em to death or
shoot em. It's got so a colored man is hung if he don't keep his eyes
down on the ground when passing by a white, and sometimes he's shot
anyhow. Theres so many lynchings that I hear it's common to pass by a
tree with two to four bodies hanging there. Saddest thing in the world.
A colored man can't be who he is and has to see himself through a white
man's eyes as filthy and less than human. Like I said, these people here
haven't seen that, but they've heard of it, an its on their minds most
of the day and night."

"So, what's Junie to do with Jim Crow?"

"So, we're back to that. Well, Junie's got lots friends like him. The
Gullah think he's up to somethin."

"Is he?"

"Hmmm, not sure, Ben. He told us he was. But I'll tell you what
I do think. I think Junie's scared plum silly of these Gullah. He was
raised with all this voodoo and root around him. He sure knows about
Bones. I think he was following you and Tilly to see who you was an
what you was up to and never knowing that he'd end up smack in front
of a party. If he hadn't been drunk, he'd a probably high tailed it away."

CHAPTER 19

Ben, Henny, and Tilly held hands and swung their arms as they walked down to the market grounds on Christmas Eve, Aunt Letty beside them.

"Wow," Ben said. "Look at that tree."

It was a standing tradition that early Christmas Eve morning Long Robby and his friends cut the largest spruce they found in the woods and set it up in the park. A cardboard angel, kept from year to year, was put on the top of the tree, and the Gullah women decorated it with red oilcloth bows. Mr. Trainey, in an annual burst of generosity, donated apples, pears, and nuts, and and red peppermint candy canes to hang on the tree. In late day, before dusk, every child waited, excited, to be given one of these treasures as their names were called by Long Robby.

There was always music which they felt opened the heavenly door. Christmas Day would be spent in the prayer house singing, praying, and shouting out their gratitude to the Lord. No matter what had happened or was going to happen, gratitude was always within the Gullah.

Christmas morning, Aunt Letty wrapped a wool throw around her shoulders and stoked the fire. The warm weather they had enjoyed for the past few months was gone. She didn't care what it was like outside as long as she was warm inside, but she had something to do this morning, and it wasn't inside this warm house. She looked over at Tilly curled up in a ball sleeping. She never believed she could love this much again. It was time for her to go to Hallelujah Cemetery. No one would be there this early, and she liked being alone with her family.

She got back in bed and cuddled Tilly to her, kissing her forehead. "Merry Christmas, honey."

Tilly roused sleepily, smiled at Aunt Letty, got out of bed, and walked over to the tall chest they shared. Long Robby had seen the chest out in the streets in town where the residents left things no longer wanted to be taken by others and brought it to Letty after Tilly began living with her.

Tilly pulled a chair to the front edge of the drawers, climbed up, and reached over the top ledge. When she had what she was looking for, she clasped it in her hand, got down, and grinned as she ran to Aunt Letty.

"Chile, what on earth?"

When Tilly opened her hand, Aunt Letty gasped, glad she was sitting down. On Tilly's palm was a small white silver-colored hair comb with five large brilliant white stones across the top. Aunt Letty looked from Tilly's hand to her face, so shaken she could barely speak. She didn't know what kind of stones they were, but she knew the comb was special.

"Tilly, where'd you get this?"

Tilly opened her hand and looked sadly at the little comb.

"Oh, Tilly," she said, wrapping her arms around her. She was so befuddled she felt dizzy. Letty jerked her head up suddenly, feeling stupid. Of course, she knew exactly where Tilly got the comb. She reached under Tilly's chin and lifted her head so she could look at her. She brushed back the dark strands of hair that covered her face and said, tenderly, "Tilly, it be so beautiful. I never had anything in my life so beautiful."

Tilly smiled.

She was the image of the woman in the locket, Letty thought. Her uncle must have brought the comb with the locket. "Don't push her," he had said, and she hadn't, but she wondered what might still be in Tilly's head.

She took Tilly's face in her hands and asked softly, "Tilly, do you know who this belonged to?"

Tilly slowly shook her head.

How can this child tell me anything? I ain't asking no more bout this. It's just one more of the mysteries.

She hugged Tilly to her and closed her eyes to all the darkness surrounding this beautiful child. *If it ever come out, dear Lord, let it come easy.*

She let go of Tilly and walked over to the chest. She opened the middle drawer where she kept her valuables in a wooden inlaid box. Among them were her mama's gold earrings, a long strand of jet beads Miss Jenny had given her mother, and a ring with a ruby on it that had belonged to Miss Jenny when she was a child. It had been Pet's birthstone, and she had wanted Letty to have it. She picked up a large shiny dark brown acorn, twice the size of most acorns, and rubbed it in her hands. Bones found it soon after she joined him in the woods. He had put it in her hand and said, "This be luck for you, Letty. From now on." She looked at the little bird toy that Tilly had asked her to put away for her last summer and smiled. Tilly had finally been ready to let it go.

Along with the other treasures was the gold locket. It was engraved with initials she couldn't make out, and inside was the picture of the lovely woman who Letty was sure was Tilly's mother. She shook her head in wonder. *Just who could she be? This fancy-looking woman.* The picture showed only her head and bare shoulders, her black hair pulled up with ringlets flowing down. Not frizzy, but soft curls surrounding her creamy, light-colored skin. Just like Tilly's.

Letty looked over at Tilly, who was playing with the corn stalk doll Henny and Ben had given her Christmas Eve. The diamond comb was fastened on the side of the woman's hair where it was pulled up. She wasn't wearing any other jewelry that she could see.

She put the comb in the box, closed the drawer, and walked over to Tilly, who seemed to be okay now, content to play with the doll. *Maybe someday it will all make sense.*

"Honey, there be somethin I gotta do. There's biscuit on de table and those sugar cakes you like. When Orie comes a little later, she be bringin a pot of gumbo."

Letty leaned down and kissed Tilly on the cheek. "I won't be long, honey." She wrapped the wool shawl around her shoulders and walked out into the misty palette of grays.

As soon as Letty was gone, Tilly rolled over under the quilt and buried her face in the pillow. Her body shook with sobs as silent as the room. She lay away from the wet pillow and screamed and screamed in silence. At last, exhausted, she stared up at the wood ceiling. She pulled the edge of the sheet where Miss Emmy had embroidered it for Aunt Letty and rubbed it gently against her face and looked out the window at the gloomy day.

Letty stood at the iron gate to Hallelujah cemetery and respectfully asked permission of the spirits to let her enter. No doubt in her mind there were plenty around that day. She walked over to a far corner of the fenced graveyard, closing her eyes as she passed graves so as not to disturb their spirits.

She kneeled before a mound with a small wooden marker that had been painted white with the words, *Pet, our beloved,* and below that the dates, 1885 - 1888. Beneath were the words, *Our Mama, 1844 - 1888.* She leaned over and lay her head on the soft grass that covered the grave of her daughter and mother and spoke to her child.

"I love you, my lil baby girl. I'll never forget when my mama put you in my arms. That was de sweetest thing I ever felt. No lil chile could have been loved more than you. I want you to know dat, baby. No one will ever take your place in my heart. Not ever. Not a day I don't feel your lil arms around my neck." Letty wiped her eyes on the shawl. "So, when you see Tilly with me, you remember what I say. No one can take your place.

"But God give me Tilly so I wouldn't be sufferin over you all de time. She found her own place in my heart right beside you." The emotion Letty was feeling overcame her, and she collapsed back on the grave, weeping.

"This be Christmas, Pet, so I been thinkin about dat lil ring Miss Jenny gave me when you was born. Bones has your doll baby to keep for me. I ain't never goin to give dat baby doll to no one. You were holdin dat baby doll when it flew outta your hand. Can't think about dat, Pet." Letty squeezed her eyes shut against the memory. "You'll always be my beloved, baby. Til we be together again." She leaned down and kissed the earth above Pet and moved over to where she thought her mama might be.

"Oh, Mama, I wish you was beside me more than I can bear sometime. I be thinking if only my mama was here and then I hear a door close, or a wind go by, and I know you are there right beside me, but I sure wish we could sit down and talk. I wish we could have a cuppa life everlasting tea together. I know I'll be seein you soon, Mama. Don't know why but I think dat's de truth. I'll be singin for you today. I never forget what you told me, Mama—dat music be de path to de soul. Amen. We got our music, don't we?"

"Hello, Papa. You was a good man, Papa."

Letty stood back, looking appreciatively at her family. "Ya'll be all I got but Orie and Tilly. You, Mama and Papa, Grandma and uncles and Aunt Susie, I'm glad you're close by. Been nice visiting with ya'll. Always is. But Orie's made gumbo. An then we're going to the prayer house and sing all day an mebbe all night."

CHAPTER 20

"Merry Christmas, Henny." Ben walked into the kitchen in his long johns.

Henny, bending over to the oven, straightened up and smiled. "And the same to you, son. I'm putting this fresh ham back in to warm up for breakfast."

"Boy, that sounds good, Henny," he said, rubbing his arms and moving over to the warmth of the oven. "But I been lying in bed thinking of something I wanna do right now. I've never taken you out in my boat. I was thinking, well, that would be kinda like a Christmas present, if ya wanna go."

"Ben, I can't think of anything I'd like more," Henny said, genuinely pleased.

"If we leave now, we can see the sun come up."

"Let's go. Soon's I get on clothes fit for the chill out there."

Henny walked down to the cove with his arm slung over Ben's shoulder. "It's been a while since I was out in these waters, Ben. I'm really happy we're doing this together."

"Me too, Henny."

Henny sat beside Ben on the wood slat seat of the bateau, each with a paddle in their hands, as they glided down the tidal creek. The fog rose like a veil, leaving visible only what surrounded them, the marsh banks beginning to move with life, a white heron dipping his beak for small fish his keen eyes see, and the deep croak of a bullfrog disturbed by the sudden shrill cries of shore birds awakening.

"This is the perfect way to start a day."

"It's the time when I'm out here the most, Henny. I love being here any time, but this is the best. When everything around begins to stir. When the sun first starts comin up. Even when it's chilly or bone chilly like it is today, it's pretty to me."

They sat silently as the little boat drifted out into the marsh, allowing their senses to be seduced by the tranquil beauty surrounding them as scarlet color swelled in the sky.

"Ben, this is the best Christmas present I could have. Thank you, son."

Ben grinned. "Almost as good as breakfast sounds to me. My stomach is growling."

"Then we better head on home." Henny chuckled.

Henny walked in the house and said, "Let's fix our plates and go sit where it's warm an more comfortable than these pine chairs."

They piled their plates with ham, grits, and stewed apples and sat before the fire. "Dig in, boy."

After every grain of grits was gone, they both sighed and leaned back in the chairs.

Ben picked up a broken piece of kindling and threw it in the fire. "You don't think much of the Gullah's religion, do you?"

Henny looked at him, surprised. "Now why in the world would you say somethin like that?"

"Just seems to me you don't like it much. And telling me you hadn't been to one of their Thanksgivings in the market because of too much religion."

Henny squirmed around, trying to make himself more comfortable against the lumpy old pillow. He reached for his pipe and held it in his hand. "I reckon I did say that." He turned the pipe around, looking at it. "It's not that I don't like the Gullah's religion, Ben. I have a lot of respect for those people. Can't say I'd ever dislike anything they did. Religion or not. It's just that they got their ways and I guess I got mine."

"Henny, what are your ways? You asked me if I believed in God. Do you believe in God?"

Henny stared into the fire for a long time before answering. "I've never put what I think into words, Ben."

Ben, embarrassed, said, "I'm sorry, Henny, I didn't mean to ask you somethin you didn't wanna talk about."

"You're not, Ben. I'd talk to you about most anything. I grew up with a lot of love, Ben. I was a little boy when my mama died, but as long as she lived, she showed me what I meant to her. An Pop, too. An them to each other. That's a good feeling, knowing you're loved. I think that has a lot to do with how I feel bout the people I know and sometimes folks I don't know. Just seems we're all in this together. Someone said, made of the same cloth. That's the way I feel about it. An that's the way I feel when I'm out in nature. Like we was this morning and you are every day. From pretty early on, I've spent a lot of time on the water and in the woods. Maybe not as much as I used to, but alone in all that beauty when everything is still, except for creature sounds, I feel at home. I feel a part of everything around me. There's this feeling that comes up from so deep in me I nearly cry. Sometimes I do. I don't know about God, but I know I'm not alone. I know there's somethin beyond what we can see that did all this so perfectly."

They sat quietly before the fire, Ben thinking he'd never told anyone he loved them. He'd find a way to tell or show Henny how much he loved him.

⁓

Early afternoon, Henny was looking out toward the river when he saw Tilly running like a filly up the hill. He walked outside on the porch and called to her. "Now you're the last person I expected to see today, young lady." She ran into his open arms, then looked around and pointed to the inside of the house.

"No," said Henny with a twinkle in his eyes. "You'll find him behind the house. He's been out there with the sling shot you an Aunt Letty gave him for at least an hour." Before he could ask how she happened to be there, she had skipped down the steps and headed toward the back of the house. Henny shook his head, amused, and watched Tilly's long legs flying around the corner. He smiled and walked back to the warmth of the house.

Ben had made a paper target and tacked it to a square board, which he nailed on a pine tree. There was only the bullseye on the paper because he didn't consider hitting anywhere else. He reached into a bucket of small rocks beside him, fit it inside the leather sling, leveled his aim at the black circle, and let go. "Bullseye," he yelled, flinging up his arms and dancing in a circle. It was then he saw Tilly, grinning wider than usual. His face lit up.

"Tilly, how come you're here? Henny said you'd be gone all day."

She spread her arms and twirled around.

"Tilly," he said, holding out the sling shot, "I never had nothing that was so much fun in my life. And Bones made it," he yelled.

He grabbed her hand and pulled her until they were inside the house. "Henny, look who's here!"

Henny walked out of the kitchen, wiping his hands on a dish cloth. "I'm ahead of you on that one, boy. I saw her first." He ruffled the top of Ben's unruly hair and winked at Tilly.

She grinned and held out her hand to show the ring Aunt Letty had given her.

"Gee, that's really pretty. I like that red stone on it."

Henny moved closer and held Tilly's hand. "Tilly, I think this is somethin very special, an that means Aunt Letty thinks you are mighty special.

Tilly put her hand against her chest and smiled.

"Tilly, I'm glad you're here." He looked at Henny. "I haven't been

back to the tabby house since Tilly and I were there and Junie showed
up. You said ya hadn't never been there, Henny. Let's go now."

Tilly's grin faded.

"Aw, Tilly, Junie won't be there."

"He's probably right, Tilly. I don't see why he was there to begin
with. If it suits you, Tilly, I'm all for going."

Tilly reluctantly nodded.

"Well," Ben said impatiently, "let's go."

They walked through the woods and down the drive, glancing
somewhat warily around them, knowing it was unlikely, and particularly
on Christmas, for anyone to be around, but still the thought lingered.

Henny looked at the house and all around the grounds and down
to the marsh. "Someone did a nice job on this place. I guess we'll never
know who it was."

Ben showed him the walled garden, with Tilly tagging along
unenthusiastically. They sat on the bench while Ben told them how he
wanted to work in the garden, bring it back to life. "I've been thinking
about that for a long time."

"I hope you can do that, Ben. As for me, my old bones are aching
to get back home and get put on my bed for a nap. But this has been
a nice treat, seeing this pretty place."

Tilly picked up something by the gate and took it to Henny.

"This yours, Ben?"

"I've never seen that, Henny. What is it?"

"It's a surveying tape measure. Pop had one when we were staking
out our property line before building our house." He pointed to the
small round metal tape in a circular roll attached to a wood handle.
A small metal handle was adhered to the mechanism. "You turn this
and it cranks the tape. If it's not yours, Ben, someone walking through
dropped it. Maybe someone was here surveying this property."

"Henny, you know who was here. Junie. Why's he doing this
surveying?" He was so upset he choked on his words.

"Calm down, son. I can't imagine what Junie would want with this
property. He owns the biggest tract of land on this edge of the coast."

"He asked about it, Henny. To Mr. Moody. I know it's him that left that tape measure."

Henny looked off at the marsh and then around the property again. "Mebbe so, Ben. But it don't make sense."

They arrived home to find Aunt Letty sitting on the porch. "It be about time ya'll got back here."

They stared at her as if she were a spirit, then ran to hug her, except Henny, who beamed when he saw the basket of pastries, cakes, cookies and, of course, ham biscuits.

"You know, Henny, what the prayer house means to me. But somethin happened today when I let Tilly leave. A loneliness settled in dat wouldn't let go and I thought, God ain't just heah. He's where my Tilly is, too, an my friends. So here I am." She squeezed Tilly to her and slyly lifted a slip of her red turban just enough to reveal the little comb.

Sometime after midnight, Ben and Henny walked Aunt Letty and Tilly home, all sleepy and ready for bed. They agreed it was the most wonderful Christmas they ever had and one they would always remember.

CHAPTER 21

On New Year's Eve afternoon, everyone gathered in the market square for the burning of the Christmas tree. Later they would all gather in the prayer house for the Watch Night Service and be on their knees before midnight, bringing in the New Year in prayer. After midnight, they read the Emancipation Proclamation. This was a sacred tradition to the Gullah and one they always observed. However, the earlier tree burning had become a tradition as well.

"That tree sure looks naked," Ben said, looking at the spruce shorn of its red bows and candy canes. "The burning means more than getting rid of it, don't it?"

"Yep, it's symbolic of a way to clear away past regrets or sorrows," Henny interrupted. "It's a way of saying the past is past, let's get on with what's going on now. Sorta like painting—wash a board with turpentine and it's ready for a new paint job. Or, you might say, to clear away the old and open the doors to new journeys. Kinda like you setting out in your boat on water you don't know. Never can tell what's around the bend."

"Henny," Ben said sarcastically, "I know every bend in every creek, stream, river, fork, tributary, or saltwater marsh in this county."

Henny put his arm around Ben's shoulder, laughing. "Just having some fun with you."

Ben nudged Henny to look at Long Robby dancing a jig to Ragbone Harvey's music. "Yep, better tie up your boot strings and tighten your belt. There's gonna be fiddling and stomping today," Ragbone called out.

Ben rolled his eyes. "Not me, Henny. Watching the tree burn'll be about as close as I come to any stomping."

Henny looked toward the river. He wished he could explain to himself the uneasy feeling he'd been having lately. He forced the thought out of his mind and listened to the strains of Ragbone playing "The Maple Leaf Rag."

Long Robby called to everyone to gather in a circle around the square. "I ain't goin to explain to you why we do this. If you don't know by now, you better go home." Laughter filled the air. "No wind today but keep your distance and watch for sparks."

Tilly, Aunt Letty, Henny, and Ben stood together, everyone in a jovial mood, counting down the numbers to zero at the top of their lungs as Long Robby handed a torch to Rufus, who set the tree ablaze, flames leaping to the top. With all the attention on the fire, no one noticed that Tilly wasn't standing with them until Aunt Letty reached for her hand and saw her lying at her feet unconscience. Aunt Letty screamed, hysterically, and Henny quickly swooped the girl up in his arms.

He headed for Letty's house, Letty trying to keep up and Ben beside her. By the time Henny lay Tilly on the bed, she was coming around. She sat up and threw herself at a terrified Letty.

"Oh, my baby," Letty said over and over while she rocked her against her chest. "What scared you, Tilly? What frightened you so bad?"

It seemed pretty clear to Henny, and he said so.

"The fire, Letty. Somethin about the fire. She was standing along with us until Rufus torched the tree. Had to be the fire. That's a lot of fire for someone who never saw anything like it. Musta scared her."

He looked at Aunt Letty's distraught face. "You know something else it could be, Letty?"

Letty wrapped Tilly up in the quilt, holding her as close as she could. "No, Henny, I don't, but oh Lord, I wish I did." Tears streamed down her face.

Ben stood motionless, not knowing what to say or do.

Henny reached over and stroked Tilly's head, straightened up, and put his arm around Ben. "We're going, Letty. If you need us, you know where we are. I expect Orie'll be here soon as she hears what happened." He looked at the fireplace, the wood ready to light.

"Letty, does she mind a fire in the grate?"

"No, she don't."

She was so upset Henny almost decided to stay until Orie got there. He looked at Letty and said, "I think you are better alone with her now."

With his arm still around Ben's shoulder, they walked home. "She gonna be all right, Henny?"

"Don't know, Ben," he answered honestly.

Letty lay, staring at the ceiling long after Orie had left and Tilly was asleep. She heard the familiar sound she had been waiting for. She knew he was coming. She carefully removed herself from Tilly's arms, got up, and walked into the only other room in the small house. Tears began to flow when she saw him.

"Bones, what's goin on with my girl? Why is she so afraid of de fire?" She shook her head in consternation. "Even if I ask, she couldn't tell me."

She sat down on the daybed she used as a couch, her arms lying limp in her lap. "I know there are times when she be upset and tries to hide it." She put her hands on his arms. "What's goin on, Bones?"

"Letty, what you be doin is all dat lil girl needs now. I think there's times she's beginnin to remember somethin. You just have to wait for her, Letty."

She looked piercingly into Bones' deep-set eyes. "I think you knows, Bones. I think you knows. Will she ever talk? Will she ever remember all dat happened? Her uncle said her parents died. Dat is all I know. I think he was tryin to tell me about how they died, but he never got it out of his mouth."

"Letty." He sat down beside her. "If I know dat, I be tellin you. Some things don't come to me. But my feelin says she's goin to know all there be to know someday."

"Is this de trouble you were talkin about in de deep woods? What you see comin?"

"No. Dat be somethin else."

"Can't you stop it? When dat trouble goin to happen, Bones?"

"No, Letty. I can't stop dat. It'd make things worse for us if I did. Bad for everyone here. I think it be comin soon."

Letty looked away, frightened.

"Letty. I won't be around for a while." He stared into the fireless grate and back at Letty. "You goin to be fine." He walked over to the fireplace. "I'm goin to light this for you. It be gettin colder."

Her eyes were as round and white as a full moon. "Bones, you're scarin me."

"I don't mean to scare you, Letty. Just tellin you what I know like I always do."

"What's goin to happen?"

Bones eyes glazed over. "Can't say, Letty."

Letty jerked around and squinted at him. "You expect me to stay cooped up in here with this girl like chickens?"

"No need to stay in de house, Letty. Or stop what you do every day."

"Where're you goin, Bones?"

He looked at her tenderly. "You know I'm always with you, Letty."

In the woods she had watched him leave for days at a time, sometimes more. She had always known he was different from the rest of the Gullah. She knew most of the story about the gift of the mantle from King Oosafella, and she knew how special that was. He was far removed from the root doctors she knew about. Often, he didn't seem to be a part of this world, and it got more like that as time went by.

She repeated, "When you comin back, Bones?"

He looked at her, his eyes black as a bat cave.

"Can't say."

He got up and walked out the door. He was closer to her than anyone alive, and at times she missed him so much it hurt. But, at least, he came when he came.

Letty got back in the bed and held Tilly close, her mind a jungle of twisted thoughts. *An who's not goin to be fine?* She turned that over and over in her head until she feared she would go crazy.

In the morning, Letty lay in bed without moving a finger, waiting for Tilly to wake up. She didn't know what to expect. She was afraid that she would be agitated from the memory of the tree burning. She also harbored a shred of hope that the incident might have opened a door to Tilly's memory. But when Tilly opened her eyes, she smiled at Letty without a sign of anything disturbing having happened the night before. Letty leaned over her and swept her dark hair away from her face. "You all right, baby?"

Tilly smiled again and leaned against Aunt Letty.

Letty held Tilly's face in her hands. "Tilly, did you have a good time yesterday?"

Tilly frowned and looked quizzically into Letty's face. She nodded but blinked, staring off with a blank expression, and got out of bed.

Letty sank back against the wall and closed her eyes. *She don't remember. Dat chile don't remember nothin.*

CHAPTER 22

Ben walked in the house, the door banging behind him. He went back and closed it. "Sorry, Henny." He walked over to the fire and warmed his hands. "That wind is so fierce I couldn't throw a line. Ain't no way I can stay out in that without being blown out to sea."

"Yeah, glad it wasn't like this a couple of nights ago. Oh, I got news for you. I saw Orie and Aunt Letty is gonna keep Tilly home for another day."

Ben sighed. "Did she say what got into Tilly?"

"No, she didn't." Henny glanced at Ben's downcast expression. "Ben, how about some checkers?"

"Ah, thanks, Henny, but I was thinking of going into town. Got some things I wanna do there if that's okay? Anything I can get you?"

He looked at his tobacco tin. "Yep, you can get me some pipe tobacco. Big can. Oh, and get about three pounds of dried lima beans while you're at it. Mack's out of em."

Ben knew exactly what he wanted to do. He'd been thinking for a couple of weeks what he could get for Henny that he would really like. That old cushion in his chair was falling apart, and he was going to get him the one he'd seen in the window of a nice store downtown.

It was covered all over with pictures of pines and cones. *Henny'll like that.* If it took all the money in his pocket, he didn't care.

He passed the bank on the far end of the three-block business part of town where most of the shops and stores were, taking notice of flyers, flapping in the wind, put anywhere they could be put. He grabbed one and ran across the street to the grocery to get Henny's tobacco and beans. He'd go back for the pillow. The wind was gusting and pushed him across the street. He looked around. *Not many people gonna be out in this wind.*

"Hi, Mr. Moody."

"Well, hello, Ben. I'm glad to see you. My first customer in an hour." He chuckled. "The ladies don't want their hair mussed up with this wind."

"Sorry about that, Mr. Moody. All I need is a can of tobacco for Henny's pipe and dried lima beans."

"I'll have the tobacco up here by the register, Ben. You'll find the beans in the back with the other barrels."

Ben started to walk to the back but stopped and held up the flyer. "Mr. Moody, I seen these in windows and nailed to trees all over town. A circus is coming here?"

Mr. Moody's face brightened. "Yes, indeed! The circus is coming to town, Ben."

Ben's eyes lit up. "Gosh, Mr. Moody, that's great."

"It just happened a few days ago. Surprised all of us. The owner of the circus came to see the mayor who then called in the town council, of which I am a member." He smiled proudly. "Mr. Barnes, the owner, bills the show as The Greatest Small Circus in the World. There will be a fine band, as well. Mr. Barnes, having just lost his conductor to a bigger circus, has hired a renowned New York City conductor who was seeking employment in the South."

"When are they coming, Mr. Moody?"

"Next week. We had to move fast to meet their needs, but now the whole deal is signed and sealed."

Ben was delirious with joy. "Golly, Mr. Moody. I can't wait to tell Henny an . . . " He hesitated, thinking of Tilly. "And everybody."

Mr. Moody slapped him on the back, chuckling. "Well, go get your beans."

What neither Mr. Moody nor the town council knew was how deeply concerned and disappointed Mr. Barnes felt upon meeting his new conductor for the first time. He found him pompous, and far from appearing distinguished, he was on the far side of shabby. As for his companion, he looked as scurrilous as any thug found in a dark alley. Nevertheless, Mr. Barnes prayed he was wrong. After all, appearances weren't always important.

It had been decided, not without laborious arguments, that the large open field behind the square would serve the needs of the circus. It was fronted by the Bay and banked by a deep forest on the other side. The small dirt road that led from the Gullah's property to town came out where the woods met this vacant land. This was a fairly quick walk from the Gullah community, but as far as the road being used frequently, it was more a convenience for the Gullah employees of the town residents. The populace of Belleview didn't expect any Gullah would come to the parade or circus. As a matter of fact, they had given it little consideration, but they would have no objections as long as they knew their place.

CHAPTER 23

Henny was sitting around a fire he had just stoked when Ben, laden with his packages, pushed open the door with his arm and blurted out excitedly, "Henny, a circus is coming to town."

"I know a circus is coming to town." He picked up the webbing hook and began to work a net.

Ben, surprised, stared at Henny. "You knew about the circus?"

"Only heard today." He shook his head side to side. "Seems bad timing with this wind but by next week it should be calmed down." He shrugged. "Could be calm as a sleeping cat tomorrow."

He put his net down beside him. "Long Robby told me bout it. He said he was worried." He stared out of the window and watched four or five buzzards heading for the woods. "Ben, I hate to say it, but I don't think the Gullah ought to go around town when the circus comes."

Ben frowned. "Why, Henny?"

"Well, things, like I told you, just ain't good between the whites and coloreds now."

He looked down at his net. "The Gullah have been protected being out here, almost hidden away, but bringing in the circus means the town might not only bring in the militia but a bunch of strangers, and I'm just not too happy about that."

"Henny, what about the sheriff?"

Henny chuckled. "Ben, Belleview's sheriff's more of a playmate to the kids in town than a law man. He's a good man, but nothing never happens in Belleview, and I doubt he'd know what to do if it did."

"Well then, if there was trouble, wouldn't this militia keep somethin from happening?"

Henny raised his brows and let out another long sigh. "I don't know, Ben. I don't much think so." He stopped his weaving and looked at Ben. "The militia's just a bunch of men, just like any other white man."

"Where's the militia from, Henny? All I've heard for the last two days is everyone talking bout the militia being here. Who are they?"

"Soldiers. The Fort just opened a few days ago across the river in Baytown. So we got the army here now."

Ben looked at Henny, concerned.

Henny threw the net on the floor. "They are probably good boys, or at least most of em. I just don't like the idea of the military being around here." He reached for his pipe then put it down. "Those young men have been brought here to be trained for somethin, and the only thing I know soldiers are trained for is war. We just had a war, durn it. An I don't like the idea of strangers coming here and stirring things up in this peaceful place."

Ben stared at Henny, shocked at this burst of anger from the amiable man he knew.

"And like I said, they're white men working for the government, and I ain't seen the government protecting the coloreds lately."

He let out a long sigh, pulled out the lumpy pillow, and pitched it across the room.

"That's just my feeling." He looked apologetically at Ben. "I'm sorry to be so ornery. I'm just an ignorant old lowlander, Ben. The last time we had any soldiers around here was during the war. Fifty years ago. I wasn't born til after it was over, but I know what it did to people. Not just the whites but the Gullah too. Mighta freed the enslaved people but look at em now. Scared to death and with good reason. Well, that's enough of that."

He looked over at Ben, who was still standing and trying to take in all Henny was saying. "Whatcha got under your arm, boy?"

Ben, jarred back to the moment, looked down at the wrapped pillow. "I forgot. It's for you, Henny," he said, smiling.

Henny opened the package and stared at the pillow. Without looking up, he said, "No one's ever given me nothing, Ben." He got up and put his arms around Ben. "Thank ya, son."

"Aw, Henny," Ben said, embarrassed at the mist he had seen in Henny's eyes. "It's just an old pillow."

"It's far more than a pillow, Ben. It's the kindness of your heart. I've told you before I regretted that I didn't ask you to come live with me sooner." He chuckled. "Except for maybe when you floated up in that basket." He winked at Ben. "Did Ben Clary tell you what the Gullah thought when he brought you up to the market from the marsh?"

"No, but he told me I spoiled his plans of heading further down south."

Henny chuckled. "Ben, you can't imagine the fuss when Ben Clary told em how he found you. They thought you was another Moses. You was lying in that big wooden bowl smiling at all those people. They was so excited they called the pastor. Ben Clary didn't tell you that?"

"Not that I remember. Who's Moses?"

"The Gullah thought that meant God had favored them with a miracle."

"Who's Moses?"

"I ain't sure but some important person in the Bible who was found in the marshes, too. They kept yelling, 'He been sent by de Lawd to us.' Pa and I looked at each other knowing what was coming and hightailed it home."

Seeing Ben's confusion, he explained, "We were the only whites nearby. Ben Clary was passing through. No Gullah family was going to take in a white child, Moses or not.

"Ben, I been thinking ever since you come to live with me what I missed all those years. But Ben Clary was a good man. He settled in that old shack down the river and took care of you like you was his own. Had plenty of help, too. Even after the pastor convinced them you wasn't another Moses. No one knew where you came from but thought some sharecroppers passing through had set you afloat. Ben Clary told me that you saved his life. After he lost his farm in Virginia and his wife died having a baby, he just started walking."

"He told me that, Henny."

"So, now here we are. You and me."

⁓

"I just talked to Rufus, Henny. Long Robby's going to take anyone with him who wants to go to the circus. Are you going?"

"I'd go with you, Ben, if you were going alone. This may be the greatest small show on earth, but sitting here by the fire watching it crackle and spark is all the show I need.

"If you're going to be with Long Robby, I ain't got nothing to worry about. He'll keep ya'll roped in so tight a flea couldn't get to you. Rufus going? And Tilly?"

"Yeah, they're both as excited as the younger kids."

"I'll have to say I'm surprised that Aunt Letty is letting Tilly go."

"Me too." Ben grinned. "Aunt Letty said if Long Robby was taking us, it'd be fine."

"Rufus is older than you, right?"

"I think he's about two or three years older than me."

"He's a good boy, Ben. I'm glad he's your friend. Long Robby says he's going away to school next year. Doesn't want to be a fisherman."

"He and Long Robby are real close, Henny. I'm surprised at that. What's he gonna do away at school?" Ben frowned at the idea.

"Ben, a lot of young people are going up north. And not only the young. In many cities hundreds of coloreds have already gone north. I wouldn't be surprised to see that happening around here soon. Some of it has to do with the way the Gullah are treated here, and some of it is there ain't no opportunity for them here no more. Rufus is getting a good education at the Gullah school on St. John's Island. What would Rufus do here?"

"Well, I'd sure work for his dad if I was him."

"That's cause you've been on the water all your life and you love it. Lottsa kids today don't see it that way."

CHAPTER 24

Most of the Gullah didn't go to the parade after hearing the soldiers from the fort were going to be guarding the shops and homes in the event visitors got out of hand. To the Gullah, that read, "They be watchin for us to do anything, and that is to steal."

However, there were about a dozen parents and their children who met with Long Robby in the market. He made it clear there would be soldiers around and it was mandatory that they all stay together. "So as long as you know dat, we be off to see de parade."

Tilly, Ben, and Rufus laughed and ran a little ahead.

Following behind Long Robby, the train of Gullah parents and children danced, skipped, and jumped around the entire twenty minutes it took to walk to town.

The three blocks of downtown and the block past the square led to the grounds where the circus tent was installed. The road along the square was already lined with people of all ages. The ladies were attired in fancy long dresses, frilly big hats, and umbrellas. Not to be outdone, the gents wore their Sunday best, vests, and bowler hats. Children screamed and jumped up and down next to their parents.

The Gullah looked at this scene, knowing they were not invited to join the whites with the best view along the street. They were accustomed to this and were just grateful for a chance to see the parade, no matter how far back they had to stand. Long Robby had already decided they would be safer and more accepted if they were closer to the end of the parade, back against the forest, which was next to the ground where the circus would set up. He guessed that most of the militia would be closer to the stores, but some could be by the houses as well. *Best to stay out of sight and out of mind.*

The air was electric with excitement, all the Gullah holding their breath in anticipation. They heard the strains of music first, before the band was in sight, and grins spread across their faces. This was foreign music to their ears, but it was "moving" music. It was feet-shuffling music, and they began to sway and clap until Long Robby shushed them. But that didn't stop the delight they felt or the swaying in their colorful dresses and turbans.

"Look," one of the children yelled, pointing toward the sounds coming toward them.

Leading the parade, strutting proudly to "Stars and Strips Forever," was the owner and ringmaster, Mr. Hanibal Barnes, dressed in a bright red jacket, white shirt, frilled at the neck, white pants, tall black boots, and a black top hat, which he tipped as he bowed to the thrilled audience lined up along the street.

He was followed by two very scantily dressed girls in tight-fitting red satin costumes, adorned with gold ruffles well above their knees, revealing black lace stockings and gold shoes. Gold feathers swayed in the breeze on small caps perched on their very blond heads. But it was the low bodices, barely containing full bosoms, that caused the Victorian ladies to cover their eyes with fans. Their gasps could be heard to the bay while their husbands smiled. The girls held a gold banner stretched between them painted in black glitter, "THE MOST SPECTACULAR CIRCUS OF ALL TIME."

The band leader pranced behind them, missing the baton with almost every pitch in the air. He was dressed in a tight white one-piece suit, adorned with gold braids, epaulets, and buttons, a white cap with gold braids, and what seemed to be no end of pearly white teeth under a pencil slim mustache on his pasty face. However, the blue uniformed band he led was magnificent, having been trained well by the former conductor.

Oohs and *Ahhs* were heard up and down the street. The thrilling sounds of the trumpets, saxophones, and trombones rang through the air, piccolos trilled, and the drum section took the watcher's breath away and caused a massive breakout of goose bumps. Ben stared in wonder, his own heart soaring, and he wished more than anything in the world he was marching in that band.

The band was followed by gilt cages of leopards, lions, and monkeys, most of them sleeping. The Gullah felt a kinship with these animals, believing they had lived in the land their ancestors came from, but they had seen a few cats living in the woods around them, which they knew had not come from Africa.

One spectacular act followed another. A little boy yelled to the crowd that he was going to join the circus.

At the end of this magnificent parade was a small elephant, painted in colorful designs on his trunk and legs, a red velvet blanket covering his upper body and a gold crown topping his head. On his shoulders was the most beautiful girl Ben had ever seen. She wore a glittering white costume that clung to her shapely body from the low bodice to her thighs, over which a colorful flowered silk cape flowed down her perfect, white-stockinged legs. Her headdress was the same as the elephant's, making them a fetching pair.

The Gullah looked at the elephant in reverence, feeling a tightness in their chests. They had heard hand-down stories about elephants. They never dreamed they would see one and would never forget this day. Although it hurt them to see such a special animal taken away from the wilds of its home.

The candy applecart was the last of the parade. Ben had brought some pennies and nickels and ran as fast as he could to get the apples for the children, but in truth, he was beside himself to get closer to the girl on the elephant. He could hardly pull himself away from the elephant's side, moving along with it and gazing adoringly at the girl of his dreams until he stumbled on the brick street and remembered why he was there. He bought a dozen of the tooth-cracking treats from a clown who patted him on the head and helped him arrange the candy apples on sticks between his fingers to take back.

All the children's hands were reaching eagerly for them. Long Robby laughed and said, "Dat's mighty fine of you, Ben."

Ben was as happy as he could remember being. He was in love for the first time. "This's been a perfect day, Long Robby."

Long Robby spread one long arm around Ben and Tilly and the other around Rufus's shoulder as they watched the last of the parade arrive on the grounds in front of them.

All the entertainers began to scatter, and workers pulled the cages to the back of the field. The Gullah lost interest, particularly since the music had stopped.

Long Robby said it was time to go home. "We seen the best, ya'll."

There weren't many of the children begging to stay. Their heads were still swimming with color and clowns. And they were still crunching on the candy apples. It had been a wonderful time, all agreed, even Long Robby, who was grateful it had gone so well.

"Rufus, I don't see no problem in ya'll stayin a little longer. Just keep your eyes fixed around ya." His own opened wide in warning. "Any sign of trouble or if the militia come, you got to get out of here as fast as your legs can take you. We don't know nothin bout those soldiers." He stared at them warily. "You understand dat?"

"You can count on dat, Dad."

"Okay, have fun."

Seeing Ben's worshipful eyes fixed on the beautiful girl who was now standing next to the elephant, Long Robby whispered in his ear, "Dat lil filly caught your eye?"

Ben blushed. "Aw, no, just watching the elephant."

Long Robby laughed in good cheer and poked him in the ribs.

Embarrassed, Ben started to walk away, but at that moment, the girl he loved was walking toward him, smiling. His heart flew up into his throat when she held out her arms. He knew he must be on fire, and that she, and everyone else, could see the flames. He stood there like a moron, he thought, not able to move as she put her arms around his neck and kissed him slowly on the mouth, smiled sweetly, and walked back to the elephant being led to the back of the grounds.

Ben felt like a block of smoldering cinder. He stood, unable to look at her, not believing what had happened. His body was crawling with new sensations that were embarrassing to him. *Oh gosh,* he thought. *Oh gosh.* He moved further back against the trees, all mixed up with raw feelings.

Rufus and Long Robby were doubled over laughing, not noticing the glower on Tilly's face.

"Looks like she got you, boy," Long Robby called as he walked away toward home.

Suddenly the wailing cry of the elephant caught Rufus, Ben, and Tilly's attention. They looked back at where the elephant had been tied and frowned. The girl had left, but there were two men dressed up in clown's costumes, but without painted faces or wigs, who were fooling with the rope that tied the small elephant down.

Rufus said, "I don't know what they be doin to dat elephant, but he sure don't look like he likes it."

"Rufus, I think one of them is that band leader."

The elephant was being led close to the marsh, swinging his trunk and occasionally crying. It looked like the men were poking something into its sides.

"Where're they taking it?"

"Looks like they're walkin towards the fence dat separates de homes from de circus grounds."

"Well, maybe they're just moving it to some other place to tie it up."

"Maybe so."

Rufus said, "Gladys, the Hackney's maid, told me yesterday dat no one was to go over dat fence."

Tilly grabbed Ben's arm and put her hand over her mouth.

"Rufus, look at that!"

"Dat's no clown act, Ben!"

The men were getting out of the clown suits and were trying to climb the fence, poking their feet on the slats between the boards. They watched, baffled, as the men jumped down on the other side of the fence and began running along the marsh in front of the mansions.

"Maybe they are just running away from the circus, Rufus. Should we tell someone?"

"Who'd we tell, Ben? I can't go to anyone over there and tell em their elephant is loose an two clowns are over the fence." He clenched his jaw. "Anyway, it's none of our business an I don't want to be involved in anythin to do with this. If there be trouble, there'll be soldiers from Fort Fairfield up and down de street, Dad said."

"Rufus, why don't we go home and forget those men?"

Tilly was nodding.

"I'm all for dat, Ben. Let's go."

They gave one last look at the men, who had suddenly changed course from the water and were now running toward the Hackneys' house.

"Oh no!" both boys exclaimed, alarmed.

Tilly grabbed Ben's arm and pointed across the street. Ragbone, who must have been watching the men also, was running around the back of the Hackneys' house, where the circus people were heading.

"Oh Lordy. I gotta go get him." He looked at Rufus. "You know this could be bad. Take Tilly to Henny's. Get out of here now, Rufus, and don't let no one come here. No one."

"I'm not leaving you, Ben. Not alone."

"Rufus, ya gotta go now and take Tilly. You know what your dad said."

"Tilly can go home with Emmy an her sister over there. I'm not leaving you."

Frustrated, Ben said, "We don't know what those guys are up to, Rufus, but you can count on the militia being here before we cross the street once they hear bout those guys. You get your hide going or I'll drag you and Tilly home. And then Gladys might be dead."

"I don't want to do this, Ben. What about you?"

"I ain't Gullah."

Rufus grabbed Tilly's hand, and she pulled away, running to Ben. "You can't stay with me, Tilly. You gotta go with Rufus."

She hung on to his waist, fighting Rufus, who finally threw her over his shoulder. She made a furious face at Ben and beat on Rufus' back as he ran down the road.

Ben raced across the street and around the back of the house. He had no idea where the two men were, nor Ragbone for that matter. Nor Gladys and the kids. He threw open the unhinged back door, and as he did, the two circus men crawled out of a second-floor window, stepped onto the porch roof, jumped to the ground, and ran toward the marsh. Relieved, Ben sped up the kitchen stairs two at a time to the second-floor landing, calling Ragbone all the way up.

Ragbone was standing in the bedroom surrounded by a shiny, colorful assortment of necklaces, rings, and other jewelry, which were scattered out to the hall.

"Ben, I sure be glad to see you. Those villains broke in de back door an got hold of Miz Hackney's fine things. They scrambled outta dat window." He pointed to an open window in the bedroom. "I reckon when they heard me comin up de stairs."

Ben ran to the window. "Yeah, I saw em. Pretty easy to get to the ground from here. Ragbone, we gotta get outta here fast."

A voice called from the closet, "Ben, it's me."

Gladys slowly opened the door, shaking like a leaf in a storm, talking so fast her words were tumbling over each other.

"I heard em breakin in de back door, Ben. I grabbed James, David, and Annie dat was playing Parcheesi right by me heah upstairs, and we been hidin in Miz Hackney's closet. I never been so scared in my life. I heard all this mumbling bout getting as much as they could into bags.

Then I hear Ragbone callin from the kitchen. Lawd a mercy. Then one of them say, 'Let's get out of here.'"

Ben, distraught, said, "Gladys. You gotta get back in that closet and don't you come out for anything until the Hackneys get home."

Instead, she looked at Ragbone and said, "You ain't got de sense of a billy goat, Ragbone. Get yourself outta here, you crazy old man."

"I'm fine, Gladys." He smiled calmly at her. "Those fine soldiers'll be here soon to get those thiefs."

She put her hands on her head and shook it. "Ragbone."

She turned frantically to Ben. "They'll kill him, Ben. He told me before you got here dat he saw de hoodlums goin to de back of this house and figured they was up to somethin bad. He said he saw de soldiers from de fort further on down de street and asked a young white boy standin close by to run and get em fast."

She caught her breath. "Oh, Ben, this be bad. I told Ragbone to go out de back door quick, but he say his little grandsons are waitin for him by de front steps. Ben, he thinks those soldiers be his friends."

"She's right, Ragbone. We gotta leave now."

He glanced at Gladys, who looked like a feather could knock her over. "Gladys. Get back in that closet. Are the kids okay?"

Before she closed the closet door, she said, "I scared em so bad they're still huddled up in de back of de closet. I told em de soldiers were comin and if they found em they would feed em to de gators."

"Gladys, the soldiers."

He reached for Ragbone's arm, knowing it was too late as the soldiers ran up the steps.

He stood dazed as they walked toward Ragbone, who smiled, tipped his hat, and said, "We been waitin for you gentlemen." He held out his hand to the soldiers.

"You stand where you are," one of the soldiers demanded.

Another waved his hand across the floor and said, "You trying to get off with this loot?"

Ragbone looked over at him, surprised, and put his hands in his pockets. "No sir, I been waitin on you to come and get those thiefs."

"What's that you got in your pocket, nigger?"

Ben gasped and said, "Ragbone, stand still. Please, don't move."

Ragbone started walking toward the soldier, pulling something out of his pocket.

"Stop!" one of the soldiers yelled.

Hurt spreading across his face, Ragbone looked back at the soldier. "I only got my harmonica, sir."

Two little curly-headed boys not much more than toddlers ran up the stairs calling, "Pappy, Pappy," and rushed into Ragbone's arms, tears streaming down their faces.

"Damn you, get those pickaninnies away from you."

Ben lurched for the children, but one of the soldiers pushed him away with the butt of his rifle and demanded, "You stay over there."

"They're just my lil granchillun," Ragbone said, hugging them closer to him. "They mean no harm. They just be scared."

Saddened, Ragbone reached for his pocket and started to pull out the harmonica. "I told you all I got is this."

All three soldiers raised their rifles and fired at the same time, hitting Ragbone and the children, tearing into the boys' small backs and sending a shower of blood in the air. Like slow motion, they all fell to the floor together.

Ben, stunned, unwilling to believe what he had seen, heard an involuntary scream coming from the depths of his being. He leaned over Ragbone and the children, sobbing. Crazed with rage, he picked up the harmonica and shook it at the soldiers. "You bloody murderers. You killed him. He ain't the one who stole the jewels. You bloody bastards, you killed em."

The soldier standing nearest him sneered, and Ben jumped up and knocked him down, sending his rifle skidding across the floor. Ben quickly reached for the gun as another soldier yelled, "Why, you ain't nothing but a filthy nigger lover, are you?" He slammed the butt of his rifle against Ben's head, sending him reeling against the sharp edge of the door jam. Blood splattered over the walls as Ben slumped unconscious to the floor.

Henny reached the stair landing just in time to see this and howled, "Noooo." He flung his body over Ben. Tears flooding down his face, he cried out, "You ignorant, filthy bunch of scum."

Seemingly out of nowhere, the sheriff, mayor, the Hackneys, and a few others were in the hall, staring aghast at the grotesque, bloody scene.

The sheriff yelled, "You idiots. What have you done?"

"Oh my God," someone cried at the sight of Ragbone and his two little grandsons lying in a pool of blood.

Mr. Hackney touched Henny's shoulder as he sobbed over Ben's body.

"He's alive," Henny choked out.

Horrified and shaken to her bones, Mrs. Hackney kneeled over Ragbone and the children, caressing one of the little boy's curly heads matted with blood, and began crying.

"You monsters. You've killed these precious little children and this sweet, gentle old man." She glared at the soldiers. "How could you?" she screamed, enraged.

The mayor, his face misshapen with anger, shouted, "What you have done is unforgivable. Get out of here. NOW."

One of the soldiers said, arrogantly, "Why are you in such an uproar, mister? We were called here."

The sheriff grabbed the soldier by the collar. "You better get out of my sight. Tomorrow your commander will hear of this."

He looked down at the little children, tears spilling from his eyes. "Not more than four or five. Babies." He glared at the surly soldiers. "You can count on that. You are a shame to our country."

The militia, angered, left in a huff, and as they did, Gladys slowly opened the door, her sweet brown face red from crying.

"Gladys!" Both Mr. and Mrs. Hackney pushed aside the glittering objects on the floor and went to her. Mable Hackney took Gladys' hands in hers. "The children?"

At the sound of their mother's voice, all three ran out of the closet into her arms. She held them tightly to her and said, beside herself with shock, "Thank God you are safe."

Mr. Hackney reached out and put his hand on Gladys' shoulder. "You four have been in that closet the entire time?"

"Yes, sir," Gladys whimpered. "Since when I heard de thiefs breaking in."

He shook his head, deeply upset. "My God!"

Mrs. Hackney reached for Gladys' arm and held it gently. "Take the children downstairs to the back-sitting room where they won't hear what has to be done. Give them anything they want."

Bill Hackney kneeled by Henny and told him who he was. "Ben is a special young friend of ours. Please, let me call an ambulance, Mister . . . ?"

"Findley," Henny managed to say. He picked up Ragbone's harmonica laying by Ben's hand and put it in his pocket.

"He's been badly hurt, Mr. Findley."

"He's alive."

A younger man knelt down with them. "I'm a doctor, Mr. Findley. I can't help that poor old man and the children." He shook his head sadly. "Please let me look at your boy. I can help him."

"Thank you, doctor, but I want to take my boy home."

"It won't take long to look at his wounds, Mr. Findley."

"I dunno what good looking will do, doctor, but go ahead. Won't change my mind bout taking him home."

"Do you know what happened to him?"

Henny gently moved his hand across Ben's face and head where it was swelling. "I saw that soldier smack my boy with his gun. So hard it woulda dented a wall. It knocked him over there." He pointed to the sharp door jam.

"I would be surprised if he didn't have a concussion. Looking at his head, it looks like two bad blows. It would be better to take him to the hospital where he could be cared for in case of a cerebral hemorrhage, Mr. Findley."

Henny looked at him, tears streaming down his face. "Thank you. I appreciate that, but I want him home." And, to himself, he said, "Letty's medicine is stronger than any the hospital ever heard of."

"You are aware of the severity of a cerebral hemorrhage, Mr. Findley?"

"Are you sayin he could die, doctor?"

The young doctor hesitated. "He could. Without care."

"Thank you, doctor, but I wanna take my boy home."

"All right then, Mr. Findley, we are not going to argue with you. You know the dangers."

"I'll take you home, Mr. Findley," Mr. Hackney said. He looked over at Ragbone and his grandsons. "I'm heartsick over this. How can we take Ragbone and the little boys to his family?"

"I'd appreciate them bein taken to the Gullah docks. Somebody'll be there to take them to the Island."

Mr. Hackney sighed, leaned down, and took off Ragbone's, hat which lay askew on his head.

"How could those men do this? They don't come any better than this sweet old man." He looked at the little boys. "Just starting life. Those precious little beings."

When the car pulled up at Henny's house, Aunt Letty was standing on the porch looking frightened and with her arms wrapped around her chest. Mr. Hackney's chauffeur, who looked more like he belonged in a boxing ring than a fancy car, gently lifted Ben out of the large back seat where Henny was holding him.

Aunt Letty opened the front door, her heart pounding as she saw Ben lying so helplessly in the man's arms. Her eyes shifted to Henny and welled with tears.

"It's bad, Letty."

She followed him to Ben's room.

After Ben was laid down in his bed, Henny thanked Mr. Hackney and his chauffeur, Plummer. "You've been very kind, sir."

"Those soldiers will be dealt with."

Henny kept a blank face but knew that would never happen.

CHAPTER 25

Aunt Letty looked down at the seemingly lifeless form on the bed and said quietly, "Dear God help us." Tears streamed down her face. "Oh, Henny, what happened? What happened?"

"At the Hackneys's." Henny lay his head on the bed. "I saw the soldier hit Ben hard enough to kill him."

"Who, Henny? I dunno nothin but what Rufus told me bout Ben runnin to get Ragbones. I came on here to find you."

"The soldiers. They killed Ragbones." He hesitated then said, stumbling on his words, "And his two little grandsons."

She flopped on the small wooden chair by the bed and laid her head on the quilt. "Oh Henny," she finally said, her voice choking with emotion. "I can't wrap my mind around dat now."

She laid her hands on Ben's head and sat there looking at him. "My heart can't handle all this at once, Henny. I can't think bout anythin but this boy here now." *And Bones,* she thought. *This be it. What he said was coming. But why couldn't he help?*

After a few minutes, she said, "This shirt someone wrapped around his head is soaked with blood, Henny." She unwrapped the cloth and shook her head. "Dat's a nasty cut on his head, but it's not too deep, thank de Lawd." She ran her hand over the bruised and swelling side of his face and head, tears welling in her eyes. "But it's de inside of his head dat matters."

She looked at Henny's dispirited face. "I need things from home, and I gotta see about Tilly. Orie's staying with her." She put the quilt, crumpled up at the foot of the bed, over Ben and smoothed her hand lovingly over the side of his face.

Henny, barely above a whisper, said, "Save my boy, Letty."

She put her hand on his shoulder, squeezed it, and left.

She didn't tell him that she had been restless all afternoon, feeling danger so close she could taste it, trying to believe she was just imagining things, just nervous. When Rufus came running to her stall holding onto Tilly, she knew something bad had happened.

Orie met Aunt Letty on the porch of her house, her expression full of questions. "I got Tilly settled down with wild cherry tea, Letty. She's sleepin now. Letty, what happened?"

"Henny saw it, Orie. Ben got a bad blow on his head from a soldier's rifle. Orie, Ragbone is dead and two of his little grandsons with him. Shot by soldiers. I don't know more than dat now."

Orie stretched her hands to the sky. "Jesus, Jesus, what you be doin?" she cried. "First Jimmy, now dis?"

"If dat make you feel better, then yell it all out, Orie, but it be de soldiers to blame, not Jesus. How long can you stay with Tilly?"

"I'll send word to Miss Rebecca. She'll have to do, but she got Stella if she needs her."

"Come to de kitchen with me." Aunt Letty gathered cobwebs for the bleeding, marsh grass soaking in sea water to make a poultice for bruising, and Life Everlasting tea for everything else. She put them in a basket and walked outside to a darkening sky, turned around, and went back inside.

"What'd you forget?"

"A needle."

"Looks like a storm coming in. An I'm sure as I'm starin up at those black clouds dat Tilly is staring out dat window. An don't you turn and look. Lawd a mercy, Orie. What am I goin to tell dat girl?"

They held each other close, both wishing the swiftly moving clouds would blow away all the heartache they felt facing them.

As she walked back to Henny's, she saw a car carrying Ragbone and the little boys down to the dock where Long Robby was waiting to take them home. She bowed, her hands in prayer. "Goodbye, my sweet friend," she said sadly.

When she got back to Henny's, she stood at Ben's room, the door cracked open just enough to see him sitting in the little wood chair next to Ben. His tall body looked so small hunched over, his head on his chest and hands folded in his lap. He didn't look up when she entered the room. Ben lay back with his mouth open, his bloody hair matted to his face, his strong young body so limp. Henny had removed his shoes and blood-spattered clothes and covered him back up with the quilt. She looked at his young, beautiful face and then at Henny, who had gone back into a motionless kind of stupor. She put her hand on his shoulder. "Henny, go get one of your more comfortable chairs an let me get there. We're going to get this boy well."

CHAPTER 26

Gladys brought news about the circus and events from town. Mr. Barnes was angry at his stupidity for hiring someone sight un-seen, but he had no interest in their thieving caper. Or in the militia's cruel actions. What was done was done. He quickly packed up his circus and was out of town before dusk.

The thieves were found in the marsh trying to get away from an alligator swimming toward them.

What was taken of Mrs. Hackney's jewelry was returned to her.

The three soldiers responded to demands they be punished by claiming to be innocent of any crime. They had been called to the house for a burglary. They found the suspect in the house standing with the jewelry. They ordered him to stop. When he refused, they acted accordingly. The boys just got in the way of the bullets. They were excused and with more praise than admonishment.

The only question was whether Ben's name would be added to those murdered.

⟳

By the end of the first week, both Henny and Aunt Letty were as attuned to Ben's young body as a mother was to her newborn as to every breath he took. They knew every beat of his heart as if it were their own. It was what they couldn't see that concerned them.

"How do we know if his brain's bleeding, Letty?"

She reached over and rubbed his shoulder. "When he wakes up, Henny. We'll know."

"Letty, I'm surprised that Tilly hasn't found a way to get away from Orie."

"Orie had to go back to work, but Nellie's caring for her. Tilly knows dat she can't see Ben now."

After a few days of no change in Ben, Henny was distraught. "I keep thinking of what that doctor said, Letty. I shoulda let him take Ben to the hospital."

"It can take time for head wounds, Henny, but today looking at him I feel in my bones that he's comin outta this."

"I ain't loved many people, Letty. My ma died when I was not much more than a toddler. I sure loved Pa. An when I was just over bein a little shirt-tail guy, I had a fancy for a pretty girl on the farm next to ours. Only she didn't fancy me. Never had another chance for romance, living here. But I love that boy."

Aunt Letty was gently patting Ben's face with a damp cloth when she heard a movement outside the door.

They both turned to see Tilly standing there. Without a word, she walked over to the bed, crawled up on it, and curled against Ben, her face next to his.

Aunt Letty and Henny looked at each other and smiled.

"Let's just let them be, Henny. This may be the medicine we've been needin."

When they heard someone else out in the hall, Aunt Letty went to see who it was then returned and said, "That was Nellie. She be upset about Tilly gettin away from her."

She looked at Tilly, who was stroking Ben's arm, looking like all the joy in the world had gone off with the circus and wouldn't come back unless Ben awakened.

"I'll give her a little more time with him, Henny, then I gotta go."

"You'll come back?"

"I'll be comin after the market closes. And I'll help you get some broth down Ben. I'll bring Tilly with me." She rolled her eyes. "Like I got a choice. But if anythin happens, if there be any reason you need me, ring dat bell you have on de side of this house."

The next morning, Henny was looking out the window at the dreariness of the winter when he heard Ben call him, barely above a whisper.

Henny knelt by Ben's side, tearful. "I'm here, Ben. I've been here." He rubbed his hand over Ben's head and lay his on the bed and let the tears come.

When he could control his feelings, he looked at Ben and said, "I'm so happy to have you back. I was afraid I had lost you."

Ben stared blankly at him, turned his face away, and closed his eyes.

For the next few days, he seemed to sleep.

One afternoon when Letty brought over dinner he told her, "I think he's awake more than he's letting on."

"You may be right."

Gradually Ben kept his eyes open more during the day but said little. As his memory began to return, he talked about the circus, the clowns, and the elephant. Then one day he asked about Ragbone. "He's dead, ain't he?"

"Yes, Ben, he is."

When Aunt Letty brought dinner, Henny said, "There's still something not right about him."

Aunt Letty lit into him. "After what dat boy's been through, you think he's goin to just snap back to bein the Ben we know? Ben'll never be the Ben he was. Lawd knows, Henny! He's holdin in a lot of grief. You know dat." She shook her head. "Dat's gonna come out sooner or later, and I hope sooner. I know how dat be."

CHAPTER 27

As the weeks passed, Ben's strength returned, and he walked around the house and helped Henny with simple chores and sat silently by the fire. He looked out the windows often but made no attempt to go outside except to the privy.

It had been well over two months since they brought Ben home. He ate everything placed before him and walked as sturdily as ever. The vicious bruise on his face and head was slowly fading, and the gash, expertly sewn together by Aunt Letty, was healing nicely.

One sunny day, Henny asked him if he wanted to take a walk, but Ben thanked him and went to his room. Henny tried several times more to make conversation but finally gave up.

The day ended much as it started. Ben was so listless and uncommunicative it got Henny down. He went outside, wrapped his arms around himself, and walked down to the river. The moon was almost full and casting its light like a torch on the water. He looked up at the round mystical orb, not a cloud to hide its brilliance. Crying out, he said, "Old girl, I wish you could talk. I'm not one to ask for things, but I need help. It'd be mighty kind if whatever made ya so spectacular would send some answers my way."

Henny bolted up in bed. It was still dark outside, but he was certain he heard the front door close. He ran onto the front porch barefooted to see Ben, an old jacket of Pop's slung over his shoulders, heading straight to the cove. He stood shivering in the early morning chill. "Well, I guess there's no place better to get it all out than where you're going, son."

Henny went inside, made coffee, and ate two of Aunt Letty's hot cross buns, dressed warmly, and went back outside and sat on the porch steps.

Ben untied his boat from the myrtle tree and pushed it into the river. He rowed until he reached Moss Creek and followed it to the sound. There was just enough moonlight to see the patches of marsh grass. He lay the oars by his feet and waited, floating with the light wake. He felt Pop next to him, talking to him as he had one early morning long ago.

"Ya never know what's gonna be round the bend in the river, Ben. It can be good or it can break your heart. Here I was heading south with misery and blame for the loss of my family. I had thrown a line over to catch dinner and decided to join the fish instead when you come sailing up in that bowl right at my feet."

Ben's bateau bobbed and turned with the ripple from a heron diving nearby. He paddled the bataeu around to face east as the first crimson glow of morning slowly surfaced until the flames flushed the sky and the sea below.

"It's magic, Ben. The most magical and beautiful thing I know. Every morning it comes up and makes a new day, dayclean the Gullah call it. All this flaming magic burning away the past and when it's done it gives us a whole new start. That's life, son. It comes, it goes, and it comes again."

Ben felt the hurt throbbing in his bones, his chest, his head. It was rushing up like a wave in a storm. He began to shake with anger until his boat shook and swayed. He leaned over and grabbed the oars, beating them against the hull with fury as raw as the red glow on the water. He picked up an oar and slashed at the golden-brown spikes of spartina, flushing out stalking Ibis from the marsh, his boat swinging from side to side. He beat the air and bellowed at the sun, now white throwing off its majestic fiery cape. He howled with rage until someone called, "Hey, you okay?" He looked over at the fisherman, blinded with tears, and paddled home.

Henny saw him coming, running toward him, sobbing. He stood up and opened his arms, holding Ben close to him.

"It was my fault, Henny. I might as well have pulled the trigger on Ragbone and those little boys." He gulped for air between sobs.

"What are you talking bout, son? The soldiers killed em."

Ben was shaking so hard he crumpled to the ground. "No, Henny. Ragbone was in reach of me. I had time to grab him and get him away. And the little boys were standing so close I coulda held them back. I could've saved them. Henny, I was scared."

Henny held him in his arms, letting him cry out all the pent-up pain until the sobs were dried out.

"Let's go inside, son." He reached around under Ben's arm and helped him into the house. "Let's sit down here on the floor in front of the fire and let it warm us." He put his arm around Ben's shoulder. "An let all that hurt burn up with those logs. Ben, sometimes people are in the wrong place at the wrong time. An it doesn't have nothing to do with nobody else. Just bad luck. What happened was a terrible, terrible thing, but it ain't your fault Ragbone or the children died. As for being scared, don't you know there ain't nobody that is not scared when faced with danger, as you were, and no one to help? None of this is your fault." He wiped away Ben's tears with his hand.

"It keeps going round and round in my head that I coulda done something."

"Ben, that's a question everyone living asks at some time or other, and you can go in circles for the rest of your life trying to get an answer on that. I hate to say this, but if it's anyone's fault, it's Ragbone's. Good old man without an ounce of sense. He shouldn'a been there with those little boys. An their mama shoulda known better than to let them go with Ragbone."

Ben's face was swollen and red. He leaned forward toward the fire, his arms across his bent knees. He slowly shook his head. "I can't get that outta my head, Henny. There must have been some way I coulda saved them."

"I'm so sorry. I wish I could help ya with that, Ben. I'd do anything if I could. But you need to stop blaming yourself for everything that happens to other people. As far as Ragbone, it was his choice to be there, not yours. Those soldiers knew they was going to find a Gullah man there. The little white boy he sent told em, I bet you anything. Ragbone was dead the minute that boy told em there was trouble."

"Henny," he gulped back more sobs, "I loved Ragbone." The tears flowed down his already drenched face.

"I know you did, an he loved you." He walked into the kitchen and grabbed a dish cloth. "Go ahead and use this to blow your nose and dry your face."

They sat by the fire until the embers were dying. Henny shook his head as he pushed against the floor to help steady him as he stood up. "Not as spry as I was."

"I'll miss Ragbone, Henny. I'll really miss him."

"I know you will, boy." His face brightened. "I have something in the other room come to think of it that might help a little."

When he brought the harmonica to Ben, his mouth fell open and he stared at it. Finally, a small smile formed. "There's nothing I'd rather have, Henny."

CHAPTER 28

The next day as the two walked toward the market, Henny said, "Look at that sky. It's so blue I could swim in it." He swung his arms around at the fresh sunny morning air, warmer than it had been in months.

Tilly was helping Aunt Letty when she saw Ben and ran toward them, beaming.

Henny started laughing. "Well, looks like someone wants to see you."

"Hi, Tilly."

She ran straight at him, throwing her arms around his waist so tight he gasped.

"Let go some," he said, prying her arms away. "I can't breathe." He put his arm over her shoulder as they walked to Aunt Letty's booth where she waited with a huge smile spread across her warm brown skin. She wrapped her arms around him, and he melted into her softness. He leaned down and lay his head against her bosom and closed his eyes. Aunt Letty looked over at Henny and smiled and then lay her turbaned head against Ben's.

When Ben pulled away from her arms, he said, "Thank you, Aunt Letty. I know how much you did for me. I felt you there when you came. I couldn't tell you, but I felt you."

"Ben, dat makes me feel so good." She gave him another quick squeeze and reached for a hot cross bun to give him. "Welcome back!"

"How about you, Henny?"

"No thanks, Letty. I see Long Robby heading our way, and I would bet that sugar bun on his wantin to see Ben."

Long Robby, with a broad grin, walked up and put both hands on Ben's shoulders and said, "I'm mighty glad to see you lookin so good, Ben." Then he pulled him to his chest, holding him tightly. "Thank you for sending my boy home. He would of been lying on de ground like poor Ragbone and his baby granchillun."

Ben blushed as Long Robby struggled to hold back tears. "Thank you, Long Robby, but I didn't have much to do with that."

"I think you did. Rufus told me he tried to stay and help you, but you made him bring Tilly back here. You're a fine young man. Sometime soon why don't you come on down to de docks and let's have a chat?"

"I will, Long Robby. Thank you." He looked at the river, thinking how much he had missed it. "Long Robby, has there been anything going on down the river since I been gone? Henny says he's been so busy with me he don't know nothing."

"We don't go near that island, Ben. But de boats come into de sound and harbor. As long as they leave us alone, we figure dat's their bizness."

"And Junie?"

"Not a word. Which probably means he be up to somethin."

⌐)

Sitting around the dining table after dinner, Ben and Henny talked about his conversation with Long Robby.

"I think Long Robby might be thinking of adding me to his crew on one of his boats with Jimmy gone, and I just heard a couple of the others talking about going north."

"You look like you ain't so keen on that idea."

"I dunno, Henny. I ain't never worked for no one else."

Henny sat back in his chair and lit his pipe, staring at the ceiling. "Well, no doubt about it, that would be a big change for you. You wouldn't have all the spare time you got now for one thing."

"But it'd be fun to be with those guys. And I'd make more money."

Henny chuckled. "Seems to me you're doing pretty good with the oysters and other seafood. There's no reason, if you stay by yourself, you couldn't have a good business all year round."

He got up and walked onto the porch, Ben behind him. "The weather's getting warmer every day. Spring's about here, and summer's round the bend." He tapped out the ashes from his pipe against the porch rail and watched until they were dead. "Let's go play checkers."

Ben respected Henny's request to take it easy for a little while longer and spent most of his days helping him with his nets, learning the craft of roping the cotton into the circular shape for casting for shrimp. Henny was considered an artist and the best around the county. He never forgot how priviledged he was to have a craft brought over from Africa, and so special to the Gullah, given to him by his fisherman friend.

~

It was almost the end of March when Ben pushed his boat out into the river and along the creeks and estuary. When he wasn't fishing or netting shrimp or getting oysters from the thick beds, he lay back and floated through the masses of rose-colored day lilies blooming in the fields, woods, and on the banks. Migrating birds were returning from their winter away, and he was ecstatic to be alive and doing what he loved most.

Ben sold what he brought to the market, and much to his surprise and delight, he had daily orders from the cooks of town residents for fresh fish and particularly oysters. The season for them would end soon. He made a point of spending time with the fishermen at the dock and the ones working for Long Robby.

Long Robby was standing on shore waiting for him one early morning as he was coming in with a load of shrimp.

As he got closer, Long Robby yelled, "Hey, Ben, when you finish today, will you stop by the house? I wanna talk to you, an I think Sassy's got a pot of beans and rice cookin."

"I sure will, Long Robby."

Long Robby didn't waste any time coming to the point. "Ben, you been doin a good job in dat little bateau, but you're outgrowin it. I been thinkin dat you might do well with me. I've got this new smaller boat I bought from Jimmy's family, and with several of my fisherman gone now, my boys and I could use some help. What d'ya think bout dat?"

"Long Robby, I appreciate you're giving me this chance to be with you and learn what you know. I've thought a lot about it, but I just ain't ready. Not yet, anyway."

Long Robby put his big hand on Ben's shoulder. "Can't say I'm not disappointed, Ben, but I understand. When dat day comes, you got a job and be welcomed at dat." He squeezed Ben's shoulder affectionately. "You know I mean dat."

That night he told Henny, "I don't want to be a part of someone else's fishing yet. He said when I did want to join em, I had a job."

"I think you did the right thing. And you can always get another bigger boat one of these days, if you want, saving from all you make with the town folk."

Ben grinned. "Henny, my boat's almost like my best friend. Don't know how I'd feel about being on another one."

CHAPTER 29

Ben loped over to Aunt Letty's booth like a long-legged grasshopper. "What's got into you?" she asked.

"Aunt Letty, it's April, the best month of the year, and I wanna take Tilly with me on a walk and picnic."

"Just where you plan on takin dat girl?"

"To a really pretty place I know, Aunt Letty." He held out his money. "Just give me what this will pay for."

He was smiling so broadly she chuckled and started putting various food in a bag. "Well, guess I can't spoil all dat good cheer."

Ben was looking all around. "Where is she?"

"Over playing with Freezie's lil boy." She handed him the bag and watched him run toward Emmy's booth. "You be careful an I mean it," she called after him.

Tilly ran to him, grinning. He grabbed her hand and pulled her toward the thick south woods that bordered the river. "Tilly, I haven't been back to the tabby house in so long. Aunt Letty gave us food for a picnic."

As they reached the edge of the woods, Ben stopped and looked at the wet ground ahead.

"Daggone it, Tilly. It's been raining so much lately we'd sink to our knees in this mess." He looked around at the large patches of water.

"Might's well walk in the marsh. C'mon, I know where there's an old road through these woods that'll probably be dry."

He picked up two sturdy sticks and gave one to Tilly. "Here, use this to poke out in front of you. Snakes like it here." They picked their way slowly, walking through the thick palmetto and weeds before they came to the old logging road.

"Looks okay."

She wanted him to slow down. The sun had suddenly filtered through branches, and golden streaks of light danced in the clearing. It seemed so magical to her she began to swirl in and out of the light.

Ben stopped and spun around as well, caught in this sudden delightful sensation as if time stood still.

Tilly heard it first and stopped. Then Ben. The shrill scream so close and terrifying in its pitch they stood paralyzed. At the second piercing shriek, like a dying call, Tilly began running toward the cries.

"Tilly, wait," Ben called, running after her. But she didn't stop, cutting through a mass of broken branches and twigs, following the blood-curdling sounds. She stopped suddenly, Ben running to her side. They stood frozen, looking down at a boy sprawled out in an old dugout just as the largest rattler Ben had ever seen struck the boy in the leg. As the diamondback slithered away, another crawled out from the mass of brush. The threatening sound of rattles blared from the thicket.

"I gotta get him outta there, Tilly. That's a rattler den. You stay here." But Tilly jumped down into the ditch before he could stop her, reaching the boy just as the second snake rose to strike, its venomous fangs bared in its huge open mouth. Another, coming out of the dense deadwood, rose back to strike Tilly. As Ben tried to pull her out of the way, it leapt toward her just as the other snake struck out for the boy.

Among the screams, like in a dream, the snakes turned into brown sticks on the ground. Two black arms, which appeared from nowhere, reached out and lifted Tilly and the boy.

Ben scrambled out of the pit, looking grayer than a ghost's shadow, his heart pounding, and gaped at the wooden sticks.

Tilly was shaking so hard Bones smiled at her kindly and said, "It be fine now, lil Tilly. You be a brave girl."

He put her down next to Ben then wasted no time laying the stricken boy down on a bed of leaves. The boy had passed out of consciousness, more from fright than the bite. Bones tore off his knickers to where he had been bitten on his calf, revealing the vicious-looking, swollen, and blood-red-oozing bite. He knelt and placed his large bony hand within inches of the wound and with low gutteral chants began drawing the thick green poison into his palm. When there was nothing left of the venom in the boy's body, he leaned back and blew what seemed an endless stream of fiery breath into his cupped hands until there was no more smoke. He then held his scorched hands to the Sun and asked reverently, "Heal."

Ben, reeling with nausea from fright, watched as Bones' hands returned to normal, then wobbled over a few steps, leaned over, and retched until he slid to his knees. Tilly was already on all fours, green as Ben was gray, staring at the black earth in a daze.

"Ben," Bones called. "I need your help. I know you don't feel good, but I need you."

Ben, still in shock, looked up at him, speechless.

"I need you to go to Letty. It's not far on the road from here. Tell her we be comin to her house with Master Beau and he be just fine but to get some snake-bite remedy ready an some Life Everlasting. She needs to send someone to tell Orie."

Ben pulled himself up, trying to make sense of his surroundings, and started walking toward the Gullah community. Finally, getting his bearings, he began a wobbly run.

"Ben," Bones added, "no need to be tellin her nothing more than dat. No need for her to know Tilly be in dat ditch."

Bones walked back through the tumble of limbs and picked up two crutches where they had landed when Beau fell into the pit. He reached a hand over the brown sticks in the pit and said, "Be what you are."

Tilly got up and started backing away from the pit as the snakes came to life.

"Tilly, they be a part of nature and no need to fear em when they be left alone." He smiled at her as he picked up Beau and then her and walked toward Aunt Letty's house, Beau's crutches under his arm.

⌒

Aunt Letty was waiting on the porch with Ben, who had told her the gory story of Beau in the snake pit and how Bones had changed the snakes into sticks. The only detail he left out was that he and Tilly had been in the dugout with the boy. There was no question of her trust in Bones and his healing powers, but big worries were on her mind other than the snake bite. Orie!

"Dat boy ain't never been outta his house alone." She spoke to a vision she was holding of the Mortons' household more than to Ben. "What in de world got into him? What could of happened? And where was Orie?" She closed her eyes, uneasy.

"Aunt Letty, who's that boy?"

"You know bout him. He's de boy Orie takes care of at de Mortons's."

"The boy with the hurt foot?"

"Dat's de one. His name be Juan Beauregard Morton, but they call him Beau."

Ben scratched his head and screwed up his face. "I never heard of anyone with that kind of name."

"Orie tole me that Juan is for some famous friend of his father's that lives across the water, and Beauregard is from some general in de family."

"How old is he?"

"About your age, maybe a year older." She squinted at him. "How old are you?"

"Fourteen."

"Well, maybe Beau's a little older. Maybe a year." She pressed her lips together. "Dat be a sad boy, Ben."

Ben raised his eyebrows. "Cause of his foot?"

"Reckon so."

"How'd he get it?"

"Born with it." She winced and felt the old familiar pain when there was talk of Beau's wronged foot. "He can't walk without someone to help him. Just cries and stays in his room." She sat on the steps and sighed. "I just don't know how he got away from Orie."

Ben's eyes had widened into circles. "If he had a twisted foot, how did he get out in those woods?"

Aunt Letty turned to him, exasperated. "You askin me dat?"

"Well, here they come."

Tilly wiggled out of Bones' arms and ran to Aunt Letty as soon as she saw her.

"Oh, baby." Aunt Letty held her close, laying her head on Tilly's.

"Bones." She gave him a smile of gratitude and said, "Put him on my bed."

Beau had awakened and was crying softly.

"Master Beau," Bones said, "you be just fine now. Your mama'll be heah soon, and Letty's gonna make you feel a whole lot better."

He smiled at the boy and turned to Aunt Letty. "I'm goin. He be fine with you. All de poison be gone, Letty."

Aunt Letty held his hands close to her heart. "I'm mighty thankful, Bones."

"I always be close, Letty." He looked at her with an expression of love and left.

Her eyes followed him until he was out of sight. "You're always close to me except when it suits you," she said. Then felt ashamed of herself.

⌒

The 1914 Rolls Royce Silver Ghost bumped down the road minutes after Bones' departure. Aunt Letty already had a poultice of aloe, Angelica bark, and some swamp grass on Beau's snake wound. The swelling and discoloring around the bite was so gruesome she feared Miss Rebecca would get the vapors if it was not covered. Hopefully the remedies would bring the swelling down quickly enough to settle everyone's digestion.

Miss Rebecca didn't wait for Brian, her chauffeur, to open the door before jumping out before the large, sleek car had stopped. She ran into Aunt Letty's bedroom and threw herself on top of Beau. She was too scared to sob, sucking in her breath with short gasps.

"What happened to you?" When he turned his head away and didn't answer, she looked at Letty frantically.

Aunt Letty, looking more and more uncomfortable, not sure who Miss Rebecca was going to blame, said, "From what I understand, he was in de woods off dat old road dat runs from town."

"And?"

"I reckon he got bit by a snake."

To her credit, Miss Rebecca didn't scream right away but just stared open mouthed at Aunt Letty before yelling, "What kind of a snake?"

Letty glanced at Orie, who had tears running down her face, and mumbled to herself, *Oh Lordy.* "A rattler, Miss Becky, but Beau be just fine."

"A rattlesnake?" she shrieked. "And he is lying here on your bed like he is taking a nap?" She looked around the house and yelled, "Brian! Brian!"

She glared at Orie. "This is all your fault."

"I know it don't look like it, Miss Rebecca, but Master Beau is fine. All de poison is gone." Aunt Letty nodded emphatically.

When Brian rushed into the room, she told him to take Beau to the car, that they were going straight to the hospital. She looked menacingly at Orie again and said, "If I ever want to see your face again, I'll let you know."

Orie was crying so hard she slumped on the floor.

"It's not her fault, Mama," Beau cried out. "I told her I was going to take a nap. It's not her fault." He started crying and reaching for Orie from Brian's arms. "Orie."

"He's fine, Miss Rebecca." Aunt Letty crossed her heart. "Bones be there and got de poison out right away."

Ben and Tilly watched them leave and thought they saw Beau

looking out of the back window through the dust that was kicked up from the elegant automobile as it bumped down the road.

"Do you think we'll ever see him again?" Ben asked Tilly.

She just stood looking at the dust trail.

They heard several days later from Orie, who was back in Miss Rebecca's good graces, that the doctor at the hospital said there must have been a mistake in communication between the Gullah woman and Mrs. Morton. Beau showed only a scratch and bruise, which he treated and sent them home.

If Beau talked to his mother and father about why he left home, Orie didn't know what he said to them. However, he told her he wanted to die but changed his mind after he jumped into the pit.

CHAPTER 30

The cool breezes and sweet blooms and scents of spring melted into the fiery grasp of summer. The community had experienced this sweltering heat before many times and groaned when the mosquitoes, larger than shrimp, relished their skin. Even the sweat pouring off their bodies didn't wash the insects away.

The Gullah women carried large fans made of palmetto fronds and swatted as they fanned. All the vendors closed the market early. Most of the Town, at least the wealthier customers who sent their cooks to shop at the stalls, had gone to their summer houses.

Long Robby went into town and got rolls of extra-fine netting, which everyone in the commune stretched over their doors and windows, but even so, sandflies managed to get through the meshing, making nights a torment. Women made net hoods for themselves and children, knowing well the dangers of malaria, which had killed so many of the slaves who worked the rice fields.

Henny rigged a fan out of sawed-off paddles, an empty string spool, and rope to pull the makeshift gadget. It brought more laughs than breeze.

Ben decided it would be worth getting his head lopped off just for a swim in Goose Neck Pond. Without telling anyone, he paddled down the river to the forbidden stream where the rum runners had threatened him and killed Jimmy. As he suspected, no one nor anything unordinary was there. *What fool would be here now?* he thought.

He and Tilly spent every minute they could in the deep black water. They tied a rope Henny gave them to an overhanging limb and swung out over the pond to see how high they could go before splashing into the cool water. And, late in the day before reluctantly leaving, they floated on their backs, blissfully innocent to anything but the quiet world of nature surrounding them.

In late August, Long Robby and Sassy held a fish fry for the entire Gullah community in honor of Rufus, who was leaving for the north. He and four of his friends from the Island school had been accepted to the respected Howard University in Washington, DC. It was a bittersweet affair with feelings all around of pride and sadness. Rufus said he was not coming back except to visit. Many of the boys as well as their elders in neighboring counties had already gone north. But Rufus was the first to leave this home community where he had grown up, and there were many wet eyes. When Ben asked him why he was not coming back after college, he said, "And do what, Ben? Be a butler for one of de town residents?"

The party was fun and the fish fry sensational. Jackroo and Matt, despite the loss of Ragbone, played their banjo and drums well into the night for dancing and singing.

The next morning, all the partygoers wearily followed Rufus and his family down the road to town and watched Long Robby and Rufus, suitcase in hand, walk toward the bus stop until they were out of sight.

In late September, the strong winds from a hurricane heading out into the Atlantic from further South brought relief, and the vendors began spending more time at the market. Aunt Letty, sitting on a chair in her booth, said, "Don't know what I be doing here. Most of my customers are up in some mountains watching trees. Willie Mae said Miss Becky sent word to Mr. Morton not to expect her home until after the last of the red, gold, and yellow leaves were on the ground."

The Gullah community didn't hear the luxury touring cars returning to Belleview, but it didn't take long for them to know the town residents had returned home. Tilly was the first to see Orie running down the road waving her arms at everyone in sight. She fell into Aunt Letty's arms, laughing and yelling out how glad she was to be home.

That night, sitting at a park table, Orie told Letty and Tilly all about the summer away, not rubbing in the perfect weather in the high mountains. "I guess I got good news and not good for me news. Beau decided to let some doctor in New York operate on his foot."

"Oh, Orie, that is such good news," Aunt Letty remarked. "Dat be de best news I ever heard."

"The bad news is they want me to go with Miss Becky. Dat means all winter being there."

"Oh no, Orie. Can't they find one closer?"

"There was one from Charleston a longtime ago. He say he couldn't fix Beau's foot. There be some problem with his leg, too, where it joins his foot. He said there's a doctor somewhere else dat knows how, but he would have to cut de back of his foot and Beau would have to wear some kind of metal thing all de way up to his knee and he might not ever walk right. And Beau would have to be older anyway."

Aunt Letty looked at her accusingly.

"Don't look at me dat way, Letty. I didn't know about all dat until now. But Miss Becky told me last week dat they're goin to New York City where there's a doctor doin somethin new an they're going to fix dat boy's foot. Sometimes I look in dat boy's eyes and he be lookin off somewhere like I ain't there. Spendin too much time in his own head."

"Oh, Orie, what am I gonna do without you? When are you goin?" Aunt Letty asked, distressed.

"In November." She dropped her shoulders and shook her head woefully. "Oh, I forgot, Letty. Miss Becky wants to see you."

"Why she want to see me?"

"I ain't too sure."

On the appointed day, Letty was led to the breakfast room, a cheerful, lovely room with flowered curtains on each side of large windows that faced the garden where she had sat once before with Miss Becky. When Rebecca Morton joined Aunt Letty, Orie set down a pitcher of sweet tea and glasses and walked back to the kitchen where she could hear every word.

"I've invited you here, Letty, because I felt sending a message by Orie would not express the gratitude we feel toward Tilly and Ben except in an impersonal way. I hope you don't mind coming here?"

"No, mam."

"We want to do something for each of the young people. Orie told us of the difficulty of giving Tilly and Ben a proper education where you live. Beau will be in the north all of the winter and probably into spring. His tutor, Tim, a student at the Citadel, will be available during that time. If you are interested in his coaching them, it would make us very happy to offer it. We could work out an arrangement when Beau returns. What do you think?"

Letty was certain Rebecca Morton had no idea of how surprised she was. And under that surprise was a cauldron of mixed feelings. She knew Miss Becky meant this kindly, but it was not something she had ever experienced—this kind of paying back. She stared at the table for some time then answered, "I really don't know, Miss Becky. Ben can read and write, an I ain't sure bout him, but I'll ask. As for Tilly, she been readin books for some time. She be a smart girl." She studied the table. "You may know dat some of the kids goin to the island school are leavin here and going up north. I don't think Ben or Tilly will be leavin."

"I understand that, Letty, but an education is still valuable and enjoyable. You let me know. They are fine young people, Letty. I'm quite impressed with their bravery." She looked at a shelf in the next room. "Letty, we have books I will send over by Brian that Tilly might like." She studied Letty. "I think this doctor we are taking Beau to will be able to answer the question you have been waiting for all these years, Letty. I hope that will settle your fears once and for all."

"Orie says there's another doctor who saw Master Beau, Miss Becky."

"That was a long time ago. We asked him how to fix Beau's foot, Letty, not what caused it."

"Yes'm."

"It's good to see you, Letty."

She stopped and looked back. "I forgot. Beau would like to see Ben and Tilly before he goes. If they would like to come here some afternoon fairly soon, please let Orie know."

"I'd be happy to do that."

When Mrs. Morton's news was told to the pair that night, there was nothing but silence until Ben, frowning, said, "Aw, I dunno."

He looked up at Henny with a pathetic expression. "I know schooling is good, Henny, but I just don't see it for me. Not that kind of schoolin."

"For land's sake, boy." Shocked, Henny said, "Why in the dickens did you say something foolish like that?" He shook his head, frowning. "You've got a good brain on you."

Ben looked him in the eye. "If I want to know something, I'll ask." He looked uneasy. "Ah, Henny. I can't see me reading about things that don't mean nothing to me. It's what's around here that matters to me. I just want to learn more about all of it. How to keep it like it is. When I go over to the island with Tilly, I talk to Mr. Smalls when I can. He knows more about this place than anyone. He says this is a fragile eco-system and is very special and that it's important to take care of it. That's what I want to learn to do. We've got all this beautiful water, the salt marsh, all this wildlife and fish we gotta take care of." He made a face and looked away. "Not sit in some room learning something I don't care about."

Henny smiled. "Well, there's certainly nothing wrong with that plan, Ben."

Aunt Letty, who had been listening, turned to Tilly. "What about you, Tilly?"

She shook her head from side to side, holding up a copy of Dickens that Sassy had arranged for her to borrow from the island school, and pointed to Aunt Letty's house where a pile of books had been delivered.

That night in bed, Ben thought about Rufus and his school friends. That was different. He never saw those boys now. A lump settled in his throat. *I miss Rufus*, he thought.

CHAPTER 31

It was a glorious day with blue skies and cool weather. The sun felt like rose petals on the skin. The hardwoods were rich in color now. The color lasted longer here than further north, but not much longer.

Ben ran to Aunt Letty's booth, looking happier than a pelican with a beak full of fish, and said, "C'mon, Tilly. Aunt Letty, we're going down the marsh and won't be back until late afternoon."

She watched them leave, hand in hand, as they turned away from the market. "He don't even ask anymore. When did they grow so big they don't even ask if they can do something?" she muttered to herself.

"Tilly, we can have a picnic at the tabby house. Henny gave me some fried chicken, and Aunt Letty biscuits. The last time I was there last summer, the mosquitoes and pests kept after me until I had to leave. But it's cooler now."

Tilly reached for his hand and gave it a squeeze, smiling at him.

Ben smiled back and squeezed her hand. "I'm glad you are with me, Tilly. I sure am glad Aunt Letty gave us this bag of food, too. I'm hungry."

After they had walked a good distance through the woods, they came to the stream flowing over scattered, moss-covered rocks. "I don't know the name of these wispy kinda blue-ish purple plants that come in the fall, but I'm learning a lot from Mr. Moody about all the wildflowers. I look at his seed books whenever I can after my work is done." They stepped over to the other side and ran through the wild azaleas and redbud on to the drive and walked to the garden.

"Mr. Moody is going to show me how to cut them back. They look bad, but maybe in a year they will come back and look just like they used to. He is helping me with plants and flowers that like it here and that bees and butterflies and birds come to."

He walked over to the pond and leaned his hand into the cool water. "This is a spring pond. I expect they built the garden round it." They sat on a broken tabby bench.

"It's too cold to swim today, but it sure is nice in the summer. Except for the mosquitoes." He grimaced at the thought.

Tilly smiled. *It's our place.*

"Do you want to eat down by the marsh? It's pretty there."

She nodded.

They walked down the lawn and lay on the ground above the water. It was warm in the bright sun, which was sending out flickers of light over the landscape.

After eating the picnic of sausage biscuits, fried chicken legs, and fruit, they lay back and looked for animal shapes in the few clouds moving through the sky. Ben played his harmonica and sang some of the old songs he'd learned from Ben Clary and Ragbone until, drowsy from the food and sun, both fell asleep.

Ben brushed away something that was shaking him until Tilly grabbed him with both hands and jarred him awake. Startled, Ben bolted up and saw Tilly frantically pointing to a skiff motoring along the edge of the marsh. It wasn't close enough to see who was in it. "Probably some fisherman, Tilly."

He watched as the boat got closer, then cried frantically to her, "Tilly! That's Junie, and he's got two dogs in that boat with him. An there's another man with him. We gotta get outta here." He grabbed her hand and pulled her up with him. "Run fast as you can." He looked at her terrified face. "Keep running with me. They're further away from us than we are to those woods across from the house. Stay close to the edge of the trees here," he gasped between breaths. "I don't think he can see us yet."

They heard the boat motor stop, and Ben said, already panting, "Okay, Tilly, run straight across to the back of the house. They can't see us there. Then run as fast as you can and plow into the woods. If they see us, they can't catch us, but those dogs can."

They had hardly gone any distance when they heard the dogs howling.

"It's okay, Tilly. They can't catch up with us now," he lied. "But we gotta run fast." He pushed back a large limb for her and winced at the look on her face. "That stream is pretty close. Those dogs can't get our scent there."

He didn't want to tell her that the dogs would find them. He knew they would. He had seen dogs running after game. And Long Robby told him no slave got away if the dogs were on their scent. He couldn't think about that now. "We gotta run faster, Tilly."

She was breathing so hard he could hear her above his own hard breath. He reached over to take her arm and help her, but he tripped on a loose branch and fell. He felt their feet thundering on the ground. And the deep baying of the large dogs was getting so close.

Jumping up as fast as he ever had in his life, Ben began to run, half carrying Tilly with him. "The stream," he whispered. "Over there."

They ran into the shallow water, the rocks slowing them down. Those dogs were trained to kill; he knew that. And he wasn't sure if running in water would keep the dogs from smelling them as he had heard, but it was their only chance. "Keep on going, Tilly," he panted. "We don't have far to go."

Tilly was struggling to keep up, even with Ben's slowed pace. She tried to jump over a larger rock and fell hard against the sharp edge.

Ben heard the splash and turned to see her open mouth silent scream. "Oh Lordy, Tilly," he grimaced, "that gash looks bad." He swooped her up and jumped out of the water. "We gotta get out of here quick or there'll be blood in the water and everywhere else. No hiding for us then." He pulled off his shirt and wrapped up her leg. She was grimacing with pain, and he said, panting for air, "I know that hurts awful, Tilly, but we can't stop. I'll carry you as long as I can."

She bore her face in his shoulder as the tears ran down her face. "We aren't far now, Tilly. Try to keep my shirt around your leg so it don't bleed on the ground."

He heard voices, but they didn't sound close. However, the dogs' barking was so loud his heart pounded. "Tilly, I gotta slow down." He wasn't sure how long he could hold Tilly. He was a strong boy used to running but not this fast for so long carrying somebody else.

Tilly was hanging onto his neck with one hand and holding the shirt around her bleeding leg with the other. His shirt was soaking with blood and had been dripping on the leaves almost since he wrapped it around her leg. *Those dogs'll be all over that blood. We ain't got a chance.*

As quick as he had that thought, a wolf howl sounded through the forest like an omen. Just as suddenly, there was a shrill whistle, and the deadly howling of the dogs stopped. Ben slowed down, not believing his ears. Tilly leaned back to look at him.

"I don't know, Tilly." When the silence remained, Ben caught his breath, too drained mentally and physically to think and leaned against a tree with Tilly in his arms.

"I'm taking you to Aunt Letty. I don't care if she does kill me."

Aunt Letty was packing up for the day when she saw Ben carrying Tilly, the blood-soaked shirt hanging down from her leg. She took a shaky breath, put her hand on her heart, and leaned against the table for support. But she didn't panic as Ben had feared.

In a steady voice after looking into Ben's face and seeing how near collapsing he was, she said, "Put her down here on de table and you sit down."

She leaned down and brushed Tilly's hair away from her tear-streaked face. "Oh, honey, I know how dat must hurt you." She reached for a clean cotton rag from a basket, wound it around the gash, and felt up and down Tilly's leg. "How did this happen, Ben?"

"She fell running in the creek, Aunt Letty."

"We can talk bout dat later. I need to get her home. Dat's a deep cut, but she didn't break any bones. Go get Long Robby. I need him. I saw him down at de docks, but get anyone there."

Ben got up slowly and ran as fast as his aching body would allow.

"You're gonna be fine, honey." She reached for another cloth and gently wiped away the tears. "I can't bear to see you hurtin so bad, Tilly."

Long Robby, with Ben following at some distance, loped more than ran to Aunt Letty. When he saw Tilly on the table, he frowned. "What happened, Letty?"

"Don't know yet, but she has a bad cut, and I need you to take her to our house." She turned to Ben. "You better come, too, Ben. She can't tell us nothin."

⁎

After Tilly's wound was covered in cobwebs to stop the bleeding, Aunt Letty put a small amount of nightshade in a glass of everlasting tea to sedate her. When the bleeding had stopped, she cleaned it in turpentine and made a poultice of sassafras to clean the blood and inflammation.

"She be goin to sleep now for awhile."

"She goin to have pain, Letty. You got comfrey and poke root?"

She gave him a disgusted look. "You ask me dat?"

"Wasn't thinkin, Letty."

Ben was leaning back against some pillows propped on the wall.

Aunt Letty looked at him without expression. "I have a strong feelin there's more to this than Tilly fallin in de creek, Ben."

He looked her straight in the eye. "Yes, mam, there was. I'd never of taken Tilly back to the tabby house if I'd thought Junie was gonna show up. Everybody kept saying he didn't have no use for that place."

"What?" Both Aunt Letty and Long Robby said in unison.

Aunt Letty slumped over, her head in her hands.

Ben sank back down against the wall.

"What happened, son?" Long Robby asked. "Take your time."

Ben told them every detail from first seeing the boat to getting Tilly to Aunt Letty.

Aunt Letty put her head in her hands. "Oh, Long Robby, he said he was going to get Tilly."

"Don't sound to me, Letty, like he was huntin Ben and Tilly down."

"No, Long Robby. I know he didn't even see us for a while. At least I don't see how they could. They was just trollin along the marsh like they was looking for something in the woods. Long Robby, if ya'll don't think he has a reason for going there, then why does he keep going there?"

"I don't know, Ben." He put his long, strong arm around Ben's shoulders and looked at him soberly. "Don't go back there until we know more. Junie is a bad sort, and ya never know what he's up to. I don't think he has anythin to do with it, but I just heard that a Gullah family in Charleston dat's been livin and farmin on land they bought after de war was evicted by law. The old man refused to leave his house, and they put him in jail." He shook his head sadly.

Aunt Letty's jaw dropped. "How can they do dat to someone who owns their land?"

"Looks like de law or any white man who wants property dat belongs to a Gullah family can make a lyin claim against him. Dat poor old man's son didn't do nothin to dat white woman like they say. They just want his land. I hear dat's how they get land now. Good waterfront land. They don't think it should belong to us. Dat's what's happenin, Letty. All over."

CHAPTER 32

T he following week, Letty arrived at the Mortons' back door with Tilly and Ben, Tilly with a blue bandage wrapped around her leg and covered by her dress, much to her gratification.

They followed Orie and Letty to the Mortons' living room but stopped at the door, gaping at the opulence of the home.

Letty knew the downstairs of the house from many years of helping Orie with parties, but it never failed to take her breath away at how fine it was: the velvet and silk material, fine furniture, crystal chandeliers, and large portraits of stern-faced whiskered men and prissy women. She particularly liked the beautiful carved wood on the tall ceilings. *Dat musta taken some doin,* she thought. *Done by our enslaved people, no doubt.*

"I be waitin for you down in de kitchen." She looked at them sternly. "Don't ya'll be lookin at dat boy's foot!" With that, she nudged them both toward Orie to walk up the carved winding staircase.

When they reached the bedroom door, she smiled at the two who had been silent since entering the house. "You'll be just fine," she said and opened the door.

"Beau, here be your guests."

Tilly and Ben stood spellbound by the extraordinary room before them. Each *objet d'art* in this eccentric menagerie was as carefully arranged as were the colors in the Matisse on the wall.

Beau sat in a narrow velvet-covered armchair, a woven shawl covering his lap and legs. Behind him was a long library table with burn marks as if it had been scorched in a fire, made less noticeable by careful sanding and waxing. It was cluttered with papers, books, and framed photos of family and a chess set where he had been playing when they entered.

Quite composed, Beau smiled. "Thank you for coming."

Tilly smiled back but stayed by Orie's side.

Ben, who never felt more ill at ease, cleared his throat. "How're you feeling?"

"I never felt too bad. Mostly, it was getting over being so frightened." Beau smiled. "I wanted to thank you. If you hadn't found me, well . . . I would be dead. You were very brave." He looked at Tilly and smiled.

"It was lucky we were there."

"Please, come sit down."

There were two antique wood chairs covered in a patterned silk on either side of a round mahogany table with silver trays of cakes and cookies and a large pitcher of lemonade in front of two panel windows looking over a garden. When they were seated, Orie poured the lemonade and said, "I be leavin you now, Beau. Pull de bell cord if you need me."

She put her hand on Ben's shoulders. "I'll be back in an hour."

Beau watched as Ben and Tilly took in every detail of his large sitting room.

"I ain't never seen anything like this," Ben said, bewildered by all around him.

"It took a while to get it like this."

The walls, with the exception of one, were a rich deep green covered with interesting art and drawings; a hand-crafted brass and steel Civil War sword hung next to an odd-shaped one

"That is a Samurai sword," Beau said, noticing Ben staring at it. "The Samurai were the early military nobility in Japan."

Photographs, Native American artifacts, and Aboriginal, African, and other tribal masks hung on the walls. Leather books from floor to ceiling were on one side of the room. On another was a magnificent mural, painted in such detail it seemed a small elephant was walking out of the wall. Ben flinched and involuntarily backed up a bit, which made Beau laugh.

"Looks real, doesn't it? I went with my dad on a safari to Africa a couple of years ago. I was carried by two natives on a bamboo chair through the plains. It was great fun. Dad and his friends were fortunate to hire the big game hunter, Frederick Selous, to take us. My father had the mural painted for me from sketches done by an artist hired by the group to travel with them."

In a round, ornate brass cage reaching to the ceiling was a tiny monkey high up in a small tree staring at them as if warning them not to come near.

"Chi Chi was a present from the Governor of Brazil after we visited the rainforest. Actually, we just went down the Amazon River in a boat. He is called a finger monkey and is the smallest monkey in the world. Unfortunately, they don't live long. He came to us last year and will live about nine or ten more years maybe. I would let him out, but he likes to bite. He is called finger monkey because he clings to fingers and isn't much larger."

There was a model of the first horse-drawn carriage and later models to the present-day Model T Ford sitting on small wall shelves.

There was so much to see Ben almost missed the car sitting in one corner of the room. He gasped! It was sleek, long, and black and was large enough to sit in.

"That is an exact model of Dad's new car. It is a Lozier touring car. Dad was a friend of Mr. Lozier, who died last year, but his son had this model brought to us as soon as Dad's Lozier was ready for delivery. He made this car for me. The Lozier is the best car made in this country and the most expensive. It was a gift but would have cost Dad $7,500 if not." He quickly lowered his head, embarrassed. "That was crass of me to mention the price. I'm sorry. I could drive it on the road if I wanted to."

He pointed to a gilded cage with a small parrot. "Pedro won't talk now. He's shy around new people." He said in a smaller voice, "Actually, you are the only friends who have been in here. If I may call you friends."

Ben was so mesmerized he didn't answer immediately.

Beau laughed. "I hope we will be friends."

"Oh, uh, yeah," Ben stuttered. "Sure," he said, feeling more awkward by the moment.

Tilly, who had been sitting in the chair eating a cookie, got up and walked over to Beau and took both of his hands in hers and smiled.

Beau, obviously pleased, smiled back and said, "Thank you, Tilly."

Ben turned away, annoyed. He glared at the painted plains of the Serengeti: a cheetah chasing gazelles; lions devouring a kill, buzzards circling above; tigers playing with their young. A lazy leopard rested on a large limb, and monkeys and zebras, birds—all a mystery to him.

Rankled, he blurted out, "There was an elephant at the circus, and our woods are full of wild animals."

"You are fortunate, Ben. You have so much more to see and do than I, living where you are. However, I am not sure I want to go into any woods again any time soon." He laughed.

Ben squeezed his eyes shut, humiliated. "Oh," he said in a strained voice, not looking back at Beau. "The woods are full of sticks and stones. I can't imagine what it would be like to see all you've seen."

Suddenly an odd voice resounded in the room. *"Give Pedro a cookie. Give Pedro a cookie. Give Pedro a cookie."*

⁓

"He's really nice, Henny," Ben said, after relating the events of the afternoon. "It would've been a lot better if Tilly wasn't there."

"Tilly? Why're you being hard on Tilly? She's your best friend."

"I just don't think I wanna be around her for a while. She's just a child."

Henny studied him, put his feet up on the porch rail, and lit his pipe. "Well, reckon you don't have to, do you? Maybe you and Beau can be friends now."

"Ahh, he ain't like Rufus, Henny. I think he's a nice, but he lives in that big house with stuff I've never seen before and does things that

I never heard of before. I dunno. And anyway, he's got that hurt foot."

Henny saw the emotions running through Ben's mind and wished he could say something to make him feel better, but this was an experience he would have to come to grips with himself. He'd run into someone he had no way of understanding. And he suspected that while Tilly may have found Beau and his surroundings different, she didn't care. He puffed on his pipe and looked out over the river. His boy's feelings were hurt by something, and he was pretty sure it had to do with Tilly.

CHAPTER 33

Ben found Henny out cutting wood. "I told ya I'd do that, Henny."

"I know you did, but sometimes it just feels good to swing an ax."

"Henny, I'm goin back to the tabby house. I gotta go back. It's all I can think about. I gotta see if anything is going on there."

Henny stopped swinging the ax and looked at him, shaking his head, bothered. "We talked bout this, Ben. You said you was going to stay away from that place."

"Henny, it's been a month now since Tilly and me was there. If Junie's doing something around there, I wanna see what."

"I can't stop you." Henny swung the ax through a log. "Just be careful, Ben."

Frustrated, Ben walked back to the house and made a pork sandwich. He walked back outside and asked, "I gotta satisfy myself."

⁓

Ben pushed through wild azaleas and trees past the house where he could see the entire property down to the marsh. *There ain't nobody here.* Cautiously, he ran across the road to the house and smiled. *It don't look like no one's even been here.* He ran to the enwalled garden and spun around, arms wide, and said to the entangled grey twigs and weeds. *You're going to be so beautiful, just like I think ya used to be.* Excited, he started pulling up the dead roots and tall weeds. *I need tools,* he realized. *I'll come back here tomorrow with everything I need.*

He jauntily sauntered back across the wild grass lawn, whistling "Noah and the Whale." The air was crisp, the sun smiled down, and Ben smiled back. *What a great day,* he thought just before he heard the unmistakable sound of horse hooves pounding on the road toward him. Startled, he thought, *Oh Lordy. I'm hexed. I gotta be.*

He was too far from the garden or the house to take shelter there. He quickly looked around, saw the nearest large oak, ran to it, and jumped onto the low limb, climbing as far as he could get before eight to ten men reined in right beneath him. He only recognized three of them, Junie and the two with him who chased him and Tilly on Halloween last year. He'd had a lifetime of scampering up trees and wasn't afraid of falling, but if one of them looked up, he was a goner. He leaned back against the huge trunk of the old tree and planted his feet firmly on the limb.

"This is a pretty place, Junie. Never knew it was here."

"Yeah, it's hidden away. That's what made me think of it."

"Who owns it? Looks like they abandoned it," another voice pitched in.

"Don't know about that. I've asked a few people, and no one seems to know anything, but I remember Daddy telling me his granddaddy thought he saw the man who built this place."

"What d'ya say? Think it will work for us? We need some place to meet and make our plans. And it would be a good place to store the rum barrels if there was trouble over on the river."

"Now that's got to be the most asinine thing I ever heard, Junie. How do you think we would get all that hooch here?"

"The water, dumbass. This marsh opens up to the water."

"Nah, too far."

"I don't like it, Junie. I agree with Sim. We need a place closer to where the boat comes in, for one thing."

"I've been looking around and haven't seen anything better that would fit all our needs." He looked back at the house. "Well, maybe you're right. There've been kids here the last couple of times I was here."

Dave laughed. "Yeah, I heard about that from Sim. You sicked the dogs on em and then called them off. Something scare you, Junie? Something like a wolf's cry?"

The men roared with laughter.

Junie glared at them. "I didn't want to hurt my boys in all that scrub."

"Yeah! Like the woods would hurt those pampered killers."

Junie ignored them, angry. "Okay, we can decide on some place better later on."

They turned their horses to canter off when one of the men said, "What's that over there?" and trotted over to the sandwich Ben hadn't eaten and dropped when he climbed the tree. "Looks like someone's been here."

The men reined the horses around, looking.

"Let's go home. It probably belongs to some darky passing through looking for work. Y'all go on. I want to talk to Sim."

Sim slipped off his horse and tethered him to a limb.

Junie swung his leg over the saddle and jumped to the ground and threw the reins over his horse's neck for him to nibble on the grass.

"What you got on your mind, Junie? This place spooks me."

"You're a weirdo! Let's sit on this big limb." He looked around. "One of the things I like about this place is all the big trees." He looked up to where Ben was hiding behind the trunk. "I wonder how old they are?"

Ben shifted his footing and slid further around the trunk and was barely out of sight when a piece of bark fell on Sim's shoulder. Sim looked up. "A scampering squirrel. What do you want to talk about, Junie?"

"Sim, I want this place. I met some northerners when I was up there who have the money to buy this property for a game lodge. That's the talk up there now. They see the birds flyin south, and they wanna follow. This is perfect. It has everything, wildlife, the marsh leading to open water, coves. All this land around that wasn't cleared for crops. I've been here several times and beyond the birds and fish you saw the other day when we were coasting offshore all the possibility of there being a plenty of wildlife. Some of the deer almost came out to say hello. All I need is to find some way of getting it. That idiot lawyer in town threatened me, but his threats don't stand up, and he knows it."

"I don't know why you want to get into business with the Yankees, anyway. We got our hands full with the Klan and getting the rum business goin. Forget it." He shivered. "I don't like it here. That property where the Gullah live is a hundred times better than this. At least it's there for the taking, not like the trouble of getting this one."

Junie's jaw stuck out like a bulldog. "You can bet your new boots I'm going to get that land. They stole it from me. But getting it will take some time. I like the idea of doing business with those men up north. I'd like their respect."

"Well, what do you want me to do about it? I ain't got no magic wand."

"Help me find out who owns this place, if anyone does. You know more people in this county than I do. Anyway, they don't seem to cotton up to me."

Sim laughed. "You're something else, Junie Savage. Why would you expect them to like you, the way you've always treated folks around here? Forget those high-faluttin people you want to impress. We got all we can handle here."

⌒

Ben stayed where he was until the men were out of sight. For the second time in two months, he ran back home without stopping. His heart was racing, and he dropped down beside Henny on the porch, panting.

"What got you running back here out of breath?"

"Junie, Henny. Junie and his friends. They nearly got me."

When he got his breath, he told Henny all of what he'd heard.

Henny chewed on his pipe stem, shook his head, and sighed. "Forget the lodge. That ain't gonna happen, and Junie knows that. It's the other reasons they looked at the house that bother me." He shook his greying brown head, frowning. "Junie and his kind are gonna stir up the devils in hell to do their business until they're in their graves." He looked over to Ben and smiled. "Don't let this get to you, boy. Tomorrow we'll let Long Robby in on what you heard. I don't see how Junie can get the Gullah property, but if there is a way, he darn sure will try."

CHAPTER 34

Ben and Henny cut a small spruce for Christmas and put it in a far corner away from the fireplace. The four had decided against presents this year but just the gift of warm friendships and love.

Henny, however, put a box under the tree on Christmas morning.

Ben looked up, surprised. "I thought there wasn't gonna be presents, Henny."

"Just open that box."

Ben stared down at the contents of the brown paper package. "Oh, Henny."

"You've never had new clothes, boy. You been wearing someone else's for too long."

"Henny, this is really nice of you," he said, his voice cracking. He looked down at the brown pants and brown checked coat. "Henny, these are the first new clothes I've ever had."

"It's about time, son." Henny patted him on the back. "It musta crossed your mind that Pop's clothes don't fit you no more." He spread his arms out. "Just look at you. Those pants are above the ankle an inch, and you're squeezin outta that shirt." He looked over at Ben's feet. "We'll get new boots when we go to town. Looks like your toes are pushing through those old ones of Pop's. Like I said, boy, you're growin up. It's time you dressed like other boys your age."

"Ah, Henny, I do thank you."

"You're sure welcome, son. Thought you might like this, too." He handed him a large brown paper bag with a red ribbon on it that Mr. Moody had given him. Henny smiled when he saw the expression of pure delight on Ben's face when Ben tore off the paper.

"Thought so," he said softly, noticing Ben's obvious delight.

Ben, speechless, stared at the cast net, just the right size for his bateau.

"Guess ya don't like it, huh?"

"Henny," Ben finally managed to say, "I never thought I'd have a net. Specially one of yours. Ah, Henny. Aw, Henny, thank you."

"Well, I'm pleased you like it. I thought you could use a net instead of that old pot. I was thinking about getting you a gun. Pop gave me a .22 when I was your age, taught me how to use it safely. What to shoot and what not to. But I thought this wasn't the right time for a gun."

Ben was shaking his head, his eyes widening with alarm. "No, Henny, I don't never want a gun. I don't never want to kill nothing. Not anyone or no living thing."

"I understand, boy." He smiled at him. "Come on, let's go get doozied up for Letty and Tilly."

Ben blushed at the admiring looks from Aunt Letty and Tilly.

"Those new clothes sure look good on you, Ben," Aunt Letty said with Tilly grinning at him.

It was a wonderful day of talking about good old times, singing songs that they all knew, sitting around the kitchen table until all the quail, corn pudding, and other scrumptious fixings Aunt Letty and Henny prepared were gone. At the end of the day, Henny poured a drop of peach brandy in two glasses, filled them with water, and gave them to Tilly and Ben. He then poured a glass for himself and Aunt Letty and toasted to warm friendships.

"It'll soon be another year, Letty. We've had our bad times but some mighty good ones, too."

"We sure have, Henny." She started to say, "An no sign of Junie," but the words froze on her lips. As hard as she tried to push such feelings away, the more they reeled inside her head. Junie was always on the edge of her mind. Most of the time a far edge, but she knew, deep in her bones, they would not be free of Junie this coming year.

CHAPTER 35

Early one morning in late February, Henny was sitting on his front porch steps watching Aunt Letty huffing and puffing as she walked toward him.

"You okay, Letty?"

"Yeah, I'm okay. Just too fat."

"You're not fat, Letty. Well, mebbe just enough to round you out here and there."

"Don't go gettin sassy with me. I ain't in the mood for it." She looked around. "Where's Tilly?"

"Gone fishing with Ben. C'mon and sit up here. I heard you were after a hag."

She bunched out her lips and glared at him. "No sense in pretendin you care about hags, Henny. I know you don't believe in em."

Henny never could come to totally believing in hags. Or haints or boodaddies, for that matter. Hags were supposed to be mean old spirits who slipped out of their skin at night to find someone to ride on their back, jumping up and down to get the breath out of them. The hag could get through a keyhole or any tiny place they wanted and get on someone's back or chest and ride them all night until the person being ridden was plumb worn out and that person being ridden didn't dare move for fear the hag would steal their skin. Before the sun came up, the hag would skidadle back to their own skin—or they would burn up. Then the next night they were at it again. And just anybody was good bait for the hag. They were foolish about counting straws in a broom or holes in things, and if they got into an open salt bottle, they got so excited about counting every grain they'd forget what time it was and sometimes just burn up right there before your eyes. That was a bit too much for Henny. But he respected Aunt Letty as he did all the Gullah with their rich beliefs, and he was going to listen to her about this hag.

"Well." He chuckled. "I like a good story."

"Hmmp!"

"For someone who can't talk, Tilly did a pretty good job of showing us how Willie Mae landed in your lap. Why wasn't that worthless girl working at the Mortons's?"

Aunt Letty frowned at him. "Willie Mae ain't worthless. She's just young, and I reckon she was worried sick about her sister Stella. But Tilly saw Willie Mae before I did and pointed to dat wild-eyed girl runnin towards us like a haint got her scent."

Henny laughed. "She sure must of been running fast if she thought a haint was after her. Haints are really bad, right?"

"You wanna here about this or not?" She turned to face him with another withering look.

"I'm sorry, just couldn't help myself."

"Well, she ran right to me, fallin in my arms sobbin. She said de hag done rode poor Stella to de gates of Hebb'n. I told her I didn't mess with hags no more. They be more trouble than they be worth. Anyway, they usually get all de air they want and go on off. But Willie Mae was screechin, 'She be dead before sundown,' over and over.

"So, like some old fool, I go on to Stella's house." Aunt Letty stared out into space. "I walked through de indigo blue door seein more stuff than I've ever seen in one room. There was brooms, strainers, sieves, an salt was spread from de front door and every window to circling de bed where Stella lay. Her whole family was around her and a bunch of other kin, moanin and groanin like she be already dead. I felt shivers down my spine.

"That girl looked more like a cadaver than sweet Stella. 'Lawd have mercy,' I blurted out, and everyone in dat room say, 'Lawd have mercy,' like a chorus at a funeral."

Henny listened attentively, his pipe paused in the air.

"I asked how long she been rode by dat hag, and her mama, cryin her eyes out, said she don't know. They just saw her yesterday like this. Dat started de whole room wailing a chorus, 'Our Stella goin to de promised land.'

"So, I looked up and told Jesus to get himself down and help me. I'm tellin you, and this be the truth, the moment I called on Jesus, a beautiful glow filled dat room. Dat family in de holiness of dat room looked up at de ceilin as if they expected de pearly gates to open for Stella to float through."

Henny, with that, leaned back against the step and bit his lip to keep from laughing.

"Dat's de truth, Henny. Don't you go lookin dat way or I won't finish."

"Sorry, Letty."

"Well, I told em we were goin to be prayin if it took all day and night. We hadn't been prayin long before de candles start flickerin. Our voices were quiverin, but we kept on prayin. Then another prayer or two and we hear this scratchin at de door, but we kept on shakin in our chairs. About the middle of the night, de whole house starts shakin. Then we begin shoutin our prayers. But just short of dayclean, there was a streak of lightnin just out de door to light up de world. We grabbed a hold of each other but kept on prayin loud as we could when all of a sudden rain started beatin down on dat tin roof like it come to save us and Stella. You know hags don't like water."

"It didn't rain here."

"Well, it sure rained there, and the scariest scream I ever heard in my life shook the earth. We all fell on de floor coverin our heads until we were sure dat hag was gone to hell. Then outta de blue we hear a fretful voice askin, 'What ya'll doing heah in my house?'"

Henny leaned over and said, as sincerely as he could muster, "Letty, that sure was some hag. And I'm mighty glad Stella is still among us. Let's go in and have some breakfast."

"Thank you, Henny, but I wanna go home. Thank you for keepin Tilly. I hope they get here soon before I fall asleep here on this step."

"You're in luck, Letty. Looks to me like that's Tilly and Ben coming up from the docks."

Before he reached the steps to the house, Ben called, "We've been talking to Long Robby. Hi, Aunt Letty." He waved as Tilly ran to sit by her.

"Did he say anything about Rufus?" Henny asked.

"Yeah. Said he was homesick but likes his school. Said all the talk was about the war overseas. That the president didn't want any part of the war. That was about it as far as Rufus was concerned."

"So, what else did he have to say?"

Ben's face lit up. "Henny, Long Robby and some of the fellas have been frog gigging down the river. He said those frogs are some of the heaviest yammed ones he's ever seen."

"Where is it?"

Ben started to tell him, hesitated, and quickly glanced at Aunt Letty before answering. "Well, it's that stream just beyond the one where all that trouble was. And not a sight of anyone around, he said."

"Yeah, I know the one. Nice little stream until it runs straight into a backwater slough that's about as stinking and nasty as any swamp around. Devil's Blood, it's called."

Ben laughed. "Yeah, Long Robby calls it Black Death. It's the longest swamp anywhere around, and he says people have gone in there and never come out it's so tangled with limbs an reeds."

"Does Long Robby gig in there?"

"Henny, you know Long Robby. He ain't afraid of nothing, and I reckon he does, but he said those big toads along that stream were haruumping like they was singing a bedtime song."

Henny smiled. "So, I guess you got a notion to go gigging, huh?"

"Long Robby said he'd lend me the gig and he has a new light. You oughta see it. It's a woodbox with a large tin ring on the side holding the light. Brand new. Cost him four dollars. Called a search lantern. It's brighter than a flashlight."

"You better be leaving Tilly outta whatever you're thinkin bout." Letty wrestled with getting up from the stairs. "I ain't listenin to no more of this nonsense. C'mon, Tilly, we're goin home."

Henny looked up at Letty, his eyes twinkling. "Now, Letty, there's nothing to fear down that stream but mebbe brushing up against a ghost or two."

She glared at him. "You stay outta this, Henny Findley."

"Aunt Letty, I been going out in my boat down that river and every stream and other waters around here as long as I can remember. I know em. I sleep on my boat down em all the time or used to. An the rum runners are gone. Ain't nothing to bother us. But I wouldn't go near that backwater swamp if I had a knife to my throat."

He cringed but then remembered she didn't know about that time he had a knife to his throat. "There's a full moon tonight, an there's nothing like looking up at it with it glittering down all over everything just like magic."

Aunt Letty looked at him, knowing much better than he would ever likely know what it was like to live and sleep with only the raw sounds and smells of nature around. The moon so big you felt you could walk into it. But she gave him a cold look and said, "It be magic if I let Tilly go anywhere with you at night and down some river where bad things happen. That's final, and I'm tired and goin home."

"I know you're tired, Letty. That hag done wore you out. Go home and rest, and they can talk to you about it later."

She bristled and put her hands on her hips and asked, "And just what bizness it be of yours?"

Tilly leaned back toward Ben as Aunt Letty dragged her away, and they shared sad faces.

There was no more said about frog gigging for a few days, except for Ben's lamenting to Henny. "Why is Aunt Letty so hard on her going or doing anything like frog gigging?"

"She's got her mind set, boy. Might as well forget Tilly going with you."

A few days later, Ben walked into the house calling, "Henny! Look what Long Robby sent with me."

Henny raised his eyebrows, delighted to see what he guessed were frog legs in the small burlap bag Ben was carrying. "Now that's the way I like to get em. Ready to cook," he said when Ben dumped the heavy yammed legs on the table. "Let's get them on ice and we'll have them for supper."

"Maybe if we ask Tilly and Aunt Letty and she sees Long Robby don't have no problem getting them from that stream, she'll let Tilly go gigging with me. Long Robby said there's no one around there no more."

"Boy, you just don't let up. I told you. When she sets her mind, she sets her mind."

Henny sat back and looked at Ben. He wasn't a boy anymore. Letty noticed how fast he was growing. That was her fear, not the stream. At least that's what he thought. She saw the tall, muscled young man Ben was growing to be, and good looking. A tanned complexion was replacing the freckles. Henny had long wondered who Ben's parents were. With that shock of blond hair, his kin coulda been those Swedes that settled down the river for awhile. They were good people, not the kind to set a baby loose on a saltwater marsh. Another mystery.

Ben hadn't seemed to notice the change in Tilly. She had grown lovelier and more beguiling with each day, and only the straight frocks she wore covered the new rounds of her body. Ben may not have noticed, but he would. That's what got to Aunt Letty. And then what? They lived in a world where color mattered. Henny closed his eyes in sadness for what he, and Letty for that matter, feared might come.

"Henny?" Ben asked, concerned. "What ya thinking?"

Jarred loose from his thoughts, he said, "Oh, about that war. From what I hear coming down the river, I don't think we're gonna be pulled into it. The president don't want to go into war."

"I hope not, Henny. The guys at the dock don't want no part of it, either."

He stretched to look out the window. "If I'm seeing right, we got company."

"Who?"

"Stella and Tilly are beating a track here."

They got up and met them on the porch, but before Henny could say anything, Stella blurted out, "Henny, Mr. Morton's real sick, and Aunt Letty had to go help Willie Mae."

"What's wrong with Mr. Morton, Stella?"

"Mr. Morton went to Atlanta on business, and there's a lot of the grippe there. The hospital don't want him there, but they sent a nurse, and the doctor will come every day, they say."

"Hmm, and just Willie Mae there to take care of Mr. Morton."

"That's right, and Willie Mae be my sister and I love her, but she don't know an egg from a ball. Anyway, Miz Morton can't come home, and she needs Orie there. Beau be gettin ready to have de second operation on his foot. I guess they be hopin Aunt Letty can help with de cookin and help Mr. Morton, too."

"Does Mrs. Morton know about this?"

"No. Mr Morton don't want to upset her. Nothin she could do."

Henny looked at Tilly and smiled. "Well, now. I bet that means we're gonna have our girl with us for awhile."

"Wow, that's great, Tilly. You can go fishing with me. And you can have my bed."

"Okay," Henny said and slapped his knees, "I'll borrow a cot from Long Robby."

The next day, Ben and Tilly ran into the house calling Henny.

"Long Robby says the town's cooks are always asking about frog legs. Henny, if I could get three or four frogs a night, I could make more money than I can with shrimp. Or anything else."

"Yeah, I bet you could. Would Long Robby lend you the gig and light?"

"He said I could use his stuff when they weren't until I could get my own. I can make my own gig."

"Sounds good to me."

"Henny, there just ain't no good reason Tilly can't go with me, you know that."

He looked over at Tilly's downcast face. "I can't buck Aunt Letty, and you know that."

"Henny, Aunt Letty left you in charge of Tilly. That's as much as sayin you got a right to say what she can and can't do."

Henny chuckled, picked up his pipe, and sat down by the fire. "Ya'll go on off somewhere and give me some peace."

CHAPTER 36

"Ben, I never meant anything more than I do this. If you see anything peculiar, no matter what, you better hightail it back here or there'll be two of us skinning you alive." He looked Ben solidly in the eye. "I mean that."

"I will, Henny, I promise." He was giddy with happiness. "But there won't be nothing peculiar. I know that. And there's still almost a full moon, and we can see pretty much what's around us even without the search light."

Long Robby had told them both where he found the most frogs along the designated stream and had instructed Tilly how to hold the light.

"Go easy with the gig, Ben. Once Tilly has the frog mesmerized with the light, take aim carefully then shoot the gig to the mark fast. That frog'll cry like a baby when you got em. One thing to remember. There's a breeze tonight. Don't let your boat drift too close to that swamp. Your boat's small, but it's still hard to turn in a little current when you get down that stream with all the tall grass and willows." He handed them a small potato sack to hold the frogs once gigged. "Wet it down before you leave. That'll keep em nice and fresh."

It was a perfect night—the moon still large enough to cast a beautiful light, all the stars were out, and the air was just cool enough. The two couldn't have been happier when they turned into the stream. Tilly sat behind Ben as he inched the boat in and kept the light steadily on the bank, switching it from one side to the other. Within minutes, she had a big yammed frog in her light.

"Great, Tilly. Hold it right on em."

Ben poled close to the bank with his oar and positioned his gig high to jab the toad when they heard rustling leaves followed by someone with a light approaching the bank.

"Tilly, shut off the light and get down in the boat."

Ben tried to ease his boat toward a bunch of tall reeds as the man shined the light out into the water.

"Who's out there?"

Ben grimaced and could feel Tilly's heart pounding against his back where she pressed against it. He'd know that voice anywhere. There was no doubt in this mind it was the same man who wanted to slit his throat. He put the gig in the hull and reached for his slingshot and a rock.

"Just us, sir. Trying to gig some frogs."

"Lemme see you," he called out and shined his light on Ben's boat.

Ben shielded his eyes and said, "We'll leave if we're bothering you. Just thought we could get some frogs tonight. Heard there was a lot of em here."

The man leaned over and shined his light on Ben's face. "You're that boy I caught in the woods." He straightened up, laughing. "I told you what I'd do to you if I ever saw you again, remember? A nice slit throat just like your friend got."

Enraged, Ben put the rock in the sling and whispered to Tilly to turn the light on the rum runner when he said to.

"Who you got in there with you?" He shined his light on Tilly's face. "Well, now, look what we got here. If it ain't that little half and half. Ain't that what Junie called you?" He laughed again. "Looks like it's gonna be a good night after all."

"Now, Tilly," Ben whispered.

Ben aimed at the man's forehead and let the rock fly.

"Yowww," the man screeched.

"Tilly, keep that light on him."

The rum runner was clutching the space between his eyes, falling over backward, howling in pain as his light rolled into the water.

Ben heard his friends running toward the screams. "Hang on tight, Tilly."

He started paddling away. He had no choice but to go to the swamp! If he tried turning around, they'd catch em for sure. The angry voices were on the bank surrounding the wounded man now.

"Out there. That kid," he moaned.

The men shined their lights out on the stream, catching sight of the boat as it cleared the bank.

A bullet whizzed past so close, Ben yelled to Tilly to climb in front of him as he tried to pick up speed. Another shot missed them by a foot, then someone said, "I lost em. Let's run down the bank. I wanna get those kids."

Ben headed toward the swamp as fast as he could. *Oh my gosh. They're gonna get us,* he thought as the voices got closer.

Ben dug his paddle quickly between the reeds and slid into the muddy, stinking backwater. The men were running down the bank yelling obscenities.

Finally, one of the men yelled, "Ah, let em go. They can't do nothin. The swamp'll get em anyway. Let's go. I ain't going in that foul-smelling slough."

Ben almost cried out with relief as he heard them leave. He headed toward a large clump of tall grass and a pile of logs jammed together. It was lit from the moonlight, and they both cringed at what they saw ahead. Never had they seen anyplace as foreboding or downright evil looking.

Neither Ben nor Tilly moved until long after the last sound of the departing men.

"Tilly," Ben said as quietly as he could. "We gotta stay here." His voice was cracking. "I don't know how long before Henny will get worried and someone will come for us. We gotta stay here anyway. The boat's stuck in the mud."

He pulled her up next to him and wrapped his arms around her. He was used to the night sounds, but he knew she had to be terrified. It was the scariest place he had ever been, and even he felt spooked. They listened to the owls and ducks, bats, and other night birds and watched the beavers and raccoons prowling about. And the harumping of the frogs. He knew there were gators in there but was pretty sure they would leave them alone. The breeze turned cold and the night eerier. They sat huddled together for what felt like hours. *Henny will miss us soon, I know he will.* It was the cats he heard lived deep in the swamp that kept him on edge.

As if he conjured it, Ben watched, gasping, as a huge, smoky cat dragging its long tail walked slowly toward them. He reached for his sling but slowly put it down in his lap as the cougar came closer. It held them enchanted with glistening eyes as if they were friends, put both feet on the bow, and pushed them out of the swamp into the stream. As if by magic, the boat skimmed the water past the place where the men, now gone, had been and turned into the river where they sailed smoothly to the docks without Ben touching the oars. "Tilly." Ben's voice was quavery, and he felt Tilly's body trembling next to him. "I ain't talking to nobody bout any of this. I can't." Without looking at him, she slowly nodded her head up and down.

"Well, there ya are. I was beginning to get a little worried about you," Henny yelled out to them. "Must have been some good frogging."

Ben pulled the boat up on shore and lay the gig and lantern on the dock, then he and Tilly walked toward the house, past Henny and Long Robby as if they didn't see them.

Long Robby and Henny looked at each other and shrugged.

"I guess it didn't go so good for them, Henny."

They decided not to mention the frog gigging to Ben again, thinking his pride must be hurt.

CHAPTER 37

Aunt Letty was asleep in the servants' quarters at the Morton house when Bones awakened her.

She frowned. "Where you been?"

"Away, Letty. I saw de King."

"You saw de King? King Oosafella?'

"Yes. He be comin heah."

"When?" she almost shouted.

"I just know he be comin. I expect he thinks it's time to settle some things."

She knit her brows. "What sort of things, Bones?"

"Junie."

She frowned. "What's he goin to do? Junie's mine, Bones."

"He be doin what he needs to do, Letty. Junie and his pa hurt you bad, Letty, but de King's feelins go way back. Back long before Junie."

She let his words settle in. "I'm gonna be there, Bones. I got my stake in this."

"You will be, Letty. I promise dat." He took her hand and held it.

"Bones, where is de King? Where do he live?"

"All over, Letty."

"What are you talkin about? All over where?"

Bones stared out the window. "The King lives wherever he wants to, Letty. He can be anywhere."

"Is he still a man?"

He turned his smile on her. "He be more spirit. Sometimes he's a man and other times he's what he wants to be. In Africa, he's a white lion, like when he came down from a star."

Letty stared with a look of reverence. "Oh, Bones, I sure would like to see de King."

"You will, Letty. You will. I came to tell you dat I'm goin to get rid of de rum runners. Our people here are gonna get hurt if I don't."

"I didn't know they was back."

"They be."

"How are you goin to do dat, Bones?"

"You be seein. But dat ain't all, Letty. It be time to finish this evil dat lives amongst us."

He didn't usually tell her what he was doing. "I miss you, Bones. All these years and I still miss de forest and bein with you. I always will."

She ran her hand across his kind face, loving the bony structure. What most saw as ugly she saw as beautiful.

After he left, she lay thinking about what he had told her. "Well, I sure ain't going near that swampy hell hole of an island where the rum runners and ghosts be," she said aloud and drifted off to sleep.

After a couple of weeks, Aunt Letty was back in her stall with Tilly beside her. Mr. Morton had recuperated quickly with her care, Life Everlasting tea, and poultices. And Willie Mae had learned to cook shrimp and grits, working alongside Aunt Letty.

They had received word from Mrs. Morton that Beau's operation went very well, and he would walk just fine with a cane for support, which appealed to his refined sensibilities. They planned to come home in late spring. And they were thrilled that Beau had been accepted into the school of law at Georgetown University. His excellent tutoring had granted him early admission. He would be leaving in the late summer. The other children just wanted to come home, along with Orie and Brian, who had enough of the cold winter.

CHAPTER 38

"It's April, Tilly. This time last year we was going to the tabby house and we found Beau in the ditch with the snakes."

She nodded, laughing.

"Yeah, but it wasn't funny then. Then we went last fall and nearly got caught by Junie and the dogs." He thought about the time he'd gone to the tabby house and nearly nearly gotten caught by Junie and his friends. That had been so scary. Junie wanted it for their hangout. *Thank goodness the men didn't like it.*

"Junie and his klan friends ain't there now, Tilly. I checked the other day. It's so nice today. Why don't we go there?"

Tilly smiled and grabbed his hand, running along with him.

Ben watched her run through the tabby walls surrounding the garden.

"It's a mess in here now, Tilly, but I'm working on it like we talked about. Mostly cutting back on those plants like Mr. Moody showed me. I'll clean up the weeds around the pond. I wanted to get the seeds in earlier so we would have a garden now, but it didn't work out. We'll have a fall garden." He looked up to her. "It's funny, Tilly. I almost feel like this place is mine. I don't think it belongs to anyone."

She walked over to him and squeezed his hand, smiling at him in a way that made him uneasy.

"Let's go down to the water. You can almost see the whole shoreline from there. Look, Tilly, not a cloud in the sky."

She poked him and pointed up behind where he was looking.

His jaw dropped. "That's crazy. There is only that one little, tiny cloud sitting up there, and it's black as mud. Tilly, I've never seen nothing like that. It's just sitting there like it's waiting for something to do."

With that, a bolt of lightning shot straight down to the ground from the black cloud, followed by an explosion that rocked the ground under their feet. Flames filled the sky, followed by clouds of smoke billowing up like giant mushrooms high in the sky.

"Holy smoke! Whatever that lightning hit . . . Oh my gosh, Tilly, we gotta go. It's over by home." He turned to grab her hand. "Let's go. Tilly? Let's go now."

She just stared at the smoke until he grabbed her arm and ran.

The entire Gullah village was in the commons or by the river. The flames had dropped below the trees, but the smoke still covered a massive area just down the river from them. But even the smoke seemed to be smoldering out.

"That's mighty odd," Long Robby said to Henny as he walked up. "That blast was big enough it should still be burnin and the sky filled with smoke."

One of the fishermen said, "I was out trollin and saw dat lightnin streak down, but when I looked up, there wasn't nothin up there."

"I'd bet my boat it's where that sumpy island is," another fisherman said.

Ben squeezed Tilly's hand.

"That's crazy," someone else said. "Just lightnin out of de blue and from nothing?"

Ben looked at Tilly. *It's that island. That spooky island.*

"It's dying out," Henny said, dumbfounded. "That fire is burning out."

"Let's go down there and see what's goin on," Long Robby said.

All the fishermen ran for their boats, taking on as many of the others standing around as they could.

Henny looked over at Ben. "I think I'll go see what happened down there. You wanna go?"

"No, Henny," Ben said, backing up along side Tilly. "I don't think so."

Henny looked at him inquisitively. "Okay. I thought you'd be the first down there."

Ben just shrugged nonchalantly. "Nah, you can tell me about it."

Henny gave him an odd look and joined the others.

⁀

When the group arrived where they thought the explosion occurred, there was only steam and bubbles rising from a large expanse of water. The little island that had been the cause of so much turbulence and heartache was gone. The group gawked, astonished.

"Dat bolt of lightnin sunk de island dat was here," Billy John said. "I didn't know dat river was deep enough to hold dat island."

But the others just stared at the empty space.

No one noticed the fragment of a charred barrel floating away amongst the bubbles and steam.

When Aunt Letty heard, she smiled to herself and went on with her baking.

⁀

The *Belleview Gazette* ran a full-page account of the loss of the island. As much about it as they were aware. Mrs. Mable Vanderpool, a notable citizen of Belleview, wrote an article comparing it to the lost civilization of Atlantis but, she wrote, no one knew where Atlantis was lost. An op-ed sent in by another citizen said he had heard of lots of islands sinking in the Pacific. The following day Miss Libby Hackney, the librarian, replied to Mrs. Vanderpool's article with the information that she would be able to find Atlantis in Plato. The local naturalist answered the op-ed that Belleview and the entire corridor was Lowcountry and not subject to high tides or rising seas and it was foolish to compare it to those in the Pacific. Except for some interest around the area, the news soon died. Probably because they hadn't seen it sink, they didn't believe it, or it was just not of interest to the majority of citizens who were more interested in the sand beaches than the river. The Gullah were just relieved that the pestilent island was gone.

There was one citizen, however, who did not forget the sunken island and fumed with malicious intent. He was sure there was more to it than an act of nature. He was all too aware of the Gullah and their ways, particularly of one. Bones. Junie decided to bide his time. It was his property that had sunk, and but for the fact he had imbibed a spot too much of the rum while tasting its value the night before, he would have been on the bottom of the river and sound with the dead.

CHAPTER 39

After the last suitcase was unloaded from Rebecca Morton's car and she, Beau, and the rest of the children were back inside their home, Orie moved up in the front seat beside Brian, and they headed to the Gullah commune with the horn honking all the way.

Orie hung out the window calling and waving to everyone they passed. When she saw Aunt Letty, her arms raised to the sky, high stepping as lively as a filly, Brian had to jerk to a stop as Orie threw the door open, jumped out, and went into her sister's arms. They held onto each other so long those gathered around to greet Orie laughed and pulled them apart.

"Tell me, Orie. Tell me what de doctor said. Is Beau's foot okay?"

"Miss Becky says she wants to talk to you herself." Her laughter trilled through the commune. "You didn't do nothin to cause Beau's foot to be like dat, Letty. De doctor told de Mortons it was somethin called genetics." She grinned. "Dat be de truth, Letty. You can stop you're grievin now."

Aunt Letty pulled Orie back in her arms, tears running down her cheeks. "Oh, Orie, God's smilin on me today. Dat's de best news I ever got."

At dusk they all gathered around the campfire where a kettle of frogmore stew hung and listened to Orie talk about the months they had been away.

"Things are so different there. They ain't as friendly to colored folks as I thought they would be, but we was mostly in dat big house Miss Rebecca rented. Most of de talk up there is about de war overseas. Miss Rebecca say de president don't want it, but dè Germans be doin bad things, so nobody knows what he gonna do."

The next afternoon those in the market stopped what they were doing and stared, dumbstruck at the sight moving swiftly toward them. Beau greeted them all politely, waved to Aunt Letty, and asked from the driver's seat of his miniature Lozier touring car if they could tell him where he might find Tilly and Ben.

"Beau, it be mighty fine to see you home and lookin so well," Aunt Letty said, coming toward him. "Hmmm mmm, dat sure is a mighty fine car you got there."

"It might be getting a little too small for me, Aunt Letty," he said and laughed.

"Ben and Tilly are down at de docks. They're pretty much straight ahead of you. I know they'll be glad to see you back."

"Thank you, Aunt Letty," he said and was off in a small poof of dust.

"Beau," Ben called out when he recognized him and his little car. Tilly and Ben ran to meet him. "It's good to see you back." He looked over the little Lozier they had seen in his room. "Boy, that is really keen."

Beau looked at Tilly grinning at him. "I'm sorry it isn't big enough to take you for a ride." He was still looking at Tilly, which was not lost upon Ben.

After small talk about his trip and a mention of the wonderful success with his foot, they walked, Beau with his cane, toward the benches in the community park. Ben was surprised that he didn't feel as shy around Beau he had before, but genuinely glad to see him.

"I wanted to find some memento as a way of thanking you for saving my life, but I couldn't think of anything that satisfied me. I realized there is nothing that could ever compensate for your bravery but the knowledge that you saved a life." He smiled warmly, which he hoped would show them the depth of his sincerity. This had not been easy for him. He had practiced his smile in the mirror of his bedroom, thinking about Tilly and Ben and what they had done for him, until he could actually feel what he wanted to portray as genuine gratitude. A cold bitterness had been with him for so long. Because of his deformity and the fact he was the center of so much attention, he had developed a persona that now felt deplorable. He had relied on his intellect and was calculating and controlling, and for the first time in his life, he wanted to change. He worked at it until he gradually felt his heart melting. He was learning to care about others. And it surprised him that it made him happy.

Ben was thinking that he liked this odd guy. "Thanks, Beau. I'm not so sure it was us that saved you, though." He looked at Tilly and back at Beau. "Ya gotta give credit to Bones for that."

Tilly nodded and smiled.

Beau laughed. "I don't think it was Bones who risked his life jumping into that pit with me." He smiled at Tilly. "I have to go now. I have only a couple of months, if that, to get ready to leave for Washington. I will stay there after my graduation from law school for awhile. Maybe I'll come home once or twice, but I won't be going into the war if our country does."

"Then you'll come back here?"

"Oh yes, and join my family's firm. I'll be the fourth generation to do so."

Tilly stood up with Ben, and although she didn't hug Beau, she looked at him with such warmth Beau quickly got into the little car and left, embarrassed by his feelings for her.

CHAPTER 40

S ummer came with less of the sweltering heat typical of Lowcountry, and Ben and Tilly spent it exploring the woods, swimming in the ponds, playing the games they loved, often with Aunt Letty and Henny. Ben, with Henny's help, built a barbecue pit, and they cooked fish and small game that Henny brought home—squirrels, rabbits, dove, or quail. Occasionally, he would make a trade with Dicky Short for pork spareribs and would invite Orie, Emmy and Billy John, Long Robby and his family, Nellie and Joe, and whoever else was on his mind for a well-into-night fest. A little corn whiskey added to the jovialtity.

Despite the mosquitoes that swarmed and the humid air, Ben spent as much time as he could out in his boat, often debating the idea of joining Long Robby. They didn't hear anymore directly from Beau, but Orie said he would be leaving on the train for Washington soon. It had been a wonderful spring and summer, and at the first sign of autumn, when they could smell it in the cooler air and the sourwood turned red, they were grateful that all had gone well for so many months without any news of Junie. Although superstition didn't let them say that to each other, or anyone else.

It was October when Junie surfaced, making his first move by paying a visit to Beau's father, Michael Morton.

The October sun was outdoing itself shining away any clouds that tried to steal its glory. Long Robby was kneeling, cleaning his traps, when Willie Mae ran up to him.

"Willie Mae, what brings you down here?"

"Mr. Morton sent me to tell you he wants to see you, Long Robby. And could he come to your house this afternoon?" Willie Mae sat down on the railing and looked up and around. "I plumb love this time of year."

"Why does he want to see me, Willie Mae?"

"Lawd knows. He don't tell me nothin. He just wants to know what time suits you."

Long Robby sat looking down at the traps until Willie Mae asked, "You heah me?"

"I heard you, Willie Mae." He got up, cleaned up his work, and put the traps back in his boat. "Well, whatever it is it ain't goin to be good. I know dat. Tell him anytime after two this afternoon be fine. And I be waitin for him at de road in town."

A little after two, Mr. Morton with Long Robby beside him in the touring car passed through the commune, stirring up enough interest for the news to travel quickly. Long Robby didn't look out the window at the anxious faces watching as they passed by. He would talk to them later if need be.

When they pulled up in front of Long Robby's house, he introduced him to Sassy. "It's such a nice day, Mr. Morton, you might want to sit out heah on de porch."

"That would be quite nice. Thank you."

He looked at Long Robby. "As long as I have known you, I don't know your last name."

"It's Cinque', Mr. Morton. When my people got to de Savage plantation, we had to take de master's name, but when my grandaddy left Granterre he took back our own name."

"Cinque'. I like that. Do you know where your family is from in Africa?"

"Yessir, I do. About sixty-five years ago, a kin of ours led a revolt on a slave ship headed here an it made a lotta news. He was tried and found innocent, and de whole lot of slaves was returned to Sierra Leone. I'm right proud of dat, but de Cinque's always were rulers."

"That's very interesting, Long Robby. And unusual. I can imagine it did cause quite a stir. Good for Mr. Cinque'." He studied his hands in his lap. "Long Robby, I'm sorry to have to bring this news to you, but Mr. Junie Savage came to see me yesterday. He's interested in this property. As you may know when Belleview burned in 1907, not only the courthouse burned but my father's and my law office burned as well. I know a little about property deeds, grants, and memorials, but without the actual recordings of property, I'm somewhat at a loss to give him any information. My father would have known more than I do, but he died last year."

"Junie Savage's daddy tried to keep us from gettin this land when my daddy went to see your grandaddy."

"Do you have a deed?"

"No, sir. It was put in a community trust. Mose, my daddy, knew all de problems with de plantation land bein given to de former enslaved people by the military who was in charge here and then their havin to give it all back to the original owners after de war. But he also knew dat wasn't de case around here."

"That's right. I'm familiar with the allocation of land not only in Belleview County but on St. John's Island as well. Those former slaves around here were the first freedmen of the war, and they had powerful allies in the missionaries when it came to St. John's Island, and the Union military supervisors as well. The missionaries fought for the rights of the freedmen and established the school that is there now. Belleview County was the only county in the country where an ex-slave could buy land. And under the Union's jurisdiction property certification was assigned to individual households giving them plots of plantation land for farming. There were a quarter of colored farmers in the South who owned their land by 1900."

"My grandaddy was given ten acres, which he farmed til he died."

"Those were interesting but disturbing times. But what I have to find out now is what you have here, Long Robby. A law for homesteading just passed in 1862, but I don't believe that was used here."

Long Robby excused himself and went into the house, returning with a neat folder of papers he handed to Mr. Morton.

"Long Robby, I assume your father discussed these documents with you?"

"Yessir. My daddy and three of his friends acted as trustees over the property until my parents died in de hurricane. I took his place. Daddy told me your grandaddy had a fight with Mr. Savage, but de court said Mr. Savage didn't have evidence showin he owned this land."

"I'd like to take this file home and study it if that's all right with you?"

"That be fine with me. I ain't goin to say nothin to no one here yet I don't think."

"I will more than likely have to go to Charleston and search through old records. The present Mr. Savage says Grandterre was a land grant issued in 1726. He has an old paper that has been in a safe declaring this, but it is not legal and only gives the acreage but not any description of lines. There were no recordings of title until after 1785. Mr. Savage may be threatening your claim, but he has a lot to prove. Keep faith."

He smiled at Sassy and Long Robby. "It was very nice meeting you, Sassy. Thank you for the delicious tea." He tipped his hat and left.

⁀

"Oh, Emmie, how could you leave us? You and Billy John have been here all your lives." Aunt Letty wiped the tears from her face. "I just can't stand it. You can't go, Emmy. You just can't."

"There's too much hate and danger closing in around us, Aunt Letty. Billy John and I been thinkin about this since last year. We got chillun to think about. And it ain't just de foulness we be facin here. I been scrapin pennies in de market. Didn't used to matter when Billy John was making money on our crops, but now they got all those new shops downtown. We keep cuttin de prices on tomatoes and other things but seems de people in Belleview like de stores that got all those fancy groceries lined up on de shelves."

Aunt Letty put her head in her hands. "I'll never get over this, Emmy. But I hear you. I see it comin for all of us. How long are we going to keep de market runnin? Oh, Emmy, I can't bear to see you go."

"Aunt Letty, so many Gullah Geechee are already gone from around here. Dat island a little down south is being taken over by rich folks up north. They be just pushin out de people who been livin there all their lives and their kin before them. All de people goin north—they call it de great migration."

Aunt Letty looked around her at all at the familiarity of their home place and thought of how much she loved it and all the activities and holidays. *Always being there for one another.*

"Yes, Emmy, I fear dat we're lookin at changes we ain't gonna like." She put her arms around Emmy. "Please, let us know someway how you and Billy John are. I'll be thinkin of you every day."

"And I you, Aunt Letty." Tears streaked down her face. "I be lettin you know bout us as soon as we get settled in Chicago where Billy John's brothers been livin."

⌒

Michael Morton sent word for Long Robby to come to his office two weeks later. "I have good news but also some news you are not going to like, Long Robby. I asked you to come here so we could talk about it more freely without upsetting everyone at your home who might see me."

"Yes, sir." Long Robby sat like stone on ice over a fiery pit.

"I found records in Charleston about the Savage property but nothing at all about the property your community owns. You won't have to worry about that any longer. I'll see to it that you have a recorded deed. That might stand up better if there ever was a problem." He looked at Long Robby, regretting what he had to tell him next.

"Did you ever suspect the Savages owned the old warehouses?"

Long Robby looked down between his legs at the floor. "It crossed my mind, Mr. Morton, but I figured he'd a claimed them if he'd known." He sighed, distress flickering over his strong face. "The warehouses be right on de docks."

"Mr. Savage suspected he owned them and asked me to find out, and unfortunately he does own them." He shook his head sadly. "I'm so sorry, Long Robby."

"Ain't your fault, Mr. Morton." Long Robby looked out the window toward the marsh and his people. "Whats he goin to do with de cotton gins?"

"I don't know. He has no use for them. My guess is that he'll sell them. I'm fairly sure he needs the money. He lost about everything he had when the boll weevil took his crops of cotton. The boll weevil was responsible for a lot of loss in Belleville and its surrounds." He shook his head, sadly. "For our family as well. Sea Island Cotton was a particularly desirable strain, a higher quality cotton, that made Belleview the wealthiest and most cultured town of its size in America. You may know that." He smiled half-heartedly at Long Robby. "Well, cotton or no cotton, there's no telling about that man, Long Robby, but if selling is his intention, I may be able to help. I won't go into that now. We will have to wait and see what he does. You have your land, and that is the best news we could have expected."

He got up and patted Long Robby on his back. "You are a very fine man. The Gullah community is fortunate to have you take care of all their needs."

Long Robby laughed. "I reckon there be a few times where I can help, sir, but not all."

Long Robby made the good and bad news known to everyone in the commune that night. "We just have to wait and see what he does now. Mr. Savage is pretty angry about his not ownin this land."

Junie Savage wasted no time letting them know how he felt. On Thanksgiving Day, when he knew they would all be together in the park, he and six of his cronies thundered in on horses. Junie reined close to the crowd and yelled angrily, "Ya'll listen to me and listen good. You are going to pay for that land, and ya can damn well count on that."

As they galloped off, there wasn't a soul present who doubted his word.

CHAPTER 41

Winter brought the ducks returning to the marsh. Ben looked up at the black flocks of birds and said, "Hunters'll be swarming in like those ducks pretty soon, Tilly, and if it's like it was last year, more strangers than ever will be coming."

He finished stacking the wood he had chopped and looked out at Tilly, who was leaning against a tree.

"I talked to Long Robby down at the docks this morning. Rufus wrote that the president sent someone over to talk to England and Germany about ending the war. He said it looked like it worked."

He took off his heavy gloves and stuck them in his coat pocket. "Let's go inside and sit with Henny. If you wanna stay for dinner, why don't you go ask Aunt Letty to come? I'll go in and start on the shrimp."

He looked at her again and frowned. "Why ya got your hair up on your head?"

She rolled her eyes as she walked away, swishing her new green skirt further up above her ankles.

Ben felt his face getting warm. *What's gotten into her?*

He let the front door bang a little and slumped down in the chair next to Henny by the fire.

"Nothing in the world like a warm fire on a cold, nasty day." When Ben didn't answer, he looked over at him. "What's eating you?"

"Nothing. It's that girl. She is getting so weird, Henny."

Henny closed his eyes and chuckled to himself. "If you hadn't noticed, Tilly is a young lady now. She's not the kid you played with. And you're not the same kid she played with. Thought of that?"

Ben got up from his chair and said gruffly, "I'm gonna go clean up." He stopped and added, "I think Tilly and Aunt Letty might be coming for dinner. I'll get the shrimp peeled and headed if you'll make shrimp and grits?"

"Sounds good to me." He watched Ben thoughtfully as he walked away and rested his chin in his hand.

After dinner, the four sat around the fire and talked about Junie and the cotton warehouses.

Henny said, "We know that devil won't sit still until he has gotten back at ya'll with something dirty. I hate to say that, Letty, but you know better than anyone."

She stared into the fire. She had never talked to anyone but Orie about what Bones told her. But besides Orie, these were the people closest to her.

"Bones came to see me. He said dat de King was comin to take care of some things. I been thinkin bout dat."

"The King?" Ben almost jumped out of the chair.

"Well, that's something, Letty." Henny turned in his chair to face her. "When?"

She squirmed in her chair. "I dunno dat."

"Take care of what things, Aunt Letty?"

"I don't know nothin but dat he's comin. Just thought I'd tell ya'll."

"Well, that's something, Letty. I don't know what to say."

Ben stared at her, mouth agape.

No one spoke until Tilly spread her arms out to the others and raised her eyebrows.

Henny said, "Letty, you wanna tell Tilly about the King?"

"No, if anyone tells dat story, it gotta be Long Robby."

"Well, if that's the case, why don't we go see Long Robby? I'd like to hear it again. I'm not sure I even know the whole story."

"Me neither." Ben sat up, excited.

"It's still early."

She got up from her chair and said, "I don't mind hearin it again neither."

Long Robby jovially invited them all in to sit around his big hearth in their large, comfortable living room. When told what they wanted, he frowned and stared in the fire. "Lawd a mercy. It's been a while since I thought about King Oosafella, but maybe it will all come back to me." He laughed and leaned back in his chair.

Sassy brought out a large platter of cookies and hot chocolate.

"Legend has it dat before Africa knew time, a star burned through the sky, its bright light nearly blindin those who watched. It landed near a village where de old Queen S'Tonga lived. When she and her tribe went to see the star, there was nothin there but white lions. No one had ever seen white lions, and they were so beautiful it took their breath away. The lions and de Queen and her tribe sat down on the ground and stared at each other in what was said to be Godly grace. As if nothin else existed. After some time, a huge white male lion who seemed to be head of de rest walked over to Queen S'Tonga, lifted his paw, and placed it on her head. Before their eyes, de Queen changed to a beautiful young woman and de lion changed to de man we call King Oosafella.

"De King and Queen had many children and lived happily in de jungle with all the wild animals and de white lions for countless years. Then one day he heard about de slave ships dat were comin to his land and taking his people. It's said you could hear his roar all over Africa. There really wasn't anythin he could do about it in spite of his powers. And he had powers beyond any dat had ever been heard of.

"One of his younger daughters, Jinga, asked him to let her go with her husband to this land where their people were being taken and see if she could help them. He agreed but told her he would not be able to help her if she were in trouble. She carried de white lion gene and wasn't afraid.

"When de boat landed in Charleston, the master of Grandterre was there to buy lots of slaves. He had de largest plantation on our coast here. None of de Savages was any good. When de first Judson saw Jinga, he couldn't stand de thought of not havin her. All de slave buyers wanted Jinga. She was dat beautiful. Savage wanted her for his mistress no matter what she cost. She knew dat and played up to him so he would buy her husband and friends who had come with her on de ship.

"The King and Jinga had a way of talkin to each other in their dreams. He knew exactly what was happenin there. Savage had built her a nice house, and while it was bein built, she told Judson she would let him come to her when it was finished. The King taught her in their dreams how to put a spell on him. So every night when he came to her, there wasn't nothin he could do but just look at her pitifully. Angry and frustrated, he would go off and wander through the woods, doubtin himself.

"All de while, she and her husband helped many, many slaves escape without Judson ever suspectin her. And she taught de enslaved people all about herbs and plants and how to treat with them and how to poison someone if they needed to. Most Africans knew about herbs and plants but not as much as she did. It be said that her knowledge and teachins is de reason de people here have de knowledge about herbs and plants they do. The white plantation owners thought knowin about herbs was witchcraft, but Savage let her do it. He let her do anythin she wanted.

"Jinga and her husband stayed close together but not so Savage would suspect anythin. Jinga had a way of bein with child and not showin it. The first year she had de child who was the grandfather or great-grandfather or however many grandfathers back of Bones."

"One night when Savage went to Jinga, she gave him an herb, telling him dat it would fix de problem he had of bein with her. He gladly took it, but within minutes, he was hallucinating, running outside screaming and yelling in some language no one could understand. All those enslaved watched as he ran into de marsh grass and out to de water. He never came back. His family looked on, glad to see him go, it's said.

"But his son, Judson, thought she had something to do with his father's craziness. He watched her carefully. An he took a dislikin to Jinga's husband even though he didn't know he was Jinga's husband. One day when Judson Jr. was drunk, he lashed Jinga's husband to death. Jinga's lion gene came out in her fury, turnin her into a fierce white lioness, and she clawed Judson Jr. to death. She was shot and killed. The King couldn't save her as he had told her when she left. But he grieved and sent word through a dream to her son that he would come someday to take care of dat evil family.

"Jinga's son married and had several sons and daughters who had children who then had children. One of them was Bones. And he was de boy de King had been waitin for. There was no doubt he gave the mantle to Bones, though no one knows when he came."

"Why's he coming here, Aunt Letty?"

She didn't answer and continued to gaze into the fire.

CHAPTER 42

Henny looked at Aunt Letty standing on the wide brick walkway between the docks and the warehouses. "Letty, what are you doing down here?"

"Looking at these old warehouses, Henny. I thought last night I ain't really seen em. They just been here like an old dog lying in the same spot, and I thought they always would just be here."

"I think we all feel that way, Letty. Except for Ben. Can you imagine the boy living in this moldy old place full of rats?"

"No, Henny. I can't."

"Long Robby," Henny said as his friend walked up to them. "Ben tells me he's been to see you."

"I hope he decides to join me, Henny. I just lost two more of my men who are goin north."

"You ain't alone. There's more spaces empty in de market. Makes me so sad I almost hate bein there."

"We been so busy just livin our lives like we always have, not payin attention to what's goin on around us, except for Junie and Jim Crow, it snook up on us. If de president wins this fall, I have a feeling he'll get us in this war."

"How's Rufus, Long Robby?"

"Oh, I dunno. His letters don't sound like a boy having fun. I think he misses home." Henny sighed. "If there be a war, he and Ben will likely go."

"I hate to think of that," Henny said and looked over at Aunt Letty. "Letty, pull that lip back in or that pelican flyin over is gonna sit on it."

Walking back to the square, Henny said, "Come to think on it, I've been meaning to ask you if you found those papers we were talking about. The ones Tilly's uncle left."

Letty looked off toward the water. "I don't know where they are."

Henny gasped. "You lost them papers, Letty. Those papers that could tell us bout Tilly?"

"Those papers. I don't know what I done with em, Henny. I plumb forgot. Been too long ago. I didn't think they was much at de time. All wrinkled up and dirty."

"Letty." He looked at her, dumbfounded. "Those papers might tell us everything we want to know bout Tilly."

"I don't think so," she said defensively. "I don't even remember what he said bout em. But I don't know where they are now and dat's dat."

CHAPTER 43

"That must be a good book, Tilly. You ain't looked up from it for an hour or more." Ben got up from the quilt he and Tilly had spread along the riverbank.

Tilly held up the book so he could see the title.

"*Moby Dick*. Don't know that one. Tilly, I think I'll go for a swim at Goose Neck. Wanna go?"

She nodded and pointed to her house and the need for her bathing suit.

"Too bad you ain't a boy. You wouldn't need it."

He laughed when she gave him a dirty look and walked away.

Ben's memory flashed back to that first time he took her to Goose Neck, about three or four years ago, and she wore that thing that made her look like a bloated clown. It swallowed her whole. He laughed out loud. She was a good sport. She was so little then. And there was the man who wanted to slit his throat. He sobered at the thought and pushed the memory out of his mind.

Aunt Letty walked in the door as Tilly dropped the bathing dress over her head. "Honey, you take my breath away."

Tilly leaned down and hugged her.

Tilly had become an accomplished seamstress after Emmy gave Aunt Letty her sewing machine when she left. She studied the Sears

Roebuck catalogue until the pages were torn.

She ordered bright yellow material from Mr. Moody and followed one of the patterns for a bathing suit. It was sleeveless, had a nipped-in waist held by a bow, and rows of tiny ruffles down the skirt ending above her knees. It was the latest fashion and was daring. Her day clothes came down to her ankles.

Aunt Letty smiled. Tilly had blossomed. "You be a dream, precious."

Tilly slipped into a colorful cotton cover, kissed Aunt Letty and ran to Ben's boat.

She waved a bag at him as she neared the boat, and he grinned back.

She took his hand when he held it out and stretched one long, bare, shapely leg over the side. Ben sucked in a deep breath and turned quickly away as soon as she was in the boat.

He rowed to the tree where he tied up the bateau and jumped out without looking at Tilly. "I'm going on. You come when you want to."

Hurt spread across her face, but she swung her legs over the side and followed him.

"Oh, this water feels good. We didn't get here at all last summer. Tilly, do you remember when . . . " He stopped in mid-sentence, gaping at her in the new swim-dress as she took off the coat and lay it across a branch.

"You ain't got no clothes on," he yelled and got out of the water. "What's happening to you anyway?" He glared at her. "C'mon, we're going home."

Tears sprang into Tilly's eyes. She ran up to him and banged on his chest with both fists and walked away, leaving him with his own fists balled. *I don't like her anymore. She's changed too much.*

When she walked in the door, Aunt Letty took one look and gathered her in her arms. "I don't know what happened, Tilly, but I have a pretty good idea. De numbskull. But don't worry, honey. He'll get over it."

And he did. They both were standing by Aunt Letty's booth in early August when they saw a familiar figure walking up the road toward them. They ran to Rufus and threw their arms around him.

"I can't believe you're here, Rufus. I can't believe it."

"I didn't want to stay up there any longer, Ben," he said with his arm around Tilly. He stood back and looked at both of them. "An I can't believe how you've both grown. Ben, you be two heads taller." He looked at Tilly and took a deep breath. "Oh my gosh, Tilly. You are beautiful."

She smiled at him and kissed him on the cheek.

Annoyed, Ben said louder than he meant to, "Rufus, does your dad know about your coming home?"

"No. I just walked out and hitchhiked here startin a few days ago. Have you seen him?"

"No, but I think he may be at the dock. He's lost some men and has been working all the time."

"I know. One of the reasons I came. I'm goin to help him, Ben. He needs me, and if we go to war, I want to be here before I go."

⁀)

Long Robby was overjoyed to see his son and even more so when he told his father his intention. "An I think Ben will join you, too, Dad. He talks about it."

Ben, Tilly, and Rufus spent August and most of September together and some of the time with Aunt Letty and Henny. They played kick ball, barbecued whatever they caught, fish or fowl, and sometimes Dicky Smart's spareribs. They went back to Goose Neck pond many times, Tilly, wearing her old long, and she knew ugly, swimming dress.

As fall once again began to show its changing colors, Ben went to the tabby house alone. He had a clear vision of what he wanted to do there. He had seen pictures in magazines that touched his senses deeply. He loved the natural world, but the garden had been a dream most of his life. He ordered the seeds as he had once before and started cleaning the debris away at times when Tilly or Rufus were busy with other things.

Just when the trees were at their most colorful, Ben asked Rufus and Tilly if they wanted to go to the tabby house with him. He wanted to surprise Tilly with all the work he had done. But when he invited

Rufus to go with them, Tilly felt her heart had turned on her. That was their place. It always had been. She started to leave with some excuse, but Rufus said he had to go home and help his dad repair the roof.

"You know, Ben, I really like doin things like dat. My grandfather was a master builder. I bet I could do well at building. But for now, I'm with Dad."

"Okay, we'll see you later. C'mon, Tilly."

She nodded, half wishing she could make him angry by not going but doubted he would care.

They walked slowly through the woods close to the marsh, Ben reminding her of Beau and the snake pit as he always did when they walked to the tabby plantation. She smiled. She couldn't stay mad at Ben. He had been her best friend since she came to the commune. Well, pretty soon after, anyway. She felt such warmth toward him she reached out for his hand, and he surprised her by taking it.

"Tilly, every time we come here, something bad happens. I sure hope nothing does today. I feel too good."

He showed her the work he had been doing in the garden and how the original plants were coming back. "They'll have buds in the spring. Look at that camelia. It's already got buds, and there will be other kinds blooming in the spring." He told her about the seeds he ordered before from Mr. Moody and the flowers that would bloom in the spring. They walked down to the river and sprawled out where the sun had warmed the grass.

Tilly turned over on her stomach and opened a book she brought with her and began reading. She was the picture of contentment, and Ben couldn't take his eyes off of her. He smiled. *I didn't mean it when I said I didn't like her. She's my best friend. I don't know what I would have done without her all these years.* He wanted to tell her how sorry he was for being such a jerk. His heart flooded with warmth. He would tell her later.

He reached over and trailed the back of his forefinger down her hand where she held the book, and she turned to look up at him.

"Tilly, I'm going back to the house. I been thinking a lot about this place. Mebbe no one owns it like no one owned the Gullah property. It's been in ruins for a long time. I think I'll check out the back property that looks out on the long road that we took the first time I brought you here."

She smiled at him and waved him on.

He walked through the brush but found more dead limbs than anything and was about to go back and join Tilly when he heard horses on the oak-lined road and stared unbelieving. They were unmistakeable. A mass of white hoods and cloaks coming toward him.

He gasped. *I don't believe what I'm seeing.* They were far enough away for him to get to Tilly. But what then? He raced back around the house to see Tilly walking toward the garden gate. *Thank God.* He ran to her, picked her up in his arms, and dashed inside the garden, leaping over bushes to get in back of the tallest and thickest growth of leafy plants, slipping the book under her head.

Startled, she tried to get his attention.

"Stay still, Tilly. Don't move an inch."

He lay on top of her, covering her body with his and wrapped his arms around her chest. His heart was pounding as he tried to regain his breath. *At least they can't see her if they find us,* he thought irrationally. *That's ridiculous. They'll kill both of us.*

Suddenly the roar of hooves and whinnying of horses surrounded them. He instinctively held Tilly closer to him, holding his breath.

The men were laughing and congratulating one another.

"Our first run, Junie, and we got five of those niggers."

"Didn't even have to pull em outta the house. They just came running out, their hands in the air, like we were their saviors."

Another round of boisterous laughter.

Junie said, "Let's meet at my place as usual and plan our next joy ride." He roared with laughter.

"Why not the Gullah down the road?"

"No," Junie said harshly. "They'd know it was me getting back at em. An they got ways," he said more softly. "We'll save that until we can get all of them together. When they're praying." He laughed raucously again. "Let's get one of the churches near here. Be nice if it's full."

Another round of laughter.

"Let's get going."

After the last sound of hooves had faded, Ben lay there feeling he was in a bad dream. The horror of the words he'd just heard pounded in his head like a drum. He was filled with rage. And fear. He needed to get back to Long Robby. He had to know about this. Ben knew about the Klan and knew what they did, but to be there and listen to the raw hatred of the men made it real. Children. Babies.

His body stiffened, and then he felt Tilly squirming under him.

"Tilly. I'm sorry, I must be crushing you."

He started to pull his arms out from under her when it became painfully clear to him that he was holding her breasts and had been since they lay down behind the bushes. *Oh God, no!* A wave of heat flushed through his body. He grit his teeth, jerked his hands out from beneath her, carefully raised his body from hers, and moved to her side. He dropped his head in his hands, moaning to himself, "You idiot," which he repeated like a mantra until he could get up.

Tilly was still lying on the ground with her eyes closed.

Loathing himself, he said in a voice he didn't recognize, "We gotta go."

She gradually pushed herself up and brushed off the leaves and dirt from her dress. She didn't look at him but walked toward the path they took to the commune.

Ben's throat was so constricted he couldn't have said anything if he wanted to. They walked silently through the woods until they were home. He took her to Aunt Letty and left without looking back.

He didn't see Long Robby at the docks and ran to Henny's, still cursing himself. *I can't think bout that now. I gotta get my mind on what Junie and those guys said.*

He told Henny every word as he had carefully remembered them. "I don't know what they've done, but it sounded like they killed a family in Botown."

Henny grimaced. "Probably burned them, Ben. The Klan is ruthless, and burning is what they do. They're filthy cowards, and how God let such trash on this earth is beyond me." He put his face in his hands, shaking his head. "C'mon. Long Robby can find out about what they did, and more to the point, we need to tell him what they said."

The next morning when the Gullah community met, there were only half the residents as would have been there a year ago.

"About Botown." Long Robby said angrily, "De Klan got hold of a young couple and their three little children, tied em to a stake, and set em on fire. The house, too. A neighbor saw de whole thing and hid until he could get to Sheriff McTeer." He choked and closed his eyes. "They won't stop now. This is what Junie's been plannin all along. We have to watch every move we make. Nothin is safe now. I'd hate to see one more of us leavin here, but if you got a mind to do that, now's the time. It ain't never gonna be like it was for us round here now."

Later that day, Ben found Long Robby sitting in his boat looking out at the sound.

"Long Robby, I'd like to fish with you if you still want me."

"Ben, you don't know how happy that makes me." He got out of the boat and hugged Ben. "You and Rufus with me. Nothing could be better than that. C'mon, Rufus is out pulling in some limbs to cut. Should be back by now and Sassy's got a pot of gumbo on the stove. We'll holler to Henny to come. How bout dat? Been a sad day. Spending the evening with friends will take some of that hurt away.

Walking home from Long Robby and Sassy's house Henny said, "I think ya made a good decision, Ben. I know you love dat boat, but you begun to look like a giant in a teacup. You waited til the time was right."

"My boat still suits me fine, Henny," Ben said, a little offended. "I ain't making the money I was with the new seafood store in town, and it don't make sense not to go with Long Robby. He supplies that store with his catch and others, too. Oh, I saw Mr. Hackney in town earlier, and he started to say something to me and then looked like he changed his mind."

"Hmm, wonder what that coulda been. Probably bout that little family. By the way, where's Tilly? I ain't seen her since this morning with Letty."

Ben picked up a pinecone and pitched it out across the yard. "I dunno."

Ben and Rufus stood by the spread of BBQ at Dickie Smart's farm gnawing on ribs and, as Ben said, in hog heaven. The entire commune had been invited as well as Ben and Henny for Dickie's birthday.

"Ben, as much as I love Dickie's pig, I can't eat BBQ without thinkin of Junie dat Halloween he came ridin in on us."

"Rufus, that is one memory I'd just as soon forget."

"Yeah," he said and sighed. "Junie never lets up. De Klan burned down de little Baptist church on de edge of Botown. No one was in it. Dad had talked to Sheriff McTeer in de next county and our sheriff, too. The sheriffs did what they could to warn de Gullah Geechee churches round here. Dat was bout all they could do. Every Gullah around heah be scared silly now."

"There's gotta be a way of stopping him, Rufus."

"Ha! Junie and his buddies can do anything they want and get away with it. And dat's a fact." He looked at Ben. "I haven't seen you with Tilly lately. You two okay?"

Ben swallowed hard. He knew this question would be coming sooner or later from Rufus.

"Tilly's a nice girl, but we outgrew each other. It was fun being with her when we were kids. But that's changed."

Rufus raised his eyebrows. "Well, childhood friends don't always grow apart." He looked across the yard where Tilly was sitting with Aunt Letty and Orie. "Ben, have you actually looked at dat girl lately?"

Ben blushed and hung his head down. "Been too busy lately to go to the market."

"Huh, you expect me to believe dat? What's going on, Ben?"

"Nothing's going on, Rufus," Ben answered, irritated. "Can we talk about something else?"

"Sure. I see some of my former school friends. Let's go over where they are. If you are really not interested in Tilly, there's a girl I think you might like."

⁓

Henny had been waiting to catch Aunt Letty alone and jumped at the chance when he saw Orie and Tilly leave the table where the three were sitting.

"Letty, what's going on with those two kids?"

She rolled her eyes at him. "What's goin on is they ain't kids, you goon."

After he had digested what she said, he blew out a long stream of air. "Oh, so that's it. Guess I am a goon. Ben goes around like half a person. Looks miserable."

"I reckon they both are. This time I ain't sure what to think. All I know is my baby is hurtin, Henny, and I can't bear dat."

"Has she tried to let you know anything?"

"How? She ain't been cryin dat I know of. Just mopin round. And I ain't askin nothin."

"Time, Letty. Time will tell."

"Time, humph."

⁓

Fishing with Long Robby was far more enjoyable than Ben had imagined. He was either on Long Robby's boat or on one of the other boats with a few of the crew he had known all his life. It was serious business, unlike his days on his own boat, trolling and hand netting and enjoying the small streams and marsh. This was casting nets, pulling in traps, line fishing at times, fighting the tidal waves, but it was always fun. The good humor was abounding no matter which boat he was on.

He and Rufus had become inseparable, and when they were not on the water, they were with Rufus's old friends from the island school. Victoria Smalls, the girl Rufus chose for Ben, was sweet, pretty, and witty, and he liked her, and he liked being with her. He never allowed himself to compare Victoria to Tilly. He never passed the market if he could help it, and when he did, there was such an ache in him, he cursed himself.

One afternoon near Christmas, Henny found Ben sitting on the back stoop, leaning over his knees with his head in his hands. He didn't miss seeing Ben quickly swipe at his eyes. Henny didn't say anything but put his hand affectionately on Ben's shoulder.

Ben didn't look at him but said, "Just tired, Henny. I like being with Long Robby, but it's hard work. Not like it was on my boat. Nothing's like it was."

"Have you seen Tilly, Ben?"

Ben braced. "No, only a couple of times with Aunt Letty at the market. She okay?"

It was the first time Ben had been willing to talk about Tilly, and Henny was surprised. And pleased. "I think so. Aunt Letty says she spends a lot of time sewing and reading."

He stood up, taller than Henny now. "I'm meeting Rufus and the gang over on the island later. I may be late coming home. But I think I'll go spend some time on my boat now. I haven't been on it lately."

"I'll see ya later then, son." Henny watched after him until he was out of sight.

CHAPTER 44

Christmas was as festive as ever. As always, Long Robby brought the biggest tree he and the others could carry from the woods to the park.

Christmas Eve the children yelled and jumped around until Long Robby called their names for a present. There were ring dances and singing—always singing.

Henny looked across the colorful turbaned heads to where Tilly and Aunt Letty stood. Despite all the gaiety surrounding him, he felt sad. He missed them.

Ben had noticed them earlier. Tilly looked so pretty in the red dress that draped around the curves of her figure. He let himself look at her longer than he had since that day at the tabby ruins. He winced and said, "Henny, I'm going back to the house."

"I'll go with you, son."

They walked a bit before Henny said, "Ben, I'm going to ask Letty and Tilly to come spend Christmas with us tomorrow like they usually do. I can't stand this, this whatever it is that is messing up our times together. I don't know how you feel bout it, but that's the way it is."

Ben breathed deeply and let his breath carry a moment of grief to his toes. "I'm sorry, Henny."

"Will you be here?" Henny asked with an edge to his voice.

"I guess not, Henny. Victoria's family invited all their friends to a party. I promised her I'd be there." He hated the way he was feeling and dug his fingernails into his palms. "I'll be with you in the morning like always, Henny."

Henny's chest tightened in disappointment but not surprise.

Christmas Day was not the same as those other times when they sat around the kitchen table laughing, eating every morsel of the delicious food, telling stories, and enjoying each other's company until wee hours. Not even that morning when Ben and Henny were together on the creeks as they were every Christmas.

Later, when Aunt Letty and Tilly joined Henny, they sat around the fireplace as Henny poured the peach brandy into the glasses, this time including Tilly's.

"Let's drink up to good times ahead," Henny said, thinking of what he feared was ahead as Germany sank more neutral ships in the North Atlantic. "An it will be if Wilson keeps us outta this war."

"Amen, Henny, I'll sure drink to dat."

In late February, Mr. Hackney sent word to Long Robby that he and a group of friends would like to talk to the Gullah community in front of the old warehouses.

"Oh Lord," groaned Long Robby to the remaining residents gathered in the prayer house. "I been waiting on this. Only good thing about it be we'll know what either Junie's up to or someone else's up to. Either one's goin to be bad for us. Guess you be prepared for dat."

At the given time for the meeting, the Gullah community waited for Mr. Hackney and the group of men he said would be with him. The fishermen's boats were lined up along the docks like sentinels. The Gullah stood on the large old brick path between the warehouses and the docks, their strong emotions and vivid imaginations taking them down, and the docks, the boats, and the warehouses with them, all sinking slowly to the bottom of the dark river.

When the two automobiles pulled up and the group of white men greeted them warmly, it made little difference in their feelings.

After Mr. Hackney introduced his friends, he said, "We want you to know about the decisions that have been made regarding the warehouses and what our intentions for them are. Mr. Morton told Long Robby sometime ago, and of course as you now know, Mr. Savage owned the warehouses. We made him an offer, which he accepted. While that may be of some relief to you, we are not unaware of how our plan will affect your community. For one thing, it will invade your privacy. We are truly sorry about that.

"We will start remodeling the warehouses in late March, maintaining the brick structure and character of the old buildings. The bottom floor will provide spaces for shops, and offices will occupy the second floor. We brought the architect's plans for you to look at. While you may resent this intrusion, we think you will not be too displeased with the outcome. In many ways, the shops and offices will increase your revenue. And we count on the activity we anticipate as increasing ours. As you know, there is a burgeoning growth in the barrier islands as well as in our town and others along the coast. These new citizens bring money. So we trade our quiet lives for more income and more advantages for our families. I'm speaking of your community as well as the town. It's progress."

"Mr. Hackney, what is this going to do to our fishing bizness?"

"We see nothing to interfere with your fishing business, Long Robby. In fact, I expect you will profit greatly. You already supply our town fish monger with your catch as well as your individual customers. Can you imagine how your business will grow with all the people moving into the area?"

He looked over to Aunt Letty, who was having her own thoughts, which showed plainly on her face.

"Letty, there is not a baker like you south of New York City, and I doubt anyone there can touch your cakes and pies. If you open in one of the new shops, you will have not only every maid from every household but her mistress as customers as well. Visitors strolling this walkway you are standing on will line up for a ham biscuit." He smiled. "We plan to offer a shop rental to you at half price the first year." He smiled again.

Aunt Letty remained silent.

"In addition to the warehouses, we negotiated a piece of land on Junie Savage's property where it adjoins your property to serve as a road to the walk. We were not surprised at his willingness to sell it. We are pretty sure he is running short of cash. The property runs from town to a point where it meets your property line by the water. It will not touch your land. There will be a nice parking area for cars, and if you permit, we will landscape this large brick path and make it enticing for visitors to walk here." He gestured toward the boats and nodded to Long Robby. "It just occurred to me a seafood restaurant would be a very welcome addition. Again, Long Robby, more income. Fresh seafood!"

"What's going to keep them from comin on up into our park?"

"We don't know, but we will try to work something out."

"When all this be finished?"

"We count on every detail being completed by November of this year. We want the Christmas trade."

"My people are havin a hard time dealin with all de changes we been goin through, Mr. Hackney. Now we be lookin at what you be plannin to do here. I know you have our interest at heart, but this ain't goin to bring back what we had."

"No, Long Robby. It won't." He looked around the group. "However, I genuinely hope that in some way the changes here will come to give you some satisfaction."

With that, the men got in the cars and drove away.

There wasn't one Gullah face with a smile on it as they all walked home.

⌒

There were reports of more KKK atrocities every month if not more often: burning of houses empty or full, burnings of small farms and churches, some empty or full. It seemed to the Gullah all their fears came suddenly and like a flaming ball. All this violence to the fragile stability of their lives. Progress, Mr. Hackney called it. It was just as Aunt Letty had feared and predicted months ago.

There were a few vendors who stayed with the market. Nellie with her jams said she had so much family in the commune and on Sapelo Island that moving away was not a thought in her head. Her blood went back to Bilali, the Muslim slave caught in Africa and taken to the islands first but brought back to Sapelo as head driver for the plantation there two hundred years ago. He was an important man and the father of future generations.

But Freezy packed up her table of chipped dishes, cups, old stainless ware, and other items that had been sitting on her table for months. Tom Cat gave the used and worn toys to all the Gullah children, and along with half a dozen more of the market vendors, he left for the north, hoping for kinder treatment and jobs.

Gone with them were the colorfully adorned booths and the constant chatter, the gossip whispered from stall to stall, the laughter and friendship. The market was left in ghostly silence. The prayer house, once the center of all discussion about anything, always overflowing so that many had to sit on logs outside to be a part of the shouts and songs and fervent cries to God, where one had to swoon standing up because there was no room to fall, was now half full, but no less fervent in worship.

Gone was the long turbaned train of women gaily balancing large baskets on their heads. Those who remained put all of their effort into holidays. Dicky Short still roasted his pigs for Halloween, and Long Robby cut down the largest tree the men could carry from the forest for Christmas.

Aunt Letty, looking around at the empty stalls, said to Nellie, "Don't make much sense to set up here anymore. What you gonna do?"

"I talked to a couple of the shops in town, Aunt Letty. They'll carry my jams, but they'll keep half of de money. Maybe when those new shops come to de warehouses, it might open up somethin for us."

"Dat's what I been thinkin. I have a good business with de town folk now as long as de maids come for what I bake. I been thinkin even if my pies and cakes are better than someone who might set up shop in town, those people dat buy from me now might find it a whole lot easier to send their maids down de street."

CHAPTER 46

Henny called to Ben coming up from the docks. "Sit down with me, Ben. I've been sitting here looking out at all the flowering trees and the plants that seemed to have sprung up overnight."

Ben stretched out in one of the porch chairs. "I guess you heard."

"Just did. It's not like we didn't know it was coming, Ben, but somehow it seems like a rude shock." He shook his head, grievously. "The war to end all wars, Wilson says."

"It's been all Rufus and I have been talking about all morning since the word got to us. Henny, we decided not to wait for the draft. We hear they're taking colored volunteers. All Rufus' friends are gonna leave day after tomorrow for Charleston and sign up." He hesitated before saying, "Rufus and I are going with them, Henny."

Henny felt his heart stop. "That soon?"

Ben fiddled with his harmonica. "I reckon so. I can pass for eighteen. I almost am anyway. But from what I hear, that don't matter. I'd be drafted anyway. I might as well get in now rather than wait and fidget bout it."

Henny let out a long sigh. "I hate to see you go, son." He shook his head sadly. "But as you say, you'd have to go sooner or later."

They sat listening to the birds singing and looking out over the field at the wildflowers swaying in the breeze. It was a lovely day. Too lovely to have to talk about war.

"Ben, I'm gonna ask you. You don't have to answer me. I been watching you skirt around Tilly for months. If you see her go one way, you go another. But I seen how you look at her when you thought no one was watching you. I know you, son. I know that tender heart. I don't know what happened to you and Tilly to cause this distance between you, but I think it's time to talk about it. You can't go off without getting it right between you."

Ben leaned over, his elbows on his knees, and lay his face on his balled fists. Tears welled. "I don't know anything anymore, Henny. I'm so mixed up I don't know what I feel."

Henny studied him for a minute. "I may be wrong, Ben, but I think something happened to make you see Tilly differently and it scared ya. She's not a little girl anymore. She's a lovely, desirable young woman."

Ben opened his fists and held his face in his hands, trying to hold back the tears. "She changed so quick, Henny. All I kept seeing was this same person I'd always known, an all of a sudden she was someone else. And I didn't know what to feel. She screwed me all up, Henny. How could I have all these new feelings about a little girl? That's what I felt, Henny. I was feeling things I didn't think I ought to feel." He stopped to get his breath. "I couldn't get near her without feeling that."

Henny moved his chair over close to Ben and reached out to rub his back and neck softly. "What happened, Ben?"

Ben sat up, his face blotched with tears, and rubbed his eyes. He told Henny everything that happened the afternoon at the tabby ruins. About the tenderness he felt for Tilly as they lay on the grass. He told about the Klan, which Henny already knew about, and then he told him of the moment he realized he was holding Tilly's breasts.

"I didn't mean to do that, Henny. I just wrapped my arms around her trying to protect her like I always have. When I felt them." He winced and cleared his throat. "When I knew what was in my hands I reacted. I couldn't stop. I got off her, but she knew. She knew what happened. I couldn't get over it, Henny. I hated myself for wanting her." The tears flowed. "I was so ashamed, Henny."

"Are ya still?"

"No. I've had a lot of time to think about it. But what a fool I was not to know what was happening sooner."

"Love is a funny thing, Ben. It can be there all along, loving someone as a friend, and then without warning it twists your heart inside out til it takes over your whole being. Love crazy it's called."

"That's part of what I felt. Crazy."

"And love."

"Yes."

"That's nothing to be ashamed of. I always felt something like this would happen someday. As close as you two are. Are you gonna tell her how ya feel?"

"I don't know, Henny. Now with my going off, it don't make much sense. Rufus, the other guys, and me leave in two days. I think I'll just let it be. After the war, we can see how we feel. I don't know what I'd say to her now."

"That's up to you, son. Just be sure that's what you really want."

The next morning, Ben and Henny got up early to glide along the creeks and inlets to the marsh in time to see the red sun come out of the depths. They sat quietly as he rose, the Lord of the skies, casting down his shining glory. *Dayclean.* Off with the old, on with the new.

"I'm gonna miss you, son. I'll be waiting on the porch looking til I see you."

Ben put the oars down and let the boat float among the reeds. "Henny, I've never told you what you mean to me. How your taking me into your home with you was the happiest day of my life. I wanted to tell you that before I left. Just how wonderful living with you has been."

He looked out over the marsh of greens and blues. "I'll be so happy to be back here with you an everyone."

Henny teared up and put his arm around Ben's shoulder, unable to speak as the boat drifted through the new shoots of the marsh.

"Henny, I want to say goodbye to Aunt Letty."

"We'll find her. I'll bet she's down at the docks looking at what they're doing to the warehouses. That's the source of entertainment lately."

And she was. She and Nellie were leaning back against the rails of the docks watching them haul out all the old remains of the interiors. When she saw Ben coming, she hollered, "C'mon down heah and see what they be doin to your old home."

The four of them looked upon the changes happening so quickly to the old buildings.

"Well, those rattling bunch of boards and rat nests never meant much to me. They was just a place to live."

Nellie said, "As far as I'm concerned, they may turn out to be our salvation." She put her hand on Ben's arm and smiled warmly. "We're goin to miss you, Ben. There has hardly been a day since you came to us dat I ain't seen you. You bring yourself back here soon."

"Thank you, Miss Nellie. I hope to."

Nellie said, "I be seein you later, Letty," and walked away.

"Ben, if you hadn't come to see me, I was gonna find you and whip your bottom." Aunt Letty reached out her arms to Ben.

He wrapped her in a hug, holding her a long time. "It would be kinda hard to get me over your knee now, Aunt Letty."

She reached up and rubbed his ear. "There's other parts." They both laughed, remembering the time she pulled his ear.

"I'd never leave to go anywhere that I didn't come see you. I love you, Aunt Letty. I've always loved you." He put his arms around her, both of their eyes welling up. "I'm gonna miss you." He rubbed his tummy and closed his eyes. "And I'll be dreaming of hot biscuits."

"You get yourself back here safe and sound, young man."

"I will. Just as soon as this war is over. I'll be back here." He looked at her, his sadness evident. "Aunt Letty, tell Tilly goodbye for me."

She looked into his eyes, her own heart heavy, wanting to tell him where he could find her. "I will, honey."

Later in the day toward sunset, Ben, who had been packing a few things in a small cloth bag, like his harmonica and knife, walked out to the kitchen where Henny was making shrimp and grits, Ben's favorite food.

"Henny, I want to go back to the tabby house. The garden is so pretty. Just as I thought it would be. The flowers are blooming now, roses too. I'd like to see it again and get a picture of it in my mind."

"You go on. I'll have dinner ready when you get back. And just keep away from trouble."

Ben walked onto the grounds of the place he had come to feel was a part of him. He sat on the old tabby bench overlooking the spring pond, the reflection of the trees, bushes, and spring flowers all shimmering on the surface with camellias, gardenias, roses, lilies, hyacinths, daffodils, the blooming redbuds, and dogwood blossoms.

His chest hurt. *Why can't I stop thinking about her? Oh, I miss you, Tilly.*

A pebble dropped into the stillness of the water, making expanding rings, and in the middle of the circle was Tilly's face. Startled he stared, unbelieving, sure his imagination had conjured this vision, when he felt her hand on his shoulder.

"Tilly."

Ben and Tilly lay wrapped in the thin, worn piece of blanket Aunt Letty thrust in her hands as she ran out the door. "Wrap it around your shoulders, baby. It's a little cool."

When Ben wasn't at Henny's, she didn't need to ask where he was.

Now in the dim light of the waking dawn, Ben slowly roused and pulled Tilly closer to his body. He nuzzled the softness around her neck, kissed her gently on her forehead, nose, and mouth, and wiggled his toes against her feet where they were entangled with his on the dewy grass.

"We have to go, Tilly."

She turned in his arms to face him, smoothing away the strands of yellow hair from his eyes, and pressed her lips against his. He turned her over on her back, memorizing every beautiful part of her.

"I wish I didn't have to go, Tilly. I wish we could stay here forever."

She smiled with such an expression of love that for a moment he wanted to grab her and run away.

"Someday. When I come home, we'll find a way to be together. I know that. It's what I'll think about the whole time I'm gone." He pulled her up and cradled her face in his hands. "I love you, Tilly. I think I've always loved you."

Arm in arm, they walked back to the commune, stopping where the grass was worn away. Where the market had been. Where he had first seen Tilly years ago—a scrawny, dirty, frightened urchin under Aunt Letty's table.

Ben groaned more than sighed out what he was feeling and pulled her to him, burying his face in her neck.

"We've always been together. I don't want to let go of you." They held each other breathing in the memories from the smells and sounds of the marsh and land.

"Tilly, the bus leaves for Charleston at noon. Will you and Aunt Letty come to Henny's and my house earlier? I don't want to be away from you more than I have to before I go."

She nodded, kissed him on the mouth, and walked toward her cabin.

When Ben got home, Henny was sitting on the steps, a smile on his kindly face.

"C'mon in. I got breakfast ready. Thought I'd fill you up in case the army don't."

They didn't talk about Ben's night with Tilly. They sat by the fire, lit for the cool spring morning, talking about Ben's leaving home. He had never been further than town. They talked about the Gullah community. What it would be like now. They didn't say more about their feelings for one another, but it was there, like the fire, warm and comforting.

Mid-morning, Letty and Tilly arrived, brown sacks in hand.

"Take these biscuits and buns with ya, Ben. You won't find these bittles where you're going."

Ben hugged her. "Aunt Letty, they'll be gone before I get to Charleston."

Tilly took Ben's hands and led him toward his room. Standing by the window, she opened her hand, which held a tiny wooden bird. She reached over to Ben and made a sign with the bird pointing to him and his flying back to her as the ducks returned to the lowcountry every winter. Then she took his hand and put her gift in it.

Ben stared at the tiny bird, trying to remember where he had seen it.

Tilly smiled, took the diminutive object back and pointed to her hand, and then put it against her heart.

Ben's mouth fell open. "Of course. I remember, Tilly. It's part of your toy. The little bird on a mast."

She nodded.

Ben ran his fingers over the smooth white surface, the little head turned out on its body with an expression as if all were well. He was torn with emotion, remembering that lost little girl that night.

Tilly smiled and placed her hand on her heart and then his.

"Thank you, Tilly." He gathered her in his arms. "I will come home to you. I promise you that. I want you to believe that. No matter what, I'll be back here with you as soon as I can. And I'll keep this little fella with me until I do." His eyes misted. "I promise you that. It's so small I'll keep it in my pocket. Nothin could take it from me."

CHAPTER 46

There wasn't any special gathering to see the boys off to war. The feelings, whatever they might be, were between each family. But as Long Robby and Sassy and their young family, Rufus, his schoolmates and friends and their families, Tilly, Aunt Letty, Henny, and Ben walked toward the bus station in Belleview, it seemed like a parade. The young colored men were proud. They were going to serve their country as equals with the whites. They were considered heroes in their community. They were volunteering, expecting respect and appreciation now and on their return.

It was good they did not know as they boarded the bus with pride that they would be treated with extreme hostility when they arrived for training. That they would never receive equal treatment. They would be delegated to segregated units. Very few sent to combat but were limited to serving labor battalions and never treated with respect.

However, they did not know this, and as the bus left Belleview, each window was a frame for a smiling brown face.

Ben's eyes were fixed on Tilly, his heart longing for the day he would come home. As the bus rolled away, he caught sight of a tall young man watching, far enough away not to be noticed. *Beau.*

Several days later, Henny was walking down to the docks and saw a lone figure heading toward the commune. He waited until he could see who it was.

"Rufus?"

"Yeah, it's me, Henny. Those white soldiers at de recruitment center didn't want any part of me. Henny, they say I have flat feet."

Henny almost chuckled. "Well, I'd be thankful for that if I were you, Rufus."

"Henny, all my buddies have gone to fight. Some may not come back. What am I supposed to do?"

"Help your daddy. Long Robby needs ya now more than ever."

"Well, I guess you're right bout dat. But it doesn't keep me from feelin bad bout not bein there doing my share."

"Have Ben and the other boys left for the training camp?"

"They were leavin when I got on the bus home. De recruitin officer told em they were de last bunch of coloreds de army was takin. De war department had cut off enlistin more volunteers. Said they had reached their quota for coloreds." He shook his head. "If dat isn't something. Won't white folks ever realize it be only de color of skin dat makes us different from one another?"

"That's a question I can't answer, Rufus. There's a lotta reasons why some poor ignorant people can't see that. C'mon. I'll walk to the docks with you. I know someone who'll be mighty happy to see you."

CHAPTER 47

The heat of summer had barely begun when Tilly got sick, vomiting all morning.

When it started, she thought she was dying and tried to hide her fear and misery from Aunt Letty so as not to worry her.

However, Aunt Letty was a midwife and aware there were more signs of pregnancy than morning sickness.

She followed Tilly to where she was hiding behind the outdoor kitchen and put her arms around the clammy, wretched girl.

"C'mon inside, honey."

Tilly, too weak to care anymore, gratefully let Aunt Letty take her back in the house.

Aunt Letty helped her on the bed and put a soothing cloth of Life Everlasting tea on her forehead and held her hands in hers. A bowl for more retching was nearby.

"Tilly, my sweet girl, you don't know what's going on with you?"

Tilly slowly shook her head, tears beginning to stream down her face.

"Your gonna have a baby, Tilly. I ain't too surprised. Sometimes all it takes is one time. You're a strong girl. There's no need to be afraid. You love Ben. Just remember he is a part of that baby in you. I'll help you with the sickness. It'll be over soon, an we'll live with happiness in our hearts til that blessed baby come to us."

She wiped the tears from Tilly's face with the cloth and leaned down to kiss her forehead.

"There's a lot of love around here for you, Tilly. You just know that. No one's judging you here. Just lovin you."

As the summer sent sweltering waves of heat, Henny attached a hose to his cistern, and he, Aunt Letty, and Tilly took turns spraying each other.

In the evenings, they were often joined by Orie, Nellie, and Joe at either Henny's or Long Robbie and Sassy's for barbecue or just sitting and talking of times past. Rarely, if ever, was Junie or Jim Crow mentioned. The Klan burnings had stopped nearby, and the summer was passing peacefully.

Tilly hadn't heard from Ben, so Henny made another trip to the post office in Belleview and was told mail was months behind. The news said none of the recruits would be going overseas until at least February or March when the government got the draft sorted out.

Tilly and Rufus formed a friendship, and when he wasn't fishing, they went on long walks around the commune or sat talking upon the benches the owners of the warehouses placed along the walkway. One afternoon, Rufus appeared on Aunt Letty's porch with an exquisitely made cradle. Tilly was so touched she put her arms on his shoulders and kissed him on the cheek. Even with his dark skin she could see he was blushing.

Tilly put her hands over her heart and smiled.

Tilly blossomed in pregnancy, and as the winds of a coming fall swept away the scorching heat of summer, she began walking to the tabby ruins when she wasn't helping Aunt Letty. When the bench became too uncomfortable, she hesitantly asked Rufus to take the folding lounge chair Henny had given her to the garden. She had never shared the place that meant so much to her and Ben, but it was either asking for Rufus' help or her not going. As she suspected, Rufus found the garden enchanting but left after setting it up for her, seeming to understand her need to be there alone. He had begun to come around to the house or shop more often, which she knew Aunt Letty noticed as well. She wasn't that concerned but hoped nothing would interfere with their friendship. Rufus was lonely, too, and she liked him. He was the company she needed to take her mind off of her concern for Ben.

Ben's spring and summer flowers were now part of the brown earth. The dogwood leaves were aflame, and the perennials of fall were dying back, but there were chrysanthemums, vibrant purple beauty berry, winter roses, primroses and azaleas, and always the beautiful fragrant boxwood.

On one nice day after a November heavy rain when there was a cool breeze and the sun was ablaze in the blue sky, Tilly looked at Aunt Letty and pointed in the direction of the tabby house.

"Just take care, honey. There'll be some muddy spots along the way." She put her arms around Tilly and kissed her brow. "You ain't got but six weeks now before that precious little one comes to us."

Tilly lay back in the easy chair Rufus had placed near the pond, her hands resting on her belly, feeling the movements of her baby, thinking about Ben and the last night she was there with him. She smiled and caressed her stomach, feeling love for the baby inside her. It was because of that night he was there. The comforting thoughts and warmth of the sun lulled her like a lullaby into a deep, tranquil sleep.

Startled by loud banging noises and raucous voices, Tilly bolted up in the chair. Regaining her senses, she became alarmed, remembering the men who had come here when she was with Ben. She got out of the chair stealthily and crept behind the bushes, leaning against the wall. They were too far away for her to hear their words well, but their angry voices terrified her. And the banging. *What were they doing?*

They hadn't come to the garden before, and if they did, she doubted they would notice her behind the thick brush of garden plants. Maybe they weren't the same hateful men who burned babies and children. *Maybe.* But she felt they were. She would stay hidden in the bushes until they were gone. *The chair! Her shawl was on the chair.* What if they did come to the garden and saw it? A cold shiver ran through her body.

She cradled her stomach in her arms, silently humming and swaying gently to soothe her child and herself.

As the voices grew louder and the men began to chant, she heard another voice. One she knew. She crawled further along the wall, closer to the gate opening, hoping to hear better. It was Rufus. Rufus yelling, "Where is she? What have you done with her?"

Tears streaming down her face, she instinctively leaned further into the wall, branches tearing her skin. What was happening? Why was Rufus there?

"Well, we got you," a muffled but grating voice shouted back. "An you're not gonna be here long enough to care about anyone else."

Again, the roaring, maddening chants blared out like trumpets, reaching a horrendous peak. Then a lone cry. It was Rufus. She knew that. As quickly as she could through the tangled bushes she crawled to the gate and carefully looked out.

She wasn't aware of her piercing scream as it soared over white shrouds, torches, and Rufus roped to the wooden cross. She was held within the unearthly wail of agony and pain as memory spirited her over this shadowed land to another place, another time, to white columns, ancient trees, a child's swing hanging still as death. She was the child watching from her bedroom window as blotches of white and torches of fire danced around the wooden cross where her parents burned. She watched that child, without a sound, until she was snatched from the window by her uncle.

Tilly saw all that before her vision blurred into darkness and she was lifted into Bones' arms. She didn't see Bones leap through the fire and rescue Rufus from the cross. She didn't see the tall white candles, which replaced the white cloaks, melt into the earth as Bones carried her away. Nor did she see Rufus running beside him back to Aunt Letty.

Tilly had not awakened when Bones put her on the bed and told Aunt Letty what he knew Tilly saw.

"Oh my good Lord, Bones. No tellin what be goin through her mind." She looked lovingly down at Tilly and kissed her forehead.

"Rufus, go get Orie. Tell her she gotta come right now.

"Bones, you go, too." She looked him in the eye. "Stay near."

Aunt Letty removed Tilly's clothes and checked to see if there were any signs of the baby coming, then lay a blanket over her. *There may not be no sign, but dat baby be comin. Soon. An I oughta know.* She thought of all the little babies she had delivered. Each so special. But this one was Tilly's. *Her Tilly.*

As soon as she laid a cloth wrung out in Life Everlasting tea on Tilly's forehead, she began to moan. Her eyes were closed, but she began turning her head side to side slowly, the whimpers becoming more distressed. She opened her eyes and looked around, not seeming to know where she was. She started sobbing and reached her arms out to Aunt Letty.

"Oh, my precious Tilly," Aunt Letty crooned, tears streaking down her face. "You're home now. Everythin be fine now."

Tilly leaned into Aunt Letty chest and whispered in a strained, weak voice, "Mama."

Aunt Letty was overcome with emotion. Not only to hear Tilly speak, but for her to say words she never thought she would hear again when she lost Pet. To her, the most beautiful words in the world. Love flowed through her like a song. "I'm heah," was all she could say as she rocked Tilly back and forth, sobbing with her.

By the time Orie arrived, Tilly had fallen back into the darkness. Orie knelt beside them and took Aunt Letty's hand.

"Rufus told me what Tilly saw. He said he was almost done with, the flames touching his feet, when Bones came. Tilly was passed out when Bones got there."

"Bones told me most of dat, too, but it be what Tilly saw in her mind I want to know. Well, dat will come later when she's ready to talk about it."

With a look of total surprise, Orie's head jerked up. "Talk?" she almost shouted, catching herself and slapping her hands over her mouth. Still excited but in a lower voice she asked, "Tilly be talkin, Letty?"

Letty dabbed at her tears and took a moment to answer. "Orie, she said, 'Mama.' To me."

"I told you long ago, Letty. This girl was meant for you." Orie brushed Tilly's hair away from her face. "Letty, what does her voice sound like?"

"Not right. Scratchy and weak. I guess time will tell on dat. But she be talkin, Orie. Dat's de gift Heaven sent to us even if what caused it be heartbreakin."

"Her uncle. He told you, didn't he?"

"A little but it was hard to understand him. He was so sick, and I could hardly hear him most of de time. But I knew what he was sayin was bad. Too much for a little girl to see." Aunt Letty dipped the poultice in the tea, wrung it out, and put it back on Tilly's forehead.

"Orie, I believe with all dat's in me dat this baby is makin its way to come before sunlean. It's been through hell and high water today, and I think it wants to come out."

"Any signs of dat?"

"No, there ain't no signs, but I feel it, Orie. I hear it inside its sack. I hear it murmurin. I feel it in de spirits comin down from my mama and her mama. This baby comin, an I need you to get things from de kitchen for me. This baby is comin early, but Tilly's strong, and dat baby inside her is strong."

They sat beside Tilly, the sisters, waiting, and when the first pain jarred Tilly awake, they were ready.

A red-faced little boy announced his entrance into the world with a cry the fishermen heard in the channel.

Aunt Letty, who had been up most of the night, not only tending the tiny baby but helping him suckle his mother, told Tilly when she was fully awake, "This boy's got his daddy's lungs, Tilly."

Her voice still weak and strained, Tilly said, "And blond hair."

"And he's got your beauty, Tilly, but his hair ain't blond. It be as red as de new morning sky."

"Does Henny know?"

"He sure does. Orie told him last night. An dat you be talkin, honey. He'll come over later this afternoon when you've had a good chance to rest."

The following morning, Tilly said, "I've been thinking of naming him Benjamin Findley Clary. I think Ben would like that."

"Honey, I think Henny'll be de one who'll like dat." She laughed. "Benjamin Findley Clary, born into our world on November 9, 1917."

As they knew he would be, Henny was beside himself. "How about calling him Finn, Tilly? My dad was called that because of his red hair. I think it's a name for redheads in Scotland."

"It's perfect."

Overcome with joy, Henny went to the post office in town and sent off a letter to the war department asking if there was any news on Ben Clary. He mentioned that Ben had a son and he wanted him to know. And once more he said his own prayer to who might listen, asking to hear something about his boy.

Near dayclean, Bones, as quiet as the moon, slipped in and stood over Finn's cradle. He smiled then left as quietly as he had come.

CHAPTER 48

Tilly's voice got stronger, and over the next few weeks while her baby slept in Aunt Letty's arms, she told Aunt Letty how the burning cross brought back memories that had been too painful to remember. She stopped talking when the pain of remembering became too much for her. When she remembered how happy she had been with her mommy and daddy and how much she loved them.

"I was just a little girl. What I saw. How could I live with that? My mommy and daddy. Watching them die.

"I was sitting at the window watching when my uncle came. We ran down the stairs as the flames started up. We ran past them and out the back to my grandmother's house. She lived next door. Mommy, Daddy, and I used to walk over there in the afternoon for tea. I don't know what happened to my grandmother. For a long time, I kept seeing my mommy's face and then it would go away." She was crying so hard Aunt Letty took her in her arms.

"Shh, shhh. Dat's enough now, Tilly. Just let it come when it wants. It'll all pass by in time. It's too sad to hold onto an you got this precious little boy and Ben when he comes back, an you always got me lovin you."

Tilly told her, clutching Aunt Letty's hand, that when Uncle Louie saw the men in white coming down the long, tree-lined road to her grandmother's house, he picked her up and ran to the marsh.

Her grandmother had hidden the beloved help down in a secret passageway that had been made during the war. "She promised Uncle Louie she would join them below where they would be safe if the house burned. I remember all that now. It keeps coming back. Oh, Mama."

"Shh, that's enough for now."

On other days, she told what she remembered about Uncle Louie and what they went through to get to this place. "We stayed in the marsh for a long time, walking along the shore. I think that's when Uncle Louie began getting sick. He was coughing so hard. We hid during the day most of the time, then he watched for wagons and sometimes cars he felt were safe enough to stop for rides.

"We slept wherever we could. A lot of the time he hid me so he could beg for food. Or we picked what we could out of farms or gardens. Uncle Louie told me because they had different-colored skin, people would think he stole me. He seemed to be always frightened. He got so sick and kept saying he had to get me to some place. I know he was so glad to get here. I had forgotten everything. Things would happen or I would see something, and it would frighten me. And I didn't know why."

When the trauma of the memories was wrung out of her, Tilly slept for long periods of time except when she was nursing or the baby was asleep. He was a good, healthy baby for one born early, and she and Aunt Letty were grateful for that.

Finn brought life back into the Gullah community. On the days Tilly, carrying Finn, and Aunt Letty and often Henny walked to the docks to see how close the workers were to finishing the warehouses, there would be a crowd gathered within minutes to oooh and ahh over the little red-haired fella.

~

Tilly didn't hear from Ben until late January. She read the letter, walked to the wall, and angrily beat against it.

"Lawdy sakes. What be de matter, chile?"

"Ben's gone. He's been gone. He doesn't know about Finn, and I don't know where he is." She began to cry.

"Now just stop dat. You done cried enough, and it ain't good for you or Finn. Tell me what he said."

Tilly blew her nose and read parts of the letter that would interest her. "He was at a basic training camp in Virginia after leaving here. He says he'll be leaving in a few weeks to go overseas with a special group called the American Expedition Forces. They told him he was selected because of his size, strength, and agility. '*I laughed at that, Tilly. I didn't know what agility meant for one thing. I do now and I reckon that's right. I can get around pretty good. Whew, we sure have worked hard, Tilly. Not like fishing in one of the streams at home.*'

"He couldn't tell me where he was going. He wrote this in July. And he asked me if I had gotten his letters."

Again, Henny went to the post office and was told they were ill informed as to what was happening to all the letters sent out but heard most were stacked up somewhere or lost.

CHAPTER 49

The warehouse shops were finally completed in February, and the Gullah were invited to a festive ceremony on the old path. The brick had been cleaned and polished to a rich burnish. The architects had added attractive touches of copper, brass, and iron to the old brick buildings, bringing sighs of admiration and comments like, "Who'd a believed it!"

There were two buildings and eight nice-sized shops in each, all of which had been spoken for. Henny and Rufus helped Aunt Letty set up her space with her complaining the entire move. It had been obvious to her that the wood stove she had always used was not going to work in the new shop. She complained so bitterly when the owners refused to let her have it moved to the new shop, they offered to set up the kitchen for her, mostly due to the insistence of their wives. She was to pay the improvements off at a very low cost over time.

"Hmphh," was her response to the new and latest model gas stove. "They think what I bake is gonna taste de same from this pile of metal?" But, secretly, she was excited and enthusiastic, as was Tilly, about trying the new equipment and being in the Dock Shops, as they were called.

From the beginning, there was more business than any of the shop keepers could have imagined. During opening hours, there was a constant cortege of fashionable shoppers along the attractive promenade. When the Gullah proprietors had a moment to spare, they stood just outside their door looking for friends to call to or for a quick wave, bringing back memories of the gaiety of the market.

～

The winter passed without incident. Finn was fattening up. And as close as Tilly and Aunt Letty were before, they now became inseparable. They worked together at the bakery all day and played with Finn all evening. Henny felt left out and told them so. They laughed but started spending more time with him, and when it was helpful, they took the cradle to his house, between feedings, much to his delight. There was still no word from Ben, but when one or the island boys came home on crutches, Rufus asked him if he knew anything about Ben. He hadn't seen him but heard some time ago that he was in the trenches, maybe in Nancy, but he wasn't sure.

"Nancy is not a good place to be, from what I've heard."

In early July, Henny was sitting on his porch working on a net for Long Robby's new boat when he saw Beau Morton walking toward his house. He jumped up to greet him, stretching out his hand.

"Beau, this is a nice surprise. Wish I had a cooler place for us to sit but c'mon up here and tell me what's on your mind."

"I'm afraid it's not good news, Mr. Findley. It's from the war department. The soldier who was to deliver it to you didn't know how to get here and left it at the post office who sent it to my law firm. Why, I am not sure. Perhaps they didn't know how to reach you, although that seems rather ignorant."

Henny stared at the envelope, his hands shaking so badly, he couldn't open it.

"May I help you?"

"Please."

Henny stared at the letter. It was the usual form letter. *"We regret to inform you that your ward, Ben Clary, is missing in action . . . "*

For the second time in his life, Henry was frozen with fear. He had a flash of Ben as a boy lying unconscious in bed, so afraid he was losing him. Now he was at war, and Henny was not able to envision anything around the young man he considered his boy. He sat, looking at the words, now a blur, on the page.

Henny turned to Beau, choked up, and asked, "What do you think this means, Beau?"

"I wish I knew, Mr. Findley. I hope it means he's just missing now. They don't know where he is, but that doesn't mean he is somewhere, alive and well."

Henny looked at him with such sadness that Beau's usual reserve melted, and it was a minute before he could say, "I'm so sorry. I wish I could tell you somethin more positive."

"You gave me hope, Beau. Thank you.

"Beau, I guess this is as good a time as any to bring this up. There's something I been meaning to see your dad about for a long time. Maybe you could help me with it." He told Beau what he knew of the Swedes. "I thought that maybe your dad might have known something about them. I think Ben may have belonged to them."

"I will ask him as soon as I get back to the office, Mr. Findley. I hope we will have some news for you. I can imagine how much it would mean to you to have an answer to Ben's origin."

⁓

After Beau left, Henny waited to go to Aunt Letty and Tilly's cabin until he was sure they would be home from the shop. He stood outside the door to steady himself, but Tilly saw him.

"What are you doing standing out here, Henny?" She started to laugh then saw the expression on his face. "Come in, Henny."

Little Finn was crawling on chubby legs toward him as fast as he could. Henny picked him up, sat down, and told them what the letter from the war department said. Tilly, without saying a word, took Finn from his arms and went into the bedroom. Aunt Letty stared at the floor.

"Dat boy's got to come home."

The next morning, Tilly came out of the bedroom nursing Finn and smiled at Aunt Letty. "He's all right, Mama. I know he's all right." And that was all she ever said about it.

⁓

Several days later, Beau went to Henny's house and told him what his father knew. "He did know the family, Mr. Findley. As a matter of fact, it seems he knew them fairly well. Their name was Lindstrom." He smiled. "It's interesting, Mr. Findley that *strom* in Swedish means river."

Henny just nodded.

"Dad said they were a fine young family. Close to his own age. The couple moved to Minnesota from Sweden, had several children, and traveled south until they found the land they bought. They, according to Dad, felt they had found paradise. Dad handled several legal matters for them, including the purchase of the land. They became friendly enough to invite Dad for lunch, entertained him with music. Each member of the family played a musical instrument. They played fiddles, accordians, and even the youngest played wooden whistles or flutes. And there was a baby boy. He said it was a matter of deep sadness for him when the coroner contacted him and told him of their death. It happened so quickly. As you know, yellow fever doesn't waste time killing its victims.

"I think the coroner knew Dad might have known them or done some legal work for them. Dad knew, or knows, most people who live close to Belleview. He told Dad the approximate ages of the deceased family but didn't mention the baby boy. Dad was curious about that and insisted they search around the property. When the baby wasn't found, they assumed he either crawled off into the water or an animal got him."

"That baby could have been Ben, Beau."

"Yes, Mr. Findley, he could have been. But we will never know for sure."

Henny looked down at the floor. "Beau, what happened to the Lindstroms' property?"

"The authorities asked Dad what he knew about family, but all he could tell them was they didn't have family in this country, and they hadn't mentioned if they still had family in Sweden. Without heirs, there is a certain period of time for relatives to show up. If they aren't found, the property passes to the state. In time, that property was sold and the house torn down."

"Does Mr. Morton have any papers left about the Lindstroms?"

Beau shook his head regretfully. "No. I'm afraid not. He destroyed what he had after their death."

"Well. I guess that puts the end to that. But I still want to believe, and do, that was Ben's family, Beau. I don't think I'll say anything to Tilly about this. Not now, anyway."

As Beau got up to leave, Henny stopped him. "Did your dad say what the young father did for a living?"

"Why, yes he did. He was a carpenter and doing quite well. He built the house they lived in, as a matter of fact. But he told me he loved flowers and plants and hoped to add landscaping to his work."

CHAPTER 50

The friends in the community were thoughtful of Tilly and didn't talk about Ben and the letter. Thanks to some council from Aunt Letty, they gave her needed space. Not so Rufus. He hung around her like a fly over honey. Tilly was thinking of how she could say something to him without hurting his feelings when Long Robby did it for her. He took Rufus aside and told him, "Rufus, you be headed for a broken heart. Tilly's only got one love and only ever gonna have one love, be he dead or alive. You get your mind off her, boy."

Rufus moped around for a few days but heeded his father's words. He spent more time on the island, visiting his friend who had come home wounded, Victoria and her brother, and a few others who had been too young to enlist. In late August after staying longer in the night than usual, he was crossing the sound, battling the waves, when he saw flames on the Gullah commune shoreline.

"Oh my God," he screamed. The boats. He sounded the horn on the open fishing boat, praying that someone could hear it. By the time he got close enough to see what was happening, there was such a mass of flames he steered away from the docks and tied his boat down on a post where the path to the shops began. He ran as close to the flames as he could and was able to reach the emergency alarm on a piling set away from the wooden docks. Within minutes, Long Robby and the rest of the fishermen along with just about everyone else living within earshot was staring at the red embers of the crumbling wood pilings, the docks, and burning boats.

It was only after they all turned away in heartbreak that they saw the damage to the warehouse shops. The windows had been smashed and buckets of grease thrown inside, covering all the contents.

There was nothing they could do in the middle of the night but let the flames die. With heavy hearts, and too soon for rage, they all went home.

"We're ruined, Dad," Rufus moaned the next morning.

"No, we ain't, Rufus. We sure ain't ruined. We just got a mess to clean up, build new docks, and get new boats."

Rufus looked at him like he had been affected mentally by the fire.

"Rufus, when Mr. Hackney brought his insurance man to see de warehouses, he invited me to talk to him. Mr. Hackney encouraged me to get insurance because I would be taking away bizness from some white biznesses who sold fish. Some questionable white folk who might not like de competition. He told me of a colored man in Wilmington who set up a food store near an established white man's store. He took all de colored business away from dat white man. De colored man's store burned down and he with it. So I reckoned what he said made sense."

He looked at the mess. "We got some work to do, but I got insurance to pay for new pilins. Rufus," he slapped him on the back, "we be getting new boats. We ain't got time to build boats now. We gotta get back in dat water and get fish or we'll lose our new customers. We be goin to Charleston to buy brand new boats, and we ain't hangin out de back of an old wagon to get there neither. We be goin by train."

Crews came in to clean the damage to the Dock Shops, and within two weeks, no one would have known there had been a greasy, nasty mess in the boutiques. The contents of the shops needed to be replaced, which was a problem for some.

Nellie bemoaned her jellies and jams. "What am I going to do, Letty?"

"Make more."

It didn't take much thinking to know who was behind the fire and shop destruction. But, once again, the Gullah were resigned to turn their heads.

The tenants of the shops were busy moving back in when Johnny, the wounded soldier friend of Rufus, pulled his skiff along side one of the new docks. Rufus and Long Robby helped him tie up as a friendly gesture.

"You haven't seen all this since it's been finished, Johnny. What dya think about it?"

"Mighty fine, Mr. Cinque. I'm sure sorry about all de trouble you've had."

"Well, it's over now." Long Robby looked Johnny up and down. "Well, if you don't look sharp in dat uniform. You goin to a shindig?"

Johnny laughed. "No, I just want to walk up and down that street in Belleview in my uniform. I want those folks to see how proud I am I fought in the war for them."

Long Robby brushed aside the concern that flashed through his mind. "Well, boy, I am sure they will be as proud of you as I am."

"Do you want me to go with you, Johnny? I'd be happy to."

"Thanks, Rufus, but I'm not in any danger now, not in my uniform. The war changed things for us."

When Johnny didn't come back that afternoon and the skiff remained at the dock, Rufus became worried and walked to his house and told his dad.

Long Robby frowned. "Rufus, maybe he's just browsin around." He rubbed his chin and sighed. "I know it's somethin to think about, but who'd hurt a soldier, no matter his color?"

"You know who, Dad."

They waited another two hours and walked into town to look for him. They asked in the various stores if he had been seen. Some said they had seen him walking much earlier. The rest shook their heads no. It was late, and the stores were closing. They walked back home and sat at the docks, hoping he would come.

It wasn't until dusk when Brian, the Hackney's chauffeur, driving back from Sandsboro, noticed something unusual on a tree beside the Belleview sign at the entrance to town. He stopped long enough to see a young Gullah boy in an army uniform hanging from a limb.

The town was in an uproar. The Gullah in the community and those on the island were devastated, enraged, and ready to fight, no matter what happened to them. They called a meeting of everyone in both places, the island and the commune, for the next morning. They couldn't count on the town to do anything. They never could.

The meeting was held. But as usual, under such circumstances, the Gullah knew there was nothing they could do but scream out their frustration into the marsh and to God.

CHAPTER 51

Aunt Letty, Tilly, and Finn were cuddled together in her bed, talking late into the night about the young soldier friend of Rufus', the sadness that had come to them over the years, how the trauma of Tilly's parents' death still haunted her but was easing with the help of Aunt Letty's love and wisdom about pain. They laughed at remembered funny times like when Aunt Letty pulled Ben's ear and caught Tilly's mischievous look after she had done the same. Tilly giggled remembering the circus girl who kissed Ben and how jealous she had been. She loved him then; she had almost always loved him. She told Aunt Letty how grateful she was for the unseen hand that led her to the loving woman who became her mama.

When Tilly's head slipped from Aunt Letty's shoulder, she gently tucked her in along with Finn, pressing her lips against their two heads. One dark, one red.

She lay down on the day bed where she insisted on sleeping now that Finn had grown out of his cradle and let the happiness she felt at that moment fill her heart. She thought of her life, of those she had loved: her mama and papa, little Pet, Orie, and her friends here. But most of all, she thought of the precious gift of the girl and her baby asleep in the other room and gave thanks to her God.

She heard him open the door and waited until Bones was beside her. She knew he was coming.

"Wrap something over you, Letty, and come with me."

They walked to the kitchen behind the house before Bones said anything more.

"Letty, de king is here."

Her eyebrows flew up. "The king is here?"

"Letty, he's come to take care of our misery. And his. It be time now."

"Now? Meaning *now*?"

"Tonight. As soon as you get dressed. It be Junie, Letty. If you still want to be de one to do this, you gotta come now."

She leaned against the wall of her old beloved kitchen and closed her eyes. She had so much to live for. Tilly and Finn needed her. Was revenge worth it if something happened to her?

"I know what you be thinkin, Letty. It be up to you."

"I've hated that beast since I was a girl, Bones. I've wanted him dead all these years. Somehow, now, it don't seem as important to me. I'm worn out, Bones. I can hardly get my breath walkin. I don't want Tilly to know. I just want time with them."

"I know dat, Letty. I just lettin you know."

Bones started out the door. "Bones. Wait. I be sorry if I don't go."

Bones led Letty through the old slaves' woods where she walked to see him every Thanksgiving. There was nothing alive there but the trees, shrunk and bony with age like the bones scattered about the broken markers.

She had never been afraid of passing through here. She always felt the spirits of her ancestors nearby. Tonight, she shivered at the silence and stayed close to Bones.

Slowly, coming almost as eerily as fog moves in unexpected, there was a faint humming. She was imagining things, she told herself. The spirituals were first sung here by those crying out their pain and longing. That was what she heard. It was in her mind. She was good at imagining.

That's a lie, Letty Savage. You be only good at imaginin Junie dead.

Bones was next to her. She didn't have anything to be afraid of. She had never been afraid of anything but Junie. Her people had endured almost three hundred years of inhuman diabolical treatment by the Savages, and tonight she was going to end the history of that evil line of monsters forever.

Letty stopped, and Bones took her hand to lead her on. "Bones, what's that hummin? I ain't crazy. And it be gettin louder."

"It's de spirits, Letty."

As the murmuring sounds took over the woods, a low rumbling began shaking the ground beneath them. Letty didn't say more to Bones but stayed by his side, certain the earth would explode under her feet.

"They be restless, Letty."

They left the woods and stood on the lawn of Grandterre and faced the magnificent structure of the plantation, a symbol of what was once called the gracious south.

"Bones, it be as beautiful a place as it ever was. The grandest of all de plantations anywhere. I heard dat over and over. Just look at it. Those big white columns across dat wide porch. How can anythin be so beautiful have such meaness about it?"

Letty's mind's eye circled the house: mean dogs barking, her mother in the kitchen, her father tending the fireplace, her grandmother singing to her. The images flew by. She and Orie as children, Pet, little Pet running to her, dogs, then faster, too fast to see it or know it, great-grandmothers, great-great-grandfathers in the fields, cotton, slaves dying in rice fields, children crying, whips, singing, singing in the fields, praying in the woods, screams, spectral shapes flashed, slaves, chains, the first bought, Jinga, language born, Gullah Geechee, Gullah Geechee.

Peace settled over her. It flowed through her as sweet brandy and warmed her being.

As if prodded by her ancestors, Letty looked up as an explosive crack shattered the night sky, opening the heavens to blinding light. Then there was darkness, as black as Satan's den.

A sound roared from above, "Come. Come."

"Bones, dat's a lion. A white lion."

"Dat be de king. King Oosafella, Letty."

The fierce expression on the white face against the black sky didn't frighten her. She welcomed it.

"Come," the resonate voice howled again.

Then it was deathly silent, and she and Bones watched as the skeletal forms of all the slaves who had lived and died at Grandterre came out of the woods. They marched, humming louder and louder, toward the old plantation.

Letty put her hand on Bones' arm. "Look, Bones. Look at de door."

Junie stood, wild-eyed, naked, a half-empty bottle in his outstretched hand. His dogs cowed behind him. He turned to run back in the house but was met by the marching ghosts, moaning. He hollered for help, threw the bottle down, and ran out onto the lawn to Letty and Bones.

"You did this," he screamed. "You make them leave," he demanded, his voice quavering.

The bones of his slaves closed in and surrounded him, marching in place, waiting.

Terrified, Junie fell to his knees. "Why are you doing this to me? I was your master."

The deafening marching pounded on the ground before him as the humming got louder.

Junie knelt before Letty. "Make them go away, Letty. You and I were friends."

Bones took out a long knife and handed it to Letty.

Junie hunched over at the sight of it. "Letty. I didn't mean to kill your girl. I was just a boy. It was Daddy who done it. I didn't do it." He was crawling on the ground, begging.

"Bones, make them go away." He shielded his face from Letty and crouched over in a ball.

"I waited all my life for this moment, Junie. I never wanted anythin more than to see you on your knees beggin. Or to feel puttin a knife through your heart."

Junie was sobbing and digging at the earth.

"But you ain't worth my soul." She handed the knife back to Bones and walked through the phantom slaves, to the edge of the woods. Bones joined her to watch as the thousands of ghosts of Gullah ancestors moved in on Junie. They watched as the unearthly forms turned, leaving a black space on the ground, and walked silently back into the woods, returning to spirit. They watched rage take expression on the King's face as he blew a stream of fire down to the bottle of alcohol lying on the floor of the old plantation porch. His work done, his image faded from the sky.

Aunt Letty looked at the scorched circle where Junie had been, begging on his knees, and felt all the pain she had carried moving out of her heart. Junie was gone. "Walk home with me, Bones. I feel a little worn out."

"You got a reason to feel dat way, Letty."

She didn't tell him of the pain in her heart. She knew he couldn't fix it. He did other things, but he couldn't fix an old ailing heart.

"I just want to go home, Bones. I want to forget all this. I never want to think of Grandterre or de Savages again."

The following day, when it was discovered the plantation had not only burned to the ground but the only remaining sign of anything ever having been there was a broken whisky bottle, they said, "Guess he got drunk and burned it all down."

⌒

It was near dawn when Aunt Letty got home, and Tilly was sitting up in bed waiting for her. "Mama! Where have you been?" When she saw Aunt Letty lean against the door, she ran to her. "Are you all right?"

"I'm fine, honey. I just need a little rest."

Tilly put her arm around her and led her to the bed and lay as close to her as she could. "I love you, Mama." Tilly reached over and pushed a strand of Letty's hair away from her face, twining her fingers between the strands. She wiped a tear from Aunt Letty's cheeks and put her face next to hers. "Why are you crying, Mama? I love you so much. I don't know what I would do without you."

"I be fine, honey. Just tired."

Finn crawled on top of Aunt Letty, put his little hands on her face, and said clearly, "Mama."

"Did you hear that?" Tilly jumped up in the bed, laughing. "Finn called you Mama." She grabbed her little boy and squeezed him. "Finn, you little rascal!"

Aunt Letty smiled. Finn's first word. *Mama.* Then she closed her eyes.

Out of nowhere, Bones' cry pierced the air.

"What was that?" She pulled her little boy closer to her and looked over to Aunt Letty, who had not moved. At that moment, she knew. "Mama. Mama?" She tried to lift Aunt Letty's head to make her look at her. She put her arms around her, pulling her up close.

"Please, Mama, talk to me! Please, please," she sobbed. "Mama, Mama, don't leave me!"

"Mama!" she screamed.

CHAPTER 52

Orie, her eyes nearly swollen shut, opened the door of Aunt Letty's house to Henny.

"It ain't goin to do no good," she said, tears flowing. "Tilly won't see you or no one else. Not even little Finn. She shut herself up with Letty. Won't come out."

Henny, too pained to talk, walked in anyway and took Finn out of Orie's arms.

"Dat chile be almost as bad as Tilly. He looks at dat room calling, 'Mama, Mama.'"

Henny looked up at Orie.

"Dat baby be talkin, Henny. At least he say, 'Mama.'" She looked up at the heavens. "An he don't mean Tilly."

"How do you know that?"

"Because when I got here, Tilly was holdin him and he was cryin and pointin to Letty callin, 'Mama.'"

Henny leaned back against the chair and closed his eyes and smiled. "I hope she knows that. Who helped you, Orie?"

"Neighbors who heard Tilly wailin. Right after Bones' scream. They was here when I got here. They helped me settle Letty in on dat bed, and soon as we did, Tilly got on dat bed with her. We tacked dat sheet up over de openin." Tears ran down her face. "What are we goin to do without my sister, Henny?"

Henny hunched over in the chair, holding Finn close to him. Barely above a whisper, he answered, "I don't know."

"I'll remember dat cry of Bones' as long as I live. Like a wild animal." She looked out de window as if seeing Bones there.

Henny didn't say anything. He had been awake all night and was sitting in front of the hearth, staring at the ashes remaining from the fire he lit the last morning Ben was home. When he heard Bones' cry of intolerable grief, it went right to his heart and hadn't come out. He had been worried about Letty for a long time. He stayed where he was sitting in front of the fireplace as long as he needed to get hold of himself before walking to Letty's.

"Nellie and Sassy are coming to help me get her ready. I found a dress in de chest of drawers with an envelope on it. Tilly musta made de dress. I can't read de papers in de envelope, but it must have somethin to do with de dress and what we're to do about de funeral. But why, Henny? Letty's not old enough to worry bout dying." She looked to Henny with such a sad expression it was more than he could handle. He looked away.

"I can't answer that, Orie. Only Tilly knows that. What makes you think the dress is for her funeral?"

"Cause there ain't nothin else she'd be wearin a dress like dat for. Least nothin I can think of. She ain't goin to a fancy ball." She shook her head in wonder. "But then I can't see dat dress for a funeral neither."

"What d'ya mean?"

Orie rolled her eyes. "You be seein."

Without looking up, he asked, "The funeral is tomorrow?"

Orie closed her eyes and sat down. "It be tomorrow." She looked toward the sheet-covered door.

"I'll help you, Orie." He handed Finn to her. "He's asleep. I'm going in to see Letty and Tilly."

He pulled back the sheet and sat on the edge of the bed. Tilly lay against Aunt Letty, her face resting on her shoulder, and it looked to him as if she had not shed a tear. He took her hand from where it was resting on Aunt Letty's chest, leaned over and kissed it, and held it on the bed between them.

"I've been waiting, Henny. Mama told me the spirit stays. She told me the soul goes to heaven and the body returns to earth but the spirit stays. But she's not here, Henny."

Henny remained silent, not knowing what to say.

"She had me make a dress for her funeral last year, and I cried. She said it was insurance like she got for the new bakery shop. I told her she couldn't ever leave me, and she said she wouldn't. She said she would never leave me. She said when she died her spirit would always be with me." She looked at Henny with such sadness in her big brown eyes that Henny bit down on his lip until he could taste blood.

"Where's my mama, Henny?"

"I don't know, Tilly. I don't know bout these things. But I know how much she loves you."

She took her hand away from his and put it on Aunt Letty's face. "Where are you, Mama? Where did you go?"

Henny snapped up his head and stared out the window. "Where did you go?" Those words shook loose a memory so old, forgotten and tied up with age, Henny stared in wonder as it unraveled and his vision cleared. If there was such a thing as a spirit remaining on this earth after death, as the Gullah believed, he was sure he knew where Letty was. But telling Tilly could hurt her.

"Honey, Orie needs to get in here and get Letty ready. Let's go be with Finn. Her spirit will come there for you as well as in here."

"NO!" She tightened her hold on Aunt Letty's body. "I am not leaving her, Henny."

He took a deep breath. "Tilly, I'm going to tell you a story I'd forgotten."

She turned to look at him.

"You know that Letty and I have been friends most of our lives. The only time I ever been at Hallelujah was when she buried her ma and little

Pet. I watched her the whole time feeling so bad for her. We were just about fifteen then. Right after her mama and Pet were in the ground, Letty just walked off. I don't know what made me follow her. Or if she ever knew I was behind her. She walked back of the Gullah houses into woods where a lot of the slaves were buried. It spooked me, but I kept following her until we got to the edge of the worst quagmire of boggy, tangled muddle of danger I ever seen. I sure wasn't going any further, but Letty kept on pushing aside the thorns and other brush. I wanted to call her back, but I didn't. I watched until she was out of sight. I never told no one bout that.

"She didn't come home for many years, and of course everyone thought she was dead. When she did, there was lots of speculation. Most, over time, decided she had been with Bones. But she went somewhere. No one asked her where she'd been. Except maybe Orie. But I'm thinking there's a place where she found Bones. Where he lives now.

"A while back, she and I were talking and maybe sipping a bit too much peach brandy. Our talking got around to when we first met. I told her how I hated to leave the little farm where I was born. But we had lost it, and Daddy found a job with Junie. I told her when I met her I knew I had a friend. She got real quiet and didn't say anything for a long while, just smiling at what she was seeing in her head. Then she said as quiet as I ever heard her, 'There's a place I never wanted to leave. And someday when I'm called, I'll go back there.'"

"I don't know, Tilly, but it might be she's there."

She sat up in the bed. "Could you take me there?"

"Well, I could take you as far as I went before."

She got out of bed. "I want to go there, Henny. If my mama is there, I want to go."

Tilly put her arms around Orie, then Sassy and Nellie, and smiled at Finn asleep in his cradle. "Orie, I'll read the letter to you, Nellie, and Sassy when I get back. It's how Mama wants her funeral to be."

The women, taken aback by her composure, watched the two walk out the door.

"She ain't let it sink in yet," Nellie said.

"No, but it will. God, help her."

⌇

Henny took Tilly through the old sacred woods with the bones lying around and the broken markers until they reached the harsh, desolate landscape where Henny stopped. "This is as far as we go."

Tilly stared at the muck and agreed. "But how did Mama get through this?"

"Beats me, Tilly. But she did."

"So she is somewhere beyond all this. Somewhere we can't see?"

"That's what I think."

"Why, Henny? Why didn't she ever tell me about this place?"

"As far as I know, she never told no one, Tilly. I don't know why."

"My mama's spirit is somewhere over there, and I can't even see where she is." Tilly stared at the place she couldn't see. Where she couldn't go. She turned and walked back to the old woods and sat on the ground, where she let her heart empty out the sorrow tormenting her.

Tilly read the letter Aunt Letty had dictated to Orie, Nellie, and Sassy. She wrote she didn't want pots or pans on her grave or anything else. She didn't want shells surrounding her body. The water may have brought her over, but she didn't have any desire to go back. All she loved was here. She didn't want anything on her grave. And she sure didn't want little Finn passed over her grave. She had no intention of coming back and haunting him. What she wanted was for Rufus to make her a pine coffin, and she wanted a lock of Tilly's hair in it with her. In case anyone thought her dress was too fancy, that was too bad. It was what she wanted because her mama and little Pet were buried in the clothes they died in. She was dressing for them as well as for herself. And she would come back and haunt anyone who put Savage behind her name on the marker. *Letty* was just fine.

Orie and Tilly had gone shopping at Mr. Moody's store, and she picked out the most beautiful and expensive material he had in the store. The shimmering deep purple silk lit up the room. Letty had looked at it with stars in her eyes. When Tilly finished making the dress, made to her instructions, Letty's eyes shined. *I never been beautiful, but I sure am goin to be at my funeral.* The dress had a high neckline with tiny pleats, puffed sleeves to the wrists where there wre rows of small ruffles, and more ruffles down the front of the dress, descending in size, rippled down to her ankles. She had insisted Mr. Wand order her red shoes. *I want nice shoes to walk around in when I be a spirit,* she told the flabbergasted man. They were in the drawer with her dress.

The letter made it clear the service in the prayer house was to be simple. She wanted the choir. She loved music and wanted the choir to sing "Amazing Grace" at her grave. She didn't want any moaning or groaning. She had, for the most part, a happy life and would rather see them singing and dancing. But not in Hallelujah, as that might upset the grave spirits of her ancestors.

When the women had prepared and dressed Aunt Letty, Henny, Long Robby, and Rufus put her on the cooling board and opened the door for those who would come to visit but not to moan. Those who passed by Aunt Letty, dressed in her unique but exquisite purple dress and red satin shoes, raised their eyes at her choice of burial attire. But she was beautiful, just as she said she would be. So beautiful it took the breath away from those who loved her.

The next morning as Tilly was dressing for the funeral, a floral truck full of flowers from the town residents arrived. Orie said, "Oh my Lord, Tilly. We don't put flowers in Hallellujah."

Tilly thought for a moment and said, "Tell the driver to take them to the Dock Shops and put them around the bakery."

"I like dat, Tilly. I was goin to tell you how upset de town is over Letty. They thought a lot of her." Orie didn't say that she suspected they thought more of Aunt Letty's baking than Aunt Letty.

The ceremony in the prayer house was just as Aunt Letty had wished and tearful despite her wishes. The choir sang "I'll Fly Away" and other sad songs, but the one that stirred the souls was "May the Work I've Done Speak for Me."

Tilly, holding Finn, led the procession, with Orie beside her, to Hallelujah. She and all of Aunt Letty's friends were dressed in the traditional clothes: high-necked white blouses with billowing sleeves and long white skirts that they all kept on hand for such occasions. No one could see the purple silk slip under Tilly's clothes as they walked along the small shell road. The cooler air from the heat of the summer was a relief and the red sourwood a sign of autumn coming. The choir, white turbans above their soulful brown faces, sang "Nearer my God to Thee" as they walked.

When each funeral guest arrived at the old iron gate to Hallelujah, there was a pause to ask, out loud, permission from the spirits to enter. "Family," they called, "we've come to put our sister away in Mother dust. Please, let us go through the gate." And only then did they enter into the realm of the dead.

After all gathered, Long Robby, Henny, Joe, and Rufus lowered Letty's casket into the ground. When the small choir sang "Amazing Grace," everyone felt God's glory. Tilly smiled, tears welling in her eyes as peace settled in. She felt a loving warmth surround her, and she knew Aunt Letty was near. She squeezed Finn to her chest while Reverend Jeremiah Barnwell recited the old funeral rite, "ashes to ashes, dust to dust," which ended the service just as Aunt Letty had desired.

Off in the distance, sitting high on an old oak limb, a young girl and a cougar watched. As the Gullah choir sang, Letty sent all the love she had in her heart to her precious Tilly and wrapped it around her. And then she smiled at the red shoes on her body's feet before romping back to the deep forest with her old friend, Nanda.

CHAPTER 53

It wasn't seven in the morning when Tilly, holding Finn, opened the door for Orie.

Surprised, she asked, "Aren't you supposed to be at the Morton's?"

"Miss Rebecca gave me de whole week off. I told her you needed help. But, to tell de truth, Tilly, I ain't really needed there no more."

"Orie, what in the world are you talking about? The Mortons love you."

"Yeah, they love me. But I think they keep me cause I be family." She shook her head. "Miss Rebecca's granma, Miss Eloise, was the best person I've ever knowed. She was Miss Jenny's sister, and after Letty left, she got Miss Eloise to take me in. I was only twelve. I'm a relic to them now."

Tilly put her arm around Orie. "That's nonsense. You are indispensable to them."

"Beau's grown now, an he don't need me nomore. I tell you, Tilly, I'd leave if I had something else to do. I love dat family, but I been there practically my whole life. I'd like to try somethin new. But what?" She looked around. "Lawd, Tilly, I forgot why I came here."

Tilly's expression was blank as she tried to digest all Orie had said.

"We gotta get Letty's clothes outta this house."

"No, we are not," Tilly said, alarmed.

"It have to be done, Tilly. If you don't get her clothes out, spirits will start movin into them."

Tilly's jaw dropped, but she didn't dare contradict Orie.

"Orie, I want Mama's clothes here with me. I need them. They are all I have left of her that I can touch."

"That may be, honey, but you still have to let them go. Today. It be de way."

Tilly looked away, exasperated. This was too much. Tears began flowing.

"Aw, honey, I be so sorry. I thought you would know about de clothes."

"How could I?"

Orie put her arms around her and led her to sit on the daybed.

"Let's talk about somethin else til you feel better."

"I don't feel bad. I hurt. I miss my mama, and I don't want to think about clothes. And I don't want to sit down. All I want is to take Finn and go where my mama is."

Orie was at a loss for words and sat with her hands in her lap.

"Oh, Tilly," she finally said, "I do understand. I miss her so much already I can't bear it." She looked at little Finn. "Dat baby don't need for you to be upset. I'll come back later, and we can talk bout this."

After Orie left, Tilly put her sleeping baby boy on the bed. "Where's your daddy? I want him home."

She lay down on the daybed until the tears stopped. She knew the Gullah's strong beliefs had merit. She picked up Finn and walked up the hill to Henny's. He was sittiing on the porch, and she told him about Orie's visit and how upset she was over the clothes.

He took Finn from her and swung him up over his head. "This little fella is almost a year old. How about that?"

"And his daddy has been gone over a year and a half, Henny. I want him home. Everything I want I can't have."

"You got Finn, Tilly, and a lot more, too. I'm gonna tell you how I feel about those clothes, all spirits aside. You have all the wonderful memories of being with Letty. That's the next best thing to having her here with you. You can pull one of those memories up any time you want and feel like you're with her."

She wanted to tell him he was wrong, that every dress in that closet was a part of her mama, but she listened to him.

"You keep those clothes around, an no matter whether some spirit comes and gets in one or not, you're not gonna be happy. One by one, those dresses will come out of that closet and smother you with longing for her. I know a little bout that. It wasn't until Ben come along and started wearing Pa's clothes that I let go of missing him so much. You and I can talk bout Ben and Letty any time you want. Now, go home and pack all her clothes up. I'll come around later and get em."

He reached over and tousled the top of her head. "I may not be your mama, Tilly, but I love you very much. I always have."

On the way home, Tilly picked up several boxes from Mr. Moody's store, and amid her sobs, she packed all of Aunt Letty's dresses neatly in them. Each dress had such meaning for her, it was all she could do to keep from taking them out again. When she had finished, she put them over by the door, turned, and stared at the chest of drawers. There was too much in the drawers to go through them now. Aunt Letty had given Tilly the bottom three drawers of the eight in the chest when she came to live with her. It was in one of these that she had put the bird toy. She had always honored Aunt Letty's space and never opened her drawers, except to help her put her funeral clothes in one drawer.

She stared at the chest. *What could be in those drawers?* She couldn't imagine Aunt Letty having any secrets, but for some reason, she felt shaky about them. *Sometimes drawers held secrets,* she thought.

She knew the first drawer was empty after Aunt Letty's funeral dress and shoes were taken out. In the next drawer were Aunt Letty's underwear, slips, stockings, turbans, and other feminine articles of clothes. She put the entire contents of the drawer into one of the boxes.

She opened the next drawer, where she found a shallow box of hair clips, lotions, lavender water, a few hair nets, and other odds and ends. She added them to the box.

She looked up at the top drawer. It was even high for Aunt Letty. Again, she felt a strange sensation. She stared at it for a long time. Maybe there was nothing in it. She had never seen Aunt Letty open it that she could remember.

She moved Aunt Letty's foot stool over to the chest and stepped on it. She took a deep breath and opened the drawer.

She grabbed the drawer and steadied herself as her eyes filled with tears. Slowly she picked up the gold necklace with the locket dangling from it, the one she had given to Aunt Letty when Louie was so sick and they needed food. She had never seen the inside of the locket. She would wait for later to open it. She saw the diamond hair comb and remembered that Christmas morning when she had given it to Aunt Letty. She had been so unhappy and lonely. There were a few more trinkets she would ask Orie about. What interested her the most was a packet of old papers stuck over in the back corner. They were in such bad condition she was afraid to pick them up for fear they would crumble.

A voice called from the door, "I thought of something after you left."

Henny walked over and looked in the drawer. "Tilly, I think you've found your past. An I'm as sure as I am standing here that at some point Letty forgot those papers was here."

"You knew about them, Henny?"

"Letty told me bout them not long after you came here. Your uncle told her they were for you. She couldn't read em."

Orie walked in and over to the chest. "What ya'll doin?"

"Orie, the clothes are packed. Can you stay and watch Finn?"

Tilly and Henny went back to his place, where they laid out the contents on his kitchen table and looked dumbfounded at the papers.

"I can't make heads nor tales outta this pile of stuff, Tilly. Some in a foreign language." He picked up a legal document. "And this looks like an old deed."

"Henny, these old newspaper clippings don't mean anything to me. There is something vaguely familiar about the photograph, but it's almost impossible to see it clearly. And this sheet of nicer-looking paper has a gold stamp on the top, but the sheet is blank."

"How would we find out what that meant?"

"Henny, I know some of these words. They are French. My mother was French."

"Well, now." He grinned. "That's somethin. If we can find someone who speaks French."

"Henny, I'm going to see Beau Morton. He may not speak French, but he will know about this document and . . . well, I can't think of anything else to do, can you?"

"No. That's the smart thing to do. Do you want me to go with you?"

She thought for a minute and said, "No, I'll be fine."

The following morning when Tilly and Finn arrived at Henny's, he took Finn. He glanced admiringly at her. She was dressed in a light green high-waisted linen dress with a shawl collar and big pearl buttons on the belt.

"Tilly, you look too lovely to be goin to see a lawyer."

Tilly put her hand on his arm. "I've just never done anything like this, and it's been so long since I've seen Beau." She looked toward town. "I want to look nice."

Henny shook his head. "You ain't got nothing to prove to Beau Morton. If anything, it's the other way around."

"Henny, the truth is I just want to know about these papers, not what Beau thinks about me." But she knew it was both. She did care how Beau saw her, and she couldn't explain that to herself.

Tilly climbed the steps to Beau's second-floor office after being directed by the receptionist downstairs.

The door was open, and when Beau saw Tilly standing in the entrance, he was obviously so surprised and pleased he jumped up from his chair and quickly went to her. "Tilly."

"Hello, Beau."

He held out a chair for her. "Please, sit down and tell me what brings you here." He cleared his throat, hoping she would not notice how moved he was to see her.

"So much has happened since we have seen each other, Beau. As you can tell, I regained my voice."

"Orie told me, Tilly. I am so happy for you."

"And my mama, Aunt Letty, died."

"I'm so sorry. I wanted to go to the funeral, but Orie said that would not be appropriate. But I want you to know that I wanted to be there. She was so good to me."

Tilly smiled.

"I sent a small bouquet of roses. I hope you got them."

"No." She shook her head. "I didn't, but I know where it is, and I'll get it after I go home today. That was so kind of you."

She reached over and touched his hand where it lay on the desk, remembering too late how Rufus had reacted as she watched Beau turn red.

"Beau, I'm here because of some papers I found yesterday. I'm told my uncle Louie gave them to Mama to keep for me. I know some French words . . . My mother was French. But I can't read it anymore. I would like for you to help me if you can."

He took the packet and leafed through them. "I speak French, Tilly. That's no problem. But the papers are very old and worn." He leafed through them. "One is a deed and not in French. Do you know anything about that?"

"I have no idea. Nor about any of the papers."

"Leave them with me, then, and I'll see what I can find out. Let me walk you home."

"Thank you, Beau, but I will be fine."

Beau watched her as she walked out into the sunshine and saw three Marines across the street watching her with less than benevolent looks. He ran down the stairs, as fast as his slight limp would allow. "Tilly, I could use some fresh air. I am walking you home."

CHAPTER 54

It was nearly a week before Orie was sent to tell Tilly that Beau would like to see her. "He said to tell me when you can meet him an he'll come get you."

"That's nice of him, Orie. But he needn't come here."

"He said to tell you that he was coming to get you."

She shook her head. "Well, if he insists, tell him to meet me at Henny's at two this afternoon, if that suits his schedule. I'll leave Finn with Henny. I can't wait to hear what he has found out."

Promptly at two, Beau arrived at Henny's, where Tilly waited for him on the porch.

They chatted as they walked to his office about her not hearing from Ben. "I know he is alive, Beau."

"I think you are right, Tilly. He is somewhere over there waiting to come home. This war is about over. I'm sure you will hear from him once it is."

Tilly looked at the papers stacked neatly in a pile on Beau's desk.

"What are they, Beau? What do they say?"

"To tell you the truth, I'm not sure. There are documents here that are perplexing to me. The few letters are personal, but in a mystifying way they all seem to be related."

He picked up the single sheet of stationery with the crest at the top.

"It is this I'm counting on. Your parents lived in New Orleans, and I think this stationary with the gold crest belonged to someone there, perhaps your mother or your grandmother. What I'd like is permission from you to go to New Orleans and see if all this," he spread his hands over the documents, "will come together in some tangible form. In other words, we will know what it means to you."

Tilly was visibly distressed. "Beau, I cannot pay you to do that."

"Tilly, for the first fourteen years of my life, I stared out of a window. Now I'm sitting in an office staring out of another window. This is not how I longed to live my life. I wanted to be a gamekeeper in Africa or an anthropologist exploring the Amazon." He laughed. "Can you imagine what a thrilling trip this will be for me?"

Tilly laughed with him. Beau was cute when he let go of his stuffiness.

"I am sure my granny, my father's mother, is dead. The Klan was coming up the road when we left."

"I think we will know all about that and soon. I have a lawyer friend from school who lives in New Orleans. He is from an old New Orleans family. Don't look for me anytime soon. It is mid-October now. It might take several weeks."

Tilly leaned across the desk, not caring if it embarrassed him. With sincere warmth, she squeezed his hand and thanked him.

⁓

Tilly was straightening up the bakery dock shop with one eye on Finn, who was edging around the cabinet doors, when Orie walked in.

"Orie, what is wrong? You look like you just ate a jar of Nellie's pickles. I haven't seen you happy in weeks. Is it Mama?"

"I guess it be a little of everythin." She sat on one of the chairs placed around the small round tables. "Of course it's Letty. It'll always be Letty. No one in this world can take her place."

Tilly picked up Finn and sat beside her.

"Okay, Orie, what is the matter?"

"Oh, Tilly." Tears welled in her eyes. "I'm not sure what it is. It's just everythin." She looked around the shop. "You got any everlasting tea?"

"No, but there's lemonade."

"I been in dat house too long. I done about everythin a body can do in all those years. I just feel useless, Tilly. An it ain't like they don't have other help."

"Then quit. Just quit! You have to be happy, Orie. I can still hear your laughter ringing out. Don't lose that. We all need to hear it."

"What you expect me to do? Change Finn's diapers? Stand on corners crying, 'Swimps, swimps,' and I can't make sweet-grass baskets."

Tilly's eyes lit up. "But you can cook, Orie. I need help here. In this bakery. I've got Finn to care for, and I can't do all the baking, what's needed here and that, too. When Mama was alive, we worked together, and Finn was in a cradle."

She closed her eyes and breathed in as if she was smelling Aunt Letty's sweet buns.

"Orie, that's the answer for both of us. You are going to come here with me. It will be your bakery as much as mine."

Orie smiled. "Tilly, those are de best words I've heard in all my life."

"And I have been thinking that I might at some time start a little dressmaking business. Just thinking, though."

Laughing happily, they toasted with their glasses of lemonade when Finn slapped his hands on the table saying, "Swimpee, swimpee."

They doubled over then looked at each other, eyes widened. "Why not?"

Rebecca Morton cried and carried on, but she understood and wanted Orie to be happy, and she knew that Orie would come if she needed her. And the family would see her often at the Dock Shops and Aunt Letty's Bakery.

⌇

The Dock Shops so exceeded the expectations of the landlords they began planning a new building next to the old original warehouses and in the exact architectural design. Everyone was pleased. Long Robby signed up for one to sell his fish and seafood, thinking he might add some fried fish and shrimp baskets. He counted on Rufus, who didn't like fishing, to run it. When he didn't get the enthusiasm from Rufus he expected, Sassy said, "I'll take dat on. De kids'll be in school, an when they ain't, they can help me."

Henny decided he didn't need a shop to sell his nets even with his booming business. "I'll just sit down at the docks and annoy everyone."

"We'll give you a violin, Henny," Long Robby teased.

One afternoon the vendors of the various small stores were sitting around the docks chatting and enjoying themselves, drinking beer or tea, as it had become their habit to do after closing for the day, when they saw a couple with teenagers walking across the Gullah park. They stopped talking and watched until the family got close enough to see who they were.

"Emmy! Billy John!" they all bellowed at the top of their lungs.

"We heard bout Aunt Letty, an we got so homesick for all of you here. We also heard about these shops." Emma looked around at the row of attractive stores.

~

Tilly was putting a rack of bread in the oven, wondering when Beau would return, when Orie said, "We need one of those fancy new double ovens that have all those racks. Like the ones I saw in the Sears Roebuck catalogue."

"Orie, we don't have the money yet." She wiped the perspiration from her forehead with her sleeve.

She turned to look at Orie. As much as she loved her, a pang of heartache settled between her ribs. *Oh, Mama, how I miss you,* she cried to herself.

Henny stuck his nose through the door, left open to let the cooler air in.

"Tilly, I see Mr. Morton's car coming across the yard."

"Oh!" She started to run out the door, went back and splashed her face with water, let her hair down from the net that held it back, and ran out past Henny.

Brian had parked the 1918 Cunningham limousine as close to the warehouses as land would permit and stood by the open back door, from which a quite attractive and not too elderly lady dressed elegantly in a deep maroon traveling suit baring her slim ankles emerged.

Tilly thought she was dreaming. This couldn't be true. But it was. Her grandmother was smiling at her.

"Granny," Tilly called, running into her arms.

"Oh, my darling girl," Annie Shepard cooed, holding Tilly close to her.

"Oh, Granny, I thought you were dead."

"And we feared the same for you and Louie. Oh, my Louie. I thought I had lost everyone I loved." She looked over and saw Henny and Orie with Finn.

She started walking toward them, brushing off Brian's arm. "Thank you, young man, but I am quite capable of walking."

Beau, who had been traveling for three days with this lively woman, held back a smile.

After introductions, she took Finn in her arms. "You smell like something good to eat, you adorable little boy. And you are heavy," she said, handing him back to Orie.

"Tilly, Beau got me a nice suite at the Inn in Belleview where we can have lunch sent up and talk. Oh, there is so much to talk about." She looked over at Beau. "And why didn't you tell me she was so beautiful? Oh, stop blushing. It doesn't become you."

Tilly and Beau exchanged amused looks.

During lunch, Beau and Annie told Tilly all the events of the past two weeks leading to their sitting there together.

"Granny, before we talk about anything else, I want to know how you got away from . . . " She shut her eyes at the memory of the white-cloaked men riding toward the plantation as she and Louie ran toward the marsh.

"I shot them, if that is what you wondered."

"What?"

"My men, Judge and Albert, have been shooting game for me since Billy died, and long before that. I know how to shoot straight if I have to. We stood at the windows waiting. When those filthy varmints lined up with their torches and called to me, we let them have it. They never knew what hit them. We kept their horses and buried the trash in the fields. Fertilizer."

"I don't know when I stopped remembering anything, Granny. I didn't remember going to your house until my memory came back. I was so confused about everything, like I was crazy. My aunt Letty made a safe world for me. A very happy one, Granny. I loved her so much. When everything came back to me and I remembered my mommy and how much I loved her, it hurt so much I almost wished I could go back to being blind to everything in my past."

Annie Shepard was quiet for a long time. "I can't imagine what you went through, Tilly. I can't bear to think of what you and Louie went through to get you here. After you left and for many months, I stayed in my room wishing I could die. There really wasn't anything for me to live for. Billy used to say my folks and I had the strength and stubbornness of a pack of mules. I finally got out of the house and rode my stallion as fast as I could over that land. And Judge, Albert, and Cheryl were there. Constantly caring for me. Don't tell me there can't be love between blacks and whites. Love is love and doesn't see color, white nor black."

She leaned back against the chair. "I think I'll rest now, darling. Come back at four this afternoon and we can talk about some of what is in that packet Louie left for you." She smiled affectionately at Beau. "You, too! I like your young man, Tilly."

Beau turned aside, embarrassed, and Tilly almost yelled, "Beau's my friend, Granny."

"Shhh, shhh, I know. Now go on, both of you."

Walking out of the Inn, Tilly said, "Beau, I can't wait until four o'clock. Tell me whatever you know."

"Mrs. Shepard will tell you about your mother's family. I could tell you some of the financial and legal matters, Tilly, but I need more time to digest them. I have a friend in Charleston who can help."

Seeing her disappointment, he added, "I will tell you something I think will please you more than all the rest if I know your sensibilities as I think I do."

"What, Beau?" She stopped, excited.

"The deed we found in the envelope is to the tabby house you mentioned. If I remember correctly, you said, 'If only it could be for the tabby house.'"

CHAPTER 55

"Granny, I loved that house from the moment Ben first took me there. Even though I was frightened at the time, I felt such a kinship to it. I know that is strange."

"No, not strange to me. That strong instinctive feeling is what we get about something connected to us without our knowing what it is. You are deeply connected to Chez Matilda."

"Chez Matilda? That was my grand-maman's name. My mother's grandmother. I was named for her."

"Chez Matilda was the name given the house when it was built."

Tilly smiled, thinking about that. "I love that, Granny, but why didn't my mother tell me about the house?"

She looked at Tilly thoughtfully. "There were probably many things she would have told you in time. Annabelle had the deed Matilda gave her to keep for you. Matilda left you the house, Tilly. That is why Louie and I put it in the envelope you found. He brought you here hoping to find the house."

"I knew he wanted to get to someplace around here."

"We knew the story behind the house, that it was in a protected area. We thought once you were here, Louie could arrange for money to be sent to him."

"And he would stay here with me?"

"Yes. He wasn't happy in New Orleans." She looked down at her folded hands and said, "It all happened so fast, Tilly. We thought we had time to plan."

She looked up at Tilly. "Do you remember visiting Matilda with your mother?"

"Yes, of course I do. We went to Paris every year until she died."

Annie looked out the window wistfully. "She died the year before your mother and father. I can't help but think what a blessing that was for her."

"I remember her funeral, Granny. How sad we were."

Annie smiled warmly and reached for Tilly's hand.

"That was the beginning of what led to my children's deaths. Your mother and father's deaths."

Tilly looked at her. "What do you mean?"

Annie once again looked down at her closed hands, thinking.

"Do you know anything about your mother's family, other than your great-grandmother, Matilda? Who you call, Grand-maman?"

Tilly sat thoughtfully. "Granny, I don't remember if I ever knew anything about my mother's family except that she was raised by her grandparents."

"Yes, your mother never knew her parents. They were killed in a sailing accident soon after your mother was born. A squall took them under."

Tilly looked aside. "I'm confused. I don't understand about the tabby house. Who did it belong to? My grand-maman never left Paris."

"I'll tell you what I know from talks with your mother." Annie put her empty teacup on the table and sat back in the chair. "David Paine was a wealthy Virginian in Paris on business. He met Matilda Fontaine at a party given by a mutual friend. Matilda was charming and admired for her beauty. They fell in love and were soon married. What I find remarkable is David Paine was a southerner and Matilda was a 'mullato.' He was aware, of course, that he would never be able to take her to his home. He was familiar with the obscurity of the Lowcountry islands and felt she would be safe there for part of the year while he worked in

Virginia. He had Chez Matilda built, and when it was completed, he travelled to see the tabby house. He found a few questionable-looking men wandering on the grounds. He left immediately. He felt like a fool, Matilda told your mother, for thinking she would be safe from harm in any part of the south. He sold his business, moved to Paris, and lived very happily with Matilda until he died many years later."

"But Granny, why did he keep Chez Matilda?"

"I don't know that, Tilly. Maybe he hoped the south would change. He had. Who knows what all his feelings or possible intentions might have been?

"Your mother, Annabelle, and my son, Patrick, met at the Sorbonne. She was so young. I know that Matilda was not happy about her leaving school, or coming over here for that matter, but those two were inseparable.

"Tilly, I want you to know I loved your mother from the moment your father brought her to our home. She was everything a mother could hope for her son. However, living where we do when you have color in your background, there is always fear even if the color isn't noticeable. We decided to say she was from Brazil and had lived in Paris for many years. Because she didn't speak Portugese, it could have been awkward otherwise since she had a French accent.

"All went well until you and your parents were in Paris for the last time. Matilda's funeral. She and David had been a popular couple and were involved in charitable affairs. *Le Matin* put a picture of Matilda on the front page and an article that went into detail about her civic work. Tragically, the article mentoned her remaining relative. Your mother.

"Louie had gotten into politics and had a nasty opponent. That man, in Paris at that time, against all odds, saw the article with your mother's name prominently in type. He couldn't wait to get home to begin the smear.

"We quickly decided that your parents and you should leave as soon as possible. Annabelle gave me some jewelry and all the important documents to put in a bank vault. We kept a few important papers, letters, and the deed at my house. Tragically, we ran out of time."

They sat quietly, and sadly, but enjoying the closeness they had found being together. Tilly reached in her purse and brought out the mast with the forlorn-looking sails still hanging from it. "Granny, there is something I want to show you. The night Louis and I left, I took a little boat my father made for me from the room. I remember grabbing it from the table by my bed. By the time I got here, the boat was gone and only the mast with these torn sails and a little bird on top was left of it. I didn't know what I had, but I knew it was so important." She raised her brows and looked at the piece of wood and cloth. "I wouldn't let go of it for a long time. Every now and then, little snatches of memory would come back to me, and this was a part of that. Then the memories would fade. I was so afraid of letting go of it. Of course, when my memory came back, I knew what it was. It was a model of our sailboat. Do you remember that boat, Granny?"

Annie smiled and reached for the remaining piece of the carving. "I do remember your father's sailboat, Tilly, very well. But I can't say I remember his carving a replica for you. I can imagine how much that means to you. We all enjoyed sailing in the bay in front of our houses. What happened to the bird?"

Tilly squeezed her hands against her purse, feeling the ache in her chest, remembering the last time she saw Ben. "I broke off the little bird from the mast—a friend called it a marsh bird—and gave it to Ben when he left to go to war."

Annie leaned over and put her hand on Tilly's. "Oh, my darling Tilly." She handed the broken carving back to Tilly. "Marsh bird. Well, your friend was right. It would have been a marsh bird. Our houses, as you know, were on the marsh." She smiled sympathetically. "I hope your Ben brings it back to you."

She looked out the window and saw Beau walking up to the Inn. "I know where your heart is, Tilly, but . . . "

"Don't finish that, Granny."

Over the next four days at breakfast, lunch, tea, dinner, and in between, there were talks of the happy days when they were all together.

"Granny, I have heard about everyone but you. I guess children take everything around them for granted. I don't know anything about you, Granny, except that I always loved being at your house with you. Grandaddy was dead, but I remember Cheryl and Albert and Judge. I remember Sunday dinner and we always had gumbo and cornbread that Cheryl made. What about you? What was your childhood like? What was Grandaddy like?"

"Oh, honey, I was just a pretty little girl who made eyes at your grandpa until he took notice. He wasn't much of a looker, but the nicest, most loving man God put on earth. I had sense to know that. My pa worked for his daddy on the cotton farm. I grew up poor. My brother died young and so drunk they didn't embalm him. The little pigs, goats, chickens, and calves and other farm animals were my friends. I wonder Billy ever saw me I was so covered in mud most of the time." She winked. "But he did, and we had a very happy, romantic marriage until he fell off the barn roof trying to mend it. Darn fool. Showing off for me."

When it was time for Annie to leave, Tilly was devastated. When the bags were being loaded on the back of Mr. Morton's car, Tilly, out of deep longing and need for all those who had left her, clung to her grandmother. "Granny, please take me home with you."

Annie looked at her with aching sadness. "Oh, my darling girl, don't you know how much I want that?" She closed her eyes. "Nothing has changed at home, Tilly. Not where I live in New Orleans. I would never take a chance with you. But you and I are a part of one another. And we are only a train ride away. We'll write, and if ever you need me, I'll be here before you can say my name. I want to know my great-grandson better. I might come and take him home with me someday and show him how to ride a horse. That red-headed little tyke. And who knows? Maybe the South will overcome this crazy hatred of coloreds. I'll come get you and keep you. I love you. Remember that."

CHAPTER 56

A few days after her grandmother left, Beau went to the bakery to find Tilly.

"I think I understand what we have here, Tilly." He looked at her and smiled. "You have inherited a nice sum of money from your parents. I have arranged for it to be transferred to our bank here. I hope that is satisfactory with you?"

Surprised, she pressed her hands down on the floured table and leaned against it. "I hadn't expected this, Beau. But the way we lived, looking back, we had to have some money. I guess all that would come to me now."

"Yes, and I think you will be pleased."

When she didn't move or say anything, Beau's enthusiasm began to dwindle. "Are you okay, Tilly?"

"I'm okay, Beau." She walked over to a chair and plopped down in it. "I know it must seem strange to you, but I just don't know how to feel about this."

"I am so sorry, Tilly. I should have broken it to you more gently."

"Give me a few days, Beau. I need time to think." She turned and smiled at him. "Don't look so concerned. You have done so much for me."

The words were on his lips: *"I would do anything for you."*

⌒

Tilly was waiting for Orie when she walked in the bakery before dawn.

"Orie, I've put Finn on a bottle. I've got his formula made and bottles ready. I'm leaving him with you and Henny. I need to go away for a couple of days."

She picked up a small satchel and walked out the door, leaving Orie with her mouth hanging open and Finn in his new playpen.

Henny was awake when she got to his house and walked out to meet her.

"I need your help, Henny, but I don't want to talk about it. I want you to help me get Ben's boat out of the shed and into the river."

"What?"

"You heard me, Henny. I left Finn with Orie, but you two will have to share caring for him. I'm going away for a couple of days. I've got some things to work out."

"I just hope you know what you're doing going off in this boat."

"Ben taught me everything."

Henny rolled his eyes and stared off.

⌒

Tilly rowed through Coosaw Creek. The gators would be sleeping on the bank, she thought, and the sweet grass was there, too dark yet to see with the silvery clouds covering the sliver of moon descending in the sky. She came out of the creek into the open salt marsh and drifted west as a hint of scarlet was heralding in a new day.

Ben, oh Ben, she thought as memories swept in from the marsh. *"Look, Tilly, have you ever seen anything so beautiful? I come here sometimes when the tide is high and just sit watching the wading birds an wild ducks as they come in. The grass is turning from gold to brown now for the winter."* Across the sound in the distance was the island he had pointed to. *"Someday, I'm going there."*

She looked out over the spartina, swaying in the breeze, and began to row. When she saw the tabby house ruins, her Chez Matilda, she pushed through the marsh grass and pulled the boat up on the shore. She took the pillow, blanket, and satchel out and carried them to the garden, ignoring the memories. All memories. She wiped the leaves from the chair, wrapped herself in the blanket, lay back against the pillow, and closed her eyes with the cool breeze brushing against her face and let the sweet autumn perfumes of Ben's garden release their magic.

Henny was out on the porch helping Finn try to walk when he saw Tilly coming up from the river. He winced, seeing a flash of Ben. He picked up Finn and went to meet her.

"Did ya find what you're looking for, honey?"

"Yes." She kissed Finn and then Henny. "Yes, I did. Thank you for keeping my boy." She took him as he reached out for her. "Mommy."

"Is Orie okay?"

"Busy. I didn't think so at first, but those shops turned out good for everybody."

"Henny, would you mind keeping Finn a little longer? I want to see Orie, and then I am going home to shower and dress. I have something to talk to Beau about."

"I'll walk with you. I saw that boy earlier down at the docks. He's grown to be a nice-lookin fella."

"And a very nice one, Henny."

He gave her a quick look. "You're seeing right much of him now, ain't ya?"

She stopped and said, "I see him because he is my lawyer."

"I hope we hear from Ben soon. The way it looks, the war's about over."

Still annoyed, she said curtly, "Ben will be home soon."

"Are you planning something for Finn's birthday?"

She frowned. "Of course I am. Why would you even think I wouldn't?"

"November ninth is running up on us. Can I help you?"

She stopped again and put an arm around his neck. "I'm sorry, Henny. I've just got some things on my mind. Of course you can. I was counting on your and Orie's help. I couldn't do much without either of you." She kissed him and ran on ahead.

CHAPTER 57

Tilly sat across from Beau. "This has become a habit."

"I'm sorry the ambience isn't better. Nor the view out the window." He smiled.

She looked out at the bleak town scene. "Beau, there is an empty office above the Dock Shops. At least the view is better."

His face lit up. "Why didn't I think of that? I guess I'm so used to tradition it never occurred to me to leave these offices."

"Beau, there are several things I want to do, and they will require money. Is there cash? In one word, Beau."

He laughed. "Yes."

"Is there enough money to restore the tabby house?"

"More than enough."

"I'll take care of some of the ideas I have and will let you know how much money I'll need. Is that all right with you?"

"That is fine with me. We need to set up a bank account for you."

"Absolutely not. Beau, I do not want the money."

Beau stared blankly at her. Again, stunned.

"What could that money bring me that I don't have or will when Ben's here? Your life is different from the way we live here, Beau. I know it may be hard to understand. But that money can help others have a better life.

"I would like for you to take all of it and put it in some kind of fund. I never want to see it. I would like for you to take care of it and pay yourself for doing it. Pay yourself well, Beau. I want you to be happy and have anything you need to do this. I'll sign over any papers you need. I just don't want any part of it except what I want to do to the tabby house."

She looked at him sitting silently, staring at her.

"I want it to help people. The people around here. I want to do things with it that will make a difference. The Penn school over on the island has been there since the war ended. They need money. I think from what I hear that center is going to be even more important to the Gullah than it is now. I want you to feel free to give to whatever cause you feel is worthy."

When he still didn't speak, she said, "Am I asking too much of you, Beau?" She put her hand to her mouth. "I'm so sorry."

"Hush up, Tilly. I may be a bit overwhelmed, but never more excited in my life. In fact, I have a feeling I am just beginning to live."

CHAPTER 58

Finn's first birthday party was a joyful occasion. All the balloons in town had been bought, blown, hung, and popped from every tree, chair, table, and what was left of the old market. Finn pushed around the little red car Beau gave him. Nellie started a ring-dance, and everyone enjoyed the usual display of mouth-smacking good food.

Rufus and two of his friends walked over to where Tilly was talking to Henny and Orie. "Tilly, I think you know Victoria an her brother Will." He threw an arm around his friend. "We are celebrating, too. We decided to go into business together as soon as we can get de backin we need."

Tilly, delighted, said, "I hope it is what I think, Rufus?"

"I think you guessed right. Will likes buildin, too, and we think with all the people movin in here that might be a good venture."

"Rufus, if that's what you want, I happen to know just the person who will back you. He will set you up in one of those dock offices and see you have all you need to get started. And I will give you your first job. How is that?"

"Wahoo! Get dat moonshine outta your pocket, Will!"

Everyone stopped talking and watched Rufus and Will dancing a jig and shouting to the treetops.

On Monday, November 11, 1918, Germany surrendered, and an armistice was signed ending the war. The Gullah reveled in celebration, taking pride in the victory they helped achieve.

Long Robby said, "All our boys will be coming home now, and I plan to hire any of them who want to fish."

All our boys, Tilly said to herself.

It would be well into 1919 before all the troops were transported home. There were hundreds of thousands of men waiting to board the largest ship floating on the Atlantic, the sister ship to the *Titanic*, which could only hold six thousand men at a crossing.

At Thanksgiving only two weeks later, Henny said, "There's only one thing that keeps this one from being the fun it was the first time I came to one of these."

"Mama. And that was my first year here."

"I seem to remember having a pretty good time with that woman and a few nips of Pa's peach brandy."

"And those pies. My gosh, all those pies she made that year." Tilly looked off in the distance. "Henny, would you keep Finn for a little while?"

He raised his eyebrows and winked. "I think Finn and I might go back to the house pretty soon. Looks like the Reverend is winding up."

"Well, you were here for the best of the day as far as you are concerned." She laughed.

≈

Tilly walked past the old slave woods and stopped at the snarly bog. "I know you are out there, Mama. I wish I could sit down and talk to you about so many things, but I think you probably know about them. Henny showed me this land. He followed you after you buried little Pet. I miss you so much. Beau is going to get someone to help me buy all the property around here. I want you and Bones to always have your home. I love you, Mama." At that moment, a red cardinal flew across the slough and landed on her shoulder, pecked her face, then flew away.

Beau moved into the dock office and hired Long Robby's son, Ry, who had just graduated from Benedict College with a degree in business. When he was settled in the bright open office, he had a visit from Tilly.

"Beau, this is wonderful. I love the way you have brought your art and other interesting objects from home."

She stood at the wide picture window looking out over the marsh. "Hmm, I can see the island from here."

"What island?"

She turned around and sat in the chair across from him. "Oh, just an island that seemed so far away when Ben and I were younger." She smiled dreamily. "Funny. It is not far away at all."

"Tilly, are you thinking of buying an island?"

"No, of course not." She laughed. "But I do want to buy something, Beau. Or I want you to. If we have the money, I want you to buy all of the Grandterre property. Every inch of it." She smiled coyly. "And when you have bought it, I want you to talk to your mother about a garden. Orie has told me she knows more about gardening than anyone."

"Whoa, one thing at a time, Miss Matilda. You have my head swimming."

Tilly leaned across the desk. "This is so important to me, Beau. Just let me finish. I want a garden to cover that land and one so beautiful that it will erase any memories of anything else ever being there. I don't know about big gardens. I think your mother does. She will know how to do this. Would you ask her for me, Beau? Please? And one other thing. I do know enough to know she will have to hire someone to help."

"A landscape architect."

"Yes. And, Beau, I want to have him hire as many people as he needs to finish within the year."

"As for my mother, I will do what I can, Tilly. I promise you that. But as for Grandterre, I know bids are coming in on that property. I'll get on to that today."

"Thank you, Beau." She smiled at him gratefully and started to walk out the door.

"Tilly, what do you hear from your fetching grandmother? I'd marry her if she'd move here. I can't give up my view."

"Moving to the docks has affected your brain."

Beau stared after her. *You are the one who has my heart,* he thought sadly.

CHAPTER 59

Over the next year, all of Tilly's dreams were realized. All but one. She believed with all her heart Ben was coming home soon. She never let herself believe otherwise.

At Tilly's subtle suggestion, the Reverend Barnwell after Sunday service at the prayer house told his congregation he would like volunteers to help him clean up the old slave woods. He thought it would be fitting for everyone there to volunteer to repair markers and bury the scattered bones. What did they think about the name Amazing Grace Cemetery?

The Gullah community had known when the Dock Shops opened there was no way to keep the Gullah community private, so they decided to make it work for them. The old market was repaired, and the original vendors moved back in with a few added stalls. Billy John set up a small farmer's market, and Emmy gave up her stall next to him so she could sell the latest style clothes at the Dock Shops. Millie Jones sold her prized sourwood honey, and Dickie Short had the most popular booth of all with his lip-smacking BBQ.

After work in the afternoon when the tourists had gone, the plaza, as the walkway was called, was a popular place for the shop owners and market vendors to sit and drink tea or lemonade.

Beau often joined them when Tilly was there.

One afternoon, Orie saw the look on Henny's face as he watched them laughing and talking. She said, "We ain't heard from Ben in two years, Henny."

"You don't have to tell me that, Orie. I live with that every moment I'm awake. I've written the war department three times but only got the same letter saying he is missing."

"Henny," she asked as gently as she could, "do you think he'll be comin home?"

He didn't answer, his eyes moist.

Orie got up and walked back in the bakery and brought out a platter of apple turnovers.

"Henny, these may not be up to Letty's, but they ain't all that bad."

When the gardens opened, Tilly and Beau, holding Finn's hands between them, walked along the old brick path winding through flowering trees and plants. It was as magnificent as she had dreamed. No one could possibly feel anything but joy here where once it had been so free of joy. The name was fitting. Glory Gardens.

Tilly ran up the dock office stairs grinning from ear to ear.

Beau looked up, surprised. "What are you so happy about?"

"Come with me." She grabbed his arm and pulled him out of his chair.

"I guess I better."

As they got into Beau's 1919 Porsche sports car, Tilly said, "I'm taking you someplace I have never gone to with anyone but Ben. Rufus just told me it is finished. I didn't go to the tabby house while Rufus and his crew were rebuilding it. I wanted to see it when it was finished. You were the one who found the plans for the original Chez Matilda in with the papers Granny had. You were the one who brought my granny to me and the deed to my house. If it weren't for you, I would never have known this house was mine. It means a lot to me for you to be with me now."

He cleared his throat. "Thank you, Tilly."

They pulled up in the front of an exquisite house. So simple it stood out like a perfect rose against the background of old oaks.

They both were so moved they stood in wonder and admiration. And, for Tilly, love for the house, love for the history behind it, and love for Ben.

She thought she knew of the feelings with which Beau was struggling. She always knew he cared for her in a way she couldn't return. She also knew he would never be able to express his feelings. He had changed, but he was still imbedded in his own culture and family life. Only once did he come close to crossing the line. It was subtle but clearly implied. They were standing on the dock plaza looking out over the marsh grass moving with the evening breeze. He turned to her with a depth of love in his eyes she had only seen in Ben's.

He caressed her face with his hand. "Tilly," he had said, "would you ever consider leaving . . . "

She couldn't bear to hurt him. This gentle sweet man of whom she was so fond. She quickly interrupted him. "Leave here? Beau, how could you even think I would ever leave here?"

He hadn't said anything more.

Now, standing with her looking at the restoration of her beloved tabby house, he asked, "What do you intend to do with this lovely home? Live in it?"

She looked at Chez Matilda, thinking how much she and Ben loved it. Even so, she didn't think they would want to live there. At least that was her feeling now. It was too far from the compound. And if Ben worked for Long Robby? "I don't know, Beau. I haven't thought that far."

He took her hands in his. "It's an exquisite house. Whatever you do here I know will be perfect."

When she looked at him, she saw the same look in his eyes as she saw on the dock. This time she gave into it. She loved Beau. Not like Ben. There would never be anyone but Ben, but her feelings for Beau were there, and this time she wouldn't deny them.

She went into his open arms and let him hold her close for a long time. When she pulled away, she reached up, put her arms around his neck, pulled his face down to hers, and kissed him softly on his mouth.

"I have always cared deeply for you, Beau. I always will."

She knew he wouldn't answer her. For which she was grateful. But there were tears in his eyes.

CHAPTER 60

Not all but many of the former residents of the Gullah community returned. They knew they would face racial conflict, but they were home, and there were jobs. Old plantations were being used by wealthy Northerners as hunting lodges, which opened work in the duck blinds, in the kitchens, or stoking fires in the guest rooms.

Beau left the docks and returned to his father's law offices. At his father's request, he said.

In many ways, the commune was like it was years before. Just different.

Late one October morning, Tilly, holding Finn's hand, pushed open the bakery door.

"Hi, Orie," he called and walked over to the window.

Tilly hung their coats up on a hook in the back of the shop.

Orie, looking at Finn, said, "Dat boy grows an inch every day."

Tilly grinned, put on an apron, and started working alongside Orie. "He takes after his daddy." She took in a deep breath of the baking cinnamon buns. "Orie, it feels so good being here. I just love getting my hands in dough." They laughed, happy to be together.

Tilly looked over at her son, his nose pressed against the shop window. "Well, something certainly has Finn's attention." She put the pan of rolls down on the countertop and walked up behind him, folded her arms around his shoulders, and looked out at what had him so engaged. She watched with Finn as hundreds of ducks darkened the sky once more as they returned to the marsh rich Lowcountry.

"Look at all those ducks coming home. I first saw them with your daddy when I was a little girl." She felt her chest tighten, then an ache began to spread over her until it felt like a volcano erupting. As the tears started, she called, "Watch Finn, Orie."

Orie looked up, mouth agape, as Tilly ran out the door.

Tilly ran, ignoring the cold, the ache consuming her. She ran until she reached the garden. She sat on the old tabby bench and sobbed. "You promised me, Ben. You promised me," she cried out, gulping between the sobs. Her eyes blurred with tears, she looked angrily at the withered and dead flowers and leaves of the plants. "You don't care he's not here. He planted you and loved you, and you don't care." She leaned over on her knees, sobbing uncontrollably. "How can you be silent when my heart is breaking? Why aren't you crying?" She sobbed until she couldn't get her breath, heaving for air. She glared at the pond. "I wish I could hurt you like I hurt. I wish I could smash into your hateful stillness and make you feel what I feel," she yelled.

Her eyes, blurred with tears, saw Ben's face looking up at her from the depths of the pond, and she fell to her knees, crawling hysterically, reaching into the water for the apparition of her love. "Ben. Oh, Ben, why won't you let me touch you?" she cried, choking on her sobs.

"C'mon, honey." Henny knelt down and covered her with his coat. "Let's get you up from there." He gently pulled her up, gathered her in his arms, and sat on the bench rocking her back and forth while she cried. He lay his head on hers, tears streaming. "Oh, sweetheart, if only that was Ben lookin back at you instead of my old scrubby mug." When the sobs slowly ceased, he helped her up and said, "You're going home with me, honey. Orie has Finn. I ran into Loriah Higgins today, and a jug sits on the kitchen table waiting for us. We're gonna sit in front of the fire until that moonshine has us as numb as a dead pole kitty. At least for another day."

"He's not coming home, Henny," she said, barely above a whisper.

"Maybe not, Tilly. But you and I've got all that love he left with us, an we'll have that til kingdom comes, an you've got a little boy whose part of him to remind ya of that every time you look at em. Now, let's go hit on that hooch."

⸏

"What are ya doin up so early?" Henny asked as he walked into the kitchen.

Tilly sat at the table, her hands around a cup of coffee, a platter of ham biscuits before her. "I'm a baker, remember?"

"And it looks like that's what you've been doing." He poured coffee into his mug, sat down beside her, and reached for one of the large flaky biscuits. He glanced over at the jug on the table.

Tilly smiled. "I can't stand that stuff, Henny. It tastes like kerosene." Her eyes twinkled. "But that glass of Pop's peach brandy? Hmm!" She rolled her eyes and smiled again. "You wouldn't give that to Ben and me when we were children."

"Of course not." He looked at the lovely young woman.

They had spoken very little yesterday as they sat before the warmth of the fire—Henny working his net with the jug beside him and Tilly leaning back against the rocker sipping on the brandy or staring at the red embers in the fireplace. They didn't need to talk. The heartache surrounded them, but so did the mystery of peace.

"Henny." Tilly knitted her brow and looked down at her hands around the cup. "I didn't sleep last night. I opened the window and let the chill come in. I wanted to listen to the night sounds, as Ben called them."

She looked up at him. "I want Ben's son to know him, Henny. I want him to know everything we can teach him, tell him, show him about Ben until he can feel him like we do. I want him to know the marsh and all that it meant to his father. That special world with all the life living in it and around it. All the beauty of this magical place with all the rivers, creeks, and veiny waterways that flow into the sound, so much you can't take it all in. That was Ben's life, Henny. I want Finn to learn about it—all he can learn about it. I want him to know this land until he cares about it as deeply as Ben did.

"And I want him to know how much Ben loved music. He took that harmonica of Ragbone's everywhere he went. He took it with him when he left here." A tear ran down her face, and she swallowed hard. "We can get another one, and you can teach Finn to play. And flowers." She shook her head, remembering. "Ben loved that garden at the tabby house. It seems silly now, but when I got older, that surprised me. He was such an outdoor, physical guy that I guess seeing him digging in that dirt and planting those seeds seemed a little odd to me." She smiled. "But not when I was younger. He could do anything, and it was perfect to me. He was my hero."

She looked at Henny again. "I want him to be Finn's hero. I want him to know what a good, kind, fine man his father was." She wiped her hands over her wet eyes and face. "I'll never stop missing him, Henny."

CHAPTER 61

In the black of the night, a tall, gaunt man walked past the tabby house down the long expanse of lawn and fell above the bank of the marsh, too exhausted to do anything but feel the earth beneath him and sleep.

The day woke him with soft golden light, nuzzling his eyelids until they were open to morning. He rubbed his eyes and looked around him. They settled on the marsh, and tears filled them. He was starved for it like a caged man aching for light. He hungered for the feel and sounds of it. The life of it. He had dreamed of this wild beauty with its massive wet garden of grasses and all God's winged and crawling creatures, and the creeks, rivers, and streams that flowed into it until it made him crazy. He wanted to stay and feel the wind against his skin and breathe in the cauldron of scents, but there was someone he longed for more. He was still bone tired. He was also dirty from walking so far. Otter Pond was close by.

He sat on the grassy edge of the pond teaming with life and wondered if the friendly little otter he called Okatie was still there. He threw a pebble into the water, and a cloud of white feathers flushed up from the far shore.

They'll come back. I wonder if they know me. I wonder if their little brains see me and wonder who I am. Or maybe they do know me, and I am missing how they tell me. They go about their life just gliding and diving, and when they want, they fly away, flapping their wings goodbye. Seems all they do, they do together. They're safe from me. I could never shoot a bird. I could never shoot anything again. We ain't meant to kill, but that's what we do. I never wanna see a gun again. The woodland trees were reflected in the pond, and he heard the sweet sounds coming from them. *This is what life is. Why don't people know that? All this beauty. This is what life is.*

He swam out in the pond, washed, and put back on his clothes.

⁓

Tilly had just knelt by a patch of dirt, a flat of annuals beside her, when Finn yelled, "Mommy, Beau's here."

She jumped up, wiped her hands on her apron, and quickly walked toward her friend. She reached out to take his outstretched hands and said, "I am so glad to see you, Beau. We miss you."

He grinned. "And I have missed you two." He knelt down for Finn to get on his shoulders.

Tilly laughed. "I think you will be sorry. He has gotten so big."

"Well, Finn, I guess a hug will have to do." He pointed toward the garden. "What are you doing over there?"

She put her arm through his and led him inside the garden gate.

"Tilly, this is beautiful. When we were last here, there wasn't a flower. Now it looks like spring is in full bloom in your garden."

"Thank you." She smiled. "And in heavenly April weather as well. It is such fun being here. Look at this day, Beau." She spread out her arms. "Blue skies, blue water, green grass, green marsh, yellow sun."

Beau laughed. "Tilly, you are delightful. It's so good to see you so happy."

"Mommy."

They turned to see Finn looking out the gate toward the house.

"Finn, what is it?" Tilly called as she and Beau ran toward the gate.

"There's a man looking at me."

Tilly looked all around, as did Beau. "Where did you see someone, Finn?"

"Over there." He pointed to the house.

Tilly was alarmed. "Beau, what do you think?"

Beau was studiously looking at the house and around it. "I wouldn't worry. Probably just someone looking to see what was here."

"Are you sure?" she asked, still concerned.

"For some reason I am, Tilly. And I have to be going. Just wanted to say hello. I saw Orie, and she told me you were here."

"Oh, Beau." She looked disappointed. "You are my only real friend. Please don't be a stranger."

He looked at her so tenderly she knew his feelings had not changed.

He took her hand, held it with more feeling than he intended, kissed it, and left, leaving Tilly and Finn to watch him get in his car and drive away.

⁓

When Beau was on the other side of the house, he slowed his car down to a near stop until he saw what he was looking for. He turned off the ignition and got out of the car.

"Hello, Beau," a calm voice called from behind an oak where Ben sat.

"Hello, Ben." His heart wrenched at the sight of this shadow of the robust young man he knew, sitting with his face blotched from tears.

Ben steadied himself against the tree and stood up. "How did you know I was here?"

Beau absentmindedly scratched his forehead and raised his brows. "One of those crazy coincidences, Ben. Although I'm beginning to wonder if there is such a thing. When I had the operation on my foot years ago, the surgeon sent me to a psychiatrist at Bellevue Hospital. His name was Eric Elliott. Seems my mind was as damaged as my foot.

"He called my dad last week and told him a young man named Ben Clary had left the hospital in the middle of the night. He knew that you lived on the marsh outside Belleview, but the only names he had were Tilly and Henny. Of course, Dad felt we should contact Henny immediately. I asked him to wait. I may have been wrong, but I was concerned that might have caused anxiety, not knowing where you were. I hoped you would come soon. Today, Dad insisted I tell Henny and Tilly. I was about to do that."

Ben colored. "I ain't going back there, Beau. I ain't never gonna be closed up again."

"You won't have to, Ben. Dad and I are seeing to that." Beau felt his eyes misting. "Dr. Elliott told Dad what you had been through in the POW camp."

"I'm alive, Beau, and for what it's worth, I'm all in one piece." He put his hand in his pocket and closed his fingers around a small object. "It was thinking of Tilly that kept me alive. I was on my way to find her when I came back to the house here and saw her out there so close, and then I heard her talking." His voice broke, and he turned away as he tried to hold back the sobs.

Beau put a hand on his shoulder, and Ben turned to face him. "I never heard her voice, Beau. All those years we were together, I never heard her talk." He looked at Beau, hardly able to get the words out. "When did she start talking?"

Beau smiled tenderly and said, "She will tell you that, Ben."

Ben's voice and body shook with emotion. "I wanted to run to her. I wanted to hold her so bad, but you were there with the little boy."

Beau flushed. "Ben, that is your son."

Ben looked surprised. "You think I don't know that? Beau, there's people who only love once. That's Tilly and me. I knew when I saw that little red-haired boy that he was mine." He rubbed his wet eyes with his fists. "After hearing my Tilly and then seeing my little son, my heart flew outta my chest. I had to wait."

"Not anymore, Ben. All you need is out there." He squeezed Ben's shoulder, got in his car, and drove down the oak-lined drive.

Ben turned and walked back to the front of the tabby house and saw Finn looking at him.

"Mommy, that man's back."

Tilly ran to where Finn stood and stared at the young blond man walking toward her. Slowly, she felt life returning and yelled, "Finn, that is your daddy." Then she screamed, "Ben." And ran, her arms open to him.

Ben grinned wide as the sea, opened his arms, and ran to his love in the splendor of the day.

ACKNOWLEDGMENTS

I f this book did not belong to Gladys Oliver, I would have dedicated it to my remarkable mother, Eloise Hackney Brooker, who believed in me, was always there. And still is.

And to my daughter, Rebecca James Williams, my wise and sensitive reader, who was with this book from the first page to the final draft.

The words *thank you* are huge. I am informed by quantum physics that by thought, speech, or script they are heard around the world. As well, to the ears of God. This book would be just pages on a shelf if not for these people. Thank you!

Mary Morris, professor at Sarah Lawrence College, and award winning author: When I saw that Mary was going to teach a workshop at the Key West Literary Seminar in 2013, I danced on my toes and attended specifically to find out if she thought the stack of pages I had written were worth finishing. For over a year she worked with me - advised cutting about two hundred pages and helped me to put the scrambled sheets into an orderly draft with chapters. If not for her expert and caring guidance, it is likely you would not be reading this book.

Mary Logue, author, teacher, editor: The Gods were smiling when I asked a friend, Pete Bissonette of Learning strategies, if he knew a good editor. Mary has meant so much to me, not only for her considerable skills at editing and genuine care for my story, but for being my loyal friend. It was she who gave my manuscript to Marly Rusoff to read!!!

Marly Rusoff of The Rusoff Agency: Marly is far, far more than the perfect agent. She is everything under the sun and moon. She is my dear friend and my blessing and shining light! She has done everything but write the book.

Joe Coccaro, executive editor of Koehler Books: for loving my book and telling me so, and for his amazing patience, generosity of spirit, kindness, and skilled editing.

Thank you, John Koehler, for wanting to publish me, and gratitude to all the Koehler team.

Sandy Goroff of Sandra Goroff and Associates, the beautiful angel on my shoulder.

Wiley Saichek of Saichek Publicity, my other angel.

Many thanks to these teachers, friends, and family whose support mattered: SL Stebel, Santa Barbara Writer's Conference, Fritz McDonald, University of Iowa summer workshop, Susan Shreve, author, retired professor at George Mason University, and awesome teacher at Breadloaf and KWLS; Gratitude for Nina McClain, for all the reading, pages of notes, suggestions, criticisms and encouragement and fifty years of close friendship before leaving too soon in May. Thank God for Sally Bradley and Pam Chew; Thanks also to Helen Johnson, Burt Peretsky, Victoria Smalls, The Laura Riding Jackson Foundation's writing group, particularly Charlotte Terry, Gertrude Terry, Joanne Mitchell, and all the blessed souls who shared news about my book on Facebook. Many thanks to Nancy Barber, Susan Whitemountain, Carol Anne Getman, Miles Frieden, Alan Kelly-Hamm, Brian Choate, Tish Stanhope, Joe Palmer, and my loved ones: Rebecca James Williams, Jennifer James, Anne Scott Vela, William Scott, Rebecca Scott, Ry James, Michael Williams, Juan Allyon, Edyth Kiser Shadburn, Rebecca Bell Savitz, and all of my big Hackney and Brooker families. All earthbound angels. A very special thanks to Boo Harrell, Bluffton, SC, who took me on a memorable trip through the marsh and into the streams and rivers, where I melded into that exquisite, magical ecosystem, heart, soul and spirit.

I met Hilary Barnwell at the Beaufort Library when I had just an idea for this story. She graciously took me to talk to her one-hundred-year-old mother-in-law, Wilhelmina Barnwell. The conversations with that wonderful Gullah lady shaped this book. I am saddened I was never was able to thank them before they entered the "spirit world."

And for my husband, Bob Ray, for love. Maybe not earthbound but still watching over me.

Gladys Roberts Oliver came to me when I was two weeks old in 1931 and remained the most beloved member of our family until she died in 1994. I hoped to find her roots on both sides of her family. We were able to trace back to the early eighteen-hundreds to Putnam County, Georgia, where we believe her mother's family was enslaved. It is possible her father's family were enslaved in Washington County. I wish I knew more.

For mighty inspiration: My father, Judge William C Brooker, Thomas Wolfe, Dr. Rufus Morgan, Gloria Steinem, Zora Neale Hurston, Toni Morrison, Oprah, Jean Houston and you, my lovely readers.

THE
GULLAH GEECHEE
LANGUAGE

In the early years of the eighteenth century, different West African tribes were enslaved on plantations along the Atlantic coastal shores from North Carolina to Florida. With a strong need to communicate with one another, and the determination to build a sense of belonging and community, they found ways to meet, taking life-threatening risks, crossing boundaries. By masterfully melding four thousand West African names, words, and phrases with the English language, they created a beautiful, strange, and captivating speech.

In a 1949 study of the Gullah people, their language, and their linguistic ties to West African languages, Lorenzo Dow Turner, an African American linguist, was able to prove Gullah was not a dialect but a distinctive African American creole language. It is poetic and melodious, the words and grammar discernible by tempo and rhythm and sometimes by stress. Gullah Geechee is spoken today throughout the Lowcountry and by many as a first language.

In this novel, the use of Gullah words such as *de* for the, *dat* for that, and the dropping of "g" at the end of words are a link to the Gullah Geechee language. The Lord's Prayer translated in Gullah below is a perfect example of the language.

From the New Testament in Gullah Sea Island Creole
De Nyew Testament

Jedus Laan People How fa Pray (Matthew 6:9 13)

Pray like dis yah, say,
'We fada wa dey een heaben, leh ebrybody hona ya name.
We pray dat soon ya gwine rule oba de wol.
Wasoneba ting ya wahn, leh um be so een dis wol.
Same like dey een heaben.
Gii we de food wa we need dis day yah an ebry day.
Fagib we fa we sin, same like we da fagib dem people wa do bad ta we
Leh we dohn hab haad test wen Satan try we.
Keep we fom ebil.'

Victoria A. Smalls,
St.Helena Island, SC
Riley Institute Fellow- Diversity Leadership initiative, Furman University
State Commissioner p SC African American Heritage Commission
Maven—the Art of Community-Rural SC-SC Arts Commission

AN INTERVIEW
WITH NOVELIST
ANNE BROOKER JAMES

BY BURT PERETSKY

Q. The Marsh Bird, your debut novel, which begins early in the nineteen hundreds, will be published on your 90th birthday. How do you feel about your late-in-life success as a writer? Tell us how and when you began writing it?

A. I don't give much thought to my age. If I did, I would be spending all my time sitting in the garden facing the sun!

I started the book about thirty years ago .... I thought I would write a very short tale just for practice. I never thought of it as a novel. But then things started coming to me, and the story developed on its own. When I was thinking of the characters I would need to move the story forward, Aunt Letty appeared, a feisty and resilient Gullah woman who was a force in her community. She spoke her mind. And along with her appeared Bones, an ageless root man who brought an element of magical realism into my story. The two orphaned children came later, one white boy, and a mixed-race young girl.

But then I married. Bob was a bit older than me and he wanted to travel, so I put the story aside but never forgot it, in fact, I continued to attend the occasional fiction writing workshop. It was only after he died, ten years ago, that I started to focus on my writing in earnest.

You create a lot of tension around unrequited love, one of many themes in your novel. Is it a theme of particular interest to you?

Unrequited love is not autobiographical; most of my loves loved me back. It was The Phantom of the Opera that got me thinking about how unrequited love is a theme of a many great stories. It keeps readers turning pages.

But I am a romantic at heart. I'm in love with a lot of things – with nature, with beauty, with beautiful old and young people, with words and with art. My characters truly love one another. That love is what keeps their bond so strong and how they ultimately succeed. I wanted to show the love between them in the book.

How important is setting to you?

Landscape has always been important to me. I love nature and wanted to capture some of the breathtaking beauty of the Lowcountry sea islands. Once you see it you never forget it. I am deeply moved by these marshes, the movement of the tides, the wildlife, the fishermen and their nets, the ancient oak trees draped with moss. There is no sunset that compares to ones I found on those sea islands.

Q. You say you are a romantic. So how do you feel about happy endings? Is this something you thought about when writing your novel?

A. I don't think I can write a book without a happy ending.

Q. The novel is seasoned with a few words from the Gullah language. How did you set about doing your research on the Gullah people and their unique language?

A. I'd lived in the South most of my life, but not in the coastal areas, so I didn't really know anything about the Gullah until many years ago when I visited a friend in the Beaufort, SC Lowcountry area. We attended the annual Gullah Festival on St Helena's Island. It was there at the historic

Penn Center that I first saw the old Brick Church, built by the enslaved for their Beaufort masters. It later became the first school for freed slaves, established even before the Civil War ended. I had no idea! I developed a great admiration for these people who have managed to retain much of their heritage, beautiful culture and language, even until this day. When my husband Bob and I moved to a nearby sea island we heard Gullah spoken nearly every day.

True Gullah is a wonderful language but if I had written my book in Gullah no one would have been able to understand it. I asked Victoria Smalls, a respected member of the Gullah community, to read the manuscript for me. She wrote a wonderful letter that guided me, not only in use of this spoken language, but also shared a few customs I was not aware of. Most of those enslaved in this area came from several West African tribes, each with their own language. Once here, they were intentionally separated from each other by their masters to make it more difficult for them to communicate with each other. But many dared cross boundaries from plantation to plantation and, in the end, they created a new, shared language, one that combined their own native languages with words spoken by their American slave owners. This is how the Gullah language, the language of their ancestors, was born.

Q. Would the Gullah people like reading The Marsh Bird?

A. I hope to Heaven that they'll like it, and that they're going to feel very proud of it. I treated them lovingly and kindly in the book as they deserved ....

Q. What might others take away from reading The Marsh Bird?

A. I want and hope that in some ways people can see, in reading the book, that we're all just one people, that there doesn't have to be this divide among us. I would love to believe that in some way this book might touch hearts to be a bit kinder and more caring of all people.

Q. Tell us about the title…

A. The Marsh Bird is a toy held tight by a traumatized young girl who was brought to the area from New Orleans after her parents died – this toy from her past meant security to her. It was actually a little sailboat that her father carved for her…. A little bird sitting on top of the sail. She's very protective of it, but she eventually gives it to the character Ben when he goes off to war. He, like her, is an orphaned child.

The little marsh bird represented love, hope, and security, something we all desperately need in this life.

CPSIA information can be obtained
at www.ICGtesting.com
Printed in the USA
LVHW090807240821
695874LV00010B/409